ICEBREAKER

A FANTASY NAVAL THRILLER

ICEBREAKER

A FANTASY NAVAL THRILLER

GLYNN STEWART

FAOLAN'S PEN
PUBLISHING
faolanspen.com

All rights reserved. For information about permission to reproduce selections from this book, contact the publisher at info@faolanspen.com or Faolan's Pen Publishing Inc., 22 King St. S, Suite 300, Waterloo, Ontario N2J 1N8, Canada.

This edition published in 2022 by:

Faolan's Pen Publishing Inc.

22 King St. S, Suite 300

Waterloo, Ontario

N2J 1N8 Canada

ISBN-13: 978-1-989674-30-7 (print)

A record of this book is available from Library and Archives Canada.

Printed in the United States of America

1 2 3 4 5 6 7 8 9 10

First edition

First printing: December 2022

Illustration by Elias Stern

Faolan's Pen Publishing logo is a trademark of Faolan's Pen Publishing Inc.

Read more books from Glynn Stewart at faolanspen.com

ACKNOWLEDGEMENTS

Above and beyond the usual credits included on the about the author page, *Icebreaker* owes a great deal to Dr Alexander Clarke, PhD Kings College London (War Studies), who tolerated my many questions, emails, and concerns around appropriate engineering and historical parallels.

Any technical errors that remain are my own.

CHAPTER I

THERE WAS SOMETHING VERY, *very* wrong with the storm to the north.

"Take a look, Jimmy," Captain Coral Amherst ordered her executive officer, gesturing toward the black clouds gathering on the horizon. The raven-haired officer stood a solid ten centimeters taller than Commander Ardan Rompa, her second-in-command—who, like every executive officer in the Navy of the Republic of the Dales, enjoyed the ancient traditional nickname of "Jimmy."

Unlike his Captain, Rompa wore a heavy multi-layered greatcoat over his black-and-white uniform. It shrouded his broad-shouldered form into near-anonymity but didn't hide the binoculars in his hands as he followed her pointing hand.

Coral wore the same sharply cut uniform, but she didn't need the Navy-issue greatcoat with its whaleskin outer layer to protect against the cold. The magic in her blood shielded her against the subfreezing temperature, just as it allowed her to inspect the storm —still ten kilometers distant, she judged—without the binoculars.

"I'm not sure I've ever seen anything like it, Skipper," Rompa finally said. "First glance, I was thinking blizzard, but..."

She nodded grimly. "You saw the ice."

It wasn't a question.

"There's no ice south of the storm," her Jimmy noted. "But what we can see of the storm has ice floes everywhere."

"It's flash-freezing the ocean," Coral told him softly. "And it's heading our way. Fast. We need to divert and find cover."

Coral had a great deal of faith in the power of her ancestral magic —but only a third of her crew were Dalebloods like her. The rest were Seabloods like her executive officer—and even heaters and greatcoats wouldn't protect them against a storm that was turning saltwater to ice in seconds.

"Yes, sir," Rompa confirmed. He eyed her sideways, the usual slight disconcert Seabloods showed at blatant use of Daleblood powers. Many Dalebloods chose not to draw attention to their gifts, allowing the Seabloods who made up roughly sixty percent of the Dales' people to pretend they *didn't* live with magic every day.

Coral didn't see the damn point.

"Our mission, Skipper?" he asked after a second as they both continued to observe the strange storm.

"There was nothing critical about *Songwriter*'s patrol," she reminded him. "We were sweeping the north coast to see if the Stelforma were trying to sneak anything past us. We can lose a few days, even a week, to avoiding a storm—an *ordinary* storm, let alone whatever the fuck this is."

Songwriter was a battleship of the line, fifteen thousand tons of steel and corn oil–fired engines driven by a trio of paddlewheels. Even if the Stelforma—the residents of the island archipelago to the south of the Dales that they weren't *quite* at war with—had sent something north, nothing with the range to be on the far side of the Dales could stand up to her.

Coral shook her head and glared at the storm.

"Find Rocchi," she ordered. "Wake him up if you have to. Then meet me in the charts room. None of the three of us know these waters well enough to find safe harbor without a map.

"And I'm not losing a Republic capital ship because I refused to respect the ocean."

Songwriter was a hundred and thirty meters long, making her one of the largest ships Coral was aware of. Compared to the cruisers of the Dales Navy, she was an immense beast—but she still had only so much space, especially after protecting the corn-oil tanks and the ammunition for her guns.

The armored citadel around and between her two steering wheels wasn't as well protected as the turrets or the main water line, but the necessity of protecting the paddlewheels created a shielded central core for the ship's command functions.

Including the charts room, where Coral had just enough time to open the oil feeds and bring up the lights before her two subordinates arrived. From the rumpled state of his uniform, she guessed that Lieutenant Ekene Rocchi had been sleeping when the Jimmy had found him.

The navigator had been the previous night's officer of the watch, so that was reasonable. She supposed.

"Skipper," he saluted crisply, his skin only slightly paler than the black of his uniform in the flickering light of the oil lamps built into *Songwriter*'s walls. "The Jimmy filled me in. We need a sheltered harbor?"

"Preferably within about twelve hours' sailing, Lieutenant," she told him. "I'm willing to bring *Songwriter* up to full power to get out of the way of that storm, but I have my suspicions about our ability to *outrun* it."

Rocchi was already opening the cabinets on the wall with the key hung around his neck. There were only four copies of that key—three were *in* the room right now, and the last was in an emergency safe in Coral's office.

Even from the light table, Coral couldn't make out the labels

Rocchi was flipping through. The dim light in the room was no impediment to her or the navigator, though she knew that Rompa would have issues without the table's covered oil lamps.

The Daleblood navigator pulled a particular chart out with a satisfied noise and crossed to the table. Unrolling it, he passed one end to Coral—who immediately passed it over to Rompa and stepped around to review the map.

Even with the tubes built to pull the smoke out from the lamps under the table and in the wall, there was still a faint smell of burning from them. But the table still highlighted the maps clearly— a necessity, as the chart room was completely enclosed by the citadel's armor.

"The big chart isn't much use for this," Rocchi noted. "I *know*, without even looking, that we're over three hundred klicks from anywhere with an actual *port*.

"I'd like to hope that this storm isn't going far enough south to hit anywhere like that," Coral told him. Ten hours at *Songwriter*'s top speed would get them three hundred kilometers—at the cost of fuel that would normally give them a range of *six* hundred kilometers at their usual twenty-kilometer-an-hour cruising speed.

Three hundred klicks straight south *might* get them away from the storm. It wasn't like the storm was *chasing* them. It just felt...wrong.

"There's something to that storm," Rompa murmured, echoing her thoughts. "A malignance I don't normally feel with weather."

"There's dark magic to that thing," she replied. "I feel it too. I'm not convinced it *won't* chase us."

While the two senior officers were voicing their misgivings, Rocchi was focusing on his work, and he stabbed a finger down, his skin a sharp contrast against the light table.

"Here. Keller's Fjord," he told them. "Charts say it's deep enough and long enough to pull *Songwriter* into the shelter of the bay. We may still get iced in."

"We *will* get iced in," Coral replied. "But we can get the ship out of ice once the storm has passed. I'm not sure I want to discover how this ship will handle being *hit* by chunks of ice delivered by state-nine wind and wave."

"State *nine?*" the navigator asked, blanching and glancing at Rompa for confirmation.

"*I* have to do math for that," the XO said bluntly. "But I'm guessing yeah. I didn't take angles and metrics, but I'd guess there were at least fifteen-meter-tall waves in that mess."

Coral, who didn't need to take angles and metrics to judge the height at that distance, smiled thinly.

"I saw ice floes twenty meters across being carried by waves as tall as they were long," she told her officers. "We are *not* letting that catch *Songwriter*. Keller's Fjord it is—pass the course to the helm as soon as you can, Lieutenant."

"Is there anything there?" Rompa asked, peering at the map. "A sheltered harbor, even this far north..."

"Keller's Landing," Rocchi told him. "One of the Seablood Landings. Too distant for much active Republic control. I'd have to check the catalog to see what we know."

The Seablood Landings were the scattered sites where the lost sheep of the Great Fleet had reached shore and settled. *Most* of the Great Fleet had made it to the Dales and joined with the Dalebloods there, but at least a hundred ships had ended up landing in effectively random locales across the northern end of the continent.

The Republic had, so far as they knew, found them all—but Keller's Landing was a thousand kilometers by land, twelve hundred by sea, from any major Republic city or port. They couldn't truly *govern* that distant a settlement, even if the Republic proclaimed ownership of all of the Landings.

"The catalog" was the listing of all territories and settlements claimed by the Republic of the Dales. It wouldn't have a lot of information on a village of a few thousand souls this far out, but it would have *some*.

And no one aboard *Songwriter* likely knew more, so it would have to do.

"Check the catalog once you've passed the course to the helm," Coral ordered. "Full power is authorized. We're two hundred–plus klicks west from Keller's Fjord, and that storm is coming south *fast*.

"Let's not get caught."

CHAPTER 2

SONGWRITER HAD A VERY NICE, enclosed bridge, designed to have hot air pumped into it from the big combustion engines in this weather and cool air pumped up from the bottom of the ship in hot climates. Albion's seas were not calm or predictable at the best of times.

And the storm bearing down on the battleship was as far from *the best of times* as Coral had seen in her thirty-plus years in the Navy. The chill in the air was already enough to send her Seablood crew inside, with greatcoats and the rest of their cold-weather gear no longer sufficient to protect them.

But Coral Amherst found the glass-enclosed bridge with its armored shutters stifling, both physically and mentally, and *Songwriter*'s designers had installed a secondary flying bridge on top of the armored citadel. It wasn't truly intended to be used to command the ship, but it had speaking tubes down to the bridge and Engineering, at least.

So, she stood on the top of her command's armored citadel, listening to the thunder of the corn-oil burners that propelled her ship, and watched the storm approach from the north.

"It just dropped below negative forty," the Daleblood rating with her pointed out as he stood by the range finder and checked a thermometer. "Or so I'm guessing. The thermometer froze."

Coral grinned, exulting in the warmth running through her body. She could feel the cold. She was *aware* of it, and it wasn't just an intellectual thing—but it couldn't hurt her. Not without getting *much* colder than this.

There were prices to be paid for calling on her magic like this, but she didn't get many chances to do so. And she wanted to see the storm coming.

"What distance do you make the storm, Seaman David?" she asked.

"Seven-point-three kilometers," he answered after putting his eye to the device and spinning several dials. "It's, uh..."

"Gaining on us," Coral finished for him. "And the temperature near it is plummeting."

"Yes, sir."

The poor young man was a Seaman First Class, a lookout rating who really had no business being the one to answer all of the Captain's questions. Unfortunately for Miron David, the *rest* of the lookout station's crew were Seablood and had been forced into the heated interior of the ship.

Coral Amherst had no intention of being forced inside, not yet. And that meant one senior rating was left playing sounding board to the Captain of a battleship with seven hundred souls aboard.

Only three hundred of that crew could go outside the hull at that moment, and many of *those* had critical roles in the machinery rooms.

Tradition put a vast gulf between her and the rating, but he was the man on the flying bridge with her. Being directly under the Captain's eye wasn't a comfortable place for any rating, though Coral would be far gentler on even a senior rating than on, say, a Chief or officer who should know better.

"Land ho!" the woman in the crow's nest suspended above them shouted down. "South by southeast, I see cliffs!"

Coral followed the angle the higher lookout had shouted, *focusing* her vision in a way that rendered binoculars and telescopes pointless for her.

It was the right time for it to be the right coast. The jagged cliffs south of them didn't *look* particularly hospitable, but they didn't need to. They just needed to have a *break* in them, somewhere close by.

She pulled the speaking tube over to herself.

"Bridge, we have the shore in sight to south by southeast," she told Rompa. "Have Rocchi check the charts and update our course."

She paused.

"Storm is getting closer," she continued. "We don't have much time to get to shelter, so let's nail that course down."

"He's on it," Rompa's voice replied. "May I note, sir, that Dr. Fredericks is now on the bridge and making agitated noises about even the Dalebloods being outside in this?"

Coral growled, but it was apparently not enough for her XO to get the hint as the ship's doctor's voice echoed out of the pipe.

"Captain," Fredericks said querulously, reminding her that— Daleblood or not—the doctor was very nearly a hundred years old. The magic in *his* blood allowed him to be hale and healthy and use seventy years of experience to serve the Dales.

"Doctor," she said calmly. "We are fine out here. The Blood sustains and we *need* people on the deck."

"The Blood demands a *price* for that, Captain," Fredericks reminded her, his tone sharp despite the waver to his voice. "I will not tell you what is necessary to command this ship. But I will warn that every hour our Dalebloods spend outside must be paid for with an equal time of necessary rest and vastly increased rations."

She swallowed down her initial retort and growled again. As Fredericks said, it wasn't his job to tell her how to command the ship. But it *was* his job to warn her of the concerns with pushing her people, and if anyone understood the limits of the magic in her people's blood, it was the old Daleblood surgeon. She'd done what she thought was necessary—but if Fredericks said she hadn't done enough, she probably hadn't done enough.

"Jimmy, pass the word to the Chiefs," she said with a sigh. "Have them pull in *everyone* we can spare."

They'd already cut the exterior crew down significantly. She glanced down at the forward twenty-centimeter turret, its pair of guns currently aligned with the ship's keel, and sighed internally.

"Pull the turret crews as well," she ordered. "The heating in those isn't up to protecting the Seabloods, and we'll see an enemy long before we'll need anyone to fire the damn guns."

"Yes, sir."

"And, Jimmy?"

"Sir?"

"Make sure the Chiefs find something for them to do," she told him with a soft chuckle. "Storm or no storm, we don't want the crew getting *bored*."

"I imagine they already have some ideas, sir."

THE PROBLEM that Coral had been concerned about since the moment they had turned away from the storm now manifested itself in full force. The storm was barely seven kilometers north of them, and they only had two and a bit kilometers left *south* of them.

As they turned east and powered along the coast, they were no longer running from the storm. Now they were running across the storm front, counting minutes and kilometers as they ran for sheltered waters.

From the flying bridge, the wind hammered into her. *Songwriter's* own thirty-kilometer-an-hour speed would have been harsh enough in this chill, but the storm's precursors were sweeping the sea as well. The water might not be flash-freezing around them yet, but the sun was already blocked by clouds, and bursts of ice pellets intermittently bombarded the ship's upper decks.

The wind was harsh and cold, pulling the already-unmeasurable temperature down even further. Coral could withstand the cold still, but she could feel the edge of fatigue starting to creep in. Reaching inside her uniform jacket, she removed the energy bar she'd stored there for just this need.

She might not have been as concerned as Dr. Fredericks would have liked, but Coral knew the limits of her magic and how to sustain them. The block of chocolate, stuffed with dried fruit, roasted nuts and pieces of flavored pure sugar, would provide enough calories to keep her going.

Out of the corner of her eye, she saw the Seaman at the range finder shiver suddenly against the cold. She turned to him sharply.

"Seaman David, report," she snapped. She needed the younger Daleblood *not* to collapse.

"Sorry, sir. Cold is getting to me. I'm... I'm..."

Coral growled and the youth quailed. Reaching inside her jacket, she pulled out a second energy bar and forced it into the sailor's hand. It took the rating a moment to realize that she wasn't angry at *him*.

"Eat this and get yourself back inside the hull," she ordered. "You're no good to anyone out here if you let your magic run out. Have the Chief send up a replacement, then report to Dr. Fredericks."

"Understood, Seaman David?"

He stared blankly at the bar in his hand and she sighed.

"Miron," she said, forcing herself to gentle her tone rather than let concern sharpen it. "Get back inside the ship. That is an order."

"Yes, sir," he managed to stammer out, moving slowly toward the door inside.

She watched him for a moment to make sure he was going to make it, then finished her energy bar as she studied the coastline south of them. They were running out of time, but she trusted Rocchi not to have doomed them.

Keller's Fjord *had* to be nearby. Focusing her vision again, she swept her gaze along the rocky coast, looking for the gap in the cliffs that would mark their safe haven.

There?

"There!" the lookout above her—who was hopefully watching her magic better than Seaman David had been, but had to be due for replacement soon—shouted. "I can see the fjord! I make it three klicks farther east—and I see a couple of fishing boats making the same run as us!"

"Let's follow them in, Jimmy," Coral ordered into the speaking pipe. "I'll be coming in once we're in the fjord. Someone have the catalog section on Keller's Landing ready for me."

Just because the town was *officially* part of the Republic didn't mean the locals were going to appreciate having a fifteen-thousand-ton *battleship* show up at their fishing wharf!

CHAPTER 3

As *Songwriter* drew closer to her destination, Coral could easily see why the main chart—the one that showed the whole known world —wouldn't have shown the fjord. The gap between cliffs that led to the hopefully sheltered inlet was *maybe* a quarter-kilometer across.

"Are we sure that the fjord is deep enough to take *Songwriter*?" she asked the speaking pipe to the bridge.

"The charts say yes, so long as we stay at the center of the inlet," Rocchi replied almost instantly. "Soundings are ten years old, from the cruiser *Dawn*. They *should* still be good, though I don't think anyone would mind a local pilot."

Coral didn't bother to reply to that. The likelihood that a Seablood Landing this distant from the main Dales had *any* Dale-bloods in their population was extremely low—and that meant that the locals were huddled into their homes around whatever heating they had.

Except...

"Seaman Askes," she shouted up to the woman in the crow's nest. "Do you still see those fishing boats?"

"No, sir," Askes called down. "They just passed the cliffs into the inlet. I can't see them anymore."

"Damn." Coral shook her head. There went the hope of asking one of the local boats to guide them in—though she couldn't blame the Seablood fishers their rush to get out of the killing cold around them. "Keep your eyes peeled for them," she ordered. "Get a signal ready to ask for navigation help."

"Aye, sir!"

If there were a dozen people left on the battleship's upper hull, Coral would have to find a third of them and physically throw the idiots into the heated interior of the ship. She could only think of half a dozen posts that *had* to be crewed no matter what. Anyone beyond that was unnecessarily risking themselves.

She was well aware that the list of those *unnecessarily risking themselves* included her, but she had faith in the power of her magic. If nothing else, she had two energy bars left in the inner pocket of her uniform jacket.

Coral might have underestimated the risk until Fredericks called her on it, but she wasn't going to let her crew freeze in the storm. She'd ask nothing of them she wouldn't ask of herself—but her crew had less ability to tell Coral no than Coral herself did.

Songwriter shifted under her, metal creaking and frigid seawater spraying across the deck as the helmsman turned the ship into the fjord. Engines growled as the steering paddlewheels surged to maximum and opposing power, turning the ship almost ninety degrees inside her own length.

"Sir!" Askes shouted down. "One of the fishing boats is still in the channel. They're flashing a lantern at us—standard code for *Follow, uncertain waters.*"

"Well." Coral leaned on the edge of the flying bridge and bestowing a beatific smile on the distant trawler whose crew were risking their lives to guide her ship in. "*Someone* may just be owed the Thanks of the Republic."

She had the authority to give the civilian crew that set of medals, and she *would* if they guided *Songwriter* in safely. She'd also make sure there was actually *money* to go with the official Thanks.

Medals, after all, were hard to eat or buy corn oil with.

"Helm, Seaman Askes is going to be calling down from the crow's nest," she said into the speaking tube. "We appear to have a volunteer guide and we're going to follow them in. *Carefully.*"

And since they were now inside the inlet and, hopefully, somewhat safe from the storm, it was time for the Captain to come inside and see what was waiting for them in Keller's Landing.

First, though...

She stepped away from the speaking tube and looked back at the storm. It was a *lot* closer, and she could see chunks of flash-frozen ice at most two kilometers away. She smiled coldly at the black clouds and gave the entire storm a single-fingered gesture older than the Republic of the Dales itself.

"I don't know what dark magic conjured you from the night," she told the storm. "But you were never going to catch *my* ship!"

THE OIL LAMPS kept the bridge well lit, even as the storm's darkness wrapped around the ship and smothered the afternoon sun to nothingness. There was a flicker to their light that never went away, but Coral and her crew were used to that.

Songwriter's bridge was one of the larger spaces on the battleship, but it contained too much equipment and too many people to be considered *spacious*. The helm was actually one level lower down in the citadel, but there was a secondary chart table in there, along with the speaking tubes to connect to a dozen separate parts of the ship, and a dozen other stations and paraphernalia required for the battleship's Captain to command her in action.

"So far, our local guide is keeping us to about the path the charts would suggest," Rocchi told her as she stepped up to the chart table.

There was a thick blue book on the side of the table, with a ribbon bookmark pulled through it. That was the catalog, she knew, and the ribbon probably marked the spot for Keller's Landing.

"She's only making fifteen klicks; we've slowed down to stay behind her," Rompa told her. "Even if she wasn't guiding us, I wouldn't want to pass her at full speed. We'd swamp her."

Coral looked past her XO, out the window at the storm-lashed cliffs surrounding them. So far, there hadn't been *anything* shallow enough to call a beach. She presumed that Keller's Landing itself was on lower ground, but the mountains around them suggested that veering from their course was a *bad* idea.

"I'm not sure we want to be going full speed through this regardless," she pointed out. "It seems like a recipe for testing how well our hull stands up to mountains, and I can *guess* how that test would end."

Like every ship in the Dales, *Songwriter* traced her lineage to the evacuation ships of the Great Fleet. Like them, her bow was designed to crush through ice, which might be very, *very* useful shortly—but it wasn't going to help them against a fifty-meter-high wall of rock.

"What do we have on the Landing?" she asked Rocchi, gesturing to the thick blue book. "I presume they *are* in the catalog?"

"Of course, sir," Rocchi confirmed. "It's...isolated, sir. According to the catalog, they were one of the last Landings to be found, and governance is still loose." He shook his head. "Based on the detailed notes, we don't even collect *taxes* in Keller's Landing. A postal ship comes through twice a year, and there's an annual stop by one of the northern corn-oil tankers. I'd *guess* they see a tramp freighter or two every year as well, and trade fish oil and whaleskin for machine parts and engines to keep the fishing fleet running."

All of which made sense to Coral. It was unlikely that a northerly community like this grew enough crops to both feed themselves *and* render corn down into fuel for their ships. That was why the northern tankers *existed*, a handful of ships that made a long circuit across the northern settlements like Keller's Landing, selling the corn-oil fuel necessary to run their engines.

That oil was probably the only thing the locals *used* Republic tender for. Their dealings with the tramp freighters would give them the currency, and they'd turn around and spend most or all of it with the tanker crews. That made collecting taxes difficult enough to not be worth it, Coral figured—and since the northern tankers *were* taxed, it was unnecessary.

"Population?" she asked. "Any idea how many boats and trawlers we're looking at?"

"The mayor sends a report into Daleheart with the postal ship once a year," Rocchi said. "Last one said about five thousand people, all Seabloods, and about thirty boats. Only four over a hundred tons."

A single ship of the Great Fleet would have landed three thousand people, plus or minus about five hundred. If there were only five thousand of them after two hundred years...

"Rough place to live," Coral observed aloud.

"The ocean is always a hard way to make a living," Rompa agreed. The XO's family were fishers in more southerly climes, she recalled. Another reason the Seablood's rise to his current rank was surprising.

Impressive, she supposed. He was a credit to his blood.

"Our trawler friend is slowing," the watcher reported. "Looks like we've got a sharp twist in the inlet coming up."

"That's good for sheltering the harbor," Coral murmured. "Even if it slows us down. Engines to one-third power. Let's stay behind the locals and follow them through. They know these waters."

She had a great deal of faith in *Songwriter*'s armor and its ability to shrug off shellfire. But *Songwriter*'s belly and keel were significantly thinner than her main belt. If the battleship's entire hull had been fifteen centimeters of face-hardened steel, Coral would be less concerned about running her aground, but even *Songwriter*'s mighty engines couldn't have moved that mass at any decent speed.

"Let's hope they're estimating our draft correctly," Rompa muttered, looking at the windows where ice pellets and snow obscured their view forward. "We run a lot deeper than any trawler ever built."

"Unless they're *idiots*, they'll err on the side of caution and take us through the deepest possible channels," Coral replied. She presumed that back-of-beyond Seablood fishers knew their own waters more than well enough to guide the battleship through safely. She *also* presumed they were smart enough not to attempt to founder *Songwriter* intentionally...

"Coming about the bend," Rocchi murmured, his gaze flickering between his charts and the windows as he spoke. Unlike Rompa, the Daleblood navigator presumably *could* make out at least the cliffs through the storm.

"We're at twelve klicks and slowing," the helm rating reported from steerage beneath them. "Turn complete."

"Map says we should be about a kilometer from the town now," the navigator told the senior officers. "If it wasn't for this mess, we'd be able to see them now. Topography says the cliffs on the west side should be dropping toward a small valley that reaches the water."

"Lighthouse at thirty degrees starboard," the crow's nest lookout announced. "Someone's burning a light to guide them all home."

Even Coral smiled at the lookout's poetic commentary—and at the news that they were definitely in the right place.

"Keep following that trawler," she ordered. "It's good to know we're where we need to be. Are we sheltered yet?"

"Mercury's still frozen," Rompa said grimly. "We're *going* to hit ice here in the inlet. The only reason it's not already solid is that this cold is ridiculously out of season. I wouldn't expect the fjord to freeze up for another month at least."

"If we are sheltered from the storm that is *flash-freezing* the fucking ocean, we can deal with normal ice," Coral pointed out acidly.

"We've effectively made two full ninety-degree turns," Rocchi reported. "There are mountains between us and the sea now, sir. We're as sheltered as we're going to get."

"Alert! Warship!"

Every eye on the bridge snapped to the speaking tube linked to the crow's nest as the lookout's words echoed through the enclosed room.

"Report," Coral barked, crossing the room to the tube before anyone else could move.

"There's a cruiser lit up in the bay. Stelforma colors!"

They were five thousand kilometers from the nearest Stelforma base. That ship had *no* business being this far north—let alone being anchored at a Republic settlement.

"Rouse the Daleblood members of the turret crews," Coral ordered levelly, searching through the storm to find the other ship. "Crew the guns."

She could *guess* how an open-ocean warship had ended up in the fjord—the same reason as *Songwriter*—but that didn't mean the Stelforma were going to be sensible.

After all, the Stelforma believed that all of the Dalebloods were irredeemably cursed by ancient evil.

CHAPTER 4

THE STORM BATTERING *Songwriter* was a pale shadow of the monster that had chased them into the fjord, but it was enough to cloud their vision and occasionally jolt the immense mass of the battleship. Their trawler guide couldn't have been *quite* as oblivious to the potential problem between the two warships, but she continued to guide the Dale ship in toward the town.

"We can't get right up to the town," Rocchi warned, the navigator's gaze fixated on the lights of the Stelforma cruiser. "But we should be able to get up to about a hundred meters."

"Take us in, navigator," Coral ordered. "Jimmy, are the guns crewed?"

"A and B turrets both report crew on hand," Rompa confirmed. "Coming about to target the Stelforma. Handy of them to light themselves up like that."

Coral could only imagine the *sound* that the turrets' hydraulics were making while moving their multi-ton weight. They would be warmed by channeled heat from the engines, keeping the fluids liquid, but only so much could be done in these kinds of temperatures.

"Range," she demanded.

"Six hundred meters to the Stelforma ship, about fifty more to the shore," a sailor reported crisply, listening to a speaking tube from one of the external platforms.

At that range, even *Songwriter*'s casemated twelve-centimeter secondary guns would have a basically flat trajectory, let alone the twenty-centimeter main cannon.

"Sir!"

Coral turned to face the interrupting sailor and arched one eyebrow at her silently.

The woman swallowed hard, quailing under her Captain's gaze.

"Speak, woman," Coral barked.

"Blue flare, sir," the sailor reported. "The Stelforma ship has seen us and fired a blue flare."

"Understood."

The Stelforma and the Republic of the Dales had been competing, clashing, feuding and fighting for over a century. There were *protocols* for when their ships met each other at sea—and while Coral's magic would allow her to talk to another Dales ship at a significant distance, there would be no Dalebloods aboard a Stelforma warship.

So, there was an agreed-upon code of colored flags and flares. *Blue* meant *we should speak*. It was basically an offer of truce but not the white flare of surrender.

It was also not the yellow flare of *back off or be fired upon* or the red flare of *surrender or be destroyed*.

"Presumptuous of them, isn't that?" Coral murmured. "They're in *our* waters."

"The storm may have driven them here, sir," Rompa pointed out quietly.

"I know that," she replied. "Signals officer!"

"Skipper?"

Despite being locked inside a metal box for several weeks, Lieutenant Hirom Uberti still managed to look perfectly tanned. He was young, he was athletic, and even Coral had to admit he was *very* pretty. Her type didn't extend to men, let alone boys, but she could see why the signals officer had been hauled in front of her for inappropriate relations *three times.*

And if even one of those incidents had involved a rating or someone under Uberti's command, she'd have broken the little shit out of the Navy. But they'd all been consensual and at least non-abusive on the surface. Just inappropriate enough that Uberti wasn't going to make it *past* Lieutenant until he learned to say no.

"Find one of your Daleblood ratings," she ordered the man. Pretty or not, the Seablood would freeze to death if he stepped outside the heated hull. "Green flare."

"Yes, sir!"

Uberti saluted and dashed away with commendable enthusiasm.

Concealing her desire to shake her head at the youth, she turned back to the windows and watched the lighthouse grow closer.

"Our trawler guide has dropped a floating flare in the water," Rocchi told her. "It's a bit farther out than I'd say is safe per the charts, but...they're the locals."

"On the other hand, we know *Songwriter*'s actual draft," Coral replied. "Still. Bring us up to their flare and drop the anchors."

She could just make out the trawler heading toward what looked like a giant shed. As they drew closer to the shore, she could see that the entirety of where she would expect to see the fishing wharfs was covered by similar structures—and what light and smoke she could see suggested that they were being heated.

"Interesting," she said.

"Skipper?" Rompa asked carefully.

"The locals have covered docks for all of their ships, even the bigger trawlers," she pointed out. "And they appear to have heating for them. This kind of storm isn't new to them."

"I've never heard of anything like it," her XO admitted.

"And that, Jimmy, is why we're going to need to talk to the

mayor," Coral told him, her gaze shifting away from the town to the Stelforma cruiser with its harsh white arc lights.

"*After* we find out what the Stelforma are doing here."

"SKIPPER, the launch is having issues getting started."

Coral leveled A Look at the Chief Petty Officer responsible for *Songwriter*'s boats. Justyn Kaloyanov was easily her own age and had served on every type of ship the Navy had. He was, in her considered opinion, one of the most useful Seabloods aboard her ship—and even with two coats wrapped around him, he probably shouldn't have been on the deck.

"And?" she asked.

Behind her, Lieutenant Johanna Calvin was sorting out a landing party of Dales Marines. She was passing out bolt-action carbines and semiautomatic pistols, checking harnesses, and, Coral knew, keeping an eye on the ship's Captain.

"The little corn-oil engines aren't meant for this kind of cold, Skipper," Kaloyanov told her bluntly. "I managed to get out for a few minutes and check out the engine. There's nothing wrong with her 'cept that she's frozen."

"Am I *rowing* over to the Stelforma ship, Chief?"

The launch's single rear driver wheel would create drag if it wasn't turning, but Coral figured her party of Daleblood boatswains and Marines, the only people she'd take into the cold, could make it work by sheer muscle power.

"You could," the Chief told her. "Or you could wait a few minutes while the oil lamps and blankets I had the boatswains set up thaw the engine enough to rev her up. Once she fires, she'll keep herself warm, but it'll take a bit."

"I expected you to have a solution, Chief," Coral replied with a chuckle. "I'm glad not to be disappointed."

"Thank you, Skipper."

"And, Chief?" Coral said calmly as Kaloyanov turned away. He paused and turned back to her, questioningly.

"Do *not* risk any more sixty-year-old Seabloods out on the decks right now," she told him softly but pointedly. "Am I clear?"

"Yes, Skipper."

Moments after her conversation with the Chief finished, Calvin was at Coral's side, extending a belt of waterproof webbing with a blocky semiautomatic and the Captain's dress sword strapped to it.

She regarded the gun with scant favor, but she put the belt on. The sword was Dalesteel, and despite its simplistic appearance, it was potentially capable of cutting the face-hardened steel that armored *Songwriter*.

In the case of this *particular* sword, it also predated the Republic's ability to make face-hardened steel. And the Republic itself, if she trusted family tradition. The art of making Dalesteel was limited to a few swordsmiths scattered through the Dales, but Coral suspected that most Dalebloods could correctly figure the core component.

The magic of the Dalebloods was literally *in* the Blood, after all.

"Party of twelve drawn up, sir," Calvin told her. "All Daleblood, as requested. Sir..."

The Marine trailed off and Coral swung a long-suffering gaze on her subordinate.

"Speak, Lieutenant," she ordered.

Calvin snapped to attention, fixing her gaze on the bulkhead behind Coral.

"Sir, Stelforma prejudices against Dalebloods are well known," she observed. "My Sergeants believe our cold-weather gear should suffice to allow a party of Seabloods to cross to the Stelforma vessel. That may defuse potential tensions, sir."

"It might," Coral agreed. "But I am disinclined, Lieutenant, to risk our Marines to soothe the mood of a foreign vessel that has no business being in waters this far north at all, let alone in this fjord and moored off the wharf of one of *our* villages.

"So, while I could take Seablood Marines and it would not, perhaps, be an unacceptable risk to them...I won't. Do you understand, Lieutenant Calvin?"

"Yes, sir!" the younger woman said crisply. "Party is turned out as instructed, Captain!"

"Then once the Chief tells us the boat has decided to cooperate, we shall be on our way."

CHAPTER 5

SONGWRITER'S HULL loomed behind them like a steel cliff as the launch hit the water. The boatswains unhooked it from the cranes and then slowly brought the harshly coughing engine up to speed, moving carefully through the water toward the Stelforma ship.

"I see five guns on this side, all casemated," Lieutenant Calvin noted—marking that the guns were mounted in an armored section, limiting their flexibility compared to turrets or open mounts. "Assuming she's got the same on the other side, *Songwriter* has her outgunned with just the secondaries."

"They're also only ten-centimeter guns," Coral pointed out as she examined the other ship. "Even at this range, she can't breach our belt armor. There's a reason we're going aboard their ship, Lieutenant."

For all that the cruiser was built by their age-old rival, its shared heritage with *Songwriter* was clear. Modern Stelforma ships were based on ships captured from the Dales over a century-plus of hot and cold war, which meant that the cruiser had basically the exact same hull form as *Songwriter*.

At, of course, about sixty percent of the scale. The cruiser—the name *Dancer* was painted on her bow, Coral realized—was eighty meters long to *Songwriter*'s hundred and forty. She had the same flared stern with a full-width driver wheel, and her side wheels flanked an upper deck structure that Coral doubted deserved the title *citadel*.

Three ten-centimeter guns were visible in single casemate mounts between the side wheels and the bow, with two more in identical mounts between the side and driver wheels. That gave the Stelforma ship a five-gun broadside—but *Songwriter* had a *six*-gun broadside from her casemated *twelve*-centimeter secondaries *and* had the two dual twenty-centimeter turrets.

Dancer was utterly outclassed. She was a fifth of *Songwriter*'s size and completely lacking in the armor that shielded the bigger ship. Her sole chance against a battleship was to be well away from it—and the storm had left the two ships no choice.

The blue flag that matched *Dancer*'s flare hung from the signal pole amidships, and Coral waited in calm silence as the senior boatswain brought the launch alongside.

"Hello, *Dancer*!" the petty officer yelled up. "Captain and party to come aboard, as requested!"

For a few seconds, there was no answer. Coral was about to order Lieutenant Calvin to break out the grappling hooks when a voice finally replied.

"We're lowering a ladder," they shouted down. "Tie off the launch to the bollards and bring the crew up too. Ain't nobody should be out in this cold, no matter what!"

"Wait here, sir," Calvin instructed Coral.

Despite a momentary flash of indignation at being ordered around, Coral obeyed. This was the Marines' territory more than hers, after all.

Calvin and two of her Marines swarmed up the rope ladder in a blur. From the surprised yelp that Coral heard from the deck, the Stelforma crew hadn't been expecting Daleblood.

"All clear, sir," Calvin shouted down.

Coral moved instantly and was on the ladder before any of the other Marines or boatswains could get onto it. She wasn't much slower than the Marines in her ascent, and stepped onto the deck of the cruiser like she owned it.

Calvin and her Marines didn't *quite* have the three heavily swathed Stelforma crew members at gunpoint—but the body language was very clear about the level of threat that was going to be tolerated.

"I am Captain Coral Amherst," she told the Stelforma. "I am here to speak to your Captain about just what your ship is doing in Republic waters."

"Of...of course, sir," one of the sailors replied. The three Stelforma appeared to be wearing at least two full sets of cold-weather gear layered over each other, rendering them indistinguishable and anonymous. "Follow me?"

"Lead on," Coral ordered.

As she and her party followed, she glanced around *Dancer*, taking in the differences between her ship and a Dales warship. The arc lights were the most immediately obvious. There were no oil lamps there—instead the arcane devices behind thick glass panels spilled a harsh white light through the storm.

Coral suspected that the arc lights and similar so-called *common magics* of the Stelforma were more engineering than magic, but she had also seen the true High Magics of the Stelforma and had to concede that *those* were just as real as the power that flowed in her own blood.

Other than the lights, the ship could have been an old Dales cruiser. Her more-modern Dales peers would have had three turrets with paired twelve-centimeter guns rather than the casemated single ten-centimeter cannon, but Coral had served on cruisers with all casemates.

It had taken a *long* time for the Dales to get turret hydraulics down to a size that made cruiser turrets practical, after all.

The clearest distinction didn't become truly visible, thanks to the storm, until they reached the entrance to the citadel. Like a Dales ship, the cruiser's name was painted above the door, but where the Republic Navy would have painted their red chevron on black flag directly on the door, the Stelforma had flanked the door with two symbols.

To port of the door was a sword on a blue circle, the symbol of the Williams Princedom. The princedom ruled over several of the largest and most industrialized islands in the Southern Archipelago, and the prince's fleet formed the core of the Stelforma navy.

On the other side was the half-green, half-blue orb-on-sun of the Stelforma themselves. Technically a church, the Stelforma were omnipresent in the archipelago's princedoms, kingdoms, and republics—and since they controlled *all* of the Stelforma's High Magics and all of the *banks*...

The Stelforma pretended to be a loose coalition of nations, but the Republic treated them as a single theocratic nation...and no one from the southern islands ever seemed to find that a problem.

INSIDE THE CITADEL, the pretense of being a Williams Princedom ship grew even more threadbare. The orb-on-sun of the Stelforma was *everywhere*. It was the default decorative element on any part of the warship that had any decoration at all.

Their hosts ushered the full party into the citadel, away from the brutal chill of the outside storm, and then paused in confusion as they considered the *very* crowded corridor full of their ancient enemies.

"Wait here, please?" one of the muffled sailors told them, and then vanished deeper into the ship.

The other two were sufficiently heavily clothed to form a physical barricade keeping Coral and her companions in the initial corridor. Given that Coral had intentionally brought enough Daleblood

Marines to *capture* the ship, likely without even much difficulty, she wasn't overly concerned.

She *was* getting impatient and considering taking the ship by storm by the time an officer finally appeared along the corridor and gestured the sailors aside. He was a tall, dark-skinned man clad in a knee-length black tunic, a few centimeters taller than Coral herself.

He met her angry glare calmly and bowed slightly.

"I had to see for myself," he told her. "I did not believe that the Dales would be so foolish."

"If you think this is a trap, you will be sorely disappointed," she said. "I am here because *you* sent up a blue flare. My standing orders require me to respect that rather than sinking this ship for being in our waters.

"But I suggest you talk quickly."

"We do not mean any harm to Keller's Landing or your vessel," the officer said swiftly. "But the Priest-Captain cannot speak with one of the Cursed. Her presence is sanctified and cannot be so polluted. You must return to your ship and send one of the untainted to speak with her."

Coral smiled at the man. He might even have been so foolish to believe it was a friendly gesture—but from the way even his darkly tanned skin paled, she doubted it.

"I have done you the favor of boarding your ship myself," she pointed out. "That is the first and last concession I am prepared to make, officer. Your 'Priest-Captain' will either speak to *me* or she will speak to *Songwriter*'s guns.

"I suggest you choose swiftly. We both know that I can order this ship sunk from here...and that *my* party will survive that."

Probably. It wasn't a theory that Coral really wanted to test—there were enough Dalebloods on *Songwriter* that she could communicate her orders via the Bloodspeech, but she was far less certain of the ability of even her people to survive the ship being obliterated by the twenty-centimeter guns.

"I..." The officer trailed off. "I will check with her..."

"No, officer," Coral told him. "You will take me and my escort to her. I am out of patience and out of time. One way or another, I am *going* to speak to the Captain of this ship. How many of your people are going to die before I do?"

He was silent for at least twenty seconds, until Coral laid her hand on the sword at her waist. That drew his gaze instantly, and he exhaled a long, twisted sigh.

"Yourself alone," he demanded.

"The Captain will bring two bodyguards," Calvin interrupted instantly. "This is not negotiable."

From the Stelforma officer's expression, that was three more Dalebloods than he wanted to take into the Priest-Captain's presence—but since Coral knew without even looking that Lieutenant Calvin *also* had her hands on her weapons, all the man could do was nod his acquiescence.

CHAPTER 6

THE DESIGNERS of the Stelforma cruiser had clearly put at least a passing thought into the need for their vessels to act as diplomats for the disparate parts of the theocracy. Coral and her pair of Marines were escorted into a conference room on the starboard side.

Coral suspected that the space served double duty as a mess for either the officers or the priests—*not* fully overlapping categories—but a lot more money had been sunk into decorating it than in the rest of the ship. Pale wood paneling had been installed on the walls to cover the bare steel of the rest of the ship, and there were heavy drapes drawn over what might even be windows on the outer hull.

Those drapes were decorated with the orb-on-sun of the Stelforma, and the large table in the center of the room had the same symbol inlaid into it. A large painting of the Abduction of the Chosen, the mythical origin of the Stelforma, was mounted on the far wall.

Even if Coral believed that the myth of the original Stelforma worshippers being stolen from paradise by giant birds to be utter fiction, she had to admit that the artist had done an amazing job with the piece. She suspected that she'd be able to count individual feathers on the immense birds and details of their victims.

Still, her main focus was on the woman standing behind the table, studying them as they entered. The Stelforma priestess stood next to a brazier giving off light, heat, and scented smoke—though *most* of the light in the room came from a set of arc lights mounted on the inner wall.

The woman wore a high-collared cassock that hung down to her shins, tightly cinched around the waist and clearly tailored closely enough to be uncomfortable in multiple areas. Still, *Dancer*'s Captain seemed unbothered by the garment as her officer approached.

"Manuel, please," she murmured as the man opened his mouth. "I warned you."

"They insisted, Your Excellency. I told them the Cursed could not—"

"She is their Captain and I need to speak to their Captain," the priestess said sharply. The entire conversation was half-whispered—a waste of effort, given Daleblood hearing. "It is what it must be. Leave us, Commander Fodor."

The officer—Commander Manuel Fodor, Coral presumed—laid his hand over his heart and bowed slightly before withdrawing.

The woman turned her attention back to Coral and her party, and spread her hands slightly. Her face and hands were the only visible skin on the woman, but both were extraordinarily pale to Coral's eyes. Most of the Stelforma she'd met were even more tanned than the people of the Dales.

"Welcome aboard *Dancer*, Captain," the priestess greeted her at last. "I am Priest-Captain Angelica Carrasco. By the grace of our Chosen Mother and the authority of Prince Francesco Williams, I am the commanding officer and First Cleric of the Williams Princedom cruiser *Dancer*."

"And you have no business in Republic waters," Coral said sharply.

"Please, Captain, introduce yourself, sit," Carrasco asked with a sigh as she settled into her own seat. "Your escorts may sit as well, if they wish. I have wine or tea, if you desire?"

"No, thank you." Coral considered the situation for a moment, then sighed herself and took a seat across from the Stelforma woman. "I am Captain Coral Amherst, commander of *Songwriter*, a battleship of the Northern Squadron.

"Tasked, I must note, to protect our northern communities from threats and to guard our waters from the Stelforma."

"We weren't in your waters, Captain Amherst," Carrasco told her. She took a moment to pick up the bottle of wine on the table and fill a ceramic cup—marked, like so much else on the ship, with the Stelforma blazon.

"We are now," she conceded after taking a sip. "It was not our plan."

"You are currently sitting in the harbor of a Republic settlement. I need more than 'it was not our plan' to not regard you as an enemy," Coral said.

"If you did not already suspect our situation, Captain Amherst, you would have fired black flares and boarded my ship," Carrasco pointed out.

"My mission is...none of your concern," she continued. "A religious expedition, let us leave it at that. We were almost a thousand kilometers north of here, actively avoiding any Republic settlement or outposts we were aware of, let alone the Dales landmass itself.

"And then we met the hellfrost storm. We ran ahead of it for *four days*, Captain Amherst. In truth? My charts of the northern coast of the Dales are insufficient for me to have found this fjord. Only the Divine guided us to Keller's Landing."

"These people are—"

"The locals have been amazingly welcoming, as any seafarer would be to an injured ship," Carrasco interrupted Coral. "I have not and will not do them any harm.

"We did not desire to enter Dales waters, and as soon as the storm passes, we will leave. If you will permit it."

Coral regarded the other woman steadily. Carrasco was pale-skinned and severe-featured, the sharp edges of her face only accentuated by the pitch black of her high-collared uniform. It was the silver buttons of the uniform that seemed out of place, not the woman's ivory-white skin and dark brown hair.

There was an austere beauty to the priestess, though given her opinion of Dalebloods, that was a pointless assessment on Coral's part.

"At least you recognize your position, unlike your officer," she finally told Carrasco. Coral may have come aboard the Stelforma woman's ship, but *Carrasco* was the supplicant there. *Dancer* was in Republic waters—and regardless of who was in the *right*, Coral's ship outmassed Carrasco's five to one.

And a very large part of that difference was armor. Even at this range, *Dancer* would need great luck or help from their Divine to have any chance of damaging *Songwriter*. The biggest problem that Coral's crew would have would be fusing their shells correctly to not explode on the other side of the Stelforma ship.

"Commander Fodor's job is to protect me and this ship," Carrasco noted. "Like many of the lay personnel aboard this ship, he regards the protection of the clergy as a higher duty."

"For my part, the preservation of this ship and her crew is my highest duty, as sworn before the Divine herself. We did not intend to violate your waters, and I beg the ancient compassion of seafarers. You *saw* the storm."

"I did."

Coral held her silence for a few moments after that, letting the other woman stew. "You are aware, I assume, of the Northern Doctrine?" she finally said. "Per treaties between the Stelforma and the Republic, you are barred from traveling north of the twentieth parallel. You have effectively confessed to me that your plan was to do so."

A thousand kilometers north of Keller's Fjord wasn't past that line—but it was a lot closer than any Stelforma ship should have been going.

"Perhaps," Carrasco conceded. "But we did not breach the twentieth parallel. We only entered your waters when running before a storm that gave us no choice. The Divine brought us to safety here. We have done no harm to the locals."

"I will be verifying that with the mayor," Coral said coldly. "But... if that is true, then I will permit you to leave safely."

Carrasco was not wrong to call on the compassion of seafarers. For the same reason that a Dales ship would rescue the survivors of a Stelforma ship they sank themselves, she could not wreck the foreign ship for finding safe harbor in *that* storm.

"Your compassion is appreciated, Captain, and will do you some credit before the Divine," Carrasco told her. "I..."

"Need something else, don't you?" Coral asked.

She could guess. If *Dancer* had more than four hundred tons of corn oil aboard, Coral wanted to know what new magic the Stelforma had created. From Carrasco's description of their flight, they'd run over *three thousand* kilometers in total to travel a thousand kilometers south and reach Keller's Landing—and they'd done so at full speed.

Dancer likely had a range of ten to twelve thousand kilometers, but that was at an economical speed. Not maximum speed. That she'd *survived* four days at full power spoke well of the Williams Princedom's engineers, but she must have drained her tanks dry doing it.

"We need fuel," Carrasco admitted, exactly as Coral had anticipated. "Our nearest base is almost four thousand kilometers away. I need..." She sighed. "We need a hundred and fifty thousand liters of diesel to make that trip."

"That's half of what Keller's Landing *has*. But only about a tenth of what I expect *Songwriter* has at full load."

Carrasco was underestimating *Songwriter*'s fuel tanks, Coral suspected—or pretending to. She was right in that Coral could give the cruiser enough fuel to get home without risking her ability to complete her patrol.

Except...

"Neither Keller's Landing nor *Songwriter* have...'diesel'?" she pointed out, carefully pronouncing the word Carrasco had used.

The Stelforma Captain paused, then took a long swallow of her wine as if she was trying to work out how to phrase something. She sighed and pinched the bridge of her nose.

"Corn oil," she said, failing to hide the exasperation in her voice. "Your corn oil is biodiesel. We boil tar for it; you mix vegetable oil with lye and wood alcohol. End result burns the same. I can run my ship on your corn oil."

Coral didn't know enough of the details of how the corn oil for the Republic was produced to know whether Carrasco was describing its manufacture correctly. She certainly wouldn't have leapt to put the Stelforma's "diesel" in her own ship—but if Carrasco was willing to put corn oil in hers, that was up to her.

"So, we do have fuel, then," she finally murmured. Regardless of her own knowledge of corn-oil production, the knowledge that the two nation's fuels were interchangeable—at least in emergencies— was important. She'd pass that up the chain—though she *hoped* someone in Daleheart already knew about it.

"I can't just fuel your ship for you, though," she continued. "Our nations are not on *nearly* good enough terms for that."

Coral was going to have to explain just letting *Dancer* go. If she *refueled* the Stelforma cruiser? She might well end up in front of a Board of Inquiry.

"I have drafts drawn on the Bank of the Chosen, as well as Chosen-registered gold and aluminum ingots," Carrasco said instantly. "I was prepared to pay the locals for fuel, but I *know* they can't access Chosen drafts and would potentially have issues using Chosen specie as cash.

"The Navy of the Republic of Dales, on the other hand..."

She wasn't wrong. If nothing else, there *was* trade between the two countries, and the Navy could cash out drafts with the merchants engaged in that business. The gold and aluminum ingots would be easily converted by anyone in the central Dales.

Just not by fishers at one of the most distant Landings.

"I will be speaking with the mayor," Coral finally said. "*If* they confirm everything you have said about your time here, my purser will find a price she judges acceptable for our fuel.

"Cause *any* difficulties while we are both anchored here, and I will destroy your ship without hesitation."

"Captain Amherst, I understand your position and your duty," Carrasco told her. "I appreciate your patience and your pragmatism. We intend no harm, and I will make certain that my crew cause no trouble.

"You have my sacred oath as a priestess of the Stelforma."

Coral grunted and rose.

"Frankly, Priest-Captain Carrasco, I trust the guns aimed at your hull more. We'll make it work. So long as the mayor confirms your assurances about the town."

"Whatever it takes for us to pass through the storm unharmed by each other's fears," Carrasco said calmly. "These are fine people here, Captain Amherst. I hope you recognize that. We have done them no harm... I must hope that our mere presence doesn't create issues for them."

Coral couldn't say anything to that. *She* wasn't going to blame the locals for selling food to a trapped warship sheltering from a storm...but there might be those who would.

And the people of Keller's Landing were probably happier *not* appearing in Navy dispatches of any kind.

CHAPTER 7

THE MASSIVE SHEDS that the locals had built over their docks had doors of assorted size. Despite a momentary urge to demand that the locals open the largest door, the one meant for the trawlers easily ten times her launch's size, Coral gestured the boatswain to take them to a door only slightly bigger than the launch itself.

"Do we knock?" Lieutenant Calvin asked, the woman eyeing the metal gate while two of the boatswains hooked an ice floe out of the way of their approach.

"I expect that they are paying attention—and it appears I am correct," Coral told her subordinate, gesturing as the gate slowly swung open in front of them. She could just pick out the sound of a motor running inside the building and the sound of chains dragging over a pulley system.

"Take us in," she ordered. "And be ready for anything, Lieutenant. These people *should* be glad to see us, but..."

The Marine officer snorted and touched the carbine hanging over her shoulder.

"Against a dozen Daleblood Marines? They *will* be glad to see us. Or else."

There was a *reason* Coral liked her Marine commander.

Glancing around her, she spent a moment taking in the interior of the boathouse as the gate closed behind them. It was warmer inside the building. Not *warm*, but warmer. Above the freezing temperature of seawater, she judged—and she spotted several large furnaces in the corners of the building, burning merrily away to keep it that way.

The gate swung shut behind them moments after the motor stopped. A clever balancing act, she supposed, and one that drew her gaze to the man standing by the motor.

Swathed in heavy whaleskin, he gestured for them to head for the shoreline. Coral let the boatswains take care of that while she looked to see who else was in the boathouse.

It was busy in there. The trawler they'd followed into Keller's Landing had come in through the big door she'd spotted, and her crew was still disembarking their catch—presumably from *before* the storm had swept in.

"I want to talk to those sailors," Coral murmured. "First, if we can."

"You're the Captain, Skipper," Calvin replied. "We'll make it happen."

The launch finally swung up to a dock, and the crew tied the boat up.

"With me, Lieutenant," Coral ordered, leaping easily from the boat to the dock. From the movement of the small crowd on the shore side of the building, someone was coming to meet her—but as she'd told Calvin, she had her own priorities.

She reached the shore and immediately turned back onto the dock holding their trawler guide. The fisherfolk only loosely acknowledged her presence as she approached, but she expected no better. They were *busy*—and the fish they were bringing in might have to sustain the community and their unexpected guests for a while, depending on how the storm went.

"I need to talk to your captain," she said loudly.

"That's me, sir," a graying but immense man told her, appearing from behind a pile of netting. He folded his arms and studied her. "Leave me crew be. We are—"

"Busy landing your catch, I understand," she said swiftly. "I wanted to thank you and your crew in person, Captain. Your guidance through the fjord saved us time, at the least, and may well have saved us from the storm and rocks alike.

"On behalf of the Republic Navy, I offer you and your crew the formal Thanks of the Republic."

A few backs straightened around her. A formal Thanks wasn't worth much out there—its main actual *value* was that it made it easier for an individual or their family to enter the assorted public services and Republic-funded academies in the main Dales—but it still meant something.

"Our fjord ain't friendly, Captain," the trawler captain told her. "We weren't going to see anyone founder out there, not when all it cost us were a few minutes and a light."

"The cost to you, Captain, doesn't change the value to myself, my crew, and the Republic," she insisted. "I ask that you provide one of my people with the roll of your crew so they can be properly recorded in the lists of the Republic Navy."

"Of course, Captain," the fisherman said with a sigh. "It shall be as you ask."

Coral smiled thinly.

"And for a more immediate recognition, I offer *my* thanks," she told him. As she spoke, she reached inside her uniform jacket and withdrew a folded cloth pouch she'd filled in her quarters before she'd left *Songwriter*.

The *Republic*, as a rule, preferred to find ways other than cash to reward people. Coral Amherst, on the other hand, was wealthy enough to buy and sell the fishing trawler without noticing—and she'd been her father's *least* favorite child when he'd written his will.

"I can't..."

She pressed the pouch into the captain's hand. The aluminum

specie inside were probably enough to fuel the trawler for a decade... or potentially buy a new trawler from one of the shipbuilders in the main Dales.

"For your crew, if nothing else," she assured him. "I'd rather pay a thousand times than risk that storm once. From myself and my crew, thank you."

"We all face the seas of Albion," the trawler captain finally said. "I will make certain my people receive your gift, Captain. But the mayor is waiting for you," he pointed out.

"I have the feeling we will be here for a while, Captain," Coral noted. "And I will always make it a priority to thank the people who help me."

SOMEWHERE IN KELLER'S LANDING, Coral suspected, there was a printing press spitting out a certain type of man. If the mayor wasn't related to the trawler captain, he certainly *looked* it. The local was another tall and broad-shouldered man with a graying beard, standing at the end of the dock and waiting patiently for her return.

"Mayor, I am Captain Coral Amherst," she introduced herself. "I would prefer to have arrived in Keller's Landing under better circumstances, but the guidance of your fisherfolk gave us safety we might have struggled with."

It cost her nothing to be appreciative, after all.

"There's a cruiser full of religious lunatics in my fjord, Captain Amherst," the mayor told her drily. "I am fucking *delighted* to see a battleship of the Dales. I am Dr. Suljo Newport, Keller's Landing's mayor." He paused and chuckled. "And our only doctor. I'm working on that, but..."

He shrugged massively.

"It's hard to get a kid from the distant Landings *into* a medical school in the Dales," he admitted. "And, well, even harder to get them to come *back* afterward."

Coral was from Daleheart itself, a bustling metropolis of over a million souls. Growing up surrounded by the other central Dales, she could barely *imagine* what living in one of the distant Landings was like. She could see the problem with getting people to leave that life to come back to fishing in frozen winters.

"Have the Stelforma been a problem?" Coral asked. "*They've* told me they haven't been, but I hardly trust their word."

"So far, they've been decent," Newport told her. "Would you care to speak somewhere more comfortable, Captain? I'm old enough that standing around gets to my bones."

"I suppose," Coral allowed. Seabloods aged much faster than Dalebloods and took that age harder. She tended to forget that weakness. "Lead on, Mayor."

Calvin fell in behind them as the local led the way through the gathered crowd. Coral studied the villagers as they walked, and realized that many of them were clearly *sleeping* in the big boathouse. It wasn't exactly *warm* in there...but it was shelter against the storm sweeping around them.

"Don't these people have homes?" she asked Newport softly.

"We don't have enough corn oil to both fuel the fishing fleet and heat every home enough to stand off the hellfrost storms," the mayor told her grimly. "We use fish oil in its place to heat some of the larger homes, but no matter how we insulate, it's not always enough."

Newport stopped at a heavy door swathed in curtains. Several heavy greatcoats of whaleskin lined in furs were waiting there—one of which was clearly his. He eyed her carefully.

"You crossed from your ship in just your uniform?" he asked.

"I am Daleblood, Mayor," she told him. "My magic protects me."

"As you wish, Captain."

Newport took a moment to brace himself and tie the greatcoat more tightly around his waist, then opened the door and led the way out into the storm.

Even walking up what had to be the main thoroughfare, the town of Keller's Landing was basically invisible through the blowing snow. It was warmer than it had been on the water, but that didn't reduce the amount of snow in the air or on the ground.

Coral followed Newport carefully, relying as much on her magic and hearing as on her sight to know where he was at any given moment. Thankfully, it was as short a trip through the storm as she expected before he was ushering her into a large, brightly lit house.

It was, presumably, Newport's own home and operating clinic—but it appeared that an entire family had been set up in sleeping bags in the front living room, clustered around a woodstove.

"Maria, can you keep everyone out of the clinic for a bit?" Newport asked one of the women. "The Republic Captain and I need to talk in some quiet."

"Most folk are avoiding the clinic as is," she told him. "We appreciate your invitation, but we don't want to intrude."

"If it's be intruded upon or watch my friends *freeze*, I'll stuff this house three times as full," Newport said bluntly. "But I need private and quiet for now."

"I'll keep the children occupied," the woman promised, glancing carefully at Coral.

"Your family?" Coral asked as she followed the mayor through a door deeper into the house.

"Only by the loosest definition," Newport replied. "My daughter's husband's brother's boyfriend's sister and her children." He shrugged. "Maria is a good one, though—and the daughter, the husband, the brother and the boyfriend are *also* around here somewhere, with their children."

Unless Coral had badly misjudged from the exterior, it was not *nearly* that big a house. Even assuming that those three families were the *only* people Newport had taken in, the place had to be getting crowded.

"I managed to get the insulation doubled over the last summer," he told her as they moved into a room set up as a small, painstakingly clean clinic ward. "And we added shutters over all of the windows to keep the heat in there.

"This house is easier to keep warm than the boat sheds, and I've space for people to bed down." He shrugged. "We do what we must."

Coral wasn't sure *she* would have been so generous as to open her home to a random collection of people who knew her family—but then, she was the third of five daughters and three of her sisters had managed enough babies for all five of them! She might not have had children, but she *did* have enough nieces and nephews that their families alone would have filled Newport's house.

"It's that hard to heat against this?" she asked.

"This is..." He sighed, pushing open the door to a small office and leading the way in. "The worst of the storm hasn't hit Keller's Landing yet. Based off the last few, it'll come in tomorrow. No one will be leaving whatever building they're in for at least a day at that point, and then we'll be *chipping* our way out of the harbor afterward."

He gestured Coral to a seat and took two cups from a cupboard. A moment later, he realized that Calvin had followed them in, and added a third cup after looking at the Marine for a few moments.

A sealed vacuum jug was waiting on the desk, and he poured three cups of steaming liquid and passed Calvin and Coral mugs.

"Mulled dilute wine," he told them. "My wife makes it from wine we bring up from the south." He chuckled. "One leftover from when I studied down there."

Coral took a seat without waiting to be asked and took a sip of the drink. The underlying wine, she suspected, was absolutely *terrible*. Exactly the kind of cheap swill poor university students would find some way to make drinkable—and the mix of spices and hot water the Newports had added to it succeeded at that.

"So, we're going to be stuck here for a bit still, I take it?" Coral asked. "How common are these storms?"

Newport was silent for a moment, staring at the wall.

"This is the first this winter," he finally said. "But...this winter hasn't really started yet. I'm worried about what's coming if this is the *start* of winter this year."

"The *first*?" she asked. "How many are you expecting?"

"Last year we had two hellfrost storms," he said quietly. "The year before, three. But it's been one or two a winter for the last ten, twelve years. Before that, we got one a year for a while...but before I left to study medicine?"

He shook his head.

"They were a once-in-a-*decade* thing then," he admitted. "It's getting worse, Captain, and I'm not sure anyone in Daleheart is even *reading* my cursed reports. I can't tell the town this...but I'm starting to think we're going to need to abandon the Landing."

Coral inhaled a sharp breath at that. She could see his point. The storms were flash-freezing the ocean. Anyone who wasn't Daleblood who stepped outside in those temperatures would be dead within minutes. If the Landing itself was getting hit by those temperatures...

"I will raise the concern with my own superiors," she promised. The Navy would have to get permission from Parliament to do something as drastic as evacuating an entire town, but they *had* the sealift to do it. *Songwriter* alone could pack a fifth of the town's population aboard for a journey of a few days—and she was one of four battleships in the Northern Squadron.

"I'll appreciate that, Captain," Newport told her. "As for the Stelforma...the worst they've done is send someone ashore to check our oil tanks without letting us know. Couple of the ladettes found him and dragged him back to shore. They took that surprisingly well —and they've paid for the food they've needed."

"That's better than I was afraid of," Coral admitted. "They've told me they need fuel, Mayor, if they're going to get home. Which explains why they were checking your oil tanks—to see whether you had a hundred and fifty thousand liters of corn oil for them to buy or steal!"

"Our tanks only hold five hundred tons when *full*," Newport pointed out. He sighed. "And we haven't been able to afford to *fill* them for half a decade or more."

Letting the Stelforma buy their fuel from the locals might allow them to fully fill the tanks for once, Coral reflected. Except that the next trip by one of the northern tankers wasn't due for just over three months. Ninety-odd days was far too long for the fishing town to go with reduced fuel supply—and the loss of fish supply might end up hurting them more than the extra fuel would help.

"It's getting that bad up here, is it?" she asked.

"I'm sixty-five years old, Captain," Newport told her. "I remember winter here being January alone. Maybe a week or so of December or February, but not much more. The fjord froze over *once* before my teen years."

He shook his head.

"Now winter stretches from October through March. The fjord freezes by mid-December—so far, at least, after the northern tanker comes through. We can usually keep a channel open until early January with fire and pickaxes, but we lose most of January and at least some of February where we can't get the boats out.

"And this year we have a hellfrost storm in *September*." He snarled the name of the month. "If we can't get a channel out of the fjord when the storm fades, we might be in serious trouble this winter."

"That, at least, I can help with," Coral told him. "*Songwriter* is a battleship, Mayor. Her bow is built to break ice—and what the hull can't handle, the guns will."

From a distance, of course. Her twenty-centimeter guns only depressed to minus five degrees, even if she *was* willing to fire heavy shells into ice next to the battleship's hull. Still, a few dozen shells along a line in her path would more than weaken the ice enough for the prow to tear through.

"If we make it through the next few days, I suppose you'll need to get out of the fjord anyway," Newport said. "We'd appreciate you clearing a channel—and we'll help if you need it. We have those pickaxes and explosives, after all."

"It's the least the Navy can do," Coral promised. "And I'll pass on my own reports to the Admiralty and Daleheart, Mayor. I *hope* that Parliament is just taking their usual time to 'assess' the situation, but one way or another, your town's concerns *will* make it onto the floor.

"You have my word."

And given that one of her sisters *was* a member of Parliament and the other three ran the Republic's second-largest shipyard, Coral Amherst knew she could keep that promise.

CHAPTER 8

Eight days. For eight miserable days, *Songwriter* was completely trapped in Keller's Fjord. For most of that, even the Dalebloods could barely venture outside the battleship's hull—and Coral was forced to order the Seablood crew to relocate around the engine room.

Heated-air piping be damned, the upper works of the ship plunged below freezing on the third day and *stayed* there until the seventh. It was difficult for Coral and her crew to even estimate the outside temperature, but she suspected they were well below the minus forty Celsius that was as low as the mercury thermometers could go.

On the seventh day, the temperature finally began to increase, but the snow and ice continued to bombard the village and the two warships at anchor.

It was late on the eighth day that the thermometers finally started unfreezing as temperatures slowly began to return to more normal ranges, and by dawn on the ninth, it was *merely* minus fifteen degrees Celsius.

That allowed Coral and Rompa to be out on *Songwriter*'s decks and to see just how bad Keller's Fjord looked. The entire inlet was ice as far as the eye could see. The open water beyond would probably be breaking up the ice left by the storm, but the temperature remained cold enough to keep the fjord locked down.

"We'll need to assess the depth," Rompa noted, her Jimmy looking across the waters. "The bow is *supposed* to be able maintain five klicks through ice a meter thick, but..."

Coral nodded her understanding.

"When was the last time *you* heard of one of our battleships *actually* using the icebreaker prow?" she finished for him. "Half the reason for the Northern Doctrine is that *we* don't go north of the twentieth parallel either."

Somewhere north of there was the mythical City of Spires, where the Seablood Great Fleet had originated. Given that the Great Fleet had definitely existed, she supposed the City of Spires had to—and because it most likely existed, the Republic of the Dales treated much of Albion's northern hemisphere as a war grave.

"I've heard of a couple of ships of the Northern Squadron pushing through ice floes and such," Rompa told her. "But never through true ice. I'll get a crew working with a drill and get a depth."

"You do that," Coral told him. "And send Kaloyanov out. I don't think we're going to need the boats, but he knows the systems for refueling."

One of the reasons *why* the Republic Navy's battleships carried so much corn oil was to allow them to replenish escorts at sea. The Navy's cruisers weren't much shorter-legged, but if they wanted to take destroyers more than a few hundred klicks from a friendly port, a reliable fuel supply was essential.

For her part, Coral wasn't even sure why the Republic *bothered* with destroyers. Some ancient tradition required them, but the half-dozen ten-centimeter guns the Dales could fit on eight hundred tons didn't seem particularly useful to her.

"Yes, sir."

She waited as the executive officer headed back into the ship, delighting in being outside again herself. The sun was shining—

weakly but shining for the first time in days—and reflecting off the sheets of ice covering the fjord.

Coral's main focus was on *Dancer*. Looking at the cruiser, she figured the ship could probably push through thirty or forty centimeters of ice. If there were any ships in the world that *didn't* draw their lines from the Great Fleet's icebreaker hulls, she'd never seen them in person.

A chill ran down her spine as she saw the Stelforma crew bringing out grimly identifiable white bundles. They lined the bodies up on the deck and covered them with a tarp against the weather. The freezing temperatures made the deck probably the best place to keep their dead, but it was still...uncomfortable to see.

She'd had enough Dalebloods on her crew to move all of the Seabloods down to the engineering spaces around the engines. The Stelforma hadn't had that option, and the three dozen bodies on the cruiser's forward hull spoke to the price.

"Captain?" Chief Kaloyanov asked from behind her. "You asked the Jimmy to send me out?"

"I did, Chief," Coral confirmed. "We made an agreement with the Stelforma that we'd refuel *Dancer* enough to get her back to their waters. Normally, we'd be sending hoses over on a boat, which would make that your area."

"Can't exactly run the launches on ice, sir," Kaloyanov pointed out.

"And I presume you have a plan."

The purser had arranged a price with the Stelforma before the cold had become utterly insurmountable. At least four of Coral's subordinates should have informed the Chief of the Boats what was going on—and she knew Chief Kaloyanov. The only way he wouldn't have an answer to the problem was if he didn't know.

"Yes, sir," the Chief confirmed.

She waited silently as he stepped up to the railing with her.

"Biggest problem is the hoses," he continued after a moment.

"They're not great with the cold and, well, we may not have enough for this distance."

He gestured to the gap between *Songwriter* and *Dancer*.

"I'm presuming we aren't going to be able to bring them closer?" he asked.

"Frankly, Chief, they're already too close for my liking."

Kaloyanov chuckled.

"I hear that, sir. Never thought I'd be this close to a Stelforma ship without shooting at it."

"Not this far out from embassies and trade ports, anyway," Coral agreed. "Can we fuel them?"

"We've got about two dozen oil-fired heaters that should be enough to keep the hoses flexible in this temperature. But I don't know if we have the right connectors—and my life would be a lot easier if they had about twenty meters of their own hoses."

"Start rolling out the hoses we've got," she ordered. "You're authorized to talk to their chiefs and sort it out. They'll be happier talking to you than one of the Dalebloods."

"Are we accommodating that bullshit?"

Coral chuckled.

"Not really, but you're the best to talk to them on the fuel lines anyway. We're pumping them a hundred and fifty thousand liters of corn oil."

"Won't help them much if they're still frozen in here," the Chief observed.

"That's on the Jimmy and me, Chief. Keller's Landing needs to get their fishing boats out, too. We're working on it."

AFTER A WEEK OF INACTIVITY, Coral was *delighted* to stand on the main deck and direct the operations of her crew. Multiple small corn-oil engines were now sputtering away on the ice outside her ship. Work crews had set up four drills in various places around the bay and were attempting to find the bottom of the ice.

On the shore behind her, she could hear the cheerful shouting of children playing in the snow—and the less-enthusiastic sounds of their parents shoveling the streets clear to allow the town to return to some semblance of normalcy.

For a while, at least. From what Newport had said, there'd be more storms. Most wouldn't be hellfrost storms, but there would be more of those, too.

She could see his point about the town potentially needing to be abandoned. She'd raise that with her superiors, as she'd promised— once she was close enough to use Bloodspeech to reach North Dale Base, anyway.

A resounding thump and crash announced a problem with the starboard crane, and she turned on her heel to see what was going on.

Stressed by the temperatures and the weight suddenly put on it, the crane's main jib had snapped as the crew were lowering a reel of thick rubber hose to the ice. The fueling line massed well over a ton and smashed into the ice from ten meters up.

"Call in!" Kaloyanov bellowed. "Everyone check in!"

Names were shouted back to the Chief—and Coral counted them off. There had been sixteen sailors in the work party around that hose reel...and sixteen names were called back to the noncom.

She sighed in relief where no one could see and then marched over to the wrecked crane.

"Report!" she barked.

"None of the equipment was designed to handle the kind of cold the hellfrost storm brought, sir," Kaloyanov told her. "We're lucky we haven't had more failures of the upper equipment."

"We can't let this slow us down, Chief. Is the hose intact?"

"Haven't had a chance to check yet," he said sharply, then quailed under her equally sharp glare. "It *should* be," he said. "We'll get it checked out and we'll check the other cranes for damage. But… it's not like even warming them up would help, sir.

"Where there's damage, it's already done, sir. We can be careful, and we can reinforce, but…frankly, *Songwriter* is going to need a lot of new pieces when we're out of here."

"We'll deal with that once we *are* out of here, Chief," she told him flatly. "For now, get those hoses hooked up and let's give the Stelforma enough fuel to get *them* out of here."

"That will make a lot of people much happier," he agreed. "I'm on it, sir."

"Good."

She stepped back, watching as Kaloyanov scrambled down a rope ladder to inspect the rubber fueling hoses. They were all stressed, she knew, but the Chief should know better than to be sharp with *her*.

"Sir," Rompa had appeared behind her.

"Jimmy."

"We've got the first measurements back on the ice," he told her. "Ice directly around *Songwriter* is pretty thin, only about ten centimeters. Heating systems have already cleared the water around the drive and steering wheels—it's the same for *Dancer*, if you've looked."

Coral hadn't looked that closely, but she nodded anyway. That made sense, after all. The entire process of heating the ship to keep the crew alive had kept the temperature of the outer hull up as well and helped reduce the ice around her. Then, as they'd begun preparing to move, all three paddlewheels had air from the engines intentionally vented through their armored cages.

Dancer presumably had similar systems.

"The wheels are intact?" she asked.

"No," Rompa said. "But that's why they're wood. Carpenters are already in our supplies, measuring the pieces we've got. We'll have new paddles by noon."

"So, we can get *Songwriter* moving, but can we keep moving?" she asked softly.

"That's what might be a problem," he admitted. "Measurements farther away are getting thicker. Nothing over seventy centimeters so far, but I'm not liking the trend."

"That's already enough that only *Songwriter* can breach through it," Coral observed. "*Dancer* can only be rated for, what, twenty centimeters?"

"I'd guess about the same," Rompa confirmed. "It's not like Captain Carrasco handed us the design schematics of her ship."

"This has been a friendly-enough encounter, but we are still enemies at the core. We'll get the locals to cut a path from their boathouses to *Songwriter* while we fuel *Dancer* and repair the paddle-wheels," she decided aloud.

"And then, sir?"

"By then, Jimmy, I'm hoping we know whether we can make the push out to open waters...or if I need to start digging out explosives."

CHAPTER 9

"This deep in the inlet, the ice varies between about ten centimeters around the ships and the boathouses, where heat is leaking out, up to about eighty centimeters once we exit the harbor," Rompa told Coral later. "We haven't done any drilling farther out. We have drills...but we don't have sleds to put them on.

"We are less prepared for this kind of situation than I would have expected."

She grunted and looked seaward.

"We're almost done fueling *Dancer*," she told him. "I'm disinclined to set out at nightfall, but I also don't want to wait much longer. Is waiting the night going to help us?"

"If it keeps getting warmer, maybe. And I wouldn't make the voyage out in the dark, sir. Oil-fired illuminators won't find every issue we might hit."

"We should ask the mayor for a pilot to guide us out," Coral realized aloud. "That will avoid some issues."

She looked out across the ice.

"It sounds like we won't be able to rely on just ramming through the ice pack," she continued. "But I am *done* being stuck in this fjord, Jimmy. We can wait until morning. No longer."

"And then, sir?" he asked, his tone very careful.

"Then we are going to discover what the damn ice thinks of twenty-centimeter high-explosive shells. *Songwriter* took too much damage from the storm and being frozen into this harbor. If I have to abort the patrol and take her back to North Dale Base anyway, I see no reason to preserve our ammunition stocks."

"We could use emplaced—"

"It will take too fucking long." Emplaced explosives would require measurement and sending people out on foot to lay the charges and the detonator wires. "No, Jimmy. I may be being driven by my own impatience, but Keller's Landing needs the fjord open. And I *very* much want *Dancer* out of Republic waters.

"No, there will be no patient and careful laying of a path. We will ram our way to the first turn, and then we will blast a path clear."

Her executive officer was silent for a moment, clearly doing math.

"It'll break up the ice pack," he finally said. "We probably won't need more than twenty shells a kilometer, using the forward turret and firing one gun at a time. It won't be fast, sir. We'll need to aim and prepare carefully."

Coral refrained from pointing out that the main guns were supposedly rated for eight rounds a minute. *Songwriter* had excellent gunners, and even she had rarely exceeded four when actually firing.

But Rompa was right. It wasn't the rate of fire that was going to matter. They'd need to place the shells with a great deal of care—and that meant they'd be lucky if they managed to breach through a kilometer of ice an hour.

"We're, what, six klicks from the sea?"

"Around that."

"Assuming we waste a quarter of our shells, that'll be a hundred and sixty rounds. A third of our ammunition."

"We'll want to rebalance between the bow and stern magazines afterward," Rompa finally assessed. "We'll have two hundred and forty shells at the stern and only eighty at the front."

"Talk to the gunnery Chiefs, get it ready," she ordered. "We leave at dawn, Jimmy. There's nothing wrong with this place...but I am very, very tired of being stuck in the damn ice."

Dawn rose chilly and pale across Keller's Fjord. Markers danced in the icy wind, showing the places where Coral's people had drilled and measured the depth of the ice.

A fur-swaddled young woman named Blanka Mochizuki stood on the flying bridge with Coral and the XO, positioned to give directions to the helm two decks below them. She seemed more than a bit disconcerted by the entire situation to Coral but game enough.

"We have a path to the boathouses?" Coral asked, looking behind her ship.

"The locals have laid charges and are ready to blast it open once we're clear," Rompa confirmed, glancing at Mochizuki. "A lot less work than clearing a path through the whole fjord."

"And the path from *Dancer*?"

"Commander Fodor says the ice between is shallow enough for them to ram through," her XO told her. "If he's wrong...well, not sure that's our problem."

"If they sink themselves in Keller's Landing's harbor, that might be our problem," Coral replied. "But we'll deal with that if it happens.

"Helm, give me one fifth forward."

The massive driver wheel in the ship's flared stern was almost as wide as the battleship's maximum beam. Covered by an armored shell to protect it from enemy fire, it was the main mechanism to get the battleship up to her usual thirty-kilometer-per-hour speed.

While the battleship's engines had been running for the last week, they hadn't been linked to any of the paddlewheels. That was terrible for the systems and was part of why Coral knew *Songwriter* was going into dry dock for an extended period when they arrived at North Dale—but the alternative had been to freeze half her crew to death.

Now the systems locked into place and the sound of the engines increased to a dull roar as *Songwriter* began to move. The sound of ice breaking began immediately, the shallower layers that had been warmed by the ship's presence giving way instantly.

That didn't last long, and the noise of the breaking ice grew louder as *Songwriter* smashed through thicker layers, her armored bow clearing the way easily so far.

"*Dancer* is moving," Rompa reported. "Slowly but surely, she'll cut our course about a half a klick behind us."

"It seems Captain Carrasco is no more interested in getting close than I am," Coral noted. "Good."

She glanced down the side of her ship and judged their speed.

"Have the helm hold us at five klicks," she ordered. "Once we clear the measured markers, we'll need to slow further, but five klicks will do for now."

It would take them fifteen minutes to clear the markers at that speed, but while Coral was impatient, she wasn't *stupid*. Keller's Fjord would yield to them with the plan they'd made—but it would still all too easily wreck even a battleship if they treated it lightly.

"RANGE IS IN. Elevation is locked. Forward turret is ready."

"Inform Chief Thurstan he may fire when ready," Coral replied to the report from the bridge.

Chief Petty Officer Erlingr Thurstan was the iron-handed disciplinarian who ran her forward turret. The senior gunnery noncommissioned officer aboard *Songwriter*, he would probably have taken over the turret crew for this task anyway.

"Miz Mochizuki, open your mouth and cover your ears," Rompa

instructed their pilot. *He* wore ear protection, Coral knew, but they didn't have many sets of those to spare.

The pilot glanced at the XO in surprise but followed the instructions.

A moment later, the forward turret's port gun fired. The shock rippled back over them, but the magic in Coral's blood allowed her to ignore it and watch the fall of the single shell. It crashed into the ice three hundred meters ahead of the battleship and detonated, sending fragments of ice everywhere. New cracks appeared in the ice pack, rippling in every direction.

"Forward turret adjusting elevation. Forward turret is ready."

Coral had already given the only order she needed to, and Thurstan clearly knew it. The gunnery officer on the bridge had barely finished the word *ready* before the gun sounded.

"Forward turret adjusting elevation..."

She half-tuned out the reports, half-consciously counting the shells as her crew worked the explosions along the main length of the fjord. It wasn't like they were *aiming*, really, just adjusting elevation. That allowed them to drop thirty shells over the course of twenty minutes.

Thanks to her magic, she was able to track the impacts out to the next bend in the fjord, a touch over a kilometer away.

"Now is the moment of truth," she murmured. "Helm! Give me five klicks forward!"

She glanced at Mochizuki.

"We're going slowly, Miz, but keep your eyes open and give the helm directions as needed."

"Of course."

The young woman had *no* idea how to be aboard a warship, Coral reflected as she swallowed a moment of irritation at Mochizuki's disrespect.

Songwriter moved smoothly enough for the first hundred meters toward the trail of shattered ice their fire had created. Coral could *hear* the ice growing thicker against her ship's hull, though. She'd never taken a battleship through ice before today, but she could already tell the difference.

"We're up to three-fifths power to maintain this speed, sir," the helm reported.

"Maintain speed up to three-quarters power," Coral ordered.

Her ship shivered beneath her, three paddlewheels pushing against the chill water to propel them deeper into the ice.

The sound of the ice went from a smooth, slow cracking noise to a sharper grinding as they drove into deeper ice. A moment of trepidation hit Coral. If they'd misjudged the area they needed to shell, they could easily get the battleship *stuck* and need to go out with pickaxes and drills to clear the last distance.

"We are three-quarters power. Maintaining power, but we are losing forward speed."

"Understood," Coral snapped.

She could *feel* her ship slow and stared at the last chunk of unshattered ice—maybe fifty meters across before they reached the bombardment zone.

Forty meters.

Thirty, but if the ship was making *two* kilometers an hour, she'd have been surprised.

Twenty.

Ten.

And she exhaled a sigh of relief as *Songwriter* broke through the last of the solid ice and began to pick up speed again.

"Hold five klicks, helm," she ordered. "We'll slow for another bombardment as we reach the next turn."

It would take them hours to get clear of Keller's Fjord—but they were going to leave a solid trail for both *Dancer* and the locals.

The hellfrost storm had given her and her people a bad week—and she had real concerns about just what its *existence* meant for Keller's Landing and the rest of the isolated northern Landings—but against the engineering and magic of the Dales, it had failed to truly trap them.

CHAPTER 10

THE CONTINENT that held the Dales stretched from the fifteenth parallel north of the equator to the twenty-fifth parallel south of Albion's center. An irregular blob some five thousand kilometers across in every direction, it was generally temperate and fertile.

It also had very even days, especially this close to the equinox. While it was considered unsafe for *Songwriter* to travel at her twenty-kilometer-per-hour cruising speed during full dark—her mirrored and oil-fired illuminators couldn't give her enough warning of dangers—she had thirteen hours of full daylight and another four or so of dusk and dawn where she could run at full speed.

That left only nine hours a day where Coral Amherst's ship had to creep along at ten klicks and seventeen where she cruised at twenty. They were pushing four hundred and fifty kilometers a day, and if she'd been able to take a direct route to North Dale Base, they'd have been there in three days.

Of course, that would have required sailing through the continent itself, and their actual course was closer to three thousand kilometers. It was two full days before they were within a thousand kilometers of the base and Coral could finally report in to her superiors.

That was far from an easy process. Bloodspeech was among the most difficult techniques of the Daleblood magics. It was the most common of the high-end techniques—it was too useful to be anything else—but it was still difficult to master and use.

Making her report to North Dale Base meant that Coral was alone in her office, staring at the flickering light of a shielded lamp as she drew a small knife from a steel case. She'd already unlocked the shield of the oil lamp and it slid aside easily, allowing her to run the blade through the flame to sterilize it.

She let it cool for a few seconds—cauterizing the wound would defeat the point, after all—and then make a small incision on her right index finger.

As blood welled to the top, she focused on the map visible in the light. They were only *barely* under the thousand-kilometer line, which meant she needed to get the direction of North Dale Base exactly right.

Hours upon hours of practice guided her hand as she drew ancient commands on her forehead in her own blood, drawing on the power that channeled through her to reach her home base.

"Admiral Siena," she said clearly. Clarity was more important than volume—and what was *also* important was that Vice Admiral Trudy Siena had designated times for receiving these communications. At this distance, she knew she couldn't enter Siena's mind loudly enough to interrupt, say, an in-person conversation.

"This is Captain Coral Amherst aboard *Songwriter*," she continued when a pulsing sensation in the runes drawn across her face told her Siena was listening. "We had to abort our patrol of the northern shore. We encountered an unusually dangerous weather event, referred to by the locals as a 'hellfrost storm.' The storm appeared to be flash-freezing the open ocean, so we took shelter at Keller's Landing.

"For eight days, my ship was trapped in the fjord and we took exterior damage from extreme cold, well below anything we are expected to withstand. A Stelforma cruiser that was carrying out scouting operations in the open sea was also trapped at Keller's Landing.

"In this instance, I judged they were fellow seafarers in distress and aided them by selling fuel from *Songwriter*'s own tanks. Given the damage we had sustained, I knew we would be unable to complete our patrol, so the reduction in range was not relevant."

She paused, considering her next words.

"Per discussions with the mayor of Keller's Landing, these hellfrost storms are becoming a more-common event. He raised serious concerns about the ability of the settlement to endure if conditions worsen. Given our own experience with the storm and the lack of Dalebloods in Keller's Landing, I believe the locals are overestimating their ability to survive."

Her impression of the fisherfolk of Keller's Landing was that they would keep trying to make it work until the hellfrost storms and the sea killed them.

"The Stelforma vessel *Dancer* headed directly out to sea to leave our territorial waters as quickly as possible," she concluded. "I will provide a written formal report on the hellfrost storm and the status of Keller's Landing once I arrive at North Dale Base."

Coral spent a moment considering if there was anything else she needed to put into this initial bare-bones report. Nothing leapt to mind.

"Report complete," she declared to the empty air. "I await your response."

Seconds ticked by in silence, then the blood on her face pulsed warm and the voice of a woman a quarter of a continent away echoed in her ears without ever sounding in the office.

"Report received, Captain Amherst," Vice Admiral Siena told her. "Remain blooded and await an extended response. *Spearfisher* will be deployed to complete your patrol, but my initial assessment of your decisions is positive.

"I must consult with the Admiralty. Patience, Captain Amherst."

The pulsing on her face faded, and Coral released the magic that had linked her to her commanding officer.

"Patience," she said aloud, her lips twisting the word into a curse. She was still just over four days from the naval base. It made *sense* that the Admiral would take her time to formulate a detailed response and consult with the Admiralty in Daleheart.

The Admiral might not be able to reach the Admiralty by Blood-speech, but she had access to the telegraph network. The communication might not be as swift or as clear as Bloodspeech, but it was more than fast enough for most purposes.

Coral wrapped a bandage around her cut finger and considered herself in the mirror. She didn't *like* leaving the Bloodspeech runes on her face, but it meant that when the Admiral reached out again, she'd be able to reply.

Plus, while a Captain at sea was mistress of her domain, she still needed to jump when an Admiral gave her orders.

Seventy-six minutes passed by the chronometer on her desk before the runes on her face warmed again, matching a tingling warning pulse that shivered through her blood. At this distance, she might not have noticed the shiver if she hadn't been wearing the runes—and that was part of why she was waiting alone in her quarters.

"Captain Amherst, this is Vice Admiral Siena. Confirm you are receiving. I await your response."

That was unusual. Coral's own magic should have told the Admiral she'd made the connection. There were reasons to make sure...but they usually meant something *important* was afoot.

"I am receiving your speech, Admiral Siena," Coral confirmed after checking the runes on her face. "I await your orders."

"These orders are not mine, Captain Amherst," Siena told her.

That admission sent a shiver through Coral's stomach. Whose orders *were* they, then?

"The Admiralty has reviewed the summary of your report. They wish to receive your written report and interview you and your senior officers as soon as possible. You are ordered to bypass North Dale Base and proceed directly to the Republic Naval Yards at Daleheart."

Daleheart was on the southern edge of the continent, another ten days' travel past North Dale Base.

"Once you arrive in Daleheart, you will turn *Songwriter* over to the Yards for a full examination and all necessary repairs. Surrendering your command, you will place yourself at the Admiralty's full disposal for their review."

Siena paused, letting Coral attempt to muster her thoughts at the series of blows. There was no reason for her to formally surrender her command when handing her ship over to a shipyard. Not unless they were expecting either the repairs or the review of her encounters in Keller's Landing to take *months*.

"You are to advise immediately if you feel that *Songwriter* cannot make the journey to Daleheart," Siena finally said. "My analysis suggests that even if you completely filled the Stelforma ship's tanks, you should retain sufficient oil aboard for the journey.

"I await your response."

Coral took a moment. Several of them—probably more than she should have—to regain her equilibrium. There *were* positive reasons she would be asked to surrender her command—promotion or transfer, usually. It was a bad sign that they were telling her in advance of the *surrender* and not of a new role, though.

Still...she had the fuel for an extra five thousand kilometers. Not much more, not running at speed, but she had it. And while *Songwriter*'s damage was pervasive, none of it was critical. Coral wouldn't want to take her ship into battle in her current state, but half a month of regular sailing would be fine.

And if there *was* some kind of real threat to Coral's own career,

Daleheart was where she had the money, connections and *power* to make a fight of it.

Exhaling the last of her fears and once more becoming *herself*, she smiled and focused her magic on the distant Admiral.

"Orders received, sir," she confirmed. "I have no concerns about *Songwriter*'s ability to make the journey to Daleheart. It may, I must note, exacerbate the temperature damage to parts of the hull, but I have full faith in the ability of the Republic Naval Yards to correct that.

"We will proceed as ordered."

CHAPTER 11

THE WEATHER at Daleheart was as opposite to the weather they'd seen at Keller's Landing as it was possible to be. Thirty-five-degree heat saw many of Coral's Seablood crew stripped to the waist. Cooler air was piped from below the waterline to the upper works, but that didn't help around the engine rooms or on the upper decks.

Coral was as unbothered by the heat as she had been by the cold. She stood on *Songwriter*'s flying bridge, watching for the first signs of home as the battleship's engines pounded beneath her feet.

The *real* first sign of Daleheart, of course, had been the pair of one-fifth-scale siblings now keeping pace with *Songwriter*. The destroyers had *no* broadside guns—there was no space between the steering paddle wheels for both engines and guns—and their entire armament was built into a two-tiered stack of forward-facing casemate mounts holding their ten-centimeter guns.

While Coral appreciated the *idea* behind the escort, nothing except a freighter or another destroyer was actually threatened by the Navy's little siblings. Even at point-blank range, the destroyer guns wouldn't breach *Songwriter*'s armor.

Impotent or not, however, the two coastal ships guided the

battleship toward home. Sniffing the air, Coral could pick out the distinct smell of the Dales' coastal industrial cities. Rotting fish, smoke, burning oil and humanity combined to create a particular aroma that could be scented before they even entered the bay.

At least for a Daleblood, anyway.

"Ship to port, thirty degrees," the lookout shouted down.

It was the fourth such announcement in the last ten minutes, but Coral turned to see who was nearby anyway. This time, it was a Stelforma trading ship, flying the flag of the York Republic. The Yorkies often used their present-but-constrained-by-the-Stelforma democracy as a basis to claim common ground with the Republic of the Dales.

At least when they needed trade access, anyway, Coral reflected.

Looking past the Stelforma ship, she finally spotted the edge of the breakwater. The lighthouse on the end of the ridge was the first major structure she'd seen. The breakwater wasn't overly habitable, a curved expanse of bare rock that marked the seaward side of the rounded bay that sheltered Daleheart's harbor.

Underneath the lighthouse was part of the second-to-last of Daleheart's defenses. To get this far, any attack would have to fight their way through the entire Republic Navy, but if they got here, the thirty twenty-centimeter guns in each of Fort Guidelight and Fort Northside would give them a bad, *bad* day.

Rounding the end of the natural breakwater, *Songwriter* made her way under the guns of the two forts into the great Daleheart Bay. Five kilometers across and deep enough for battleships through almost its entire area, the Bay was the beating heart of the Navy of the Republic of the Dales—and of the Republic itself, for that matter.

Tucked just inside the natural breakwater, positioned to dash into open water at a seeming moment's notice, was the First Division of Home Fleet. Four battleships and twelve cruisers flashed acknowledgement lights at *Songwriter* in turn as they sailed past.

"Return the salute," Coral ordered.

The illuminators on the front of the ship were already turning, the oil lamps flaring to life to allow the searchlight to be used to acknowledge the Home Fleet ships.

Songwriter's course gave them plenty of time to do so as they swung back toward the west and around the defensive squadron. The merchant ships ahead of and behind Coral's battleship would go straight from the gateway to the main docks at the far side of the Bay, where a hundred ships were already busy loading and unloading cargo and fuel.

Behind *Songwriter*, the east side of Daleheart Bay was home to the smaller docks for the effectively uncountable fishing fleet of the Republic's capital, along with the processing plants and markets that handled their cargo.

The west side, their destination, was the Republic Naval Yards. One-third-owned by the company run by Coral's sisters, the Yards built and maintained the warships of the Dales. Along the south side, the inside of the inhospitable rock of the breakwater ridge, were the docks and fueling infrastructure of Home Fleet, where the *other* eight battleships of the capital defense force were currently at anchor.

Normally, a visit to Daleheart would involve Coral bringing her ship into the open docks of the base there, but her orders were clear. She was to deliver *Songwriter* into the hands of the Republic Naval Yards.

Then, and only then, would she finally hope to understand just what going to happen in response to the events of the last month.

WHEN *SONGWRITER* WAS FINALLY TIED off, Coral mustered the crew on the upper deck.

"Sailors of the Republic," she greeted them. "We have faced the worst weather any capital ship of the Dales has ever seen. We survived. All of us—and the fate of the Stelforma crew trapped with us shows that was not guaranteed!"

She gave the hundreds of gathered sailors a rare and measured smile.

"But *Songwriter* was not built for the frigid winds of hell itself to batter her works. We saw that in our broken cranes and cracked plating. So, we have brought her here, to the greatest naval yard in the world, where the engineers and yard workers of the greatest navy in all Albion will make her right."

Coral raised a hand.

"The damage done is the fault of no sailor or officer here," she assured them fiercely. "You did your duties to the highest standard I could ask of you—and that is why we live."

That and the power that flowed in the blood of her Daleblood crew—but this wasn't the time for *that* particular point.

She gestured Rompa up next to her.

"But our masters and mistresses in the Admiralty have questions," she told her crew. "And I have been informed that they will require *all* of my time. I am ordered and required to surrender command of this ship and this crew."

She wasn't expecting any great show of emotion over that and didn't get one. Tradition didn't call for crew to become attached to their commanders like that—and never to show it if they did.

Coral had no illusions about how attached her crew was. But they had served her well, and there were traditional ways to show that for the officers wealthy enough to manage them.

"I will momentarily surrender command to Commander Rompa. You all know him. He will serve you well as the Navy decides what to do with us all. First, however, I have one last duty and privilege to discharge to you all."

She could see enough expressions to see the hope rippling through her crew. They knew the traditions as well as she did.

"A donative of one month's wages will be delivered to each of you by your superiors before the day is out," she assured them. "As a sign of my recognition of your service and seahandling. This is the one and only time I will say this, my sailors, so listen carefully:

"You never truly disappointed me and stood against weather that rose from hell itself with me. I am honored and pleased to have commanded you all."

The crew was actually completely silent as she spoke—though Coral suspected that was sheer shock at just *how* large the donative she'd just announced was. Tradition called for one day's wages per year that the Captain commanded the ship. Many Captains would spend a good chunk of their last days in command scrambling to put together the funds to meet that tradition—and *smart* Captains saved a large portion of their salary throughout their service.

Coral Amherst had commanded *Songwriter* for five years. For all of the intentional distance she'd put between herself and her crew, they'd served her well.

And she was *more* than wealthy enough to show her appreciation in a way that would matter.

"Commander Rompa?" She turned to the man who was no longer her Jimmy.

He was dressed in a plain black-and-white uniform, done up in full dress even though he must have been *sweltering* in the heat and sun, and he saluted her crisply.

"I relieve you, Captain Amherst," he told her. "I assume command of *Songwriter*."

More likely than not, Rompa's command would be temporary. He might maintain authority over the battleship for her entire refit, but he was not yet senior enough to command her in service. But his command was no less real for its likely duration, and unless he screwed it up, it would be a solid check mark in his record that would probably see him command his own cruiser within the year.

Coral Amherst knew perfectly well that Ardan Rompa wasn't going to screw it up.

"I stand relieved, Commander Rompa," she told him, returning the salute. "Take good care of our people, you hear me?"

"I will, Captain."

Coral held the salute a few seconds longer than she had to, then swallowed a sigh and nodded to her former XO.

"I think I have places to be, Ardan," she murmured.

"I got the word just before I came up," he whispered back. "There's a carriage waiting for you."

He paused, then gave her a firm nod.

"Good luck, sir."

CHAPTER 12

A DOZEN TRAIN tracks converged on the Republic Naval Yards, bringing materials and parts from across the core seven Dales. While a Dale was *now* an administrative district of the Republic, the term came from the collection of seven broad valleys whose waterways fed into Daleheart Bay.

Their slopes produced the ores necessary to forge steel of every kind, as well as most other materials the Republic needed—including the gold and aluminum coinage that underlay their economy. The valley floors themselves were the most fertile ground on the continent, producing the vast quantities of corn and grain that fed both the stomachs and the engines of the Republic of the Dales.

Coral had grown up to the sounds of engines and the smell of corn oil. The Naval Yards were readily visible—and audible—from the sprawling Amherst Estate up the hill from there. Most of the estates of Daleheart's wealthy families were up on the sides of the circular ridge that surrounded the bay, allowing them to literally look down on and keep an eye on the factories, shipyards and freighters that underpinned their income and power.

If her meeting with the Admiralty went poorly, she might well find herself back at the estate, imposing on her sisters' goodwill and familial responsibility to unleash her family's power to maintain her commission.

For now, though, she knew *exactly* where the carriage would be waiting. Daleheart had been built before the Great Fleet arrived, and records from the early days of the Dales were fragmentary at best, but Daleheart was clearly the newest of the major cities of the main Dales. It was a planned city in ways that were easily clear to the educated eye—and one of the clearest signs of that was the presence of large, smooth thoroughfares that radiated out from the bay and the circular avenues that crossed them.

Harbor Road was less than two hundred meters from the water and arced from the Naval Yards on the west side of the bay all the way around to cut through the fishers' markets on the east side. Only the south side of the bay, the breakwater ridge, was missing from Daleheart's circular road network.

Uninhabited and uninhabitable as the breakwater was, the only structures there were the lighthouse, the lighthouse's attendant forts...and a long line of smaller fortifications, intended to stop any attempted landing on the natural barrier.

Coral walked along where the Harbor Road cut through the Republic Naval Yards, keeping out of the way of the carriages and trackless train-haulers that rumbled through with their cargos. The sounds of iron-shod hooves and iron-rimmed wheels could be overwhelming to a stranger, she knew, but it was no louder than the engine room of a battleship.

And it was home to her. She knew the Admiralty would *rather* have sent the carriage directly to *Songwriter*'s dock, but the Naval Yards restricted the number of vehicles that could enter. The trackless haulers were massive and difficult to control. Any unexpected impedance would result in the destruction of the surprise carriage—and, worse, the loss of critical war matériel.

Instead, there was a parking enclosure just inside the big gates that marked the end of the military yards. She had expected to have to ask the noncommissioned officer on duty which carriage was waiting for her, but she swiftly realized that was unnecessary.

The carriage was positioned away from the other vehicles, and its black-and-white Navy livery gleamed in the sun. Two horses were still hitched, their black chitin polished to glittering by the driver currently checking their hooves for issues.

Twelve hooves took a while to check over, though Coral presumed the horses had been checked out before they'd ever left the Citadel, the command center for the Republic's military.

Stepping up to the carriage, she cleared her throat loudly and the driver looked up. The Lieutenant looked too young to have graduated the Academy yet, but his jacket and insignia confirmed his rank.

He straightened swiftly and saluted.

"Captain Amherst?"

"Yes."

"I am Lieutenant Martin Shain, on assignment to the Citadel," he swiftly introduced himself. "I'm to bring you to the South Tower immediately. Just let me wake our escort."

Escort?

Coral didn't say anything aloud, simply nodding her understanding.

Shain whistled sharply and was answered by movement in a shaded area off to one side. Four more horses were promptly led out of the shed, their chitin glittering deep purple as they entered the light.

Someone had put a great deal of work into selecting the creatures if their natural armor matched *that* closely...and Coral was unsurprised to see that all four *riders* were equally matched. All of them were the same height and wearing identical white uniforms with dark purple piping on the jackets.

Dalesguard. Each wore a sword and pistol on their belt and had a bolt-action carbine holstered on their saddles. The swords would be Dalesteel, like Coral's own blade. The women were Dalebloods—and despite their matching appearances, looks were far from the main criteria for their assignment.

The Dalesguard protected the Citadel—and the Parliament of the Dales. Parade-group troops, yes...but also the final line of defense of the military and political leaders of Coral's nation.

"Lieutenant," one of the women greeted Shain calmly. "I told you that you should bring your horses into the stable."

"I expected the Captain sooner," the young man admitted. It was not, Coral noted, an accusation thrown at her. Instead, it was an admission of error. "I also needed light to check the hooves. Extra was limping the last few blocks, and it took me a bit to find the stone he'd picked up."

"Are we ready to move?" Coral asked bluntly. "I understand that the Admiralty wishes to speak with me with some urgency."

"As soon as you're in, Captain," the Dalesguard Sergeant told her. "We'll see you the whole way safely."

A CITY of almost two million souls, Daleheart sprawled in every direction, rising up the sides of the circular ridge surrounding the Bay in carefully built terraces and then down the other side with more terraces.

The Citadel was on the top of the ridge, at the center of the northern curve. The South and North Towers were each immense structures, rising fifty meters above either side of the rocky natural wall. Further pieces of the complex sprawled down the mountainside. In pride of place in the south half of the Citadel complex was a quintet of fifty-centimeter railway cannon, absolute behemoths that had never been duplicated since their completion just before Coral was born.

Their twenty-five-meter-long barrels, though, would put a shell larger than Coral's carriage into ships *outside* the breakwater fifteen kilometers away—and the height of the South Tower meant that the

Daleblood observers above the guns could provide enough information to target those ships.

The main purpose of the Citadel, though, wasn't so much to protect the harbor as it was to protect the train tracks. Trains, after all, couldn't go over a hundred-meter-tall natural barrier. There were a couple of lower points in the ridge that had been built up over the years with ramps that could carry track at a reasonable angle, but the main railway lines into Daleheart went through a massive, reinforced tunnel blasted through the rock.

And the Citadel spread from the fortifications around the north side of that tunnel to the logistics depots around the south side. The largest military installation the Dales knew of, it housed everything from the training academies for naval and army officers to the military high command.

The Admiralty occupied the South Tower, and Coral watched through the window of the carriage as Lieutenant Shain guided his pair of black horses through the traffic around the Tower. Away from the shipyards, there were no train-haulers. The crowd here was a mix of other carriages, riders like the Dalesguard around them, and people on foot.

Their liveried carriage moved them to the front of the security line and into the grounds of the Citadel. The ridge and the towers themselves loomed as they moved deeper, the road turning backing and forth as it rose up underneath the barrels of the stupendous railway guns.

Finally, Shain pulled the carriage to a halt. An artificial edifice of sheer gray stone rose in front of them, backing onto the mountain and putting the lie to the claim that the towers were *only* fifty meters high. From there, where the South Tower met the rocky ridge that guarded Daleheart, the central command of the Navy rose at least eighty meters into the air above Coral.

Valets in the same white-and-purple uniform as the Dalesguard but lacking the armaments emerged to claim the four horses as the women dismounted. The one who'd spoken before opened the door to Coral's carriage and gestured her out.

"Lieutenant Shain is done now," she told Coral. "We will escort you the rest of the way. The Admirals have been informed of your arrival and are gathering as we speak."

The woman might have only worn the insignia of a Sergeant, but Coral knew perfectly well that treating her as a mid-level NCO would be a quick way to turn her upcoming meeting sour. The Dalesguard were special.

"Let's not keep them waiting, then," Coral replied, stepping out of the carriage. "Lead the way."

CHAPTER 13

THE PROBLEM, Coral realized, with being told she'd been summoned to speak to "the Admiralty" was the fact that the Admiralty was an administrative structure that included everything from gofers like Lieutenant Shain through the administrative officers and noncoms who managed payroll, benefits and pensions...all the way to the six Admirals who formed the Admiralty Commission.

"The Admiralty" encompassed some five *thousand* people, including over twenty Admirals. At no point in the entire chain of events leading to Coral Amherst entering the sumptuously decorated room on the very top floor of the South Tower of the Daleheart Citadel had she expected to end up in front of the entire Admiralty Commission.

And she had been very, *completely* wrong.

There were *exactly* six people in the gorgeously decorated viewing room. All of them wore the same black-and-white dress uniform as Coral herself, matching the coloring and even the heraldry of the room around them.

But all six of them had the shoulder flashes of full Admirals, and she knew each of them by face and name, if not in person. She had not been rushed back from the farthest reach of the Northern Squadron's deployments to speak to one senior Admiral and their department, as she'd assumed.

"Admirals," she greeted them all, trying to avoid a childish squeak to her voice and manner. She suspected that *anyone* would be taken aback to emerge into the room and be met with *that* much gold braid.

"Captain Amherst," the oldest of them, a Daleblood woman named Roseline Wibawa, greeted her. Wibawa was ancient, even for one of the Daleblood, and looked like every minute of her hundred-plus years was weighing on her.

But she was Daleblood and her fragile-looking frame held the iron will that had commanded the forward strike fleet during the last war with the Stelforma. A century was not nothing, not even to Coral's people, but the Admiral was still hale.

"Take a seat, Captain. Drink?"

Coral obeyed Wibawa's command. The Chief of the Admiralty Commission was, arguably, the most powerful human being in the Dales. Wibawa and her fellows answered to the President and Prime Minister, but those worthies were subject to change every five years. *Faster*, if the Prime Minister lost the confidence of Parliament.

Admiral Wibawa had been Chief of the Admiralty Commission for ten years—and a *member* of the Commission for thirty. She *was* the continuity of command of the Republic Navy.

"I do not need—"

"Captain, it is thirty-six fucking degrees out there," a dark-skinned Seablood Admiral snapped. Admiral Aurelius Tse had been executive officer of the Northern Squadron's flagship when Coral had been a brand-new ensign, thirty years ago.

Now he was the youngest and most junior member of the Commission and he had lost neither his muscular bulk nor his tone.

"Unless the Dalesguard hooked you up to a water tank on your ride up here, you are sweltering, Daleblood or not," Tse continued as he rose and poured a glass of water from an ice-filled pitcher. "You can survive, yes, but endurance is not life."

There was no universe in which Coral Amherst would argue with any member of the Commission—let alone Tse. She took the glass of water and nodded thankfully to the Admiral.

"I...do not expect to have Admirals handing me water, sir."

"No one else enters this room, Captain," Wibawa told her bluntly. "The Commission gets used to pouring their own drinks. It is a price of security."

Coral took a sip of the ice water to conceal her concern at that. If *no one else* entered the room, what was *she* doing there?

Something in her expression must have shown it anyway, because the other Seablood Admiral on the Commission laughed.

"Please, Roseline," Vanessa Hussain told the senior Admiral brightly. "We're not *quite* that locked down here. You aren't the first Captain in this room with us *today.*

"But this space is *hopefully* the most secure in the Republic. What would have been rooms on either side of us were filled in when the Tower was built. Outside has the fall to the bay, the inside a dozen of the Dalesguard. Only the Commission and those we are interviewing enter this room. *Ever.*"

That helped...and didn't, at the same time.

"I am at the Commission's disposal," Coral finally said. "As ordered, I yielded command of *Songwriter* to my executive officer to enter the yards for repairs. My understanding is that my main assignment now is to report on the events of our *visit* to Keller's Landing."

Tse chuckled.

"That's one way to put it," he observed. "It's a place to start, at least."

Coral carefully removed a folio of typed pages from inside her uniform jacket and laid it on the table. The surface was stone, a black rock polished smooth first by the artisans who'd built it and then by two hundred years of drinks and papers.

"My written report, sirs," she told them. "The original is proceeding through the usual channels, but I suspected an extra copy might come in handy."

"It will," Wibawa agreed. "But we have time, and we need to be certain. Tell us everything, Captain Amherst. Everything you experienced of this hellfrost storm. Everything the locals told you. *Everything.*"

Coral swallowed and considered how to lay it out. The best place to start was always at the beginning, she supposed.

"*Songwriter* was dispatched on a standard north-coast security patrol on August thirtieth," she began. All twelve months in the Dales calendar had thirty days, which made some math easy at least. "It was five days later, on September fifth, that we first spotted signs of unusual weather..."

IT WAS QUICKLY clear that the Commission knew *exactly* how to conduct this kind of interview. They mostly listened in silence, but when they asked questions, they drew out details or key points Coral hadn't even thought she remembered.

After an hour of near-continuous speech, she was even more grateful for the pitcher of ice water that Tse dropped off at her elbow after the first ten minutes. The Admirals were perfectly patient with her taking the time to sip water as she spoke, and the pitcher was almost empty by the time she finished describing her, in retrospective, somewhat-ridiculous decision to *bombard* her way out of the fjord.

"I'm not sure how long it would have taken for the ice to melt sufficiently for us to break out in a more-conventional fashion," she concluded, the argument sounding somewhat weak to her own voice.

"And the Stelforma left as promised?" Wibawa asked.

"We kept an eye on them for as long as we could, and there was no sign of them heading anywhere but straight out to sea," she confirmed. "From what the Chiefs told me about the fueling, it's likely they had effectively *no* fuel left when we started pumping corn oil into their tanks.

"What fuel they'd arrived at Keller's Landing with, they'd burned over the week of the storm to keep as many of their people alive as they could. They lost, from what we saw, at least thirty of their crew."

"A cruiser of that size... That's what, a tenth of Carrasco's command?" Tse asked. "More?"

"Ten ten-centimeter guns," Hussain murmured. "That makes her an *Artist*-class ship, most likely. Two thousand tons, crew two hundred and ten. Thirty-plus dead would have left her all but unable to fight."

"And we only gave her enough fuel to make it back to the Southern Archipelago," Coral confirmed. "Unless their engines are *far* more efficient than ours."

"So far as our intelligence assets can tell us, the Stelforma remain behind in the area of major combustion engines," the old Seablood Admiral told her. "An *Artist*-class ship is one of their newer long-range scout cruisers, but she still won't have the range of one of ours for the same fuel."

"I...hope that the fact our fuels are interchangeable is less news to the Commission than it was to me," Coral said. "She called it 'diesel,' said our corn oil was equivalent, just produced differently."

"The alchemical structure of the two fuels is materially identical," Admiral Danka Rodgers told her. The blonde Daleblood officer handled shipbuilding, Coral presumed, in the same way that Hussain handled intelligence. The Commission didn't have formal titles for the division of duties, but everyone in the Navy knew those divisions existed.

"We are aware of this but have kept it close to our chests as a security measure," Rodgers noted. "We were hoping that the

Stelforma either didn't realize this themselves or, hopefully, didn't know that we knew."

"Several of our war plans are based around seizing Stelforma fuel supplies," Wibawa noted. "If they don't expect us to use their fuel, those depots may be less defended." She shrugged. "Not that it will change much if we execute on those plans. It would just be...useful."

There was a long silence as Coral waited for further questions, then Tse rose from his seat with a sigh. As if in answer to some silent agreement among the six Admirals, he crossed to a section of wooden paneling on the wall and pressed on two particular slats.

A two-meter-wide chunk of the paneling popped out in two sections, allowing Tse to swing the concealed doors wide and reveal a map of Albion marked with dozens—hundreds!—of pins in a dozen different colors.

Basically all of the markers were south of the twentieth parallel, Coral noted absently. Most were concentrated around the irregular blob of the Dales itself, with the majority of the remainder sitting on the Southern Archipelago.

Outside the Dales and the Archipelago, Albion was mostly water. Republic ships had navigated the full circumference of the equator, encountering only tiny islands that were uniformly hostile to human life for one reason or another.

As she watched, Tse took an ice-blue pin from a case on the inside of one of the doors and stuck it in the map next to Keller's Landing. Scanning for similar pins, she realized there were at least twenty of them, spreading up from the north coast into the waters the Republic patrolled.

"Those pins are...hellfrost storms, aren't they?" she asked softly.

"Every one that's been reported in the last two years," Wibawa told her. "We've been lucky, in one way. You were the first of our warships to end up in the middle of one. That we know of, anyway."

"We're missing two cruisers that were in the right area," Hussain growled. "Intelligence suggests that the Stelforma are telling the truth when they say they don't know anything—though intelligence and your own encounters suggest that they're sending long-range cruisers farther north than they're supposed to."

There were two black-and-red pins in the oceans north of the Dales, Coral saw.

"If you knew this, why pull me in here?" she asked softly.

"Because, without question, you were the first Captain of the Republic Navy to end up in a hellfrost storm and live," Tse told her. "You have seen the monster encroaching upon us and you understand, I think, what this means."

Coral was still staring at the map and considering Dr. Newport's words back in Keller's Landing.

"It's getting worse," she said softly.

"Two hundred and five years ago, the Seablood were forced to flee the City of Spires," Hussain said, the woman in charge of the Republic Navy's intelligence services speaking barely above a whisper. "We have...very little information on what drove our ancestors to the sea we now name them for.

"But we know it was a dark power that came in waves of cold and death."

Coral shivered as she remembered the storm.

"There was something to that storm," she told the Commission, her voice barely louder than Hussain's. "Some dark power fueling it. It was no ordinary blizzard."

"That is what we were afraid of," Wibawa replied. "And that is why we summoned you here, Captain Amherst. Two centuries ago, a dark power overwhelmed the home of the Seabloods and launched five hundred ships on a desperate flight that brought them here.

"Now that dark power has brought its curse to *our* shores. It took longer than their ancestors feared, but the Seablood Great Fleet was followed. And we now face an enemy we know nothing about that commands a power we do not understand."

The ice-blue pins spoke to a wave of cold and death already sweeping over the northern shores of the Dales.

"What do you need of me, Admirals?" Coral asked, still staring at the map. "My magic is strong, and my will is unbroken. My life and sword are the Republic's to command."

"And command you the Republic will," Tse assured her. "But not yet."

"Not yet, sir?"

"There are auguries to be done and further reports to be compiled," Wibawa said calmly. "Much of what we need has already been done, but there remains much work.

"You are assigned one week's leave," the Chief of the Commission told her. "You will take it here in Daleheart and not leave the city. You will not be informed of your next mission through the ordinary channels. You *will* hear from the Commission before that week is out, and we *will* have a duty for you.

"One that calls for an unbroken will and powerful magic—and also for a warship commander who has seen the face of the threat."

"Why the mystery and shadows?" Coral demanded. "If you cannot trust me, why entrust me with the mission at all?"

"We trust you, Captain Amherst," Tse said flatly. "But you speak of secrets held by few outside this Commission. We will take our time to build our plan."

"We will also take our time to verify you," Hussain told her. "We believe you are the officer for this job, but we must be certain. We will review your career in great detail. We will know your flaws, your strengths."

"I am a loyal servant of the Republic," Coral ground out.

"Trust but verify," Admiral Rodgers told her. "It is a fundamental principle of our supply chains and logistics. For a mission on which the fate of the Republic may fall, why should we apply a lesser standard?"

Coral...couldn't argue with that. Their lack of trust offended her, but she supposed she saw Rodgers' point.

"You are the Admirals of the Republic," she finally forced herself to say. "I will defer to your wisdom, of course, and await word."

"You will not wait long," Tse told her. "You will see."

CHAPTER 14

IT HAD BEEN LONGER than Coral really could count since she'd truly had a stretch of time, however short, without responsibility. Even when on leave, the Captain of a ship had to keep her vessel in the back of her mind.

Her sisters had welcomed her home with the usual stiff affectionate disregard. Coral was the middle of five, with her oldest sibling almost twenty years older than her and her youngest almost twenty years younger.

Their mother had been quite...particular about her schedule. And while their father had brought the money, prestigious name and shares in industrial entities to their marriage, Coral knew damn well that their *mother* had basically run not just the estate but the entire business empire.

Mariela's death when her youngest daughter was two years old had *broken* Brendan Varlam Hamed Amherst, the unquestioned first mover of Daleheart's naval and steel industries. Fortunately for the family's fortunes, their eldest daughter Valentina Amherst had already spent over a decade apprenticing at her mother's side and had stepped into the big seat at Amherst Enterprises immediately.

It had taken two years for their father to regain sufficient composure to recognize that he *couldn't* run his industrial empire anymore and officially pass control of the board to Valentina.

That had been a quarter-century earlier, though, and Coral's eldest sister ran the family estate and businesses with a steely hand. She and Coral clashed over many things—and bonded over being the only two of the sisters without husbands or children.

Coral had already been in the Navy when Valentina had taken over. She'd missed both her youngest sister's birth and their mother's death, and she wasn't entirely sure her siblings had forgiven her for either.

Her inheritance from their father was the smallest. That had hurt then, but after fifteen years, she understood—she wasn't going to be around to help run Amherst Enterprises, and by the time her father had passed, Coral's marriage to the Navy was clear enough that everyone knew she wasn't planning on providing grandchildren.

Sitting in the garden of the estate on the fourth day, she reflected on the recognition that her father had felt the same way she did about her sisters' children: they were never to be denied anything. Not money, not opportunities, not power.

They would be taught to use those things *well*—Valentina was unquestionably the most *powerful* of the five siblings, but Coral's command of a major Republic Navy combatant was typical of the roles held by her family. Their youngest and *least*-accomplished sibling was teaching Bloodspeech at the Sunset Academy—while raising triplets.

Said triplets were currently seven years old and causing absolute *havoc* in the mansion's carefully manicured gardens. Coral was, at least theoretically, keeping an eye on them...but *her* idea of watching children very closely resembled her approach to training junior sailors.

No limbs had been broken and no one was dead. Beyond that, they could do whatever they wanted.

They might be being chased by one of the gardeners at that

moment, but Coral knew that the crotchety old Seablood would never do more than yell at the girls—and she *had* noted what the triplets had done to the topiary sea dragon that stood watch over the west gate.

There would be consequences for that. *Coral* would have taken away the girls' garden privileges, but that was their mother's call to make. So, she let the girls run away from the angry gardener and watched to make sure nothing serious happened, allowing them to take enjoyment in what was probably going to be their last time in the garden for a while.

A soft chime cut through the garden like an audible razor. Coral turned to look toward the west gate with its currently...de*pawed* topiary dragon and was on her feet before she'd even consciously identified the black-and-white-liveried Admiralty coach or the uniformed officer standing next to the bell in full dress uniform.

A household guard was already hustling over to the gate to do his job of checking strangers. Coral took a moment to locate the triplets, noting that they had also stopped and turned to look at the gate when the bell had rung.

The gardener probably hadn't heard it from this far away, but the girls were Dalebloods.

"All right, girls," she said loudly. "You've done enough damage for one afternoon, and your mother is going to be having a nice long chat with Mr. Nicotera about the poor dragon. Go inside and get to your studies. I need to speak to the nice officer at the gate."

"Does this mean you're leaving already, Aunt?" the ringleader of the redheaded trio asked sadly.

"I serve at the discretion of the Republic, girls. Remember that. Duty comes before all else for such as us. And *well* before maiming a loyal servant's favorite art project."

That was as sharp as she was going to be at the girls for that... but, like Mr. Nicotera the gardener, she too would have words for Ivory, the youngest of the Amherst sisters, about her children.

~

APPROACHING THE GATE, Coral paused to let the household guard go through the not-entirely-ritual process of validating the newcomer was who he said he was. *She* recognized Lieutenant Shain, but Hardison hadn't met the young officer before, and it was Hardison's *job* to make sure no one entered the estate grounds without reason... and escort.

As she waited, she studied the dragon topiary more closely and mellowed her planned words to her sister. The triplets hadn't done the poor plant any *favors*, but they'd only stripped the leaves. The branches remained and even had fresh buds that the girls had left alone.

Daleheart didn't really *have* seasons the way the northern part of the Dales did. Over the course of a year, it would go from averaging thirty-five degrees at thirteen hundred hours in December to thirty degrees at thirteen hundred hours in July. It would rarely breach forty at high noon or fall below twenty at night.

Seablood crew from the southern Dales had real problems with winter in the northern Dales, in Coral's experience, and even she would admit—to other Dalebloods, anyway—that her magic had to work harder than it should to keep her warm enough in the chill.

For the moment, though, Daleheart's smooth seasons meant that the topiary would regrow the leaves and the dragon would have paws again in a week or two. It was *rude* of the girls to have wrecked the most complicated artwork in the garden like that, but at least the topiary regrew.

Hardison finished his interrogation of Lieutenant Shain and opened the gate to allow the Admiralty gofer into the garden. At the sound of the hinges, Coral turned crisply on her heel and approached the youth.

From the kid's momentary choked expression, he had *not* been expecting to run into the high-ranking, hard-reputationed warship

Captain he'd been looking for in a sundress that didn't even reach her knees.

Coral's taste didn't run anywhere *near* boys, but she took a certain concealed glee in Shain's reaction. The Lieutenant's looks, uniform, and cushy appointment at the Admiralty probably allowed him to make a lot of "friends" of his own age in the city, but he was *still* distracted by her own muscular fifty-something legs.

She figured she was doing okay.

"Captain Amherst, sir!" he greeted her, snapping to attention and saluting like he *hadn't* just abortively checked out a very superior officer.

"Lieutenant Shain," she replied. "He's fine, Hardison. Admiralty courier, I suspect?"

"Yes, m'lady," the guard confirmed. "No escort, then?"

"He won't be staying long," Coral told the man. "I've got it. Go back to the shade, Hardison."

Shain was Daleblood and, in theory, could squish the Seablood guard in a moment. In practice, Coral suspected that the guard's fifteen-odd years of experience over the young officer would prove more useful than anyone expected. The man wouldn't be an Amherst household guard otherwise.

Still, he was Seablood and the sun was beating down *hard* today. Hardison would serve no one if he gave himself sunstroke. He bowed slightly to Coral and withdrew toward the sheltered and cooled guardhouse.

"Courier?" she repeated as she turned back to Shain. "Letter or verbal?"

"Both, sir," he confirmed, removing a cloth envelope from inside his uniform jacket.

The stark-white silk was plainer than Coral had expected. The silk was a product of a close, though smaller, relative of the horses that served as local transport throughout the Dales. It came out of the silkcow a vague brownish color, but the process of preparing it as silk turned it pure white.

The Navy dyed most silk they were using in a checkered diamond pattern of black and white. The stark white was a sign that Shain wasn't delivering a *Navy* letter.

Which suggested this was what she'd been waiting for.

The envelope opened readily at her touch, the fabric unfolding around the stiff card inside. It was the kind of invitation card the higher echelons of Daleheart's society sent around for their fancy parties, hand-calligraphed with names, addresses, dates and times.

It was a polite fiction to assume that the calligraphy had been done by the inviter, though Coral didn't know *anyone* who did so. Calligraphy skills were a requirement for personal secretaries in town, and there was an entire cottage industry of calligraphers who would make up the invitations for a small fee.

"You are invited to attend a private garden party at the Wibawa residence tomorrow at twenty hundred hours," Shain informed her. "The Admiral asked me to deliver the invite as a personal favor."

Coral chuckled.

"And an Admiral's 'small favors' carry the weight of ironbound orders from lesser mortals," she observed. The time on the invite matched Shain's verbal message, and she presumed the address was Admiral Wibawa's home. She would double-check, of course, before leaving.

"Yes, sir," Shain confirmed.

"Is there anything else?" she asked carefully. Asking an Admiralty gofer to play courier for a private party was sufficiently on the edge of propriety that she was surprised to see Wibawa do it, unless there was another reason for sending an officer.

She supposed the unspoken message that this wasn't *just* a party was clear.

"A verbal suggestion, sir," Shain replied, his tone uncomfortable. "The Admiral recommends you come in uniform."

Coral smiled.

"Thank you, Lieutenant Shain. That should be all I need to know, unless the Admiral gave you any other messages?"

CHAPTER 15

Admiral Roseline Wibawa was not natively part of the upper tier of Daleheart society. She'd been born in one of the eastern Dales, rising to her current rank through the fact that the Navy was, mostly, a meritocracy.

But an Admiral had to play politics, Coral knew, and Wibawa had recognized that before she'd even become a member of the Commission. The house at the address she'd been given was modest, but it was on one of the higher streets on the inside of the north side of the ridge.

The position of the house carried prestige all on its own, even if the house itself was an unremarkable two-story structure that would have fit in any middle-class community in the city. The grounds were a bit larger than they would have been lower down the ridge, but that was it. The entire stretch of the street was like that, Coral realized as she guided her horse along.

The street was at the right elevation and had the right name to be prestigious, but the twelve houses on this section were all vastly more modest than, say, the sprawling Amherst Estate. It was an interesting compromise.

It was easy to pick out which house was Wibawa's, though. Even if she hadn't had the address and been quite certain where she was going, it was the one with a Dalesguard detail out front.

"Captain Amherst," one of the white-and-purple-uniformed soldiers greeted her as she pulled her horse up. The animal buzzed concern up at her and she patted its armored neck. "Your invitation, please?"

"Of course." She dismounted and pulled the card from her uniform jacket. "Is there somewhere to stable the horse?"

"We'll take of him, sir," the Dalesguard told her, the invitation vanishing into their jacket. "The stable is shared with the rest of the street, but we have it under guard."

Coral was sure Wibawa's neighbors *loved* that part of sharing their street with an Admiral.

"Corporal Gabrielson! Escort the Captain to the gardens, please," the Dalesguard ordered crisply, waving another soldier over. "Corporal Quixada, take the Captain's horse to the stables. Make sure he gets checked over by the grooms and gets some food and a polish."

Coral passed the reins to the indicated Dalesguard with a nod.

"Take care of him," she asked. "Firefly is my sister Ivory's...and her daughters named him."

"I know the feeling, sir," Corporal Quixada said with a chuckle. "I'll make sure he's fine."

She gave the chitinous creature a quick scratch around the antennae, earning her a headbutt and a happy buzz, then turned to the other Dalesguard corporal.

"Lead on. I don't want to keep the Admiral waiting!"

THE DALESGUARD LED Coral around the outside of the house and into a back garden shrouded by hedges grown far taller than usual. Woven from bushes and trees easily six meters tall, the green walls gave the whole space a muted twilit feel.

All of her suspicions about this "party" were proven correct when she saw that there were seven people waiting for her and she knew all of them. The Admiralty Commission's members were seated casually on garden chairs array in a rough circle, at least *looking* like this was a party.

The seventh person waiting for Coral was far more familiar than the Commission and the only person standing. Valentina Amherst shared every scrap of her younger sister's height, but without the rigid physical regimen naval officers attempted to keep up, she was easily the weight of any two other people at the party.

But her Daleblood meant she was more than hale enough to stand and survey the room with cold gray eyes, even at over seventy years old.

"Eldest Sister," Coral greeted Valentina respectfully, bowing as she approached. "I did not know you would be here."

"If you did, I would be having words with my security detachment," her sister told her. "I would *hope* that it was merely family trumping orders, but one must be certain."

"Can both of you sit down?" Admiral Hussain asked tetchily. "I'm old enough and you're both tall enough that looking up at you is putting a kink in my neck."

Coral's sister gestured her to the empty pair of seats in the circle of chairs.

"An interesting party you have invited me to, Admiral," Coral told Wibawa. "Unlike my sister, I am not used to socializing with Admirals."

At least, not the six most powerful in the Dales.

"Get used to it," Valentina said bluntly. "There's more than one reason you were picked for this. That you are my sister was not one of them. That I trust you beyond blood and life itself is."

Valentina was probably the sister Coral was most *like*, but she was not the one Coral would have said she was closest to. That simple admission of trust was the most complimentary thing her eldest sister had ever said to her.

"Thank you, Eldest Sister."

"Brat," Valentina replied, a smile flickering across her lips and vanishing as swiftly as it arrived, her face returning to the stony mask of a woman of power.

"Your sister's agreement was essential," Wibawa told Coral. "But it is not why you were picked for this mission."

A uniformed Dalesguard appeared with a serving tray of drinks. That would have been a gross abuse of power if this was a normal party, but Coral suspected that security was at the top of Wibawa's priority list.

"I serve the Republic," she said after accepting a drink from the soldier. "Whatever you require of me, I volunteer."

Anything this secretive involving the amount of power and authority present in the small garden would be career-making. Or - breaking, of course...but Coral didn't *fail* at tasks she was given.

"Eager and overly confident, as always," Tse observed. "Thirty years of service hasn't changed you much, has it?"

"It has only given me the skills to support what was overconfidence in an ensign, sir," Coral replied.

Tse chuckled.

"You were disgustingly competent at twenty-two, Captain. But if there is a challenge that may break you, it is this one. Are you prepared to die for the Republic, Captain Amherst?"

She blinked in surprise. That was an implicit part of her oaths and service, the risks she took and the duties she performed. But it was rare to hear it laid out quite so bluntly.

"I would prefer not to die for nothing," she said carefully. "But I am certainly prepared to risk death in the service of the Republic, and I can certainly see missions that would require the near-certain loss of my command and death of all aboard, including myself."

"Good enough," Wibawa told her. "None of us ever plan to die in the service of the Republic. We all think we're better, stronger, faster, more immortal than the next officer over. If you recognize that risk, it will have to do."

"What is this all about, sir?" Coral asked.

There was a long silence.

"First, I think, we need to discuss some ancient history and attendant myths," Hussain said, the Seablood Admiral leaning forward over her wineglass.

Coral nodded and leaned back in her chair to see what the story was going to be.

"We know, without question, the events of the arrival of the Great Fleet," Hussain continued. "Three hundred and ninety-seven ships made it to the home Dales. Two hundred and five years ago, the Dalebloods welcomed the Seabloods as refugees, brought them into their homes and, indeed, into their government.

"We date the modern Republic from the arrival of the Great Fleet. We now also know that a hundred and nine ships made to other places on the Dales continent. Not all of those passengers survived, but there are eighty-six Landings, settlements scattered across the rest of this continent. Many have formed anchors for new administrative Dales, slowly expanded into the wilderness by Dalebloods and Seabloods working together."

All of this, as the Admiral had said, was ancient history. Coral had studied it as a child and again in more detail as a naval ensign. The arrival of the Great Fleet had shaped modern and ancient Dales alike. Even among the Dalebloods, there was little history of the time *before* that arrival—an oddity Coral had never thought to question.

"Those are the historical facts," Hussain concluded. "Five hundred and six ships made it to land on our continent's shores. Over a million Seabloods joined our ancestors, tripling the population of the Dales over the course of a *month*.

"But the Dales are fertile, and your ancestors could feed mine. Barely."

The perpetual growing season of the core Dales had probably helped turn the corner on that, Coral figured. The Seabloods would have been put to work in the fields, sowing and harvesting to make sure there was enough food for everyone.

"Our ancestors arrived as supplicants," Tse told Coral. "But the ships they sailed on proved more valuable than anyone could have guessed—and every modern ship is based on the hull forms, driver wheels and internal combustion engines of the transports of the Great Fleet.

"And yet." He shook his head. "And yet there are the myths that Hussain mentioned. Family traditions and half-forgotten journals, written after they arrived. Stories and legends." Tse shrugged. "I, for one, always assumed these were lies to soothe children who struggled with the economic and cultural disadvantages of being Seablood."

Those were still very real, Coral knew. It was *possible*, now, for the Navy to have Seablood Admirals. There had been a time when Seabloods couldn't even be *officers*.

"What stories were these?" she asked. She wasn't aware of them...but it sounded like they were the kind of thing that the Seabloods mostly kept to themselves.

"That we were never supposed to arrive as supplicants," Hussain answered. "That we were supposed to arrive with gifts of engineering and magic that the Dalebloods didn't have, to buy our place among the Dales by allowing the Dales to rival the City of Spires.

"But those gifts didn't arrive with us. My family draws lineage back to one of the transport captains, but tradition says she had an older brother who didn't make it. And *he* commanded one of what the legends calls the *lead ships*.

"These were bigger ships, with magical navigation tools that put our sextants and compasses to shame. Each was supposed to guide dozens—as many as fifty!—of the regular transports. Potentially even to guard them, as some versions of the legends say the lead ships were armed with powerful magic.

"And they carried the knowledge of the City of Spires."

"I've never heard of anything like that," Coral admitted.

"Because none of them reached the Dales," Wibawa told her flatly. "My *guess* is that they were too big and they got their stability wrong. They sailed these vessels into the hellfrost storms and they were all lost."

"Along with at least two hundred regular transports that never made it to the Dales either," Hussain said softly. "We speak of the arrival of the Great Fleet and the million-odd souls the evacuation delivered safely to these shores, but even the Seabloods try to forget that at least a quarter of the fleet never made it. As many people were lost at sea in our flight as there *were* in the Dales when we arrived."

Coral had seen ships go down in regular storms. She'd served on a cruiser that had dueled with Stelforma privateers and lost, and had been forced to swim for her life as her fellows drowned around her.

She knew, with the bone-deep certainty of one who had both been rescued and done the rescuing from sinking ships, how awful the death those people had suffered had been.

"But this is...myth, yes?" she asked slowly. "Or did we find something more?"

"We found something more," Valentina told her, her sister's tone proud. "It was Father's obsession after Mother's death. The belief that he could find one of the lead ships and acquire the knowledge and power of the City of Spires."

Coral nodded slowly. She'd known their father had put a great deal of money and effort into some project after he'd yielded control of the company, but she hadn't known *what.*

"He died before he succeeded," her sister continued. "But we had learned enough to start. We traced currents and winds, searching for a place where a ship might have foundered while being recoverable —or have been dragged somewhere recoverable by the ocean."

"You found one."

"Ten years ago," Valentina confirmed. "In many ways, it was no great treasure. Whatever magics the City of Spires worked upon her were long dead. There were no great libraries, no arsenals of magic. Just broken metal and dead dreams—and a hull unlike anything I have ever seen."

Given that Amherst Enterprises included two of the five largest civilian shipyards on the south coast of the Dales and a significant share in all three of the Republic's naval shipyards, Coral was *quite* certain her sister was aware of everything the Republic had ever built and most ships the Stelforma had built.

"Two hundred years underwater did her no favors," Rodgers noted. "But what your family's divers found was enough to bring in the Navy. We worked with your sister's people to investigate and eventually raise the wreck."

"We badly misestimated both her mass and how badly two hundred years underwater had damaged her," Valentina admitted. "Much of her disintegrated when we moved her. Her engines eluded us—we were never able to find her paddlewheels—and whatever weapons she had appear to have exploded at some point in the past.

"Some point *after* she sank," Coral's sister concluded after a moment's thought. "From the damage done, something reacted explosively to seawater once its container rusted away. *I* wouldn't have mounted a weapon on a ship that did that, but...I am not a Seablood of the City of Spires."

A grim chuckle swept around the garden. Most of this discussion, Coral recognized, was well known to the members of the Commission. Even some of the jokes had been made before. This was entirely for *her* benefit...and she wasn't entirely sure of the point of the conversation yet.

"What *did* we retrieve, then?" Coral asked slowly. "And how is relevant to this mission that has not yet been explained?"

"Between the Navy and Amherst Enterprises, we successfully retrieved two major components of the lead ship's hull," Admiral Rodgers told her. "Even the metal of her base hull had been corroded to supreme fragility by the sea, but she had a two-meter-high armor belt directly above the waterline, and she had an armored icebreaking bow.

"Both were made of a material we have never seen before, cannot duplicate, cannot analyze and cannot even *scratch*," Rodgers concluded. "Before we came to our current plan, we tested it as far as firing twenty-centimeter shells at the armor belt from under a hundred meters."

That was a tenth of the range at which even *Songwriter*'s armor would have been useless against her main guns. And they hadn't even *scratched* it?

"We were eventually able to bend the armor belt, at least," Valentina said drily. "But the size of both the armor belt and the bow were fortuitous, though we didn't realize it for a while."

"You are aware, Captain, of the new *Swordbreaker*-class battleships?" Wibawa asked.

"Supposed to be even larger than the *Oathmaker*-class ships like *Songwriter*," Coral confirmed. "There's...two under construction, I think? I haven't seen them."

She wasn't even sure where they were being built, other than *not in Daleheart* and *not in North Dale*.

"Exactly. Both were built at Easthaven," Wibawa told her. "Laid down five years ago, they are undergoing sea trials right now."

"Five years ago, I was poking at the measurements and realities of this chunk of impossible armor that we'd picked up," Valentina told Coral. "And then realized that, well, the armor belt was the wrong shape but the *bow* was the right size to fit one of the *Swords*."

Coral finally caught up.

"We built one of our most modern and powerful battleships using armor from a mythical lost city?" she asked slowly.

"Not mythical," Hussain reminded her. "Not that lost, either, really. But yes. *Icebreaker* has an adamantine bow and a layer of adamantine belt armor over her standard cemented-steel belt. Those alone mass five thousand tons, but we managed to pull it all together."

"Show her, Miz Amherst," Wibawa ordered.

Only one person in the gathering would be addressed by anything but their rank—though Coral was reasonably sure that even the Chief of the Admiralty Commission probably shouldn't be giving *orders* to the head of Amherst Enterprises.

Still, Valentina seemed unbothered. Coral's eldest sister pulled a meter-long case out from behind a decorative bush. A blood-seal keyed to Valentina herself hissed open at a touch and the older Amherst carefully removed a model of a ship and laid it on the table amidst the party.

Coral examined the model in silence for several moments. Assuming the model was the same one-to-two-hundred-and-fifty scale as the usual builder's models, the ship represented would be almost two hundred meters long—half again *Songwriter*'s length and a third again her beam.

The driver wheel was even larger, relative to the hull, than *Songwriter*'s. The steering wheels were about the same size as the smaller battleship's, lifting the same two casemated secondary guns up from the main deck. Where *Songwriter* had six secondary guns in each broadside, this ship had ten.

But the big differences were the funnels and the turrets. *Songwriter* had two funnels to clear the smoke away from her big corn-oil engines, with two turrets split forward and back.

This ship had three funnels—larger than *Songwriter*'s, she judged —and three turrets as well. The stern turret, between citadel and driver wheel, looked identical to the older ship's, but the forward deck had one turret at the usual height and another on an elevated deck attached to the central citadel.

To Coral's practiced gaze, the difference in the bow was immediately obvious. It was clearly derived from the same theory and plan as the one built into the *Oathmaker* battleships, yet it had equally clearly been designed to take advantage of a hull material that was *far* tougher than any amount of ice.

The extra armor belt was harder to pick out and she found herself hoping it was as well integrated into the actual ship as its counterpart on the model.

"*Icebreaker*," Valentina said softly. "A merger of everything we have learned about shipbuilding in two hundred years...and adamantine armor from the City of Spires."

"Your new flagship," Wibawa concluded.

CHAPTER 16

Captains didn't get flagships. Not *battleship* flagships, anyway. Senior Captains—like, say, Coral Amherst—commanded cruiser or destroyer squadrons, but then they had cruiser or destroyer flagships.

"I think, at this point, we can dispense with the formality of hedging everything with codicils and *ifs*," Admiral Tse said firmly. "We would not have progressed this far in the discussions or plans without being certain that Captain Amherst would take the mission, would we?"

"Sirs, there is no mission I would not take on for the Republic," Coral said calmly, her mix of confusion and anticipation well concealed by years of practice. If they meant for *Icebreaker* to be her *flagship*, then she had to have a *flag*.

"We know," Wibawa conceded. The old Daleblood Admiral considered Coral in silence for a long moment, then gestured to Tse. "You're the only of us to ever command her. Seems appropriate."

"*When* you accept this mission, you will be promoted to the rank of Rear Admiral," Tse told her. "A small compensation, I suppose, for potentially the most dangerous and certainly the most...unclear mission we have ever given an officer."

Coral nodded slowly.

"I am honored by your trust," she told the Commission, glancing over at her sister. "But I think we have now reached the point where we need to *discuss* that mission. It has something to do with the hellfrost storms, doesn't it?"

"And our father's legacy," Valentina told her. "In his research to find one of the lead ships, he gathered the most complete and accurate records of the landings and courses of the Great Fleet we have ever had."

Coral followed that thought through and swallowed a gasp of shock.

"We believe we know where the City of Spires is," Admiral Hussain told her, confirming her thought. "We *know*, from earlier scouting missions, that it is shrouded by a permanent weather system that resembles a hellfrost storm on an unimaginable scale."

"There is a sheet of solid ice that appears to cover the entire northern third of Albion, Amherst," Wibawa said flatly. "We believe that *Icebreaker* will be able to break through it and clear a route to the City of Spires.

"You will be accompanied by several cruisers and at least one *Oathmaker* battleship in addition to a pair of tankers. None of those ships will be able to breach the northern ice sheet. Only *Icebreaker* has the hull necessary to clear a path.

"It may prove that the other vessels are unable to make the full journey. Their heating systems and protective measures against the cold may prove insufficient. In that case, you are authorized and ordered to proceed solely with *Icebreaker*."

"*Icebreaker* was effectively custom-built for this mission," Valentina told Coral. "Ever since we decided to incorporate the adamantine bow, I have had our engineers and seers and magi working on this very challenge, this very journey."

Coral swallowed down her fear and smiled. For her oath to the

Republic, she'd have taken on this mission anyway. For an Admiral's flag? The Commission knew her levers.

"What do we expect to find at the City of Spires?" she asked. Without knowing the exact location yet, it already sounded like it was going to be a voyage into a frozen hellscape. She could do it. She *would* do it...but there had to be a point.

"We don't know for sure," Hussain admitted. "But we know that the Seabloods were driven from the City of Spires by these hellfrost storms. If legend didn't tell us that, the fact that the entire northern chunk of Albion is covered in one would suggest it!"

"We *hope* that if we break through to the City of Spires, we may find whatever dark force is behind these storms," Tse told her. "You said it yourself: the storms are not natural. Some power, some dark *thing*, unleashed them upon the City of Spires and now upon us.

"We send you to the north to find answers, Amherst. To find an enemy with the power to hide behind magic beyond anything we or the Stelforma have mastered. We *must* know why the Seabloods were driven to the seas.

"We must know why their enemy has come after us and why now."

"And once you have found them, we hope that the force we are giving you is enough to strike back," Wibawa said coldly. "Your crews will be Daleblood. We cannot risk sending the vulnerable on this mission. We *know* the Seabloods could not face this enemy.

"So, we will send you with the best Seablood engineering and the magics we have salvaged from their ancient ships—but it is Daleblood warriors and Daleblood magic you will carry to the Seabloods' ancient enemy.

"You will bring the best of both races against the enemy that defeated the Seabloods, and *you will strike back*."

"Two battleships, a handful of cruisers," Coral murmured. "Against what may as well be a god."

"We can spare no more," Admiral Rodgers said bluntly. "The Stelforma have been agitating in multiple areas. The presence of a cruiser on our north shores is concerning for many reasons. You did the right thing in sending her on her way, but her presence speaks to violations of the Northern Doctrine."

"New patrols have been ordered along the twentieth parallel," Wibawa noted. "But that, again, consumes cruisers and battleships. We have a fleet to circle the world, yes—but if we have to circle the world, we aren't left with many ships for other missions."

Coral nodded. She understood her mission now. No one actually expected her to *win*.

"I presume I am to use the tankers and at least one cruiser either as Bloodspeech relays or as physical couriers to return what we learn to the Dales?" she asked.

"Yes. We know what we are asking," Tse said quietly. "But we cannot let this enemy think we are unable to challenge them. Even if we fail, we *must* defy them with fire and blood."

The likelihood that *Icebreaker* and her escorts would return from that defiance... Coral guessed it was very, *very* low.

But she understood.

"My life is sworn to the Republic," she told the Commission, without even a side glance at her sister. "I will take this mission and I will bear our fire and our blood into the north. I will find our enemy and I will make them understand that we will not be broken without a fight."

"Good. We are still identifying your second battleship," Wibawa told her. "We'll have selected her and her Captain by the end of your one-week leave, at which point she will transport you to meet *Icebreaker* and your cruisers.

"Your duty awaits, *Admiral* Amherst."

CHAPTER 17

THE NEW UNIFORM FELT PERFECT. Coral might not have expected to make Admiral for a few more years—she'd expected a cruiser squadron first—but she'd known it was coming. She was too good at her job for anything else.

A pair of Daleblood Marines kept pace with her one step back as she walked down the floating docks that held the active ships of the Navy of the Republic of the Dales. Home Fleet was fixed, by Parliamentary Order, at three divisions in peacetime. Twelve battleships and thirty-six cruisers—though the Navy was known to deploy Home Fleet cruisers on the basis that "three divisions" referred to the capital ships.

With one division at sea, guarding the break in Daleheart's natural barrier ridge, there were eight battleships and twenty-four cruisers currently anchored along the massive dock structure flying Home Fleet's colors.

The dock had the capacity for twice that, though some of the spots meant for battleships or cruisers currently held destroyers. Given that Daleheart's docks had space for *ninety* of the tiny ships, that told Coral there were a lot more destroyers there than she would have expected.

If every dock in Daleheart was full—an unlikely scenario, given that the bay itself could hold hundreds of warships—it would contain roughly half of the Republic Navy. If *Icebreaker* and her half-sister *Swordbreaker* were fully in commission, the Navy was now up to forty-two battleships.

Plus a hundred and twenty cruisers and around two hundred destroyers in the southern ports. It was a *lot* of hulls and uniformed personnel for a nation of some forty million people.

But if the Navy was maintaining forty-two capital ships, that meant the Commission had solid intelligence that the Stelforma had *thirty*-two. That was the standard they aimed for, after all—ten more battleships than the enemy.

The Dales had no interest in mass conversion to the Stelforma faith. They didn't officially persecute those who did convert—though it was hardly a favored choice—but Parliament had refused to impose *any* state religion again and again.

And the Stelforma church's hierarchy, led by the Chosen Mother, had three times demanded that the Dales convert or be conquered. Three times, in turn, the Republic had thrown back Stelforma troops, Stelforma ships and Stelforma magic.

From her conversations, she knew that the Commission was worried about a fourth ultimatum. Parliament would *never* agree to the Stelforma's terms, so a fourth ultimatum would mean a fourth *war*.

Coral was grimly certain that the next war with the Stelforma wasn't going to be her problem. Nothing in her updated orders and information gave her any reason to believe that this wasn't a suicide mission. She had signed on to go poke a god in the eye.

She agreed with the Commission that said god *needed* to be poked in the eye. She just didn't see it as a survivable course of action and was glad that *Songwriter* hadn't been available to join her task group.

Instead, she was heading aboard the battleship *Cloudwatcher*. A handful of years older than her previous command, the *Oathmaker*-class battleship could have been *Songwriter* if Coral hadn't been intimately familiar with the latter ship.

The differences weren't even that clear to the *trained* eye. The Dales' engineering had advanced only slowly over the last two hundred years. The biggest innovation in warship design in the last hundred years had been the hydraulic turret—and that dated to around when Coral had entered the service.

She suspected there were still Daleblood officers who thought turrets were newfangled and unreliable devices, at that. There were both advantages and disadvantages to having a major ethnic group with half again the life expectancy of the rest of the population—and that was healthy for a larger portion of that lifespan.

Most Seablood officers, in her experience, needed to be put ashore and behind a desk by their mid-sixties. Few Seabloods lived much past eighty—but *Daleblood* officers could reliably serve at sea into their nineties and would live to a hundred and ten, hundred and twenty.

Still, that only slowed down the improvements in engineering that had taken the Republic Navy from the coastal cruisers that had stood off the first Stelforma invasion to the behemoth she was slated to have as her flagship.

Her survey of *Cloudwatcher* didn't trigger any alarm bells. Everything about the battleship seemed perfectly turned out. Her hull was freshly painted, her hull number and name clearly visible on her side. The Dales' flag flew from her crow's nest, but she didn't fly the colors of any squadron or formation.

Coral's little squadron wasn't formalized yet—but one of the Marines keeping step with her held a case with the first sets of pennants for her squadron.

"Come on," she instructed the two Marines, and then stepped onto the gangplank and approached the steel wall of the ship's side.

"Hello the ship! Permission to come aboard?"

"Granted, sir!" The watch officer standing by the gangplank was perfectly turned out in her dress uniform. *Cloudwatcher's* crew had known she was coming, and the Lieutenant had clearly seen her standing on the dock, surveying the ship.

A bosun's pipe whistled as Coral stepped onto the deck, and a side party of dress-uniformed officers assembled into a crisply precise line to greet her. One dark-skinned and -haired man stepped forward and gave her an even crisper salute.

"Squadron command, arriving," the noncom with the pipe said loudly as he lowered the instrument.

"Welcome aboard *Cloudwatcher*, Admiral Amherst," the man in front told her. "I'm Captain Stipe Oliversen. May I introduce my senior officers, sir?"

Tradition defined the first few moments, and Coral knew the ritual as well as Oliversen did.

"Of course, Captain."

ONLY EVERY THIRD Republic battleship was fitted out as a flagship—one for every division, plus a reserve to make sure there were always flagships available. *Cloudwatcher* wasn't one of them, but she did have space allocated to carry passengers and hold events in port.

Coral had a few minutes to make sure her stuff had been delivered to the stateroom she was going to be using until they met up with the rest of the squadron, but then she had to make her way to the officers' mess. Oliversen had invited her to a formal dinner before the ship left port, and...well, tradition and ritual defined her interactions with a Captain she didn't know.

He wouldn't be her flag captain, but he was still the commander of the second-most-powerful ship in her squadron. He was trying to make a good impression—but Coral recognized that had to go both ways.

"Admiral!" The Marines outside the mess saluted crisply as she approached. "Captain Oliversen is already present."

"Thank you," Coral told them. She noted absently that all of the Marines she'd seen so far were Dalebloods. She'd known that was going to be the case, but it was still an odd feeling.

She generally *preferred* Daleblood officers and soldiers when she could get them, but there was a value, she suspected, in having Seablood crew around. Dalebloods could power through a lot of difficulties on the strength of their magic. Seabloods *couldn't*, and that often resulted in a more thoughtful approach.

But only Dalebloods could survive the cold where they were going, so there could be no Seablood crew on *Cloudwatcher*.

There were only two men in the mess as she entered, both seated at the large dining table and clearly waiting for her. Oliversen she recognized, the Captain having guided her around the ship for several hours earlier.

The other man was a stranger to her, pale-skinned with flaming copper hair and immensely broad shoulders. He rose at the sight of her and saluted crisply.

"Admiral Amherst."

"Colonel," she returned the greeting after a moment, recognizing he wore the insignia of a Republic Navy Captain—and since courtesy demanded that only Captain Oliversen be address as Captain aboard his ship, the stranger would be addressed by the Army rank equivalent to their naval. "I don't believe we've met?"

"Not yet, sir. I'm Captain Alex O'Connor and I'm your chief of staff. Admiral Tse selected me personally."

"I see," Coral replied, a touch taken aback—and then surprised at her own surprise. Of course she needed a staff, and since nothing had suggested she'd have the time to assemble one herself, it made sense for one to be assigned to her.

"And the rest of the staff, Colonel O'Connor?" she asked.

"Our operations officer, Commander Tácito Blanc, is aboard already," O'Connor said swiftly. "Our logistics officer, Commander

Myrna Romagnoli, is due to report aboard at the twenty-fifth hour. Our Personnel and Intelligence officers are already aboard *Icebreaker*.

"Of our NCOs and sailors, thirty-two are either aboard *Cloudwatcher* or will by midnight, and twenty-nine are waiting for us on *Icebreaker*."

Coral nodded slowly. She'd never been a battleship flag captain —*Songwriter*, like *Cloudwatcher*, hadn't had flag facilities. She'd been a *cruiser* flag captain five years earlier, before taking command of *Songwriter*, but a cruiser squadron's Rear Admiral didn't have sixty-five staff!

"I will need to meet them all, I suppose," she said. "Anything I need to be aware of immediately, Colonel O'Connor?"

"Admiralty has decided to make sure we have enough cruisers for the mission," O'Connor told her. "We're holding *Cloudwatcher* here until twelve hundred hours tomorrow morning instead of sailing at midnight. That's to allow Home Fleet to shuffle personnel to give us two fully Daleblood-crewed cruisers. No one has told me which ones yet; I believe that's being left to Admiral Moreno's discretion."

Admiral Aster Moreno was the senior officer in the Republic Navy who technically still held a floating command. Coral would be stunned if the seventy-six-year-old Seablood was actually based on any of Home Fleet's warships, but she was told his mind was still sharp.

"Hopefully, the Admiral understands the importance of our mission," she noted. Moreno was *very* capable of sending her the dregs of both his cruisers and Dalebloods if he thought the Republic was better served that way.

"He would need to know more about our mission than most people already assigned to the squadron," Oliversen pointed out. "Even *I*, Admiral Amherst, have only the vaguest notion of what our mission *is*."

"For now, Captain, secrecy remains a powerful weapon in our service," Coral told him. "While our mission is not against the

Stelforma, the Commission is concerned that the Stelforma may find ways to use it against us."

They were, if nothing else, taking forty thousand tons of capital ships completely out of the balance of power. The cruisers didn't really count into that math, but a fifteen-thousand-ton battleship and a twenty-five-thousand-ton battleship definitely *did*.

"Everyone will be briefed before the squadron leaves Bluecollar," Coral promised. "For the moment, however, we must conceal our intentions. You know we are joining *Icebreaker* at Bluecollar. Beyond that?"

"Beyond that, I know we're heading north and far enough so that we need to leave our Seablood crew behind," Oliversen told her. "But I don't know how far north, where we're going there or what we expect to find."

"Hell, Captain," Coral said quietly. "I can't say more yet...but we are sailing into hell."

"That's...evocative but not necessarily useful," *Cloudwatcher*'s Captain replied. "But I understand the need for secrecy. One would hope that our people would not betray us to the book-botherers, but we can never be certain."

"There are those who say no Stelforma worshipper should be allowed in the Navy," O'Connor said, in a tone that strongly suggested he shared that opinion.

"If we bar the 'book-botherers,' as Oliversen calls them, we become no better than the Chosen Mother and her Apostles," Coral countered mildly. "If the Republic has freedom of faith, then the Stelforma are as welcome as the Christians and Buddhists."

Coral had little patience for mythical stories of mythical men in mythical places, but they brought comfort to some. The Stelforma were no worse—and no better—than the adherents of a dozen smaller cults present throughout the Republic.

Only the Stelforma wanted the Republic to declare them a state religion and impose their faith on the Republic's people. If for no other reason than the expectation that the Republic would then obey the Chosen Mother and her Apostles, as the states of the Southern Archipelago did, the Republic would never do so.

There was a long list of other reasons to defy the Stelforma, of course, including their proscriptions against the powers of the Dale-bloods. To them, everyone aboard *Cloudwatcher* was tainted and cursed, doomed to evil by the blood that ran in their veins.

"The other officers should be arriving shortly," Oliversen finally said, neither Captain appearing to want to challenge their Admiral's dictum around religion.

"I hope at least none of *them* are Stelforma?" O'Connor asked drily.

He quailed a moment later under Coral's sharp look.

"Few will follow a faith that says they are irredeemably damned," she told him mildly. "But we will be forever better served by allowing *everyone* to serve than by punishing our people for their beliefs.

"It would be through that punishment that the Stelforma would find the cracks to undermine us. So long as those who believe in immense savior birds and Chosen children feel welcome in the Republic, they are less likely to betray us to their church."

"And when their religious leaders demand that they betray us or foreswear their faith?" Oliversen asked.

"Then we punish those who betray us and those who demanded it of them," Coral replied levelly. "And we reward those who choose to subordinate their faith in the Chosen Mother to their faith in the Republic.

"Our people know the rewards for turning in those who try to bribe or blackmail them," she concluded. "I find that most Stelforma preachers in the Republic have long ago learned the consequences of preaching the damnation of the people they live amongst."

CHAPTER 18

IT WAS JUST BEFORE thirteen hundred hours—high noon—when *Cloudwatcher* finally released her mooring lines and set off for the open ocean. Two cruisers, minuscule-feeling at a fifth of her size, moved up to flank her as she moved.

For her part, Coral was standing in the very bow of the ship, well out of the way of Captain Oliversen and his crew, and was feeling unusually out of sorts. This was the first time in over a decade that she'd been aboard a ship leaving port for a new duty station and not been in command.

She distracted herself by studying the two cruisers. They were far better than she'd expected Home Fleet to be willing to give up. Part of her had expected to be given the oldest cruisers Admiral Moreno *had*, ships that more closely resembled *Dancer* than any modern Republic ship.

Instead, she'd got *Firewater* and *Stormwind*, two of the three-turret cruiser class that had acted as test beds for the turret layout of the two *Swordbreaker*-class ships. The cruisers only carried six twelve-centimeter guns total, but they were all mounted in turrets, allowing her to present all six guns on broadside and four guns forward.

Comparing the ships to *Dancer*, they were actually *smaller* than the Stelforma ship—seventy-two meters long to *Dancer*'s eighty—but they were faster, longer-ranged, and put more guns on any given target.

The last reports she had read said that the Stelforma hadn't even fully refitted their *battleships* with turreted main guns. But the reports *also* said that the Stelforma were preparing for a fourth ultimatum and a fourth holy war.

Coral's conclusion was that the Stelforma's secular leaders and military commanders weren't *idiots*, even if they were bound to the will of their religious masters. Since that was a given, she figured that one of the two reports was wrong: either the Stelforma *weren't* about to try to start a war or they were further along in upgrading their fleet than Intelligence thought.

But comparing the two escorts running alongside *Cloudwatcher*, their rear drive wheels leaving a churning wake behind them, to the ship she'd encountered in Keller's Fjord told her that the Stelforma still had a *long* way to go to match the Republic's engineering.

Numbers were the only way the Stelforma could win a naval war. If they were attacking, they'd have the chance to concentrate their forces against a portion of the Republic Navy and balance the odds—and Coral was going to be sailing away with two of the most powerful battleships the Navy had.

But all of the petty wars of mankind would be meaningless if the dark power that had overrun the City of Spires continued its southward advance. They didn't know what mind, what power or god or monster, lay behind the hellfrost storms.

Coral only knew that the hellfrost storms weren't natural. There was a power to them that no mortal could command—but she was *certain* that someone or *something* had set those storms in motion. An attack that couldn't be stopped by mundane weapons.

So, she would take her mundane weapons *past* their storms and into the heart of the enemy. Not just for the Republic. If the hellfrost had overrun as much of Albion as the reports suggested, then even consuming the Dales would only slow their true enemy down.

The Stelforma were just as doomed as the Republic if this enemy wasn't stopped. She'd take her squadron north and know, in her heart of hearts, that she was fighting for all humanity.

EVEN PUT off by not being in direct command, Coral still felt a weight lift off her shoulders as the breakwater ridge around Daleheart Bay fell behind them and out of sight. She belonged at sea. She felt more at home on the forward deck of a battleship, standing straight-backed under the ten-meter-long barrels of her main guns, then she ever did on shore.

Even her sisters didn't understand. The one woman she'd *thought* had understood had proven unable to take the long periods apart—though outside of her least charitable moments, Coral knew that Sheila had *tried*.

But the smell of sea salt and the sting of the wind on her face was home to her. More than the estate on the ridge of Daleheart. More than any individual ship, even.

"Five days to Bluecollar," O'Connor said behind her. She turned and arched an eyebrow at the man.

"Apologies if I'm interrupting, sir," he said swiftly.

"Not really," she admitted. "There is very little for you and me to do until we reach Bluecollar and the rest of the squadron. I *could* insert myself into the training of the crews, but these are all newly assembled ship's companies. The Captains should get a *little* time before the Admiral starts correcting their mistakes."

Her new chief of staff chuckled softly.

"So certain there will be mistakes?" he asked.

"Speaking from personal experience as a Captain, there are *always* mistakes," she told him. "There are always things it takes the step back from running the training to see. That is part of why we have squadron commanders and squadron staffs.

"Enjoy the journey west, Colonel O'Connor," Coral warned. "Because once we arrive in Bluecollar and formally raise the flag of Icebreaker Squadron, I am going to work you to the bone."

"I've been a member of Admiral Tse's staff for the last three years, Admiral," O'Connor pointed out. "I *look forward* to you trying to overwork me. He didn't promote me and send me to head your staff because I was *lazy*."

Coral chuckled.

"I assumed the Admiral sent me someone who could do the job," she replied. "I still expect to run you to your limits, Colonel. If for no other reason than because *I* don't necessarily know what an Admiral should be doing."

"I can tell you what Admiral Tse would be doing," her chief of staff noted. "But that doesn't mean it's what *you* should do. Tse isn't..."

She waited a moment to see if he finished the thought, but O'Connor stepped up to the railing and stared west toward their destination instead.

"Tse isn't what?" she asked.

"Well," O'Connor finally replied, his tone utterly flat. "I shouldn't have said anything, sir."

Coral sighed.

"He can't serve at sea anymore, I take it? A damn shame."

"He probably could, honestly," her chief of staff said quietly. "He's still fit enough. He's..."

The redheaded Captain shook his head and stared out at the water.

"He's dying, sir, and no one is supposed to know that," he said in a self-flagellating tone. "Tumor in his lungs. I..." He growled at himself. "I've spent most of my time recently with just him and his staff, and we're the only people who knew."

"It's fine, Alex," Coral told him. "You're right that you shouldn't have said anything, and you *could* have just told me that. But I will keep the Admiral's secret."

There was no one else far enough forward on the bow to have heard O'Connor's revelation. Coral wouldn't have regarded Tse as a mentor, let alone a friend, but she remembered serving under him fondly. Knowing he was dying...

She sighed.

"It's going to be one hell of a mission," she whispered.

"I know the details, sir," O'Connor admitted, his voice barely louder. "I helped write the briefing materials you have hidden in your stateroom.

"One way or another, I don't expect to see Admiral Tse again."

"No," Coral agreed, her gaze turning toward the north. "But we all serve the Republic as best we can."

CHAPTER 19

BLUECOLLAR WAS a large island to the west of the Dales. Like the Landings on the northern side of the continent, it had been settled by lost ships from the Great Fleet. Unlike any of the Landings, it had been settled by a *group* of lost ships, twenty-one strong.

Bluecollar's soil hadn't taken food crops easily, and the settlement had struggled for several decades before making contact with the Dales and eagerly joining the Republic. Key critical chemicals for modern industry came from Bluecollar's rocky caves—but the main industry of the island now was the Bluecollar Navy Base, the largest anchorage for the Republic Navy outside of Daleheart itself.

Like Daleheart Bay, Bluecollar had a large circular ridge around a natural lagoon. At some point in the very distant past, the island had been a volcano, and there were still signs of that across the island and its surrounding islets.

It was enough farther north than Daleheart that Coral could *feel* the difference in the air temperature. There were days she wondered how the Stelforma could survive in their southern islands, where it was even warmer than in the southern Dales.

Bluecollar shared a temperate climate with the central Dales, and the presence of the natural lagoon shielded the Western Squadron from storms and spying eyes.

As *Cloudwatcher* entered the lagoon, Coral's own spying eyes were focused on just two ships. Clearly sisters and yet clearly different, *Icebreaker* and *Swordbreaker* were at opposite ends of the anchorage. Past the anchorage, she could see the slips where the hulls for more *Swordbreaker*-class ships were taking shape, but it was the two complete ships that held her gaze.

The model the Commission had shown her had allowed her to see the shape and the form, to count guns and estimate armor and know what the ship looked like. It was something else to the see the two twenty-thousand-ton-plus battleships in person.

Swordbreaker rode higher in the water, she noted. Given that *Icebreaker* and *Swordbreaker* shared all of their hull form except the adamantine bow on *Icebreaker*—and that said adamantine bow and the attached armor belt weighed *five thousand tons*—that made sense. *Swordbreaker* was twenty thousand tons to her half-sister's twenty-five, but that still made her the *second*-largest and most powerful battleship in Albion.

Swordbreaker was the name ship of the class of ships that would actually follow. Carrying the same weapons as her specialist sister, she was lighter and likely faster and longer-ranged.

But *Icebreaker* would forever be unique unless they found another Great Fleet lead ship. The adamantine bow and armor couldn't be duplicated by Daleblood magic or Seablood engineering. It was beyond their knowledge now.

That ancient magic was the key to their journey north, and Coral's gaze focused in on the immense bulk of her new flagship. Everything about *Icebreaker* spoke to the power of the nation that had built her and the knowledge they had gathered from every people across their vast territory. She was a meld, as Wibawa had said, of the ancient magics of the City of Spires with the modern engineering of the Seabloods and the modern magics of the Dalebloods.

She would deliver her Daleblood crew into the heart of hell. But Coral knew that even the mighty battleship she was ogling was unlikely to bring her crew *out* of that heart.

Icebreaker Squadron didn't officially have squadron colors yet, but it was still easy to pick out the ships assigned to Coral's command. While the signal flags clearly directed toward the group of ships, it helped identify them because they *didn't* have the blue-green-red tricolor of the Western Squadron.

Icebreaker and the four cruisers docked around her flew the red chevron on black of the Dales from their masts but there was no squadron pennant underneath the national flag. The two fuel tankers—each easily the size of *Cloudwatcher*—docked next to *Icebreaker's* cruisers wouldn't normally have flown squadron colors, but their position next to five warships without those colors drew the eye to the lack.

There were eight sets of pennants in the case Coral had brought with her. *She* knew which colors had been assigned to Icebreaker Squadron, but until she formally assembled the squadron, they technically had no right to fly them.

"Your launch is waiting, Admiral," a Chief Boatswain advised her.

"Thank you, Chief."

She stepped past the older noncom and stopped in front of Oliversen. *Cloudwatcher's* Captain would be joining her on *Icebreaker*—the signal flags hanging from the big battleship were ordering all Captains aboard—but there was still a tradition to discharge there.

Oliversen saluted her sharply, every motion as crisp as his movements had been the entire trip. He was, perhaps, a bit *too* polished even for her—but she would learn, she supposed, whether the man could fight.

"Thank you for having us, Captain Oliversen," she told him as she returned the salute. "All of our bits and pieces are on the launch?"

"Chief?" Oliversen asked, glancing over at the boatswain. He would never have made Captain if he hadn't known when to look to his Chiefs for answers.

"So far as we know, sirs," the Chief replied.

"Then all that is left is to say that you have a fine ship, Captain Oliversen," Coral told him. "I am impressed and am glad to have her with us. We have a hell of a job ahead, but I have faith in your ship and your crew to hold up your end of the journey."

"Thank you, sir. *Cloudwatcher*'s crew would hardly wish to disappoint. It's been an honor to transport you, Admiral Amherst."

She gave him a firm nod and stepped off *Cloudwatcher*'s side, easily dropping the four meters to the launch below as several people made sharp surprised sounds.

"There *is* a ladder, sir," the boatswain noted, managing to somehow *not* sound like he was scolding an Admiral as he stabilized the boat.

Behind her, O'Connor had taken a moment to realize that, yes, his Admiral *had* just walked off the side of the battleship, but then he started down the rope ladder tied between the ship and the boat.

"Apologies, Chief, but I get so few opportunities to pull that stunt, and I *like* being Daleblood," she told the boatswain softly. "The boat is fine, right?"

He snorted. "We'll survive. Is anyone *else* going to jump down?"

"If someone *else* does it, I have to tell them off," Coral told the Chief with a chuckle. "So, let's hope not, because I'd rather not be that hypocritical."

She enjoyed the moments where she could truly lean in to the power her blood commanded. Still, as O'Connor and her other officers began to reach the boat, she pulled her formal mask back over her face and gave the boatswain a firm nod.

"Let's be about this."

CHAPTER 20

"ADMIRAL ARRIVING!"

Someone aboard *Icebreaker*—Coral would generally assume one of the Chiefs—had decided that they didn't want the new Admiral scrambling up a rope ladder. They could have laid a gangplank between the two battleships, but that would have required more time than Coral had wanted to wait.

Instead, the crew had rigged up an impromptu elevator using one of the boat cranes. A piece of sheet metal several meters long had been hooked into cables and lowered to the level of the launch's gunwales.

That surprisingly stable platform now suspended at *Icebreaker*'s deck level as Coral stepped onto her new flagship, looking up at the familiar sight of a dual twenty-centimeter turret. She carefully ignored Captain Oliversen stepping off the platform behind her and crossing to join the line of ship Captains waiting attentively for her to begin.

The second forward turret towered over everything and everyone. Only the peak of the central citadel and the fighting tops were higher than the top of the turret—and with its guns elevated to their highest angle, the ten-meter-long barrels rose higher than everything except the crow's nest.

Out of the corner of her eye, Coral noted the last of the cruiser Captains joining the audience waiting for her. The Captains were the only people who *needed* to be there, but there were other crew and officers gathered behind.

Ceremony and ritual were important. So was making sure the right people were present for that ceremony.

"Sergeant Brivio," Coral barked as she finally turned away from the guns to review her people.

The Marine who'd accompanied her from *Cloudwatcher* was already at her right hand, and she *knew* what Coral wanted. The heavy case with the pennants rested against Brivio's leg, and the Sergeant had the first set of pennants in her hands before Coral had finished speaking.

Coral took the colors from the Marine and smiled beatifically at her new subordinates.

"Captains, I am Rear Admiral Coral Amherst and I am formally activating Icebreaker Squadron...*now*."

She let the tricolor flag spill out of her hands, the smallest version barely small enough for her to hang onto the top corners and let it hang. Even without looking at it, Coral knew the colors: blue, black, white.

The colors for Icebreaker Squadron had been chosen carefully, even if *she* hadn't picked them herself.

A short and wideset blonde woman stepped forward and gave her a sharp salute.

"Captain Ekaterina Nevin of *Icebreaker*, sir," she introduced herself. She held out her hands for the flag. "May I?"

Coral passed Nevin the squadron colors, and the Captain gestured a Chief over while she examined the full set of pennants.

"Chief Mandrel, run up the colors, please," Nevin told the noncom.

Several more noncoms appeared as if by magic, and the pennants for *Icebreaker* dispersed with gratifying speed. Coral turned on her heel and surveyed her Captains. Six cruisers, two battleships and two tankers meant there were eight Captains standing on *Icebreaker*'s deck, accompanied by key officers and noncoms from their own ships and a functionally random assortment of *Icebreaker*'s own crew.

"There will be briefings on our mission to follow," Coral told the Captains. "This squadron is now officially under orders—and under my command. Does any one of you have a reason that Icebreaker Squadron cannot sail at dawn?"

It was fourteen hundred hours. Dawn would be around seven hundred hours the next day—nineteen hours away.

She knew the three ships she'd arrived with needed to refuel and replenish supplies. They'd do so from Bluecollar's stocks, reserving the supplies on the logistics ships for the mission. Nineteen hours was *doable* for that but would definitely be a challenge.

Of course, Captain Oliversen and the cruiser COs had known this was coming, and their XOs were already ashore—and the fuel and supplies they were seeking should have been waiting for them, unless the base commander was less conscientious than Coral expected.

It was the seven Captains she *hadn't* just sailed around the continent with that she wasn't sure of.

"*Icebreaker* is prepared to sail on your command," Captain Nevin said instantly. "I believe every ship that was waiting for you is fully stocked and ready to deploy."

"I have some crew ashore, but they can be retrieved well before dawn," one of the cruiser Captains reported calmly.

"We were allowing day leave, but nothing longer," another Captain confirmed. "I have eleven crew ashore, and they'll be back aboard by twenty-five hundred hours."

Or the Captain's Chiefs were going to have *very* harsh words for the men and women who missed check-in on the day it *mattered*.

"Send whatever orders you need back to your ships," Coral

ordered. "Then report to the flag mess in *Icebreaker*'s main citadel at sixteen hundred hours for a briefing followed by dinner."

Hopefully, the staff who'd been waiting for her were ready to put a meal for a dozen-plus senior officers together on short notice!

~

CORAL HAD NEVER COMMANDED a flagship battleship, but she *had* been aboard them for exactly the kind of event she was organizing. She knew what the "flag country" that took up the stern half of much of the citadel would normally look like.

The Republic went for function first, second and third—and considered the esthetics of things last, if at all. Battleships, in her opinion, had a certain stark beauty to their presence, but generally warships only carried small decorations throughout.

Stepping inside *Icebreaker*'s citadel, however, she was reminded that she'd never served on a class's name ship. The lead pair of ships of a class, it seemed, received extra attention from the builder—which made sense, she supposed.

Coming from a shipbuilding family, Coral could easily see how the lead ships would see far more dignitaries and tours than later ships. It made sense to make them more refined than the general production line of ships, and *Icebreaker*'s flag country showed that refinement and care to its highest level.

A lot of it was small. Hard-wearing dark blue carpet instead of plain steel or rubber safety mats. Gold-plated door handles instead of plain metal. The visible wood pieces had been stained and even carved in places instead of simply varnished against rot and left plain.

Some of those changes would get made over time on any ship as the Chiefs and crew added a human touch to the cold steel of their homes. To an experienced shiphandler and a woman who'd grown up among shipwrights, designers and the shipyards themselves, the difference was clear.

The furniture in her own quarters rivaled the trappings of the Amherst Estate—and as she examined the four-poster bed bolted to the floor, she discovered the maker's mark that confirmed that it was made by the same people.

Either the builders had gone all out for the admirals posted to the Republic's newest battleships...or the plan to put *her* in command of *Icebreaker* was old enough that Valentina had made arrangements in advance.

Coral had understood her command of *Icebreaker* was due to her encounter with the hellfrost storm. Now, though, she wondered.

A sharp knock on the door interrupted her musings, and she turned to study it for a silent second.

"Enter," she ordered.

O'Connor, still courtesy-titled as *Colonel* out of respect for a *different* Captain, opened the door and stepped exactly one pace inside.

"Report, O'Connor," she told him.

"I've spoken with Lieutenant France Bolkvadze," the chief of staff told her. "He's our flag mess officer. He is...very young. Just out of the Academy, in fact."

"Please tell me that's not an excuse for a failure."

"An observation only, sir," O'Connor replied. "He has several decent Chiefs, and they have things well in hand. The Lieutenant had them prep up around the thirteenth hour yesterday and today. We might have wasted some supplies yesterday, but the flag mess team is on the dinner."

"'Wasted supplies,' in this case, meaning the flag mess team found themselves *forced* to eat steak and fresh vegetables laid aside for the Admiral's dinner?" Coral asked drily.

"I didn't ask," O'Connor replied. "I presume so, but that's a normal perk of being unsure when the Admiral is going to arrive."

"Fair." She chuckled. "And our briefing?"

"My understanding is that Commander Aldith El-Ghazzawy has been fully briefed on the operation, but you may wish to touch base with her yourself before any information is given to the Captains."

While Coral had read the files she'd been given on her new senior staff, she appreciated that her chief of staff was carefully using their full names, to help her place the officers in question. She wasn't going to have a chance to meet with all of her new officers, let alone the dozens of sailors and Chiefs that made up her staff, before the briefing.

"I recognize when I'm being managed, O'Connor," she pointed out.

"Yes, sir. Apologies, sir."

She gave him a flat look.

"Just keep being *right* when you do it, and I suppose it will be fine," she told him. "Where would I find Commander El-Ghazzawy?"

CHAPTER 21

THE FLAG MESS was unexpectedly gorgeous. Even having seen the quality of the furnishings in her quarters and the small touches throughout the rest of flag country, Coral had expected something utilitarian and military.

Instead, the tables were from the same artisan cooperative that had made the furniture in her quarters. The only concession to their current location was that they were attached to bolts run through the carpet into the metal deck beneath.

Heavy tablecloths covered the table surfaces, and neatly laid-out place settings waited for the dinner to follow—on the two tables that would be required to hold tonight's guests, at least. The *other* four tables in Coral's new entertaining space were still present and covered but lacked both chairs and place settings.

Coral walked past the tables and up onto the slightly raised stage at one end of the room. A massive map of Albion covered the back of the stage, with a layer of glass in front of it to allow it to be marked up with the grease pens sitting in a gorgeous hardwood case off to one side.

She studied the projection with a wry smile. The farther north one went on the map, the less certain the information became. The same was true to the south as well, though she presumed the Stelforma had better maps of the southern regions.

Too far north and a ship hit the hellfrost storms and ice-filled seas they forged. Too far south and the humidity and heat reached a level that no human could survive. The Dalebloods potentially *could*, but the Stelforma guarded the southern latitudes of Albion as fiercely as the Republic guarded the northern ones.

The Stelforma weren't supposed to go north of the twentieth north parallel, and the Republic wasn't supposed to go south of the fortieth south parallel.

The map on the wall had details both north of the twentieth and south of the fortieth. The Republic's maps were probably good up to the thirtieth or potentially even fortieth north parallel, Coral figured. Some of that was scouting and surveying, though some of it was taken from journals and hand-drawn maps found in Seablood evacuation ships.

The southern maps were more accurate. Roughly a third of the Southern Archipelago lay south of the fortieth parallel, and Republic merchant ships still called on those islands sometimes, despite the Southern Doctrine.

That third was far more sparsely inhabited that the northern part of the archipelago, from what Coral understood. Average daytime temperatures in the forties year-round were not friendly to humans.

Toward one pole, ice and frigidity formed the Republic's concept of hell. Toward the other, a wall of blistering heat barred the way toward what the Stelforma said was their paradise.

Studying the map for another long moment, Coral saw that someone had added *one* marker to it already. A magnet on the inside of the glass held a thumbnail-sized image of *Icebreaker* in place above the map marker for Bluecollar.

And at some point between Coral's arriving on the ship and her examining the map, someone had pinned a minuscule handmade blue, black and white tricolor flag to the *Icebreaker* token to mark the presence of the entire squadron.

Smoothing her smile from her face at the sound of footsteps at the entrance, she turned back, intending to welcome her officers to the briefing, and finally spotted what had been painted on the *other* end wall.

Delicate and impossible buildings rose from an unblemished ocean like trees grown from metal instead of wood. No human hand could ever have built those spires, and the artist had woven them together like a thicket of living trees—and around the roots of the impossible structures were familiar-looking ships.

The lineage from the evacuation transports of the Great Fleet to modern ships was sufficiently direct that Coral suspected the artist had used regular freighters as models, but it had worked. The City of Spires rose from the sea that named its long-lost children and stood protectively over the boats they'd fled it in.

And now it was time to go back.

TEN CAPTAINS TOOK their seats at the tables, looking up at where Coral stood behind the lectern on the stage. Four additional officers—one Captain and three Commanders—represented Coral's staff.

All of them were Dalebloods, which still felt odd to Coral. The Republic Navy put a *lot* of effort into keeping both of their main ethnic groups represented on every ship. The official position was that segregation could only lead to discrimination—and discrimination by any standard except merit was a poison that would destroy the Navy.

Coral was familiar enough with the Navy's history to know where that position came from. It was a lesson the Republic had learned the hard way in the first war against the Stelforma. The Navy tried very hard not to make the same mistake twice—and Parliament had recognized, before Coral was even born, that where the Navy led, the Republic followed.

Neither Admiralty nor their elected masters would ever allow the Navy to backslide on that point. But for this mission…any Seabloods sent to the north would *die*.

"Well, I think at this point I'm supposed to thank you all for coming," Coral told her audience. "But that would suggest that any of you had a choice at this point."

She waited for the obligatory forced chuckle and leaned on the lectern.

"While I don't expect every officer and sailor on this mission to fully be a volunteer, I hope that you are all aware of the level of risk entailed?"

The grim, quiet nods that answered her told her more than any verbal confirmation could have. At least the Captains and senior officers knew this was likely a suicide mission.

"I know that Captain Oliversen, at least, knew we were heading north," she continued after a moment. "Given *Icebreaker*'s construction and capabilities, I imagine that is obvious to anyone who's even looked at our flagship.

"As we speak, however, intelligence suggests that the Stelforma Apostles are laying the groundwork to commit their people to a new war against the Republic. Why, then, are we sending two capital ships and a full cruiser escort in the wrong direction?"

Spines straightened and people leaned forward. She had their full attention now as she asked the question she knew they all had to be wondering.

"The answer lies in something very simple and very terrifying," Coral concluded. "*Weather.*"

Their confused looks amused her, and she stepped back to the map behind her, taking a moment to find Keller's Fjord.

"In mid-September, I was here with the battleship *Songwriter*," she told them, tapping on the fjord on the map. "We collided with a storm unlike anything I'd ever seen. Water froze to chunks of ice before our eyes, even as winds harsh enough to shift a battleship battered us.

"We took shelter in a fjord and spoke with the local mayor. These storms are called *hellfrost storms*, and they're getting more common. A *lot* more common.

"But...what does that have to do with an entire fleet squadron?" she questioned again, hoping to stay ahead of the questions.

"Three things. First, I *saw* that storm with my own eyes, people. It is not natural. There is some dark magic, some vicious power, behind these storms.

"Secondly, these storms are known to us from the journals of the Seablood Great Fleet. It is this very weather, these very storms, that overran the City of Spires and sent the Seabloods into exile."

She looked past her officers at the mural of the City on the other end of the room and considered it quietly for a moment.

"Lastly...they are getting worse, and the northern coasts of the Dales may shortly become uninhabitable," she said softly.

"Some dark power is fueling these storms," she repeated. "Some magic we do not understand, at the command of an enemy we know nothing about. An enemy that drove the Seabloods from the City of Spires and sent them to the Dales.

"An enemy that will attempt to do the same to us. But the Seabloods had less than two million people to evacuate and magic we cannot match for the production of ships. The timelines I've seen in the journals of the Great Fleet make no sense. Hundreds of ships built in months. No mortal hands can match the magic of the City.

"We have *forty* million people. And we have nowhere to evacuate them to. The Stelforma might take in the Seabloods, but they would leave the Dalebloods to what they see as our just fate."

Coral *hoped* she was doing the Stelforma a disservice. But to motivate her people, she would do their enemy that disservice.

"So, the enemy that destroyed our Seablood cousins' home has come to our shores, and we know nothing about it. We do not know where it comes from. We do not know what they want.

"Our mission is to find out. Commander El-Ghazzawy"—she gestured to the tanned-looking woman sitting among her staff officers—"will go into detail on what we know and how, but our basic mission is simple."

She pointed to the painting on the wall behind her audience.

"We are going to find the City of Spires," she said. "We are going to learn what happened to the City, and we are going to *find* who and what did it—and, if we can, learn why they're coming for us now.

"And then, barring some unexpected peaceful resolution, we are going to kill them."

Or try to, anyway.

CHAPTER 22

THEY SAILED NORTH AT DAWN. *Icebreaker* led the way, the battleship's illuminators flickering a predawn salute to her sister as they sailed past *Swordbreaker.*

The familiar pungent fumes of corn oil wafted over the flying bridge, an eternal companion to Coral Amherst and her work. "Diesel," the Stelforma Priest-Captain had called it. A fascinating word—both foreign and yet very familiar.

Bluecollar fell swiftly behind them. The two fast tankers were built for the same speed as the battleships. It would be *foolish* to test if the supply ships could manage the same thirty-klick top speed as *Icebreaker* and *Cloudwatcher*, but they could maintain the twenty-klick cruising speed easily enough.

Her six cruisers ranged out around the two capital ships once they were clear of the harbor, taking up their posts in a rough circle half a kilometer out. With a cruising speed of thirty klicks and a *top* speed of fifty, the cruisers could move a significant distance from the two battleships while still keeping up and in formation.

They wouldn't go *too* far. The cruisers probably had the range for this mission. *Probably.* If the City of Spires was in the place Intelligence had calculated, they had six thousand kilometers to go. Another six thousand to get back.

Even the modern triple-turret cruisers that made up Icebreaker Squadron's escorts were only rated for twelve thousand kilometers at cruising speed. Even *Cloudwatcher* was only rated for sixteen thousand, though fueling both cruisers from empty would only cost her about two thousand klicks of range.

That *Icebreaker* had the fuel to sail *twenty-five thousand* kilometers at her standard four-hundred-kilometer-per-day long-distance speed told Coral that the ship had basically been custom-built for this mission. *Swordbreaker* was the true template for the new battleships—too many changes had been made to *Icebreaker* for her to be a standard.

And that was *before* factoring in the adamantine armor taken from a wrecked ship of the Great Fleet. That armor had survived two hundred years immersed in salt water. Coral had to hope that immersion hadn't done it *too* much damage—though she'd made a point of trying to find the point in the belt where the Republic's engineers had fired a twenty-centimeter cannon into it at point-blank range.

She'd failed and that was reassuring. If *Icebreaker*'s own main guns couldn't breach that armor at a range she'd never fight a battle at, at least that part of her belt would stand up to anything the Stelforma could throw at her.

"Sir," a soft voice said from behind her.

Coral recognized El-Ghazzawy without looking. The Intelligence officer was *always* soft-spoken, as if she expected to be talked over at a moment's notice—or like she was going to *force* everyone to pay attention to what she was saying. Or learn the hard way that they should have.

"Commander," Coral greeted the younger woman. "Good to be back at sea?"

El-Ghazzawy stepped up to the flying bridge's railing beside her, looking uncertainly at the drop to the main deck.

"This is my first sea posting, sir," the petite woman replied softly. Coral glanced over at the woman, taking in her deep brown eyes, looking like the world could fall into them and drown, then turned her gaze back to the water with an internal smirk at herself.

The intelligence officer was ten years younger than her *and* her subordinate. But El-Ghazzawy did have very pretty eyes.

"I'm surprised," Coral told the younger woman. "I didn't think even Intelligence officers went that long without going to sea."

"I'm primarily a historian, sir," El-Ghazzawy admitted. "I work in Naval Intelligence, yes, but mostly doing deep-background analysis on..."

The silence stretched for a few seconds before the Commander realized she'd already said too much and sighed.

"On potential threat factors inside the Seablood population," she finally finished, her voice a whisper. "We haven't had trouble with them, but there are definitely groups that dislike the Seabloods' limitations in the Republic.

"In the main, the Republic has stayed sufficiently ahead of the *legitimate* grievances to undercut any chance of a dangerous movement, limiting the threat to small groups and potential minor acts of destruction and vandalism."

"Which made you the Navy's expert on the Great Fleet when my father's research bore fruit?" Coral asked.

"Exactly." The woman was quiet for a few seconds, staring out to sea. "I worked with your father, actually. He was...a presence."

"You mean he was overbearing, abrupt, usually blunt and often right?" Coral replied drily. "I loved my father, Commander, but you do not need to worry about accidentally insulting him to me. I am aware of his flaws. He is no demigod in my eyes."

"He was very, very smart," El-Ghazzawy said after a few seconds' silence. "He saw connections between documents we'd missed for a century. It wasn't just the information and research he pulled together, Admiral. He looked at *our* archives and found patterns in them we never would have seen.

"He died before his work was finished, but without him we never would have found the lead ship. We never would have had enough information to estimate the location of the City of Spires."

"Backtracking four hundred ships by hand." Coral shook her head. "I'm glad it wasn't me doing that."

Projecting a single ship's course was simple, if far from perfect, with *recent* data, let alone two-century-old weather almanacs. Projecting the hundreds that she knew El-Ghazzawy's team had gone through to get their location for the City...

"It went faster once we realized how close we were," El-Ghazzawy said. "Even without knowing about the hellfrost storms and their advance on our northern shores, to locate the City of Spires? I am an intelligence officer primarily, yes, but I am also a historian. Finding that put the names of my team in the history books."

She sighed.

"Books that are currently sealed and classified, of course."

"Until this mission is done," Coral assured her. "If history is what a historian cares about, we're going to make it, Commander. We're going to the City of Spires."

"I know. It will be fascinating."

"I do expect you to carry out the normal duties of my intelligence officer, though," Coral warned. "The rumors out of the Stelforma are concerning me."

"They should." El-Ghazzawy was silent for a moment, then sighed again. "Perhaps it is that I am a historian. Perhaps it is that I do not normally study the Stelforma's current affairs.

"But there is something going on. I fear the Admiralty may have underestimated how ready the Stelforma are. The numbers don't line up."

Coral took a moment to process that.

"The numbers?" she finally asked.

"Intelligence is very certain they know exactly how many battleships the Stelforma have in commission across the various national navies," El-Ghazzawy told her.

"Thirty-two, as I understand."

"Yes," the intelligence officer confirmed. "We're less sure on cruisers and destroyers, but we're reasonably sure we have at least as many cruisers as they do, and destroyers are only likely in the final push on their territory."

"And you disagree with those numbers?" Coral said.

"Intelligence has spies and has sent scouts past every military shipyard and anchorage we know about," El-Ghazzawy explained. "They have solid estimates on how many ships the Stelforma can build, how many they've got anchored in various bays, but..."

"That sounds relatively complete to me."

Coral watched El-Ghazzawy bite her lip as the officer marshaled her thoughts.

"I'm not doubting those numbers, sir," she finally said. "The thirty-two battleships that Intelligence has told the Admiralty the Stelforma have *exist*. Twenty newer ships with twenty-centimeter guns in turrets. Twelve older ships with eighteen-centimeter guns in casemate broadsides.

"Except at some point, the Stelforma had *thirty* ships with eighteen-centimeter guns in casemate broadsides. And we don't know where the other eighteen are."

"Broken down for scrap to build the new ones, I presume," Coral suggested.

"Logical, and the assumption Intelligence has made because we've *seen* the Stelforma scrapping some old battleships and we don't know where those older ships would be," El-Ghazzawy agreed. "But, thanks to your family's companies among others, we happen to have a very good idea of how much face-hardened steel armor plate the Stelforma foundries have produced."

Coral inhaled sharply, following El-Ghazzawy's logic. She'd grown up around shipyards, foundries and roller mills. Just plain steel-plate production didn't necessary relate to military production. Regular freighters and even buildings could use steel plate, even large and thick ones.

But face-hardened steel was battleship armor. Even cruisers called for relatively tiny amounts of it compared to the thousands of tons that went into a battleship. Those plates, if undamaged, were the *main* thing that would be recycled if a battleship was scrapped.

"And?" she asked slowly.

"They've *produced*, over the time period of their twenty-centimeter battleship program, fourteen percent more face-hardened plate than those twenty battleships needed," El-Ghazzawy said calmly. "We *know* they've scrapped four of their older battleships, which should have been enough plate for two and a half, maybe even three ships."

"Assuming some of that plate went to cruisers, that's still, what, three, maybe four extra *modern* ships? Plus however many of their older ships they didn't actually scrap," Coral said as she ran the numbers in her head.

"How is Intelligence *ignoring* this?" she demanded.

"They're not," El-Ghazzawy conceded. "But it's not *solid*. They know what all the national fleets have. We've watched the annual reviews, we've scouted the anchorages, we've counted keels in shipyards.

"We know there's missing armor plate, but there's no yards that could have used it and there's no ships built from it."

"Except we're officially barred from the southern third of the Southern Archipelago," Coral said grimly. "And while I *know* we scout the islands of the archipelago itself, the Southern Doctrine covers a large chunk of Albion, and we don't *know* if there are other islands separate from the main cluster."

"Islands, perhaps, more directly ruled by the Stelforma church itself," the intelligence officer suggested. "Or making up entire nations and national fleets we don't know about. If the Chosen Mother has a dozen battleships directly under the Stelforma flag, ships we haven't seen and don't know the location of..."

The Republic Navy had always argued that they needed a larger fleet than the Stelforma because the Stelforma nations would most likely be the first to strike. Since they'd be able to concentrate their fleets and hit wherever they wanted across the Dales, the Navy needed to be able to maintain sufficient forces to discourage attacks in multiple places.

But if there were a dozen more battleships than expected, even if half of that dozen were old ships with eighteen-centimeter guns...the balance of power drastically shifted and the Dales were in real danger.

And Coral was sailing north with two battleships as the Stelforma drafted their new ultimatum.

"Thank you, Commander," she finally told El-Ghazzawy. "I suppose it's the economics and industry that always define the final strengths, isn't it? My father used to say—"

"'Don't follow the money; follow the steel,'" the intelligence officer finished for her. "That's where I got the idea. He was, as I said, *very* smart."

CHAPTER 23

FOURTEEN HOURS A DAY at twenty kilometers an hour while the sun was clear enough to let them navigate. Twelve hours a day in darkness at ten kilometers an hour, relying on oil-fed illuminators and the cruisers to avoid any obstacles or risks.

The course Coral had plotted aboard *Cloudwatcher* and run by her staff and Captains at Bluecollar wasn't likely to have many obstacles. Weather was the risk, especially as the first week came to a close and they passed the northern end of the Dales.

They were now as far north as *Songwriter* had been when they'd met their hellfrost storm. Unlike *Songwriter*, Icebreaker Squadron wasn't going to be able to take shelter. If—*when*—they hit the hellfrost storms, they were going to have to push through.

Coral wasn't looking forward to it. So far, though, the air had been growing cooler and they'd sailed through a few hours of rain, but the weather was being entirely mundane.

And she had other concerns.

"*Firewater* is signaling a ship sighting again," O'Connor told her. He paused. "You do know you have an entire bridge, with maps and plotting stations and everything, inside the citadel, right?"

"I commanded a battleship with my own eyes from the flying bridge, Colonel," Coral replied. "I will command my squadron the same way. Any details from *Firewater* on *what* they're seeing?"

"One of Nevin's Bloodspeakers checked in with Captain Jernigan," her chief of staff replied. "He says the contact keeps coming into sight, keeping pace at about the limits of visual range for an hour or so, then dropping back.

"He thinks she's a cruiser."

"Ah." Coral smiled thinly. That was what she'd been half-expecting, half-afraid of. "I'm assuming we don't think she's one of ours?"

"Captain Jernigan has apparently attempted to Bloodspeak to her. Only silence has answered."

She nodded, considering the situation.

"Orders to *Stormwind* and..." She glanced around, mentally tracing her cruisers' current positions. "*Rockfall*, I think. Captains Asturias and Croft are to fall their ships back into strike formation around *Firewater*.

"Jernigan has temporary command. He is to take the three ships back to intercept the cruiser. Once he is certain he is close enough to be seen, they will fire yellow flares from all ships."

A yellow flare was part of the agreed-upon code with the Stelforma. There shouldn't be a Stelforma ship this far north, but it seemed extraordinarily unlikely that any Republic cruiser would be shadowing them like this.

Which meant she was Stelforma, and Coral was concerned as to how they'd even *found* her squadron. They'd been shadowing Icebreaker Squadron for three days.

Still, the yellow flares meant *back off or be fired upon*. Either the cruiser would withdraw or...

"If they do not fall back, Jernigan is authorized to engage the Stelforma ship and sink her," she finished softly.

∽

FROM THE FLAG bridge inside *Icebreaker*'s mighty armored citadel, Coral would have been dependent on reports and plotting stations to know the scent of things. As they grew nearer to their goal and the weather grew harsher, she would perhaps make that sacrifice to fulfill her duty more reliably.

At that moment, she had sent three ships off to fight and possibly die without her for the first time. In the moment, staring south and recognizing the threat, it had been the right order. Now, though...a moment of uncertainty held her heart.

She was intellectually certain she'd made the right call. Any of her cruisers were superior to any of their Stelforma counterparts—a truth that did *not* apply to *Cloudwatcher*, for example—and three could easily run down and destroy their shadow.

None of her uncertainty showed on her face. It was an unfamiliar sensation, one she took a moment to study like an insect trapped under a pane of glass. Her confidence was strong, her skills were honed, she *knew* she'd made the right call to send the cruisers back.

But it seemed some human feeling still lurked within her, despite what at least two of her exes had suggested when they'd *become* exes.

It was probably healthy, but she couldn't let it influence her. She had a job to do.

"Yellow flares!"

The shout from the crow's nest was redundant. Coral was watching the cruisers with her sharpest gaze, the smaller ships feeling almost like she could reach out and touch them. She saw the yellow signal flags go up and the yellow flares blaze into the sky at the same time as the lookout.

The Stelforma ship, unfortunately, was beyond the horizon, where Albion itself blocked her vision. Even her magic could not curve her vision around the world. It could make everything before the horizon clear to her, but the horizon barred her blood.

The cruisers continued to drive south, their rear wheels leaving frothed white wakes as they pushed toward their fifty-kilometer-per-hour maximum speed.

Or past it, Coral reflected, her gifts allowing her to estimate the distance and speed of the ships with a practiced eye. All three of the ships had broken their theoretical top speed, spending fuel eagerly in pursuit of a potential enemy.

Soon, they'd cross the horizon themselves and all she would see would be their flares. If the Stelforma weren't backing off, though... she expected to Jernigan fire off *red* flares.

Those meant *surrender or be destroyed.*

She was mentally counting down the seconds until the expected transition into hostilities when she caught the spark of a new light, rising from beyond the horizon. A green flare.

Acknowledged.

"Green flare!" the lookout shouted. "Stelforma acknowledgement!"

Fascinating. Coral leaned on the railing and considered the situation. Jernigan was already, wisely, slowing the ships she'd given him. They were dropping to their cruising speed, but they were continuing to pursue.

She'd get a report of intentions from the cruiser Captains by Bloodspeech in a few moments, she was sure, but she could tell exactly what Jernigan was thinking: he'd follow the cruiser for a few hours, make sure the Stelforma ship put real distance between her and Icebreaker Squadron, and then use his superior speed to catch up to the Squadron before nightfall.

"That's a relief," O'Connor said behind her. "I was worried they wouldn't back off."

"Fifty-fifty, Colonel," Coral told him.

"Sir?"

"They may have just been following us out of curiosity, basically," she said. "The cruiser saw us passing, and the Captain figured they'd see what was going on. They've been warned off, and they're likely near the edge of their ability to get back to base, anyway.

"I give that fifty percent odds."

"The other fifty percent, sir?" O'Connor asked.

"We had a security breach and the cruiser was tracking us for a battle group," Coral concluded flatly. "She was falling back both to try to evade our detection and to make contact with a courier or line of communications to her friends."

O'Connor was quiet for a moment.

"Jernigan may be in trouble?" he asked.

"They have the speed to get themselves out of trouble if they need to," Coral replied. "No, the problem will be tomorrow. If they can no longer track us, then whoever is in command is going to have to decide what their mission is and what it is worth.

"And if it is their mission to stop and they think it's worth it, they'll sail at full speed through the night and into tomorrow. We can't adjust our course sufficiently to really avoid a battle group catching up, so..."

She could *feel* her chief of staff doing the math versus usual Stelforma doctrine.

"They'll intercept us around noon, maybe fourteen hundred hours," he suggested.

"Fifty-fifty," she repeated. "We shall see."

CHAPTER 24

THE CRUISERS CAME LOPING BACK SHORTLY after nightfall, as Coral had expected. She'd finally returned to her office in *Icebreaker*'s citadel and opened herself up to the Bloodspeech, which allowed her to listen to Jernigan's report.

"Once they turned away, we cut speed to match them and followed for three hours," he said. The Captain was giving his own report, she noted, which was a good sign in her opinion. Others would have had the Bloodspeakers relay it.

"We made an attempt to close at one point," Jernigan noted. "They accelerated to stay out of gun range, and we let them. They aren't in violation of the Northern Doctrine at this latitude, and the Admiral didn't give us orders to start a fight.

"We broke contact about five hours ago and made to catch up with the Squadron," he concluded. "No sign of other contacts—and our stranger was a hundred klicks away from last contact with the Squadron."

That was all Coral needed to know, and she wiped the runes from her forehead—a silent message Jernigan would receive—as she considered the layout on the map.

Her formation had just slowed to ten klicks for the night. In the eight hours since contact with the Stelforma ship, they'd made a hundred and sixty kilometers—and the cruisers had followed the stranger another hundred kilometers south.

So, four hours before, the Stelforma cruiser had been...*there*. She touched the point on the map. It wasn't a straight line south, which meant they'd only been two hundred and thirty kilometers from Icebreaker Squadron's current position.

Engines and drive wheels hadn't changed much in the last century, if ever. Every attempt Coral knew of to upgrade the engines copied from the Great Fleet had resulted in a drastic loss of efficiency and speed. Unless the cruiser was drastically different from any she'd seen the Stelforma or Republic build, she likely had about the same fifty-klick top speed as Icebreaker Squadron's own cruisers.

If the stranger somehow knew exactly where *Icebreaker* and her escort were and had been able to avoid being spotted by the detached cruisers, they could easily be just out of visual range again already. *That* was probably paranoia talking, but...

They shouldn't have been able to find her squadron at all. If the cruiser had been retreating toward a battle squadron and the capital ships pushed their engines through the night and the morning...

They'd catch up around fourteen hundred hours, as she and O'Connor had calculated earlier. That would be when they'd come into view, anyway—assuming, of course, that they either re-located her squadron by dawn or knew where she was anyway.

Coral couldn't think of any way the Stelforma could know exactly where her squadron was, not without a spy on board using Blood-speech to report in, anyway. That was *possible*...but the likelihood of the Stelforma using the powers of the "Cursed" was low.

On the other hand, she'd been present for a demonstration of the Stelforma's High Magic once. Every year, at the annual celebration of the arrival of the Chosen in the Southern Archipelago, the Stelforma arranged a demonstration of the power of the Apostles.

That time, one of the Chosen Mother's black-robed right hands had arrived to mark the opening of the construction site for a new harbor fort near Dales territory—and had *built the entire seawall* for the fort over the course of a sixty-minute ritual.

She'd heard stories of the other displays, most of which had tended to be actively destructive, but in many ways, the one she'd seen was more impressive.

If the Stelforma's High Magic could build a perfectly smooth stone wall five meters high and two hundred meters long, it could do far more than destroy things. That meant it could do *subtler* things, things that the Stelforma didn't think would make good demonstrations.

Coral didn't *think* the Stelforma could track her fleet by magic she didn't understand...but she wasn't going to rule the possibility out, either.

She just had to hope they underestimated *her* people's magic as badly as she feared she underestimated theirs.

Dawn came brilliantly lit and with a chilling wind. The thermometer on the flying bridge told Coral it was hovering around five degrees—cool enough that she could see her breath in the air as she studied the south horizon.

Beneath her, she could hear and feel *Icebreaker*'s engines increasing power. The slow safe pace of night travel was over, and the squadron was getting up to speed once more.

Not for the first time, Coral wondered if slowing down overnight gained them anything. They were in open waters and safe from ice for now; the only potential obstacles there were sea life! And while whales were dangerous and could get *big*, they were also aware that *engines* meant bad news for them.

Whaleskin, after all, was tough, completely waterproof and effectively bulletproof. A regular fifty-meter-long whale could provide as much as three hundred square meters of useful skin. Plus blubber that refined into lamp oil, plus bone that was as hard as steel and tentacles that made for tough and reliable cables once dried.

From what Coral had been told, whaleboats couldn't use engines in their hunting waters. They could use them to get to the hunt and to bring their prize home, but the actual *hunt* had to be performed under sail and oar.

Which suggested to Coral that the whales would be smart enough to get out of the way of a *warship*. But doctrine and tradition said no Republic Navy ship sailed at more than ten kilometers per hour in the night.

Stelforma ships had arc lights that could pierce the night for several kilometers. *They* were under no such restriction, which was the main source of Coral's concern. If that cruiser had been a scout for a battle squadron, they'd likely spent the whole night sailing north at twenty-five klicks.

"O'Connor," she greeted her chief of staff, not even turning around as she heard him approach.

The man chuckled as he stepped up beside her.

"How many Seablood officers have you given *fits* doing that?" he asked.

"A few," she conceded. "They get used to it. I am not one of those who conceal their gifts. The Seabloods have their value to the Republic. They can damn well learn to value themselves for themselves and not feel outshone by Daleblood magic!"

Her chief of staff sighed and Coral rolled her eyes. She knew perfectly well that her attitude was impolitic—though she wasn't, unlike some she'd heard say the same, diminishing the Seabloods' value.

Dalebloods solved things through their magic. Seabloods solved things with their *brains*. Those were stereotypes, yes, but she'd seen the core truth to them again and again. She didn't think that Seablood engineers or researchers were actually smarter than their Daleblood counterparts—but she *did* think that they tended to think things through more thoroughly.

"Even around Dalebloods, that's hardly polite, sir," O'Connor reminded her.

She let that fall and studied the sea to the south of them.

"Think about it this way, Colonel," she said softly. "Jernigan is a competent Daleblood officer. He took command of an impromptu cruiser force and chased a potentially hostile contact a hundred kilometers away from the main squadron, then caught up with the help of our Bloodspeakers."

"Exactly as we wanted him to."

"It was certainly the simplest and most straightforward interpretation of his orders," Coral agreed. "But I wonder if a Seablood Captain, in his place, might have left a cruiser with the Stelforma ship for longer. Our Bloodspeakers can talk across a thousand kilometers, O'Connor. Any of the three cruisers could have kept up with the Stelforma ship until dawn and *then* rejoined the squadron, allowing us to know whether we are being pursued by a major Stelforma force."

Her chief subordinate was quiet for a few moments.

"I'm not sure a Seablood officer would have gone that far down the logic chain, sir," he finally said. "That is a lack of seniority and experience, not some difference in thinking between the bloods."

"Maybe," she allowed. "I'm not condemning Jernigan, Colonel. I would have done the same in his place. It is only now, thinking it over, that I see the other option. Seabloods, in my experience, *do* that thinking. They haven't had the magic of the blood to carry them through life."

"You're stretching, sir," O'Connor said calmly. "To justify your assumptions."

He *meant* her prejudices. She heard the word, even if he didn't say it. She didn't necessarily think he was right...but not thinking things through was *exactly* the flaw she was flagging in her own people.

"Maybe," she allowed. "But in the end, it doesn't matter today. We don't know if there's a Stelforma battle group out there. We have to operate as if there is and continue north while watching our backs."

There was another stretch of silence before her chief of staff spoke again.

"You think there is, don't you?" O'Connor asked.

"The odds of us randomly stumbling across a Stelforma cruiser a few hundred kilometers from breaching the Northern Doctrine are... low," she said grimly. "Someone was looking for us. And if they knew enough to get that cruiser that close, I have to assume they know enough to catch up to us."

CORAL WAS VERY, *very* good at her job. She was used to being right.

Just this once, she'd have been happy to be wrong.

"Hulls on the horizon!" the lookout shouted above her, and the Admiral swallowed a sigh and checked the time.

Thirteen hundred forty-two.

O'Connor had guessed around fourteen hundred hours. She'd concurred—and, it appeared, so had the Stelforma.

"Numbers?" she called up. She could see out to the horizon easily enough, but the extra twenty meters from the flying bridge to the crow's nest made a difference in how far out the horizon *was* for a given set of eyes.

"I make eight hulls," the lookout called down. "Three larger. Sailing in line, intercept course!"

"How do they even know where we *are* that closely?" O'Connor asked.

"I suspect the Stelforma High Magic has subtler tricks than they've ever shared with us," Coral replied. "I have to hope that those tricks don't help them *aim*."

Her chief of staff paled at that thought, and she smiled grimly.

"Range?" she asked.

She knew that the ships were at least sixteen kilometers distant, because *she* couldn't see them yet. The lookout's extra height gave them another nine kilometers of sight.

"I make it twenty-four kilometers," the lookout called down. "They are cruising fast, moving up at thirty klicks."

Coral turned to O'Connor.

"Your place is on the flag bridge, Colonel," she told him.

"So is yours."

"I need to see with my own eyes, O'Connor," Coral countered. "I need to be here, to command the squadron. *You* need to be inside *Icebreaker*'s armor in case something happens to me."

That wasn't the argument he'd been expecting, and he swallowed whatever he'd been about to say unspoken. Instead, he crisply saluted.

"Understood, sir."

O'Connor stepped away, and Coral turned to the signals officer waiting patiently for her orders.

"Signals and Bloodspeech to the squadron," she told the young woman. "All ships will form declining echelon on *Icebreaker*. Tankers farthest from the hostiles."

She turned toward the horizon, looking for a sign of ships she wouldn't see until they were much closer. Her squadron was only sailing at twenty klicks, which meant the Stelforma were overtaking at about ten kilometers an hour. It would *still* be almost an hour before she'd be able to see them from the flying deck.

And her *guns* would be able to hit the Stelforma well before then —and she had to assume the Stelforma ships had the same twenty-five-degree elevation as her ships on their main guns.

Which was, of course, why the flare codes existed. They would be visible well outside the range of even the twenty-centimeter guns.

"Sir."

Coral recognized El-Ghazzawy's voice and footsteps and turned to look at the intelligence officer. The Commander looked actively uncomfortable on the flying bridge, keeping her focus out to the horizon rather than the four-meter drop to the deck below.

"El-Ghazzawy," she greeted the officer. "We have little time. What do you need?"

"I heard the reports," El-Ghazzawy said quietly. "We're being hunted?"

"Potentially. At the very least, there appear to be three battleships coming up on us...and we're a long way from Stelforma waters."

"Then the reports I managed to review yesterday may be more useful than I thought," the intelligence officer told her. "A lot of information emerges from our intelligence network, Admiral, and my focus is on the past and on our current mission.

"But I did receive a summarized report from a spy who managed to observe firing tests for the Stelforma's latest battleship turrets."

Coral's initial impulse was to demand why *she* hadn't received that report. That struck her as the kind of information the Republic's flag officers needed to know. Except, of course, she *knew* how insular and conservative Republic Naval Intelligence was.

The Navy had been burned badly by relying on incorrect intelligence in the past. Intelligence tended to only give the line officers information that they had triple-confirmed...or that was immediately critical.

If she survived to make the Commission, that was something she was going to change. But for now, she understood how her service's intelligence officers worked. She just hated it.

"Explain, Commander," she finally ordered.

"Our engineers' assessment is that they're using a heavier charge for their twenty-centimeter guns, but their turrets can only elevate to twenty degrees. Estimated effective range is twenty klicks."

Coral exhaled a sharp breath.

"Ours is twenty-four," she murmured. They were already *in* their maximum range, though accuracy would suck at this distance.

"Yes, sir. This was new intel, flagged for distribution for officers likely to engage Stelforma forces in the near future." El-Ghazzawy paused. "Which didn't include us until yesterday, so I hadn't prioritized those papers."

How many secrets of the Republic and their enemies lurked unread in El-Ghazzawy's files, Coral wondered? The Intelligence officer had no support staff, and she'd brought entire cases of paper aboard with her—and received more in Bluecollar.

"Remind me to assign you some yeomen," Coral murmured. "Ones with decent clearance."

"That is not tradition, sir."

"No, it isn't," Coral agreed firmly. "Thank you, Commander El-Ghazzawy. I wish I was going to be able to use that information."

"Sir?"

"Three battleships to two," the Admiral told her staff officer calmly. "Likely four cruisers to six, but the cruisers won't really matter. Six twenty-centimeter turrets to five.

"The odds aren't in our favor, and I don't want to be the officer who starts the war the Republic is trying to defuse," she continued. "Which I'm afraid means we can't fire the first shot."

Leaving El-Ghazzawy to digest that, Coral turned to the signals officer.

"All ships to fire yellow flares," she ordered. "Let's see if we can avoid a firefight." She looked back southward grimly.

"And then order all ships to battle stations. Because while I'll *try* for peace, I'm not taking that bet."

CHAPTER 25

ICEBREAKER's BATTLE-STATIONS bells rang out clear and loud across the water. Coral noted Captain Nevin emerging from the citadel to join her on the flying bridge, as crew trooped out to the turrets and other positions across the ship's decks.

"Flare launching!" the signals officer announced, a moment before the rocket blazed into the sky from the forward deck. A few seconds after lifting off, it ignited, and a glittering yellow light ascended into the sky.

The other ships followed suit, until ten yellow stars drifted across the sky above Coral. The sight only lasted twenty seconds or so, until the flares began to die out in sequence.

She turned her gaze from the fading flares to the southern horizon. She couldn't yet see the incoming ships herself, but she knew she *would* see their flares. If she was *wrong*, the Stelforma would send up green or blue flares, backing off or requesting a discussion.

If she was right, there'd be no flares. The Stelforma would close to their maximum range, maybe even a kilometer or two inside it if the Squadron didn't fire, then open fire themselves.

They would get into range for the cruisers' guns shortly after the

Stelforma ranged on their main guns. The casemate guns on both sides had about the same range, around ten kilometers. This battle would be resolved by the main guns on the battleships and *maybe* the guns on the Republic's turreted cruisers.

"Flare spotted!"

Coral saw them moments after the lookout did, and shock took her breath away. The report of a flare had given her hope, but the sight of three red flares rising over the horizon shattered it instantly.

A red flare meant *surrender or be destroyed.*

"Well, then," she said aloud. "Captain Nevin?"

"Sir!" *Icebreaker*'s commander replied instantly.

"Bring us about," Coral ordered calmly. "We'll drive right across their bow at seventeen klicks. Signals officer! Flag and Bloodspeech to the rest of the Squadron. Warships will turn with *Icebreaker* and retain declining echelon formation.

"Tankers will break to continue north and await further signals!"

The tankers couldn't sustain thirty klicks, which meant that Coral *had* to fight. Twenty-plus thousand tons of battleship responded to Nevin's commands beneath her, *Icebreaker* turning to cut across the Stelforma formation's course at the designated range.

Now they were no longer sailing away from the Stelforma, the range was going to drop much, *much* faster.

"When do we fire, sir?" Nevin asked, the Captain's voice carefully pitched to reach Coral through the noise of the battleship's engines.

"When they do, Captain," Coral replied grimly. "Let them start this. If they don't fire, we cut across their course then turn north again."

"And if they do?"

"Then you sink the sons of bitches."

THE TENSION on *Icebreaker*'s flying bridge was thick enough to walk on as she led the way toward the enemy force. Three Stelforma battleships almost certainly outmassed and outgunned Coral's two capital ships, but to get to their own range, they *had* to sail directly at her ships as Icebreaker Squadron presented full broadsides.

The echelon formation she'd ordered put *Icebreaker* both forward and toward the enemy from the rest of the squadron. She was intentionally offering her flagship up as a target—hoping that the Stelforma would strike the adamantine armor belt that covered *Icebreaker*'s vitals.

Every instinct in her body screamed at her to open fire as the battleship's turrets trained and elevated toward the enemy—but she couldn't fire the first shots. She was going to *obliterate* this Stelforma fleet, and she wanted every record to be clear that the enemy had fired first.

"Sir, lookouts have analyzed the silhouette of the Stelforma cruisers," Blanc told her, her operations officer acting as a relay between Coral and the ship's crew—and her own staff, inside the citadel.

That Coral *still* couldn't see the enemy suggested that O'Connor was right and she should have been inside the armor herself. On the other hand, from here, she *could* see her own ships and recognize the raggedness of their formation.

They all knew what she'd meant by "declining echelon" and had done a decent job for a squadron that had done minimal formation exercises together. Comparing it to the perfectly aligned forty-five-degree angle that the Northern Squadron tended to achieve in said exercises, though, showed the value of the practice.

"I'm assuming the analysis told us something I need to know," Coral observed at her operations officer.

"They're turret ships. *Four*-turret ships."

Coral was silent for a few seconds as she processed that. Assuming that the Stelforma were using the same dual turrets as the Republic—and given how successful the southerners had been at stealing the Republic's engineering designs over the years, that seemed likely—that gave each of those cruisers an eight-gun broadside.

The southerners preferred a lighter, faster-firing gun than the Republic for their secondaries and cruisers. Those cruisers would have eight *ten*-centimeter guns instead of twelve-centimeter, but that was still a lot of guns throwing a lot of metal.

"That adds to Commander El-Ghazzawy's theory that there's a shipyard we don't know about," she told Blanc. "Because the last *I* heard, the Stelforma navies only had casemate cruisers."

"Yes, sir. That's why I wanted to flag it."

"Good call, Tácito," Coral agreed. "Thank you."

"Range is twenty kilometers, sir," the young crewwoman on the range finder informed her.

The moment of truth. They were now inside the range of the lead battleship of the Stelforma formation. Coral studied the horizon line, knowing that the ships just beyond that line would be making their own decisions over whether to fire or not.

Icebreaker's flying bridge was silent, everyone listening for a report from the lookouts above. For a few seconds, the only sound was the engines and the waves.

"Gunfire! Enemy forward turret firing! They're turning!"

Coral let out the breath she'd been holding. That was that, she supposed.

"Captain Nevin, you may return fire."

The heavyset Captain nodded silently, then starting snapping orders into the voice pipes. The range was such that their turrets, already aligned and waiting for the order, fired before the Stelforma shells landed.

The Admiral couldn't see the enemy ships, but she *definitely* saw the shells land. Water sprayed up from the impact and explosions of the two enemy weapons, roughly a hundred and fifty meters short of *Icebreaker*.

At maximum range, that was *good* shooting.

"Enemy rear turret firing!"

170

Coral tuned out the specific words, focusing on picking up the tenor of the battle. *Icebreaker's* first salvo didn't hit anything more than the enemy's first pair of shells—but she'd fired six guns in a pattern that had covered half a kilometer of distance.

Nevin's gunners didn't *hit* the Stelforma battleship, but they landed shells on both sides of her, straddling the enemy and allowing them to narrow their targeting for the second salvo.

The Stelforma's second two-shell salvo landed even farther away, but the reports from above told Coral that the lead ship's commander was holding their fire until both turrets were loaded.

The enemy column was swinging to the west, bringing themselves not quite parallel to Coral's squadron. They'd continue to close the range, but they were sacrificing closing speed to allow them to bring all of their main guns into play.

Their second battleship and *Cloudwatcher* fired at the same instant. A few seconds later, *Icebreaker* fired her second salvo.

"Hit! Multiple hits on the lead enemy!" the lookout shouted. "Both ours and *Cloudwatcher's*!"

Captain Oliversen's gunners, it seemed, were following the flagship's lead and getting it right. There was no way to be sure how many of the ten shells in the combined salvo had hit the enemy battleship, but at least some had hit their mark.

The third Stelforma battleship fired their first salvo at the same time as the first one fired her second. Eight shells landed in the water around Icebreaker Squadron—and this time, the enemy had overshot, the shells exploding in the water on the east side of Coral's ships.

The enemy shooting might be coming up short, but their armor was doing its job. They'd landed multiple hits on the lead battleship, but she was still firing full salvos.

At this distance, there was no way they could aim well enough to specifically hit turrets or paddlewheels. Just *hitting* the enemy ships at twenty kilometers was impressive enough, and Coral found herself wondering how much difference the ability to lay out a ladder of six shells instead of four was making.

Icebreaker's turrets roared a third time, sending another salvo toward the Stelforma ships. *Cloudwatcher's* shells echoed a moment later, the two ships almost synchronized.

A few moments later, the Stelforma finally found the range. Twelve shells from three ships came crashing down all around *Icebreaker*, two of them screaming in to slam against the battleship's side armor. The steep angle alone would have been enough to neutralize them, Coral suspected, but the sound of their impact was ever so slightly different than she expected.

The Stelforma had hit the adamantine armor belt, and *that* didn't care if the shells came in from above or at a perfect angle. No shell in either force's magazines could breach the magical armor from the City of Spires.

The impacts still shook the ship underneath her, and Coral knew what came next. The Republic consistently built better ships, more compact turrets and better guns than the Stelforma, but their ammunition hoists and even the turrets themselves were driven by hydraulics drawing pressure from the main corn-oil engines.

The Stelforma tended to steal most aspects of engineering from the Republic sooner or later, allowing them to keep up in the main engineering aspects of ships. Some aspects couldn't be stolen, though—and the strength and speed of Daleblood crew who could, if necessary, lift twenty-centimeter shells were among those.

The reverse was the common magics of the Stelforma—in this case, the strange arc-motors that turned their turrets and drove their ammunition hoists. Examples had made it back to the Dales, but the Republic's engineers and magi alike had failed to find the correct rituals or unguents to empower the arcane systems.

The problem was that the hydraulic-powered twenty-centimeter guns on the Republic battleships could fire up to four times a minute as a reliable maximum—and the arc-powered twenty-centimeter guns on the Stelforma ships could fire four times a minute at a *minimum*.

And now the Stelforma had the range, that was exactly what they were going to do.

"Captain Nevin, please sink one of these ships for me," Coral told her flag captain calmly as the next salvo crashed down around them. This time, eleven of the shells overshot—but the twelfth crashed into the front of the armored citadel, releasing a spray of shrapnel that only barely missed the flying bridge.

"Doing our best, sir," *Icebreaker*'s Captain replied grimly as the battleship shook under the power of her own guns.

"Hit! Multiple hits! Secondary explosion!"

The report from the lookouts was exactly what Coral was hoping for—and a few seconds later, she only counted *ten* shells in the enemy salvo. Near misses rocked *Icebreaker*, but there were no hits this time.

"Forward turret on the lead ship went up," the lookout said after a moment. "She's still afloat, but she's losing speed."

"Hit her again, Ekaterina," Coral urged Nevin—recognizing that the Captain would pass that on to the turret crews.

As if in answer, the next Stelforma salvo crashed down on *Icebreaker* like the rage of an angry god. Two shells hit the armored deck, a third hit the citadel and at least three hammered into the belt armor. Screams of pain warned Coral that people had been struck, but the battleship continued to drive forward, and her guns fired as one only a few seconds later than planned.

The delay, though, made the credit for the Stelforma ship's fate easy to award. The four shells from *Cloudwatcher* must have struck something critical—potentially a magazine exposed by the destruction of the forward turret.

The enemy fleet was still behind the horizon to Coral's gaze, but she *saw* the plume of smoke and debris marking the destruction of the lead battleship.

If any of that ship's crew escaped the explosion, they likely suffered as *Icebreaker*'s salvo of shells crashed down into the wreckage. No power on Albion could prevent that, though the thought sent a shiver of guilt down Coral's spine.

A scream of pain from the deck below, presumably as medics got someone onto a stretcher, steeled her nerve, and she met Nevin's gaze across the flying bridge.

"Target the second ship," she ordered. "Keep firing."

The order *should* have been redundant. In the absence of orders, the squadron's two battleships should have moved their fire on to the next ship—but this was the first time Republic capital ships had fired in anger in twenty years.

The destruction of the Stelforma ship had likely killed the better part of a thousand people. A moment's hesitation before continuing to fire on the next ship was reasonable, even if Coral's sympathy for the people who'd *started* this fight was limited.

"One of the cruisers is breaking off; looks like for search and rescue," the lookout above declared.

"Understood. Under no circumstances do we fire on the rescue ship unless she opens fire herself," Coral ordered. That was a sop to her conscience she could easily justify. The cruiser was out of her own range, and Coral wasn't planning on wasting shells on the cruisers while there were battlewagons to shoot at.

The next salvo—merely eight shells now—was staggered in both time and distance, proving that the lead ship had been coordinating the fire of her fellows. They'd had the range for the last salvo, but this one fell short. The following salvo was better coordinated timewise but still undershot Icebreaker Squadron.

Reports flowed around her. The next six-round salvo from *Icebreaker* was another ladder pattern aimed at the second Stelforma battleship. They'd overshot by enough that even the closest shells had gone past the enemy ships.

More shells rang against *Icebreaker*'s armor as the Stelforma found the range again, and Coral could *feel* Nevin's urge to order the Admiral into the armored citadel.

Truthfully, if Nevin *gave* that order, Coral would obey. There'd be *consequences* for that later, but the Captain was the Captain, and if she ordered the Admiral inside in a battle, even the Admiral would obey.

For now, though, Nevin controlled herself, and the ship shook underneath them.

"They hit the adamantine belt again," Coral murmured. The difference in sound probably wouldn't be clear to a Seablood, but to her it was the difference between drums and a guitar.

"Even if we didn't need the bow for the main mission, that belt was worth its weight," Nevin confirmed. "The steel *should* have held against this, but the adamantine *has* held."

The next salvo from *Icebreaker* straddled the target, at least one shell hitting, and *Cloudwatcher* followed the angle a moment later, putting three of four shells on target.

The two ships were learning the pattern. *Icebreaker* would use her extra set of guns to throw out a larger ladder pattern, and her shot clock told the smaller battleship the angle she was firing at. When the ladder hit, *Icebreaker*'s gunnery officer updated the shot clock to the best estimate of the correct angle, and then *Cloudwatcher* followed up.

Coral had been *very* lucky in her gunnery teams, she realized.

"Sir! They're breaking off!"

Coral swallowed her initial response and looked up at the crow's nest.

"Confirm that!" she snapped.

"Lead ship just turned south; the rest are following. Pulling away from us at thirty klicks."

For a moment, the urge to pursue and finish the job filled Coral head to toe, and a predatory smile crossed her lips. Then she shook herself and sighed. The mission came first.

"Signal to *Cloudwatcher*," she ordered. "Cease fire. Squadron will turn north and return to our original course.

"We have a job to do, people, and killing book-botherers *isn't* it."

"Yes, sir," Nevin confirmed softly.

The Captain met Coral's gaze and shook her head.

"We can't let this stand," she warned the Admiral.

"We won't," Coral promised. "I'll report in to the Admiralty as soon as we're definitely clear of their gun range."

The firing had stopped when the Stelforma ships had turned. It wasn't a surrender...but it was a wordless offer to end the battle. And since Coral knew, as the Stelforma hopefully *didn't*, that every ship in her squadron had given up a significant chunk of their ammunition for extra fuel, she was going to take that offer.

The mission came first.

CHAPTER 26

"Seven dead, twenty-one wounded," Nevin said grimly as the sun began to set over the squadron. "We were lucky, I suppose, but it still hurts."

Coral nodded wordlessly, studying the marks on *Icebreaker*'s deck where Stelforma shells had landed.

"I dislike the necessity of callousness," she finally said. "I will need to check on the wounded later. Right now, though, I need to know. Can *Icebreaker* carry on?"

"We can, sir," Nevin confirmed instantly. "Even the deck armor is intact. We got smacked around, but there's no serious damage. Crew losses are a bigger problem than any actual damage...and the crew losses aren't a problem."

"Thank you, Captain." Coral looked east, toward the Dales. They should still be within a thousand kilometers or so of North Dale. "Bloodspeakers have sent in reports?"

"Yes, sir."

"Carry on, Captain," she told Nevin. "Have someone let sickbay know I'll be by to check on the wounded in the morning."

Her thoughts were in turmoil as she looked at the scarring on the deck. With a silent sigh, she turned on her heel and began the long walk toward the battleship's stern. The warship's length made for a decent walk, which was good exercise *and* helped her think.

So long as she managed not to *look* agitated as she paced the length of her flagship, she would be fine. She couldn't let the crew see the Admiral being on edge, but everyone knew even Admirals needed exercise. A calm brisk walk from bow to stern and back was entirely reasonable.

Or so she told herself, anyway. She needed to think.

The attack on her command was the first round of the war the Republic had been trying to avoid. But it was *weird*. They were a long way from Stelforma waters, and kicking off the war here made no sense. If there were other attacks on the southern Dales, she could see it, but she'd have heard by now if there had been.

For whatever reason, the Stelforma had sent a full division of battleships thousands of kilometers north of their waters. The only reason she could see was specifically to intercept Icebreaker Squadron—but *why*?

Turning to look at the setting sun, she wondered if the Stelforma understood *why* the Northern Doctrine existed. It wasn't because the Republic had any secret resources, shipyards, bases or territories up there.

It was because the best guess of the Republic's historians was that the Great Fleet had landed about a million people on the continent of the Dales...and a *quarter million* had died either on the evacuation ships or in the City of Spires.

The Republic regarded everything north of the twentieth parallel as a *mass grave*. Even *they* didn't go past that line very often, which made Icebreaker Squadron's mission both unusual and uncomfortable for the Navy.

But she still wasn't sure *why* the Stelforma would have tried to blockade her—unless they either had similar feelings about the northern hemisphere or knew something about the City of Spires the Republic didn't.

Having completed two circuits of the ship, she leaned against the railing at the bow and looked down at the pale gray of the adamantine armor, and realized an entirely different possibility. If the Stelforma knew where *Icebreaker*'s armor had come from...they might be afraid that the Republic Navy would find something in the City to allow them to vastly upgrade their fleet.

That made sense to her, allowing the pieces to fall into place. The Stelforma wanted to launch a new war and, likely, believed their secret fleet was enough to allow them to overcome the Republic.

Coral figured they were underestimating the Republic's coastal defenses and destroyer flotillas, even if they had the balance of battleships right. But if the Navy could learn the magic behind *Icebreaker*'s adamantine armor, they would be able to field an indestructible fleet that the Stelforma could never overcome.

The irony was that recovering magic or weapons from the City of Spires wasn't even *on* Coral's list. She was hunting an unknown enemy, not seeking an advantage against a known one.

Though now the thought had occurred to her...

∽

"ADMIRAL. Allow me to congratulate you on a well-deserved promotion."

Vice Admiral Siena's words echoed in Coral's skull as the blood symbols on her forehead vibrated.

"Thank you, Admiral," she told her former commanding officer. Siena was still senior to her, even if she was no longer under the other woman's command. "Do you have any updates on the situation with the Stelforma, sir?"

"It's complicated, Amherst," Siena told her. "Even *my* communications with Daleheart are by telegram and Bloodspeech relay. I do not get as many details as I would like. News of this attack has proceeded to the highest levels of the Republic; I can assure you of that."

"So, it's war, then," Coral guessed.

"It seems likely. All Squadrons have been ordered to maximum readiness. All shore forts have been ordered to check ammunition stocks and test-fire their guns. Parliament has been summoned and will, from what I am hearing, be convened at dawn."

"We haven't received any ultimatums or messages from the Stelforma?" Coral asked.

"Not as of the last relay, no," Siena confirmed. "The ambassadors of the assorted Stelforma states will likely be summoned before the Cabinet prior to the debate in Parliament, given a chance to explain things."

Coral scoffed. "What explanation could justify an unprovoked attack on my squadron?"

"More, the President and Prime Minister will give them the opportunity to crucify their own commander to avoid war," the senior Admiral told her. "Not that the ambassadors are likely to know much of anything. When the Stelforma moves, the leaders of their secular nations are not always informed."

There was silence for a moment, only the slight vibration of the runes on her skin telling Coral the link was still active.

"But the Republic is moving to a war footing. I do not believe that Parliament will accept excuses this time. There is too much evidence that the Stelforma are preparing for a fourth ultimatum. If they hoped to destroy your squadron unnoticed...they were wrong."

"Are there any orders for me, sir?" Coral finally asked.

"Telegram arrived just before I Spoke to you," Siena confirmed. "You are ordered to continue your mission. No higher priority."

Coral exhaled a long breath. *No higher priority*. Her nation was about to go to war, but she was still going to head north in pursuit of a myth.

"Understood, sir."

"I can't say I do," Siena admitted. "I have not been briefed on your mission, Admiral Amherst, but I have faith in your duty to the

Republic and in the Commission. Is there any assistance the Northern Squadron can provide?"

"Two battleships and a cruiser division are still somewhere in our northern waters, Admiral Siena," Coral warned. "I'm considering sending some of my cruisers to keep tabs on them, but based on those orders, I can't divert my capital ships."

"I have a flight of cruisers already heading your way," Siena told her. "They're raising anchor as we speak and should be in the area in two days. It's not perfect, but they'll be able to locate the Stelforma if they're doing anything except running for home with their tails between their legs."

"Cruisers won't do much against battleships, sir."

"No, but once we find the pricks, I'll be able to put battleships in front of them if they head for the Dales." Siena's calm confidence suffused her voice, and Coral drew a moment of strength from it.

"Then I will leave their fate in your capable hands," she told the other Admiral. "And continue on with our mission."

"May fate and the Divine guide your way."

"Thank you."

The channel faded and Coral stared at the wall behind her desk, feeling her hands tremble with the drain of the entire day.

No higher priority.

She unwrapped an energy bar with shivering fingers and cursed as the candy fell from her hands. Glaring down at her traitorous appendages, she took a slow breath and grabbed the chunk of chocolate and dried fruit carefully.

Coral made herself eat the entire bar before she even washed the blood from her face, the trembling in her hands telling her everything she needed to know about how much keeping her vision so tightly focused all day had cost her.

Somehow, the quick conversation with Vice Admiral Siena had driven home the seriousness of her mission in a way that even the recognition of its potential sacrifices hadn't.

No higher priority.

Her country was about to fight the war she'd spent the last two decades preparing for—but her mission was unchanged.

And the plan called for her squadron to launch the first counter-attack of a war that was already being waged against the Republic. It wasn't *her* mission that was starting a second war.

They were already at war with whoever had driven the Seabloods south. In a sense, they'd been at war since before the Great Fleet had sailed.

Icebreaker Squadron would be the first force in two hundred years that the Republic had hurled into the teeth of that enemy. Designed and built by Seablood hands and crewed by Daleblood warriors, they would sail away from the war that defined this century to fight the war that had created their nation.

No higher priority.

Coral Amherst needed a drink.

CHAPTER 27

THE FIRST HELLFROST storm hit them two days later, just after they passed the twentieth parallel and officially entered graveyard waters. Coral watched it coming from the north for several hours, recognizing it early in the morning.

"We're not changing course, are we?" Nevin finally asked, standing next to her on the flying bridge.

"No," Coral agreed. "We're going to face worse as we get farther north. We *have* to be able to endure what this weather brings us."

She turned to the signals officer.

"The Squadron will form in column behind *Icebreaker*," she ordered. "All hands are to report inside the hulls, and all efforts are to be made to keep internal heating systems online. We will maintain formation through the storm.

"The other ships *need Icebreaker* to clear the way. They must hold the column."

She turned to Nevin.

"We'll need your illuminators running as long and as bright as you can manage, Captain," she told the Captain. "No matter what, we need them to be a beacon for the rest of the Squadron."

"We're on it," Nevin promised her.

The signals officer was already laying out his flags and talking into a voice pipe to have the Bloodspeakers pass on the details.

The storm was getting closer far too quickly for Coral's peace of mind, though their sailing toward it at twenty kilometers an hour certainly didn't *help* with that. She looked out at the black clouds and the ice floes flashing into existence underneath them, and concealed a shudder.

"Once you've got confirmation on those orders, get inside," she ordered the signals officer.

"Yes, sir."

Coral turned to survey the rest of the crew on the flying bridge.

"That goes for *all of you*," she snapped. "No one should be on the decks that doesn't *absolutely need to be*."

She was Daleblood. Her hearing was far better than any Seablood's—which meant she *heard* Captain Nevin's soft scoff at her words.

Coral turned a sharp eye on the blonde Captain and then smiled.

"And yes, that includes me, Captain Nevin," she told her subordinate. "I'm going inside. I will set a good example, I promise! You do the same."

"I'll be right behind you, sir," Nevin promised. "That storm doesn't look like anything I want to become more closely acquainted with than I absolutely have to."

THE ENTIRE BATTLESHIP shuddered around Coral as *Icebreaker* hit the first ice block.

From the flag bridge, her supposed battle station, she couldn't see *anything*. There were windows that would be open in more moderate weather, but heavy metal shutters had been closed as the hellfrost storm washed over her flagship.

Oil lamps flickered in the mirrored alcoves that let them light the space, and Coral found herself looking down at the chart table as the battleship crashed through another ice floe. She could hear ice pellets and snow crashing down around them outside, and despite the heating and her own temperature tolerance, she found herself shivering at the thought.

A rating came in from the door deeper into the citadel, carrying a written message that they shared with the two crew updating the chart table. One of them took a grease pen and updated the information on *Firewater* written on one of the glass boards.

The rest of the squadron was keeping up—the update was on the cruiser's fuel status, and the other ships were being updated as other messengers from the Bloodspeakers filtered in.

They should have refueled sooner, Coral knew. She was trying not to glare at the fuel levels on the board. *Icebreaker* and *Cloudwatcher* were fine, well over seventy percent. Half of the cruisers were slipping past fifty percent.

The *other* half, though, were the three ships Jernigan had taken after the first Stelforma contact. They'd cruised for half a day at full speed and burned through that much more fuel than the rest of Icebreaker Squadron.

And that left three of Coral's ships well under forty percent fuel as the storm battered them with wind, snow and ice.

"Have *Firewater*, *Stormwind* and *Rockfall* increase frequency of fuel-status reporting," Coral ordered. The advantage of being on the flag bridge instead of the flying bridge, she supposed, was that she didn't need to get anyone's attention to pass on the orders.

Everyone there was *waiting* for her to say something, to give an order. The space was as quiet as any library she'd ever been in—except, of course, for the storm outside.

The large chart table, currently covered in their best map of the northern hemisphere between the Dales and the estimated location of the City of Spires, held pride of place. Vertical glass panels formed the arms of a horseshoe anchored on that table, mostly marked with the fuel and ammunition status of the squadron in grease pen.

A dozen staffers circled that horseshoe of displays, writing on the glass panels in reverse so Coral and O'Connor could read the updates.

"What happens if the cruisers can't handle the storm?" her chief of staff murmured next to her.

"Everyone in this room is Daleblood, Colonel," Coral pointed out to her subordinate. "*Whispering* isn't going to conceal anything."

He shrugged.

"Have to make the effort to maintain morale," he told her. "And?"

She glanced over at the status reports for the rest of the squadron.

"I'm as worried about the tankers as the cruisers," she admitted. "They're bigger and more stable, but they're also heavier and more critical."

Coral shook her head.

"If the cruisers struggle, we'll refuel them and send them to Admiral Siena at North Dale," she concluded, answering his original question. "If the *tankers* struggle...we fill every void we have on *Icebreaker* and send the rest of the squadron to North Dale."

She saw O'Connor studying her out of the corner of her eye and stepped forward to review the chart on the table. They were still over two thousand kilometers from their destination. The hellfrost storm was already slowing them down, and once they hit solid ice pack, they were going to slow down even further.

At their ordinary cruising rate, they were five and a half days from the estimated location of the City of Spires. At the rate she was expecting to manage as they hit ice pack...she was estimating more like two weeks.

"You're relieved to hit one of these storms," O'Connor said softly. "I don't understand."

"I am," she admitted. "Because much as this storm sucks, we are literally going to sail into hell, Colonel O'Connor." She tapped the marker on the map for the City of Spires.

"Our best-case scenario is four, maybe five hundred kilometers of ice pack that would take us six to eight days to travel through *calm weather*. But every report I've seen says that the weather past the thirtieth parallel is basically a permanent, if somewhat calmer, hellfrost storm."

"Hence 'hell,'" O'Connor agreed.

"So, if we struggle with one traveling storm, we won't be able to take the cruisers into that hell up there," she told him. "And if we tried, without knowing, we'd lose them. I'd rather take the risk of a storm now, when I can still send everyone except *Icebreaker* home in relative safety, than wait until we're elbow-deep in the abyss."

There was a long pause as her chief of staff considered her words, then he chuckled softly.

"Where *did* you pick up that metaphor?" he asked.

Coral turned a questioning gaze on him.

"My Captain used it when I was first promoted to gunnery officer," she remembered aloud. "Why?"

"You are definitely *not* farm folk," O'Connor told her. "Because the 'abyss' in question is usually the wrong end of a cow...which, if nothing else, is a lot *warmer* than this is looking to be."

She shook her head repressively.

"We're going to miss any sign of warmth before this is over, I suspect," she told him. "For now...let's just hope we get through the night."

THERE WAS no sleep to be had aboard *Icebreaker* that night. Nightfall itself was almost impossible to recognize, as the hellfrost storm continued to block out the sky above them. Without compasses and Daleblood navigational instincts, they couldn't have been sure they were even following the right course.

Winds howled around the citadel like anguished spirits, and the crash of the hull against ice—and of larger ice pellets against the upper decks—was at times as loud and terrifying as the Stelforma shellfire during the battle.

But the occasional messenger from the Bloodspeakers kept the status boards updated. All of Coral's ships were still with them as the dark settled in.

The first sign of real trouble came when a messenger arrived from the bridge and stepped into the central bubble of the flag deck with a nervous salute.

"Report, crewman," Coral ordered the young man.

"Captain Nevin's compliments, sir, but we've lost one of the stern illuminators," the rating told her. "*Cloudwatcher*'s lookout warned us, and a work party went out to try and repair it but...it's just gone, sir."

She would have preferred not to send anyone out onto the deck. The mercury thermometers that were supposed to give her the exterior temperature had frozen solid hours before. But...it was Nevin's call and the Captain had made it.

"Anyone injured?" she asked.

"No, sir. Chief said that it looked like a chunk of ice hit the base and tore the entire illuminator off. Work party closed the oil feed and checked the other two illuminators. So far, just cold-cracked glass on the others."

"Thank you, crewman," Coral told him. "Pass my compliments to Captain Nevin. I appreciate the report."

The youth vanished faster than he'd appeared, and she swallowed a moment of amusement.

"If they hadn't sealed the oil feed, we could have had a real problem," O'Connor observed. "I don't think any of us want to see a *fire* in the middle of this mess."

"All any of us want to see at this point is dawn," she said softly. "We *will*, of course, but it's going to be an uncomfortable night."

"We're heading north at ten klicks, and the storm is heading south even faster than that. We've got to pass through it sooner rather than later, don't we?"

"The storm that swept over Keller's Landing trapped us in the bay for eight days, Colonel," Coral murmured. "That's how long it took to pass over a single point on the coast. I'll be content if we clear the storm sometime *tomorrow*."

Her chief of staff looked vaguely ill at the thought.

"I'm not sure I can sleep with this noise," he admitted.

"Based off our time at Keller's Landing, you will," she told him. "Eventually."

Dalebloods could stay awake for around forty-eight hours— almost two full twenty-six-hour days. Like most uses of their gifts, it would cost them in terms of appetite and later sleep, but they could stay functional for those forty-eight hours.

They would then, in her experience, fall down almost immediately after the forty-eighth hour. It was fascinating just how neatly and consistently the timing worked out.

She didn't expect her crew to have to push that hard for *this* storm—but it was one of the powers of the Blood that they would need to complete their mission.

CHAPTER 28

EVEN SAILING into and through the storm, it took them over thirty hours to finally break clear of the clouds and ice. The sun washed over *Icebreaker*'s decks, and Coral took to the flying bridge again as soon it was no longer being pounded with ice and snow.

The air was still bone-chilling, but it was a *mere* negative ten degrees instead of below the freezing point of mercury. The magic in her blood shielded her from the worst of it, an inner heat suffusing her limbs as she surveyed the status of her squadron.

They were all still there, though there'd been moments in the night and morning when she hadn't been sure that would be the case! Their formation was a ragged mess that only barely resembled the neat line ahead they'd entered the storm with, but they were all behind *Icebreaker*, at least.

"Signals," she summoned the officer in question. "Flags and Bloodspeech to the Squadron. *Firewater, Stormwind, Rockfall* and *Silkcow* are to begin refueling operations immediately. Squadron will maintain a steady ten klicks north."

Each of her tankers could fuel two ships at one. *Silkcow* had more fuel than the other three ships but was the next-worse off after the trio she'd sent to chase off the Stelforma.

The cruiser had suffered the worst night of all of them, and she was still waiting on damage reports. So far, everyone was keeping up at the minimal speed she was demanding of them, but they couldn't keep that pace for long.

They needed to be moving. Every hour they spent idling along was an hour before they reached the City of Spires—and an hour before they could return home to fight the Stelforma. Or even have any news of what was happening back home. They were now well past the thousand-kilometer range of North Dale's Bloodspeakers.

No one from Icebreaker Squadron would know the fate of the Republic until they returned home.

"Admiral."

"Captain Nevin," Coral acknowledged her flag captain. "Damage report for *Icebreaker*?"

"Yes, sir," Nevin confirmed. "Short version: we're fine."

"Long version?"

Nevin chuckled.

"*Icebreaker* was built for this, sir," the Captain told her. "We have extra air ducts for heating, carefully chosen types of metal, and this crew was trained on what needs to be allowed to warm up slowly.

"We lost one of the stern illuminators entirely, and two of the remaining three have cracked glass or mirrors," Nevin continued. "We have spare parts for all of that, and we'll have four working stern illuminators by nightfall. Another working party is checking the side and bow illuminators. I'm expecting to have some more broken glass and mirrors, but all of it will be fixed shortly.

"Otherwise, we lost a couple of the paddle slats from the starboard wheel. Nothing that will even slow us down, and the carpenters are already on it. We'll need to lift the wheel out of the water for a few minutes while we replace them, so we'll have difficulty turning while that's the case."

"We're going straight north," Coral observed. "Shouldn't be a problem."

"My impression is we won't be going fast until tomorrow, regardless," Nevin murmured. "Nothing I'm hearing from *Silkcow* is promising."

"I'm waiting for Captain Weiss's report," Coral noted. She was hearing similar reports—not least as to why *Silkcow* was down thousands of liters of fuel compared to the other cruisers who'd stayed in escort formation. She didn't want to prejudice herself against Weiss's conclusions, though.

"It's not going to be pretty, sir," her flag captain warned. The two women surveyed the other ships in silence for a moment, watching as the four designated cruisers gathered around the tankers.

"Captain Weiss can't get away with it, because she can't sail at full speed," Nevin said, "but the other five cruiser Captains are going to lie through their teeth to say their ships are ready to fight."

"I was a cruiser Captain once myself," Coral replied. "They still survive on a diet of whisky and raw red meat, do they?"

Nevin chuckled. "I'm not sure that will ever change, sir."

"They'll obfuscate to try to stay with the squadron," Coral conceded. "I don't expect them to outright *lie*—and I'm hoping that between myself and my staff, we'll be able to see through the cowsilk."

"Good luck. *Icebreaker* is ready on your command. We weathered the storm without issues—I see no problem breaching all the way to the City of Spires now."

"You realize you probably just doomed us, Captain?"

"Oh, I'm sure we'll find *something* to make a problem, sir," the Captain said cheerfully. "But it won't be *Icebreaker*'s ability to survive the weather."

RETURNING to the flag bridge inside the citadel, Coral could tell that the damage reports had finally filtered in. O'Connor was perched on a seat, staring at the glass panels with the handwritten notes and information of the status of each ship.

"Colonel," Coral greeted him. "Status report?"

"Damage reports are coming in," he told her. "Do you want to review or have my summary?"

"Summarize for now."

"*Silkcow* is disabled," O'Connor said bluntly. "Primary axle on her drive wheel snapped in the cold."

"That shouldn't happen."

"No. There had to be a preexisting flaw in the steel, one that wouldn't show up in normal operating conditions but..."

"Somewhere between minus fifty and minus sixty isn't 'normal operating conditions,'" Coral conceded. "Damn. How hard up is she?"

"Debris pierced her stern fuel tanks, and she lost a quarter of her fuel to the sea," her chief of staff said grimly. "*Chorus of Dawn* will refuel her back up to seventy-five percent, but she can't carry more fuel than that now. And she can't make more than fifteen klicks top speed without repairs that are going to take a shipyard."

The paddles on a wheel could be replaced from the wood supplies aboard a ship. If they somehow managed to run out of replacement panels and wood planks, even a cruiser carried everything they needed to anchor at a shore somewhere with trees and *make* more panels and planks.

But the central axle of the drive wheel was a steel beam almost the full width of the ship. There was no way to fix or replace that at sea.

"The other cruisers?" she finally asked.

"Various degrees of battered and bruised," O'Connor told her. "One of *Firewater*'s turrets is out of commission, though Captain Jernigan assures me it's just ice buildup and they'll have it working shortly. *Skywriter*'s starboard wheel lost half of her paddles, and she's working on replacing it. Everyone except *Silkcow* assures me that their damage is reparable."

"I see." Coral walked over to the status panels and looked down, processing the swiftly written notes more slowly than she liked. Practice was helping, but this *was* her first squadron command. The last time she'd been on a flag bridge, she'd been one of the people writing backward on the other side of the panel.

"Your assessment, O'Connor?"

"Captain Weiss has no choice but to admit that her ship is crippled," he replied, echoing Nevin's comments on the flying bridge. "The rest of them will probably be able to make their repairs and keep up, but I worry about the cost in resources and time to do so. None will be fully online until at least tomorrow night."

"I wouldn't want to send *Silkcow* back to North Dale on her own, either," Coral observed. "What about the tankers and *Cloudwatcher*?"

"The tankers are bigger than *Cloudwatcher* and sturdily built," O'Connor noted. "They also have less in terms of upper works to *get* damaged. But they aren't really designed for this, and I wonder how well the hoses are going to hold up to sustained cold temperature."

"So do I," Coral admitted. None of the reports for the cruisers looked good. Only *Silkcow* was actually disabled, but the rest had all taken a beating.

Cloudwatcher was in better shape, though Coral wasn't entirely sure how far she trusted the report for the battleship. *Songwriter* had taken a beating from a hellfrost storm and she'd been in a sheltered harbor, not sailing through the heart of it. Though *she* hadn't been briefed on what was coming the way Oliversen had.

"Sir?" O'Connor asked softly after a moment.

"Orders to the Squadron," she told him, the decision popping fully formed into her mind. "All ships will come to a halt and fuel from the tankers, including the battleships.

"All Captains will report aboard *Icebreaker* at twenty-four hundred hours for a late meal and planning discussion."

It was, after all, theoretically possible that one of them would have an idea that would render her plan unnecessary.

CHAPTER 29

CORAL LET her stewards actually feed the Captains—and her, for that matter—before she stepped up onto the dais with the map of Albion and surveyed the gathered officers.

"It's been a rough fifty-two hours, people," she conceded. "And we're facing a pretty stark warning. *Silkcow* is crippled."

Most of the officers in the room had almost certainly worked that out, but it still sent a ripple of consternation through the room to hear the Admiral say it.

"*Firewater* had a disabled turret," she continued. "*Skywriter*'s starboard steering wheel is half-wrecked. *Rockfall* has lost *all* of her masts, lookout posts and upper range finders. *Roadrunner* and *Stormwind* have only lost their crow's nests and main range finders... or so you *tell* me."

Her gaze at those two Captains was accusatory, and neither of them met her eyes.

"None of our cruisers survived unscathed," Coral concluded. "At last count, we lost eleven crew across six ships and have another three dozen in sickbays across the Squadron."

Dalebloods could protect themselves from the cold, mostly. So long as they stayed fed and were smart about it, at least. But even magically enhanced balance and reflexes could only protect so much against slipping and falling on decks slick with ice—and no magic in all Albion would have allowed them to find the people who'd gone overboard.

"We had no deaths on the battleships or tankers," she reminded her people. "*Icebreaker* was built for this; she's fine. *Cloudwatcher*, Captain Oliversen? Your honest assessment, please."

The room was silent as every gaze turned to *Cloudwatcher's* Captain, and the Daleblood officer grimaced.

"We took a broad variety of minor damage," he admitted. "Very little of which we reported, if I'm being *honest*, but none of which was crippling or impeded our combat capabilities. Frozen rigging, a snapped panel, a door warped in its frame that we had to cut open... that sort of thing.

"I wouldn't want to go into combat in one of those storms, but I'm comfortable sailing my ship through them."

Coral nodded her thanks to him, both for the honesty and the confidence. She then turned her gaze on the other Captains.

"I am aware of the reputation and diet of the standard cruiser Captain," she told them. "But in this case, I do not believe the risk is worth it."

The room was silent, and she smiled thinly.

"Our mission is to find a force that is sending magical storms like the one we just survived against our shores," she pointed out. "We likely *will* have to fight in conditions very much like those we just sailed through, and see that type of weather weaponized against us.

"The last two days tell me that, bluntly, only the battleships have a chance at surviving that. I'm not entirely convinced that the cruisers will even make it to the City of Spires—and I am unwilling to send Captain Weiss and *Silkcow* back to North Dale on their own."

She looked past the Captains to the mural on the other wall, the one of the City of Spires itself. The artist had painted the City from written descriptions. No images had survived with the Great Fleet. If the City was half as impressive as the artist had thought, though, the concept that a million people had been driven from it was terrifying.

"I will not lead six cruisers and two thousand officers and crew into weather and war I do not believe they can survive or contribute to," she concluded. "And while I think the tankers are actually better able to survive this than the cruisers, the truth is that *Icebreaker* and *Cloudwatcher* don't *need* them."

If they filled their tanks there, the two battleships would have enough fuel aboard to sail all the way to the north pole...and then turn around and sail to the *south* pole before running out of corn oil. Ice and weather and speed would all impact their total cruising radius, but Coral had no concerns about the two ships' ability to reach the City of Spires and return home.

Let alone the ability to reach the City and die fighting.

"We will remain at this location until dawn," Coral told her assembled Captains. "We will make certain that *Icebreaker* and *Cloudwatcher* have filled their tanks as completely as possible.

"Then we will split the Squadron. *Icebreaker* and *Cloudwatcher* will continue on to the City of Spires and complete our mission, regardless of what weather or dark power bars our way," she said grimly. "Captain Jernigan will take command of the cruiser flight and escort *Silkcow* and the tankers back to North Dale Base, where you will place yourself at Vice Admiral Siena's disposal."

"Our ships did survive the storm," *Rockfall's* Captain Croft observed, her voice almost petulant.

"And you might survive the next one," Coral agreed. "But we are sailing into a region that is functionally a permanent hellfrost storm. An area that is the hell that those storms are named for. The *only* thing your cruisers could do in that area is *survive*.

"We will have work to do. If you can only survive, it will not serve."

That seemed to quiet some of the objections, though even Coral thought it was a bit harsh.

"If I may make a suggestion, Admiral?" *Firewater's* Jernigan said slowly. He was the senior Captain—hence being placed in command of the cruiser flight—and was actually older than Coral.

She wasn't sure why he'd remained a cruiser Captain instead of receiving a battleship command, and she suspected that she, born of a wealthy and socially privileged family, probably didn't want to examine that too closely.

"I am listening, Captain Jernigan," she told him. "My decision is made, however."

"I...understand the decision to send us back," he conceded. "I dislike it, but I am the Captain of a Republic cruiser. Our reputation for raw meat and suicidal bravery does have a foundation—but as an officer, I am bound to serve the best interests of the Republic, not my own desire for honor and victory."

If he wasn't going to try to argue that *his* ship could stay, Coral was at least willing to listen. She gestured for him to continue.

"In necessity we can find virtue," Jernigan noted. "Right now, this Squadron is out of touch with the Republic. We are roughly eighteen hundred kilometers from North Dale Base. But we have five intact cruisers that are fully crewed by Dalebloods and possess skilled Bloodspeakers.

"If we maintain contact with *Icebreaker* and *Cloudwatcher* and keep at least one ship in range of them, we can position the rest of the cruiser flight along the direct line to North Dale and create an impromptu Bloodspeech relay to allow you to communicate with the Republic."

Coral was silent for a second as she considered.

"That is not without risk, given that we would be leaving ships on their own in seas prone to hellfrost storms and that we fear to be prowled by Stelforma raiders," she noted.

"All of our cruisers are new turreted ships, sir," Lilit Croft pointed out. "There is nothing on the sea that I cannot either outrun or outgun."

Coral nodded slowly and turned to study the map behind her. One of her staff had helpfully moved the marker for *Icebreaker* to show the current location of the squadron, eighteen hundred kilometers north of the Dales and still fifteen hundred kilometers short of the estimated location of the City of Spires.

"One of the cruisers will still need to go farther north," she noted. "And four will be required for the relay."

They could *probably* manage with three, but slack was almost always a good thing.

"I'll take *Firewater* all the way to North Dale Base with *Silkcow* and the tankers," Jernigan suggested. "Captain Asturias's *Stormwind* is our least damaged cruiser, so I suggest that *Stormwind* accompany the squadron for one more day before breaking off to be the final relay point.

"The rest of us will, as per your orders, sail at dawn."

"It's a damn good idea, Captain Jernigan," Coral told him. "We'll do it."

And *she* would make sure that she got a report to Admiral Siena flagging that Jernigan had been the one to suggest it. That might make his command of a cruiser squadron, at least, less interim—and everything she had seen suggested the Republic was going to need the man.

CHAPTER 30

"WELL, THAT IS A...*THING*."

Coral couldn't disagree with the vague description—or the sheer awe in Captain Nevin's voice as the woman stared at the vista spreading out north of them.

"We knew we were going to hit something like this," she reminded the blonde Captain, but she couldn't blame the woman. "But it's something else to *see* it."

It was permanently cold now as the battleships approached the fortieth north parallel. Their destination, assuming the estimates and calculations were even close to correct, was roughly seven hundred kilometers to the north of them.

Less than two days' cruising through open water. Except that less than a hundred meters of open water lay in front of *Icebreaker's* bow, and even that was dotted with floating white chunks of ice.

Past that was an infinite expanse of ice.

Coral had understood the forecast and the logic that since things grew colder as they went north, sooner or later they would reach an area that was solid ice pack. She'd reviewed the calculations, redone them in her own office and known they would have to break through hundreds of kilometers of ice to reach the City.

And yet now she stared at that vast shimmering expanse and wondered at the arrogance of humanity that they were so certain that hundreds of kilometers of ice would yield to their magic and engineering.

"I suppose sitting here staring at it isn't going to get us anywhere," Nevin finally said. "I assume *Cloudwatcher* will stay behind us?"

"Based off my experience with *Songwriter*, *Cloudwatcher* will be able to break the thinner ice on her own," Coral noted. "But yes. We have an adamantine bow on *Icebreaker* for just this purpose. We knew it would be like this."

"Yup." *Icebreaker*'s Captain eyed the ice pack. "I make it only about thirty centimeters thick here. Pushing through that will be easy."

"We'll want to take it carefully. What happens when we find ice that's *too* thick?"

"Our bow is adamantine," Nevin echoed back to her. "So long as the ice is thinner than *Icebreaker*'s bow is tall, I believe we can breach it."

That wasn't *quite* how the icebreaker hull was supposed to work, Coral knew, but the Captain was probably right. Armor that had shrugged aside the Republic's best shells at close range was unlikely to be marred by mere ice.

"Permission to enter the ice, Admiral?" Nevin asked after a few seconds of silence.

Coral followed the ice off into the distance. Even her Daleblood gaze couldn't see anything but smooth white. Somewhere in the mess was their destination. Hopefully, it wasn't completely buried under the ice.

"Granted, Captain Nevin," she finally replied.

Orders were shouted and the engines rumbled fully to life

beneath them. Slowly and carefully, *Icebreaker* slid across the last remaining open water toward her destiny.

She made contact with a surprisingly soft cracking noise, the adamantine bow rising up over the ice and then crashing down on it.

Coral found herself holding her breath as the battleship plunged forward. Ice shattered beneath the ancient magic armor forged in the very city they were seeking, and the ship slowly picked up speed again.

"Maintain ten klicks for now," Nevin ordered. She turned back to Coral. "This won't be a fast process, sir. Ten klicks is taking half power, as much as our normal cruising speed. The ice is only going to get thicker."

"And you will increase power as needed," Coral told her. "If nothing else, *Cloudwatcher* is just trundling along, and we'll transfer fuel between ships if needed."

Captain Nevin's expression told Coral *everything* she needed to know about that idea. The battleships were equipped with hoses for fueling escorts if necessary, but the rubber of the hoses was suffering from the cold already.

Trying to run fuel between the two battleships would be an *endeavor*.

And Coral would still do it if it became necessary. For that moment, though, it was sufficient for *Icebreaker* to lead the way into the ice, her adamantine prow clearing a path more than wide enough for the smaller battleship to follow.

"We won't slow at night," Coral told Nevin quietly. "We can see ahead on the ice well enough to maintain ten klicks, and that will buy us some time. At ten klicks, we're looking at three days."

"Assuming the City is where the desk-warmers think it is."

"Commander El-Ghazzawy believed in her calculations enough that she's with us, Captain. The City might not be exactly where we expect it to be, and it may take some hunting to find it, but I doubt it will be far off what the Commander estimated."

"Well, if nothing else, I suppose we know the City of Spires is on *land*," Nevin noted drily. "We're not going to miss finding land."

"And we're going to be very glad for the adamantine armor if the City is hiding under the ice," Coral concluded.

CHAPTER 31

SEVENTY HOURS and seven hundred kilometers after they'd entered the ice pack, the continual grinding and cracking sound of *Icebreaker* smashing her way through the ice was starting to wear. For most of those hours, Coral had seen *nothing* of interest.

Well, she'd seen one herd of six-legged wildlife that had bolted as *Icebreaker* had approached. A distant relative of either horses or silkcows; even her sight hadn't been enough to see details before they had crossed the horizon.

The ice pack was getting thicker every day. Every *hour*. It had gone from under half a meter the first day to over two meters now. But still the battleship made her way forward, the ice giving way before them.

"Sir, we have a problem," the lookout shouted down.

"What kind of problem?" Coral demanded as Nevin turned to reply.

"Storm on the horizon, approaching fast from the west."

Coral traded a look with her flag captain.

"It shouldn't matter at this point," Nevin pointed out. "We're already at minus thirty and in the middle of the ice. What's a few flash-frozen floes in the channel we're breaching?"

"Another twenty-degree temperature drop isn't going to help much," Coral warned. "But I see no reason not to continue. We're close."

"Agreed." Nevin stepped away to give further orders, and Coral turned her gaze to the west, to see if she could spot the storm.

There was a familiar dark smudge on the horizon, and a chill ran down her spine. There was always a sense of malevolent power to the hellfrost storms—and now they had to be approaching their destination. It couldn't be coincidence that a new storm was bearing down on them now.

Turning away from the storm, she realized there was something else on the horizon. A *different* smudge to the north.

"Lookout, what's to the north?" she shouted up.

There was a moment of quiet and then a surprised voice shouted back.

"Land, sir! Or maybe a cliff made of ice...but it looks like land!"

"Shout if you spot any kind of shelter," Coral ordered, then turned back to Nevin.

"Captain?"

"I heard. A sheltered bay, even if it's already covered in ice, will give us a starting point. And, well..." The Captain shook her head. "We're about where the Commander said the Great Fleet came from. If there's land...the City may exist after all!"

"The City exists, Captain," Coral assured the other woman. "It might not be here, but it exists. And we *will* find it—but right now, those cliffs are potential shelter from the storm, and even if we think we can handle another round with the hellfrost, I'm not going to turn down shelter!"

They could survive the storm either way—assuming the storm passed, and from some of what she was seeing around them, she wasn't taking that bet—but the cliffs would turn the odds further in their favor. They hadn't lost anyone from the battleships yet.

Coral would risk her crews when she had to. But if fate gave her a shield for them, she was damn well going to take it.

As *Icebreaker* drew closer to the cliffs to the north, Coral heard El-Ghazzawy step up onto the flying bridge. Given the intelligence officer's discomfort with the elevated platform, Coral rarely saw her—but she supposed that finding the City of Spires was the culmination of the other woman's life's work.

It made sense for El-Ghazzawy to join them now they'd found land.

"Commander," Coral greeted her subordinate.

"Admiral. I have to admit, part of me wasn't sure we'd find anything."

"All we've found so far is land and another storm," Coral warned. The cliffs to the north rose from plains of frozen seawater and were streaked with ice and snow themselves. If she looked past that, though, they could have easily been a rocky coastline anywhere around the Dales.

"My calculations say that if we've hit land *here*, the City should be only a few dozen kilometers east," El-Ghazzawy told her.

Coral chuckled and glanced to the west, where the hellfrost storm was continuing to gain on them. It looked even blacker and uglier than the last. And it felt even more malevolent.

"I'd like to say that helps us pick a direction," she told El-Ghazzawy. "But, truth be told, we're just avoiding the storm."

As they spoke, the battleship turned toward the east, continuing to smash through ice now as tall as some of Coral's crew.

"That one looks...worse, doesn't it?"

"Yup."

Coral looked east along the cliffs, hoping to see some kind of break in the natural barrier.

"Sir, permission to take the engines to full power," Nevin asked, joining Coral and El-Ghazzawy at the port railing. "We're losing speed as the ice thickens and the storm is gaining."

"She's your ship, Ekaterina," Coral noted.

"And if we blow the engines trying too hard, it's your mission," Nevin replied. "It should be fine, but breaking ice at full power... It's risky."

Coral glanced westward again.

"If you and your engineers think it's safe, carry on," she ordered. "We're still hoping for *some* kind of shelter before the storm catches us."

Nevin turned away to give her orders, and Coral felt the ship tremble as her engines drew even more fuel. Five kilometers an hour became ten. Fifteen.

"Seventeen klicks," the Captain told her a few minutes later. "We're at full power. That's as fast as we're going to get."

"And the storm?" Coral asked.

"Still gaining, but we've bought ourselves a few hours. I hope the Commander is right and the City is here," Nevin said. "Because I'm hoping the City has a good harbor."

"Everything we've seen from the journals suggests that it does," El-Ghazzawy replied. "They built hundreds of ships there, after all, and our understanding is that the weather was worse than anywhere in the Dales today.

"Even putting aside the texts that *talk* about the harbor, logic alone says it must exist."

THE CLIFFS CHANGED SUDDENLY as the pair of ships headed east. They'd been relatively consistent—as consistent as any cliffs, that is—for an hour and twenty or so kilometers, then unexpectedly seemed to bulge outward.

"That is strange," El-Ghazzawy said. "I haven't seen a geological formation like that before."

Coral studied it herself for a few seconds. Unlike the intelligence officer, it *did* feel familiar to her. The shape was very different from the other cliffs, with what looked like a sharp rise and then a steep slope down the side instead of the vertical face of the shore to the west.

"It's curved," she murmured. She followed the line, her magic allowing her to trace it with ease. "It's a *circle*...like Daleheart Bay, but a lot smaller."

She estimated the curve to be the side of a circle maybe a kilometer across versus Daleheart Bay's *several* kilometers. But while the shape of the rocks was at about a quarter of the width of Daleheart Bay—and only a third or so of the height, she judged—the circular pattern was the same.

"There's a breach ahead!" the lookout shouted. "Looks big enough to turn the ships into!"

"Oh, thank Christ," Nevin declared. "Helm, stand by to maneuver. Engines, keep this up for just a bit longer!"

Coral followed the line of the strange curved rock formation until she saw the entrance to the bay. Like at Daleheart Bay, it was a very sudden transition. Like there had been an entrance to a differently sized bay, but then both sides had been violently reshaped to the strange sloping ridge.

She'd grown up in Daleheart, and she'd never considered the bay odd. Now that she saw it replicated on a different scale, though, she couldn't help but feel it was strange. Like some angry god had taken a perfectly circular scoop out of the landscape and then water had filled it up from the gap in the outer wall.

But regardless of its strangeness, the bay provided a covered shelter from the storm chasing them. It was in the right place to start their search for the City of Spires, too.

Coral didn't even need to give new orders. Nevin was giving directions to the helm and *Icebreaker* slowed, steering wheels rumbling to life on either side of the flying bridge as she began to turn inside the water she'd already cleared.

Once the battleship had turned, her main drive wheel began to turn again, pushing her forward through the ice and into the gap in the sharp ridge. A palpable sense of relief washed over the chilly flying bridge as the natural barrier came between them and the oncoming storm.

"Get us into the lee of the harbor isthmus," Coral ordered. "It's tall enough to give us some extra shelter from the storm."

Cloudwatcher was following in the trail *Icebreaker* left behind her, both battleships pulling into the bay and turning tightly to the outer rock. After two days of sailing through the ice, she could tell by the sound that the ice in the bay was shallower than in the open sea—which supported the hope that the bay was sheltered enough to protect them.

Once Coral was certain they were going to be safe, she began to look around the place they'd found themselves. A strange sense of familiarity and homesickness swept over her. There were none of the docks and neighborhoods that lined the gentler interior slopes of the circular ridge at Daleheart, but the shape of the terrain was *exactly* like her home city.

"Anyone else feeling like we're back where we started?" Captain Nevin asked, clearly seeing the same thing as Coral. "Seems strange to have crossed half the world and end up in a bay that's the same as home. I thought Daleheart Bay was unique."

"So did I," Coral agreed. "Though it has the city, and this place appears to be as barren as everything else."

"No, it's not."

Coral glanced over at El-Ghazzawy and realized the intelligence officer had been silent since they'd entered the bay. Likely, she'd been doing the same surveying and thinking as Coral, but without needing to worry about the fleet, she'd seen *something*.

"Because Daleheart Bay may have Daleheart City and the Republic, but it doesn't have *those*."

El-Ghazzawy pointed straight north, and both Coral and Nevin turned to follow her hand. For a moment, Coral thought El-Ghazzawy had just seen some kind of ice formation, a glint of light not yet smothered by the oncoming storm.

But as she focused and leaned into her magic to bring the spark of light closer, she realized what she was looking at was metal. It was metal *in* the cliff, the wreckage of what had once been a tower as tall as *Icebreaker* was long, hammered into the stone as if by the fist of the same angry god as the bay.

Now that she was looking for it, she could see debris along a length of the northern cliff as wide as the docks in Daleheart. The first tower she'd spotted was the most "intact," so to speak, but the ridge was *full* of metal and glass gleaming in the fading sun.

And then, past the top of the ridge, she spotted another glint of light and realized there was at least one intact tower in the City of Spires.

"So, we found it," Coral murmured. "I guess we may want to bring the ship around to the *north* side of the west wall."

She didn't know how long the storm was going to last...and if disaster had crushed the City of Spires, that only made it *more* imperative that they learn what happened before said disaster came to the Republic!

CHAPTER 32

THE DEBRIS CRUSHED into the side of the ridge wasn't going to hold the answers Coral and her people were looking for. It *did*, however, provide a series of solid anchors for them to hook ropes, chains and carabiners into as they ascended the ridge.

The Daleblood Marines and crew accompanying the Admiral could probably have scrambled up the steep slope easily enough, but it lacked the artificial terraces that had allowed the Republic's people to build a city into the similar ridge in Daleheart.

Adding the ropes and chains allowed them to climb it swiftly and safely. From what Coral had overheard, the Chiefs were already planning on a system of elevators and steps to make the ascent easier if they were there for any length of time.

She and El-Ghazzawy were out in front; even though the squadron commander and her intelligence officer really had no business being the lead climbers of the endeavor. Curiosity and impatience combined to send the two women to the top of the ridge ahead of everyone else.

Coral wanted to see what they were facing before the storm hit. She was prepared to investigate the city through the storm, but they wouldn't be able to get a good view once it arrived—and as she crested the ridge, she knew she'd made the right call.

The tower they'd seen from the bay was the tallest structure, but there was no question that she was looking down on the place the Seablood Great Fleet had launched from. A dozen similar but smaller towers still stood despite two centuries of neglect, and twice that many had clearly been wrecked by whatever had created the ridge Coral was standing on.

The ridge that she had finally recognized as the edge of a crater of incomprehensible size. She'd seen the impact crater left behind by twenty-centimeter shells in test firings, but she'd never connected it to Daleheart Bay. The difference in scale beggared belief.

A twenty-centimeter shell left a crater a few meters across. The bay that had been the City of Spires was a crater *nine hundred* meters across—and if *this* bay was a crater, what did that say about *Daleheart Bay?*

And if Coral could barely comprehend the theory of there being an explosive that could create this crater, what kind of weapon or natural disaster had created the one her home city was built on?

It was easier to realize that this was a crater, though, since she could *see* the wreckage created when the explosion had devastated the City of Spires. The thirteen still-standing towers were ominous obelisks in a field of destruction.

That ominousness was only heightened by the alien nature of the spires themselves. Even the artistic representations of the City of Spires that Coral had seen throughout the Republic over the years—like the one in *Icebreaker*'s flag mess—had the titular spires as *recognizable* buildings, of stone and brick and concrete.

These were something very, *very* different. Smooth-faced edifices of steel and glass rose from the twisted wreckage of similar buildings. A single one of the intact towers had to have more steel in it than either of Coral's battleships—and appeared to have more *glass* than she'd seen in her entire life.

Except that if it were *glass*, it would have disintegrated in the cold years before. Somehow, the glittering windows of the surviving towers were intact. Only the towers smashed in the destruction of the city had broken.

"What even is this place?" El-Ghazzawy whispered.

"Where the Great Fleet came from," Coral said grimly. "A home for magic and engineering beyond anything we or the Stelforma command."

Other members of the landing party were coming up behind them, but everyone was stopping to stare at the ruined city beneath them.

"What now, sir?" El-Ghazzawy asked.

"You're the historian, Commander. We need to learn everything we can about this city. What would *you* suggest?"

"I'm used to seeking history in archives of forgotten journals, not looking at a wrecked city and wondering what killed it," the intelligence officer replied. "I guess we pick a building and see what we find?"

"Well, in that case, there's only one place to start," Coral replied. She pointed to the building they'd seen from *Icebreaker*.

"Whatever and whoever built this place, we are reasonably sure they were some breed of human," she said. "And that means whoever was in charge was probably in the tallest building. Since that's the biggest still standing...I say we start there."

Leaving most of the landing party behind to set up an anchor camp on top of the ridge, Coral, El-Ghazzawy and a dozen Marines descended into the City of Spires. The Marines spread out around her, their carbines surveying the shadowy corners of the debris field.

Any actively dangerous debris was covered by ice and snow. The surface of the icefield was slick, but the Dalebloods carefully balanced across that as they trekked toward the central tower.

Coral was unsurprised to find the entrance to the tower inaccessible when they arrived. She wasn't sure how deep the ice and snow went, but she'd doubted that the entrance was above it.

"Spread out," she ordered her companions. "Let's search the perimeter, see if we can get an idea of what this looks like and if we can access the entrance."

The Marines and El-Ghazzawy obeyed, leaving Coral alone to step up to where ice met glass. A layer of frost, probably centuries old, blocked her view into the building. Her curiosity was driving her, though, and she focused into herself and removed her left glove.

Placing her hand on the frost, she channeled her magic into warming her skin, not just to protect it from the ice but to send excess heat flowing *back* into the ice. Her skin glowed with power and heat, and after a moment the frost began to melt and crack away from her hand.

The ice had been clear enough to let her see the structure of the building but not to see within in. Now a sheet of it shivered away from the building, shattering into a spray of icy debris that Coral neatly sidestepped.

Now able to see through the glass, she had to blink at the mix of the alien and the familiar she could see through the clear panel. The walls and furniture were made from materials she couldn't identify, and there were long-dead strange machines sitting on the desks...but the layout and the *types* of furniture could have been an office from the Citadel in Daleheart.

It wasn't even that it was an office. It was that it was, in several ways she couldn't quite specify, a *military* office.

"Sir?" El-Ghazzawy said. "I've been around the entire building. It's...not small. Forty-five meters a side. I estimate two hundred high."

"Take a look at this, Commander," Coral ordered, stepping back and gesturing her subordinate to the window.

El-Ghazzawy obeyed, looking through the one panel Coral had cleaned and staring for a moment. Coral suspected her own expression had been just as unsure as the Commander's, which made her feel better about her own confusion.

"That's...a military planning office," the intelligence officer finally said. "I don't recognize the machines, and I couldn't tell you what those desks are made of, but that's a map of Albion on the wall, and I see what I think is a chart table—though I don't see lines or tanks for the oil lamp."

"Neither do I," Coral murmured. "And I don't think staring through the glass is going to answer any more questions. Sergeant!"

The Marine noncom had completed his own circuit and braced to attention.

"Are we secure?"

"Sir, we are three thousand kilometers from the nearest Republic base, have no reinforcements except what's aboard the two battleships, and are in the middle of a city that creeps me the fuck out," Sergeant Stanislav Adrichem said drily. "'Secure' is relative."

"And?"

"There is nothing alive in this city, sir. And I don't think anything *has* been alive in a very long time. So, yeah, I guess we're secure."

Coral chuckled.

"All right. That leaves us with one pertinent question, then, and I have an answer for that."

"It's going to take us a while to excavate down to any of the doors," El-Ghazzawy noted. "Given how long this place has stood, I'm not sure we can break the glass, either."

"I wasn't planning on breaking it," Coral replied. "Stand back."

She drew her sword, the Dalesteel's pale red edge gleaming in the chill light as everyone looked at her.

"Dalesteel," Sergeant Adrichem said slowly. "Yeah, that'll probably work, won't it?"

"Feels like a misuse of one of the family blades," Coral conceded, "but I'm not spending a week cutting our way down through the ice, not when the Republic is at war."

From what information was coming through the Bloodspeech

relay her cruisers had set up, the Republic *wasn't*, technically, at war. The Stelforma Chosen hadn't *quite* disavowed their commander on the scene, but they were saying there'd been a miscommunication.

Except that reading between the lines of the reports she was getting, *everyone* in Daleheart figured the Stelforma were playing for time because they weren't quite ready for war—but they were playing for weeks, *maybe* months.

Or they would have disavowed their commander to keep the peace.

And that meant that Coral needed to know what had happened to the City of Spires. There was no time for patience, no time for analysis and excavation. It was the time for drastic measures.

Before anyone could even argue her words, she plunged the sword into the defrosted window. If she'd somehow managed to maintain the illusion that the towers were made of glass, she'd have lost it in that moment.

Frozen glass would have shattered under the blow. Whatever the transparent pane was, it resisted the Dalesteel point more than anything else she'd ever encountered—though despite the blades' reputations, *she* had never stabbed iron with her sword.

Still, the glass gave way and her blade plunged fifteen centimeters deep into the office's long-stale air. Once pierced, the panel sliced easily enough as she worked the edge down and sideways, until she'd opened a person-sized hole through the transparent exterior of the building.

"Aldith." She stepped back and gestured El-Ghazzawy to the hole. "We never would have made it this far without you. Would you like to go first?"

CHAPTER 33

STEPPING through the hole in the building's outer skin felt like walking into an entirely different world. Coral had expected the air to be stale and stuffy, which it was, but she'd also expected the temperature to be the same as outside.

The half-centimeter-thick transparent panel she'd cut open, after all, seemed a flimsy barrier against temperatures that froze mercury.

Instead, the inside of the building was *warm* compared to outside. Like all things, it was relative, and Coral suspected it was still well below freezing in the ancient tower. Compared to the outside chill, it was positively balmy.

"Is there heating in here or is that just insulation?" El-Ghazzawy asked aloud.

"Insulation, I think," Coral replied. "If there was still any kind of heat running, it would be above zero."

"Fair." The intelligence officer crossed to the inner wall of the room they'd cut into and examined the map tacked up there. "Come take a look at this, sir."

Coral followed the younger woman and joined her in looking at the map. It was made of a strange paper that glistened in the light filtering in from outside, but the shape of the landmasses was clear. This was Albion.

Except that it included detailed landmasses at both the north and south poles that didn't match any map she'd ever seen. The symbology was unfamiliar to her, but the geography wasn't, and she searched for a moment to find Daleheart.

It wasn't there. Even the *bay* was missing. Instead, there was a small star with strange text attached to it.

The text looked like it had been printed as part of the map, but Coral had never seen printed text that fine. Printing presses and typewriters alike used blocky and simplistic letters to make cleaning and reading easier. The letters here were simple and clear, but they were far from blocky.

"Fort Hearth," Coral read aloud. "...Fort Hearth?"

"Sir?"

"Where Daleheart and Daleheart Bay should be," Coral told El-Ghazzawy. "There's an icon for a Fort Hearth. And no Bay, for that matter."

"Huh." The intelligence officer was still scanning the whole map. "And none of the other cities of the Dales, either. No settlement details on the continent or the Southern Archipelago at all."

"There are names at the poles," Coral spotted. "Caledon at the north. Hibernia at the south. Those are...strange names."

"Yeah. Though at least one thing is familiar." El-Ghazzawy pointed to the top of the map, being careful not to touch the slick surface. Coral didn't expect the map to survive being touched, and her subordinate clearly agreed with her.

The top of the map declared it to be of Albion. At least *that* name appeared to be the same...though that raised questions of its own.

"You know, I never thought about how odd it was that everyone had the same name for the world," Coral said. "Us. The Seabloods. The Stelforma. We all call it Albion."

"Why wouldn't we?" El-Ghazzawy asked. "That's its name, after all."

"Fair," Coral murmured, though the thought continued to niggle at her. "See anything else of interest, Commander?"

"Everything?" the younger woman replied. "Except everywhere we go, we're damaging things. Look at your feet."

Coral did and saw what El-Ghazzawy meant. The floor was covered in a thick carpet that looked like it might be comfortable enough to sleep on in normal times. It was not, however, designed to handle being ten degrees below zero for two hundred years, and the fabric was shattering underneath each step they took.

"We don't have a choice, Commander. We have to investigate the place."

The Marines were carefully stepping into the building behind them, pulling out small lanterns to provide light in the dim spaces. Daleblood eyes could see in the murk, but Coral suspected it would get darker as they moved on.

"I'm not seeing any papers or books around here," Sergeant Adrichem told the two women. "What should I have the Marines look for?"

"I would say papers or books," El-Ghazzawy replied, turning to study the desks behind them. Each of them had several strange boxes—machines?—on them, though none of the setups appeared to be the same.

"Whatever these magics were, they're beyond us," the intelligence officer continued. "Based on the map, the Seabloods were still using the same language here as we do now in the Dales. I imagine we'll see differences in longer texts—there are plenty in the old journals, after all—but we should be able to read whatever we find."

"Well, this is a very large building," Coral pointed out. "Let's start with a sweep of this floor and see what we find. Sergeant, let's split your Marines three ways: one party with the Commander, one with me, and one with you.

"For now, let's try not to touch anything. We're finding the lay of the land, nothing more."

WITH THREE MARINES IN TOW, Coral took the clockwise loop of the tower. It quickly became clear that whatever the tower *had* been, its final form had been a mess. The office they'd entered through was the most organized and logically set-up place she saw—and from the maps and chart tables, she suspected it had been organizing the Great Fleet right up until the end.

The next office she entered had seen the desks dismantled and piled up to form the bases of beds. From the look of them, it had been intended as a stopgap...and then they'd become effectively permanent, long before the cold had frozen the strange blankets into permanent records of their occupants' last night.

There'd been about fifty people living and working on this floor of the tower at the end. Coral wasn't sure if they'd left before or after the explosion that had devastated the harbor, but there were no bodies. Just the signs of impromptu occupation of the area as people tried to survive a brutal winter.

The tools and fabrics and everything were different and strange, but the huddled masses of blankets and the handful of crude and unsafe firepits were familiar regardless of the materials used.

Eventually, the three parties met in the central section of the tower, a small open lobby with two doubled doors on each side. One set of doors had been forced open at some point in the past, and Coral could see the anchors where there *had* been a rope ladder or something similar.

"I'm guessing *we* didn't break the ladder," she said drily.

"You'd guess...wrong," El-Ghazzawy admitted sheepishly. "I didn't see any other way to go down, so I grabbed it. And it shattered in my hand."

"Everything in this place is frozen solid, sirs," Adrichem reminded them.

"It's enough warmer than it is outside to make us forget, I suspect," Coral said. "Lantern?"

One of the Marines passed her the light and she stepped over to the open set of doors. The flickering illumination of the oil lantern wasn't optimal, but it allowed her to see that the empty void on the other side stretched up and down from that level, probably to both the top and bottom of the tower.

They were on the third floor, she judged, and it looked like there were two levels underground.

"There was no ladder going up?" she asked.

"Only down," El-Ghazzawy confirmed. "And I couldn't find stairs. I *think* these shafts held some kind of elevator."

No Republic building designer would have put together a building that *only* had the diesel- or hydraulic-powered platforms for travel. And it was clear that the occupants of this building had lost the ability to operate their elevators before they'd left.

"Adrichem, send a couple of Marines back to the camp for rope," Coral ordered, assessing the drop to the bottom of the shaft. Maybe two dozen meters.

"Yes, sir."

"El-Ghazzawy, sweep this floor in detail," Coral continued. "The chart tables and maps in the first room may have information we missed. The City of Spires was under attack, and I suspect if there are any hints of the location of their enemy, they're in that room."

"Yes, sir. What about you?" the intelligence officer asked.

"Three Marines with me," Coral replied with a grin, gesturing to the trio who'd followed her around the main floor. "Because the advantage of us all being Dalebloods, Commander, is that we can see the bottom—and a little fall never hurt any of us!"

Without waiting for any of her subordinates to argue against her impatient and impulsive plan, Icebreaker Squadron's commanding officer stepped out into the elevator shaft and dropped.

CHAPTER 34

THANKFULLY FOR CORAL'S pride and sanity, the doors at the bottom of the shaft had also been forced open. She'd figured—it made no sense to have the ladder El-Ghazzawy had broken leading down to a closed door, after all.

"Shaft is clear," she shouted up as she climbed out. A moment later, a Marine followed her down. Two more came after them, but Coral was already looking around the space she was in.

This was the lowest basement level and clearly had been a secured space at some point. Unlike the upper floor, there was only one way out of the central elevator lobby. The south exit had been propped open, but the doors Coral could see looked like the armor of a warship.

As she approached, she realized it was more than that. They looked like *Icebreaker*'s armor—because they were made of the same adamantine as the new battleship's main belt.

There was a two-meter-wide gap between the two armored doors, and they appeared to have been forced back into slots in the wall to make that gap. Like the elevators, they'd clearly been powered at one point.

Shivering against the dark, Coral glanced back to make sure she had her Marines, then stepped through the gap in the metal doors. Her lantern picked out a reception slash security area that could have been on any secure floor of the Daleheart Citadel.

In the middle of the waiting area was a large metal desk. As Coral's lantern light played over it, she realized there was an emblem on the wall behind it. She stepped closer and opened the lantern wider.

Someone had spent a great of time with blue and white paint to create the emblem—and the paint was apparently longer-lasting than anything the Republic could make!

A pair of blue tree branches formed the sides of a circle, open at the top and closed at the bottom where the branches merged. Inside the branches, eight concentric circles surrounded a solid gold circle at the center of the flag. Each of the circles had a blue dot on it at a different place, the positions seeming basically random to Coral.

Underneath, painted in the same strangely angular script she'd seen on the map upstairs, was a single line of text.

Commonwealth of the United Nations of Earth.

CUNE.

"What does dirt have to do with anything?" Coral asked aloud. None of her Marines answered; the trio were circling the edges of the room to look for dangers.

"The doors are locked, sir," one of them told her. "Look like... normal locks?"

Coral chuckled. With everything they'd seen in this tower so far, that almost seemed odd.

"Let's take a look," she replied, stepping over to examine the door just past the main desk itself. In the Citadel, she'd have expected nameplates or something to mark who was in each door, but there were no visible labels here.

Something *buzzed* at the back of her mind, like pins and needles at the base of her neck...and then faded away as she touched the door. It was almost like some kind of magic had *tried* to wake up and failed.

"Did any of you feel that?" another Marine asked. "Like..."

"Like a Bloodspeech link but without a connection," Coral replied. "Strange."

"This place is very strange, sir. Are you certain you're safe?"

It said everything about Marines, she reflected, that the young woman wasn't asking whether the basement itself was safe or whether the *Marines* were safe. Only if Coral was safe.

"I'm as safe here as anywhere, I think, Corporal," Coral told her escorts. There *had* been something on the door, she realized. A piece of the strange slick paper the map upstairs had been made of had fallen to the floor but appeared to have been attached to the door at one point.

She doubted that even paper that had survived two hundred years in the cold would be fragile. Touching it could wreck it, but she couldn't see the face of it anyway. So she knelt, carefully, and picked up the flimsy sheet.

Commodore Alistair Findlay.

Commanding Officer. ~~*Caledon Bravo Site Spire*~~ *Hell.*

The first three location names had been scratched out, leaving only the proclamation that this place was now hell.

"Sir?"

"Stand back," she ordered. "This appears to have been the commander's office, so I'm going to open it up."

As the Marines had noted, the door was locked. She prodded it tentatively and confirmed her expectation: the door to the CO's office was heavy and almost certainly armored. The frame was similarly reinforced and angled so that she couldn't access the bolt.

It was a well-designed and secure door that would resist most intrusions. Except that she was a Daleblood with a Dalesteel sword.

Strength alone wouldn't have been enough—and as she stabbed into the doorframe, she swiftly realized that even the perfect sharpness and unyielding durability of the Dalesteel blade might not have been enough either. She worked the point for a few seconds, driving it deeper until she thought she'd punched out the other side, then slowly and carefully sawed downward.

It was a disrespectful use of the blade, but nothing else was going to serve. It took her at least a minute to cut enough of the doorframe to sever the latch. Even once she was done, the door hung closed, its weight oriented to keep it shut.

But it moved easily enough once she grasped the handle and pulled. She stepped through the door and froze as the smell changed. Even frozen for two hundred years, she knew the scent of death.

The room was smaller than she'd expected. The desk was identical to the one outside, and strange glass-like panels covered the walls behind it. Facing the desk, still seated in a wheeled chair, was a mummified corpse in a pale blue uniform.

"Commodore Findlay, I presume," she greeted the dead man quietly. "Who the *fuck* were you?"

Letting the door close behind her, she walked over to the desk and tried to judge the age of the seated man when he'd died. Even mummified and frozen, it was impossible...but her guess was that he was a *lot* older than any Seablood she'd ever met.

Surveying the desk, she shivered as she saw what Findlay's hand had been resting on when he died. He *looked* like he'd died peacefully enough, but he'd been holding what was *unquestionably* a pistol.

The weapon was smaller and smoother than any gun she'd ever seen, an elegant and finely built weapon an infinity away from the stamped-metal mass production of Coral's own sidearm. But it was definitely a gun.

"I hate to interrupt your rest," she told the corpse. "But I'm hoping you have answers of some kind for me. I've come a long way just to find ice, wreckage and a corpse."

Commodore Findlay didn't answer her, but she found herself following his gaze back to the desk. Most of what was there was strange, clearly machined metal and the same slick materials as the rest of the tower.

She recognized the gun...and after a moment, she realized there was one more thing she recognized on the desk. Findlay had died looking directly at a book, a thick-spined blue-bound...*journal?*

"I'm sorry, Commodore; it seems you may have actually tried," she murmured. "Excuse my reach."

She stepped up to the desk and reached around the mummified body and picked up the journal. It was lighter than she expected from its size, its cover chill and slick in her hands.

If the journal was her answers, she realized it might take her longer than she'd like. The paper was thinner than she'd ever seen, and she hesitated to touch it at all—and there had to be at least a thousand pages in the book.

But there was no other hope for answers. Settling into Findlay's spare chair, she laid the journal back on the desk and delicately, carefully, using all of the fine control her magic gave her, she opened the dead man's book.

CHAPTER 35

THE FIRST THING Coral noted was that the handwriting in the book was the same as the writing updating the base name on the door. Commodore Findlay had written "Hell" on his own impromptu nameplate.

That in itself raised her interest in the long-dead officer and she began to read.

Found this in the emergency supplies as we abandoned Caledon. We were just throwing everything onto the terraformer ships, anything that might be of use—along with two hundred thousand people!

God.

I almost threw this overboard as wasted mass, but I realized our computers are going to be limited at the Bravo Site. It's as good a tool as any to put together my thoughts on what the hell just happened.

Timing is important. It was 23:45 standard time—early morning in Caledon, so much as a polar base has mornings and evenings, anyway. June 6. Three hundred fifty-six Post Diaspora.

We received an unscheduled ping on the transceiver net. No precon-nection coms, no requests. Unknown origin. Triggered basic security proto-cols, but the war's over. We won.

Right?

Maybe not. It was an Augmetic strike cruiser, Apollo-class. There weren't supposed to be any Augmetic vessels operating at all, let alone one of their latest and most powerful strike cruisers.

Monitors Pride *and* Prejudice *were destroyed within minutes of the Augmetic ship's emergence from the transceiver net. Two thousand dead.*

Hostile entered high atmo above the Hibernia base—but it's not like Stellar Terraforming has guns at the backup facility. She came in too low and too fast for Colonel Walmsley's defenses to engage her before she launched a bunker-buster.

Fort Hearth was the administration center for a prison. We didn't build it to withstand orbital bombardment.

It wouldn't have mattered. Antimatter ground penetrator. The Fort is gone. Twenty-five thousand dead. Vaporized.

Caledon does have guns. Did, I guess. We couldn't afford a miss. I authorized Mind Caledon to assume control of the defensive systems. They can court-martial me for that if they want.

Caledon shot the Augmetic down. Perfect dazzle-deke-destroy. A Terraformer Base Mind shouldn't have known how to do that, but I guess the Mind listened to all of us old Navy salts talk about the war.

Except Caledon isn't a Ship Mind with half a dozen twenty-year-vets of the CUNEN backing the Mind up and thinking about the randoms and the consequences. A Terraformer Mind doesn't know to think about what happens after *you shoot the fucker down.*

Didn't know, I guess.

Augmetic cruiser hit the central Caledon Terraformer Facility at 0:26 standard time, June 7.

Mind Caledon is dead. So are fifteen thousand CUNEN and Stellar Terraforming personnel who were too close to the impact site. Destruction of the terraformer and the primary power cores created a Category Six hazard zone.

I ordered the evacuation immediately. The Bravo Site has significant stockpiles on hand, and we threw the CUNEN emergency supplies onto the terraformer ships. Thank everything that Stellar Terraforming uses big fucking ships.

And then we discovered the bastards had set charges on the transceiver net. I was counting on relief in a few weeks at worst. But that requires the transceiver net, and the Augmetics blew it apart. Without it, relief could be ten years. Maybe more. That's assuming the alert went out and there's a compression-drive ship nearby to bring a replacement net.

I'm not sure what happens when the primary terraformer goes down on a planet that wants to be a ball of mostly ice. I'd rather not find out— and I'm also not taking the civilians under my command near the prison territories.

There are almost two hundred thousand Augmetic super-soldiers in the valleys around Fort Hearth. With Walmsley and her people gone...I'm not dealing with the enemy until I know my people are safe!

There were a *lot* of words on a single page that Coral didn't understand. She could guess what "CUNEN" was, she supposed—if *CUNE* was the *Commonwealth of the United Nations of Earth*, then *CUNEN* was the Navy of said Commonwealth.

But she didn't know what "terraformers" were. Or "Stellar Terraforming." Or a "transceiver net." Even the use of "Mind" in that context suggested something very different from what she thought of.

The most confusing word, though, was "Augmetic." People with flying ships? Enemies of the Seabloods? They seemed the most likely candidates for the enemy she was hunting, except...she knew where Fort Hearth had been now. That "antimatter ground penetrator," whatever it was, had turned the site of the fort into Daleheart Bay.

And *that* meant the "valleys around Fort Hearth" could only be the central Dales. Which meant that there was only one group of people that had lived in the Dales before the Great Fleet arrived.

Except the Dalebloods didn't have some kind of flying ship that could turn a fortress into a new geographic feature. Their magic was strong, but it paled in comparison to what these "Augmetics" had done.

Commodore Findlay, though, had clearly thought the people at the Dales were the enemy. She traced her finger back through the text to the dead man's description of Fort Hearth: "Fort Hearth was the administration center for a prison."

A prison. With two hundred thousand of these "Augmetics." The pieces fell together for Coral, and she stared at the book in stunned horror.

The Dalebloods had been these Augmetics. Prisoners of war, she presumed, from the war Findlay said was over. Someone had tried to rescue them—and they'd broken something fundamental to the planet.

She wasn't sure what a "Category Six Hazard Zone" was...but she suspected that it strongly resembled a hellfrost storm.

She turned the page. She couldn't read a thousand pages of journal, but there had to be *some* answers she could find immediately.

It's worse than I thought.

Parts are better. We're at the Bravo Site and the macrofabricators are running just fine. We're setting up an admin tower above the Bravo Site main bunker and adding apartment towers all around. Got the prefab deuterium extractor and fusion core online. We have power, we have roofs, we're going to be fine here.

For now. But I'm afraid we're just buying time.

Mind Caledon activated full lockdown security protocols when the Augmetic ship was identified. I wrote that security policy. It made sense— Caledon basically was *the main terraformer. Killing Mind Caledon would take, oh, a megaton-range starship impacting at several hundred kilometers per second followed by a core overload.*

Right.

So. A planetside major Mind like Caledon generates an 11.6 zettabit security encryption key. Even another planetside Mind cannot crack that in the conceivable lifespan of the universe.

And Caledon locked down the orbital networks. We do not have surveillance. We do not have long-range communications. I am complete out of touch with the StelFormer base at Hibernia.

Worse, Caledon sealed the orbital terraformer network, and there is no way Mind Hibernia can crack Caledon's encryption.

Short of sending out ships with radios, I have no way to make contact with Mind Hibernia and the south terraformer complex. And our resources are focused on surviving.

Our resources are large, but we evacuated over a quarter-million people to a location mostly meant to act as a military fallback.

I have to hope that our message got out. Even if it didn't, CUNEN should realize there's a problem when they stop getting messages or the next supply ship can't connect to our net.

Ten years for a c-drive ship. I can keep these people safe for ten years. I have to hope that Administrator Keely can do the same for hers.

Maria at least has a functioning damn terraformer. That should keep the southern half of the planet habitable for a while yet.

"There's no enemy," she whispered. "Just...an accident."

An accident couldn't be fought. An accident couldn't be shown defiance with guns and blades. Commodore Findlay's diary told her that the doom of her world was something she could never fight, never stop.

Except that it had been over two hundred years past. If it had been that overwhelming and devastating, they'd all be dead already.

It was beginning to sink in that Coral held probably the most important historical document on the entire planet in her hands. Her own ancestors had actively buried most of their history prior to the arrival of the Great Fleet—no one living was quite sure *why*, but they were at least aware that it had been done. She suspected, now, that any records from the Seabloods that had said too much had been hidden as well, to preserve peace between the people.

Now she began to understand. In the face of needing their former enemies and captors to survive—and in said enemies and captors having lost most of their *own* knowledge of the past, her people had chosen to forget the past and focus on a future as one country.

Except that Findlay's journal told her they were probably doomed. She wasn't entirely sure *what* all of the words meant, but putting them together with what she already knew...the death of this "Mind Caledon" had begun a slow decay toward frozen ice.

Their entire world would eventually end up looking like the City of Spires—dreams of civilization buried in ice and death.

She had to wonder, though, how much of all of this the *Stelforma* knew. From the limited information on the two pages, she suspected they were descended from the people at the *southern* terraformer, this Hibernia.

A half-remembered truth of the Augmetic prisoner-of-war camp would explain a lot of the Stelforma condemnation of the Dalebloods.

Coral stared at the book open on the desk, listening to the Marines check the other offices while waiting on her. There were answers here, but no solutions. Only the truth of *why* they were all going to die.

Except...it had been a *lot* more than ten years since Findlay had started this journal. The help had never come. The Seabloods had eventually abandoned the City of Spires—and they had brought almost none of the magic and engineering that held this city together with them.

She exhaled a long sigh and flipped to the *end* of the book.

CHAPTER 36

THE BACK THIRD of the book was blank. Somehow, Coral didn't think that Findlay had kept up the journal the entire time he'd been living in the City of Spires, but hopefully it included some information on the end—on the Great Fleet.

Flipping rapidly through the blank pages, she came the last page that had been written on. The handwriting was definitely Findlay's still, but something about just the letters themselves spoke to a bone-deep exhaustion and grief like she'd never seen.

I guess that's it, then.

Auburn and Carr were trying to reboot the fusion reactor on Trailblazer. *Having one of the old terraformer ships active would have fixed our last issue. The last two evac fleet transports couldn't get through the ice on the harbor, but* Trailblazer *has a battle-steel icebreaker ram for a reason.*

I don't know what they did wrong. I never will. Full reactor overload. Everyone in the bay is dead. Every ship is gone. The bay *is gone.*

So's a good chunk of the city. If anyone else is left alive...I...I don't care. It's been too long, and I've done too much. My health implant is ancient, but it's telling me my rad dose is enough to be lethal, given my age.

Fortunately, I think the suicide function is still functioning.

239

I'm not even sure why I'm...

There were two blank lines after the writing trailed off and Coral tried to even *imagine* the grief of surviving the disaster that had overwhelmed the City of Spires. But the text continued.

No. I do know why I'm writing this. Because someone, someday, may read it. Someone from the evacuation fleet may return. Even an Augmetic might be reading this—and the prisoners are just as much victims here as we are.

And they are my people's only hope. We have sent them all south, a million strong after eighty years of babies. If the Augmetics welcome them and give them a home, they have a chance. If not...we may all be fucked anyway.

But I hope that someone is reading this. Because we found an answer, at the end, when it turns out it was far too late for us.

I sent Auburn north to Caledon two years ago, just after we started building the evac fleet. She took all of our aircraft and the only remaining Mind techs. Forty-five people.

The aircraft didn't survive. Only half the people made it home with Auburn—and they built sleds *from the airframe to carry their injured and supplies. They arrived just after the harbor finally iced fully shut.*

We were down to one last shipload anyway. Some of us, myself included, weren't planning on making the journey. I'm a hundred and forty-five standard years old. I'm too tired for this shit.

But Auburn found it. The only thing worth risking fifty of our best by going into the teeth of the storm. And the irony is that I am now left hoping that someone is reading this text, or all that risk and sacrifice will be meaningless.

In the top drawer of my desk there are two items you must take. The first is my command sigil. It is an authorization token that will give access to any CUNE facility still operational on Albion.

The second is a datakey. It is the fail-safe for the orbital network lockdown. The worst irony is that Trailblazer *had the necessary communication arrays for us to use it, but she needed her reactor online to use them.*

Now there is only one place on the planet where that datakey can be used. If you are here, you have a ship and have traveled into conditions utterly hostile to humankind.

And now a dead man must ask you to do it again.

Mind Hibernia is a secondary terraformer Mind. Protocol required that they be built to operate without external fuel or maintenance for a minimum of one thousand standard years. In this case, the Hibernia facility is powered by a geothermal bore.

Mind Hibernia must still be alive. And whoever is reading this must take my sigil and the datakey to the Southern Terraformer. The Mind will know what to do. The datakey will give them control of the orbital terraformers.

This world can be saved. But only if by some fluke of fate, some stranger is reading this.

May God go with you. I pray you exist. But my time is done. My task is done.

I will not die in agony.

~

It was madness. The words of a man long dead—words that made almost no sense to Coral Amherst. She understood perhaps two sentences in five of what she'd read. The only thing she was *certain* of was what the long-dead CUNEN officer was asking of her.

Ever so gently—and glad for her gloves!—she moved Findlay's mummified hand from the gun on the desk into his lap. Then she rolled the chair with the desiccated body back into the corner of the room to give her access to the desk.

The material and structure of the desk were strange to her. Still, it had been made for a human mind and human hands, and it only took a few moments for her to work out where the drawer had to be. Despite her temptation to cut it open with her Dalesteel blade, she prodded at a few different places until she found a release.

The drawer was shallow, likely designed to hold pens or papers or some such. Now it held two objects, both alien and strangely familiar to Coral's eyes.

The "command sigil" appeared to be solid gold, a medallion the size of her palm with the branch-flanked circles of the CUNE logo on one side and an axe-like object on the back that she thought *might* be some kind of vessel.

The "datakey" looked like nothing so much as the aluminum specie of the Stelforma Chosen. The same half-green, half-blue orb-on-sun. The same white-silver material. She presumed it was simply coated in aluminum, with whatever magic the key contained concealed inside.

The datakey was too heavy to be pure aluminum. The sigil was too light to be pure gold. Both clearly contained something else in their hearts—and from Findlay's centuries-old words, that something was *hope*.

Coral tucked the two artifacts into her uniform jacket and carefully picked up Findlay's journal. They'd need to store it carefully, but for now she'd have to carry it.

Taking one last look around the room, her gaze fell once again on the dead man, and a strange impulse took her.

She snapped to full attention and saluted Findlay.

"I don't know what an Augmetic is, Commodore Findlay," she told him. "I suspect I am one, but I don't know. I do know that all I have sworn to protect might depend on the task you left us.

"I will not fail."

If THE MARINES had heard her talking to a dead man, they showed no sign of it as Coral returned to the main reception area. Two were checking through the contents of the desk under the CUNE emblem, while the third was coordinating the lowering of a new rope from the upper floors.

"There's not much here, sir," one of the Marines at the desk said.

"Seems like they didn't use paper for much—even their weird paper. Not sure what magic they used to keep records, but it seems invisible to me."

"I don't know any more than you do, Corporal," Coral admitted, then lifted the book. "But I think I have found what we needed. We're done here for today."

"At your command, Captain."

The two Marines stepped away from the desk to fall in behind her as she returned to the elevator shaft, her brain swimming with unfamiliar words and impossible concepts.

Climbing hand over hand up a rope before anyone had managed to arrange safety equipment helped ground her, even if it got her a dirty look from Sergeant Adrichem as she emerged onto the third floor.

"Where's Commander El-Ghazzawy?" she asked the Marine.

"Here, sir."

Coral turned to find the intelligence officer passing a large roll of the odd shiny paper they kept finding over to a Marine. She realized El-Ghazzawy had several smaller rolls under one arm, and there were two more Marines laden down with the charts.

"Stealing all of their charts, I see," she observed with a chuckle.

"I tested whether I could touch them on a smaller one of what this place looked like before it exploded," El-Ghazzawy said defensively. "They've held up well."

"No, that's a good plan," Coral told her. "We need to head back to the ship before the storm gets too bad anyway. But...take this."

She handed El-Ghazzawy the journal. The younger woman stared at it like she'd just been handed the keys to the vault of the First Republic Bank.

"Is this..."

"Journal of the city's military commander, from its founding to his death, from what I can tell," Coral told her. "I've read the first pages and the last, and I think I have what we came north for.

"I need you to read the rest of it and sort out what it says about how we got here."

"Yes, sir." In that moment, Coral knew she no longer had an intelligence officer. She now had a *historian* handed potentially the most important historical document their world contained.

El-Ghazzawy passed the last of her rolled-up charts to the Marines and dug through her things to make sure she had the book in a protective bag—an act Coral thoroughly approved of.

"What now, sir?"

"We see if we can set up something to protect our entrance and fall back to the base camp," Coral replied. "And potentially back to the ship. You and I are going to have to meet with the rest of the senior officers and make a decision."

"A decision?"

"I think I may have found what we came here for," Coral repeated softly as they stepped out into the office with the forcibly opened window. "But it's not what we expected, and it's going to require a step we never even considered before.

"So, I want to get the staff officers' and Captain's opinions before I inform everyone what we're going to do."

CHAPTER 37

MORNING WAS an estimate as the storm swept over them. At this point, Coral's crews were far more comfortable operating in the incomprehensible cold and ice storms—but that still didn't make it *easy*.

And she was grimly aware that if she'd brought Seablood crew with her, they would have lost half of them by now at least. The decision to only send Daleblood officers, crew and Marines on the expedition north had felt wrong, a violation of the normal relations between the Republic's two racial groups.

But it had been even more necessary than they'd thought. This might have been where the Seabloods originated, but returning there would have been death for them.

The flag mess had seen additional braziers emerge from some storage space deeper in the hull, but even with them, the steam from the coffees was clearly visible as Coral's people filed in.

Captain Oliversen was the last to arrive, his uniform visibly damp from the melting ice. *Cloudwatcher's* commander looked surprisingly well put together despite the outside weather, speaking to the wisdom of lashing the two ships together in the shelter of the crater walls.

Coral was seated at the table next to the stage, drinking her own coffee and looking at the stand El-Ghazzawy had set up with the CUNE map of Albion next to the Republic's map on the wall.

"Let's let Captain Oliversen get some coffee into himself before we get started," she told the officers.

It was a small group, just the two Captains and her four staff officers. Seven people, including her, that had to make a decision that might just change the fate of their entire world.

"I'm fine," Oliversen replied, though his glance at the steaming tray of scrambled eggs in the middle of the table suggested differently.

"Drink and eat something, Stipe," Coral ordered flatly. "You're going to need to be at your best today. This briefing is going to be...big."

Only El-Ghazzawy really knew what they'd found in the City of Spires. The intelligence officer and historian was clearly cycling between vibrating with nervous energy and complete exhaustion.

If the intelligence officer had slept since returning to the ship with Findlay's journal, Coral would be stunned. She suspected that El-Ghazzawy had read the entire book overnight, which would hopefully give the Commander context on what they needed to do with the two magical artifacts nestled under Coral's jacket.

Obediently, Oliversen scooped eggs and bacon onto his plate, then took a melodramatically large gulp of coffee before gesturing for them to continue with the cup.

Coral glared at him semi-jokingly, which only added to the chuckles around the room until she relented.

"Commander El-Ghazzawy and I explored part of the City of Spires yesterday, before the worst of the storm hit us," she finally told them all. "My instincts of where to look for key information proved out perfectly. We found their military command bunker and the office of their commander."

She paused to let that sink in, then dropped her actual bomb.

"We also found said commander. He died around when the explosion took out the harbor here," she said softly. "He was a Seablood, as we would judge such things, but he was apparently tasked to defend all of Albion from threats beyond our understanding.

"We know this because this Commodore Alistair Findlay kept a diary, starting from the early days of the City of Spires and only ending on his death. Thanks to the Commodore, we now understand much more of the threat we face and we have a potential solution."

She sighed and shook her head.

"That is, of course, if we are prepared to take the word of a long-dead man who writes of things none of us understand, and to act precipitously based on it."

Coral had read the key pages of the diary herself. She was prepared to act on Findlay's words, but she needed her officers to follow her willingly.

"Commander El-Ghazzawy, I suspect you have read the entirety of the journal," she said, turning to her intelligence officer. "Would you care to lay out the situation for everyone? Take the time you need. We all are going to need a healthily full stomach for this."

The intelligence officer rose and walked onto the stage, putting the thick journal down on the lectern and considering the grouped officers like the teacher she'd probably been at some point.

"The first thing that is important to understand," El-Ghazzawy began, "is that we are not native to this world. Not the Dalebloods. Not the Seabloods. Not the Stelforma.

"I'm unsure, from the diary, which of the animals we know are from Albion versus were imported with the humans. But my impression is that Albion, prior to the arrival of our ancestors, was utterly uninhabitable by people."

Coral had put together that much, which meant she was waiting and ready to deploy a suppressing glare to keep her other officers silent. They needed the background El-Ghazzawy was providing.

"A massive magical endeavor was launched to transform Albion into a place humanity could live," the historian continued. "Entire cities dedicated to this task were established at the north and south poles. The people of the northern city, called Caledon, eventually became our Seabloods.

"I believe, though I have no evidence in Findlay's journal to support this, that the people of the southern city, called Hibernia, became the Stelforma."

"StelFormer," Coral murmured, then repeated it more loudly when El-Ghazzawy looked questioningly at her. "Findlay wrote that the people at Hibernia were working for Stellar Terraforming...and he called them StelFormers. I can all too easily see how that becomes *Stelforma*."

"But what about our ancestors, then?" Nevin asked softly.

"They were the entire reason for the colony," El-Ghazzawy said. "Our ancestors were prisoners, the losing side of a civil war. It is not clear what the war was *about*, only that the people Findlay called 'Augmetics' lost.

"About two hundred thousand Augmetics were settled here as a controlled penal colony. There was a fort where Daleheart Bay now is to watch over them, and they were allowed free rein in the valleys around that fort.

"The valleys we now call the central Dales. These Augmetics became the Dalebloods."

"None of this really helps us fight whatever is freezing our people to death," Oliversen noted grimly.

"Because there is no enemy to fight," Coral told them all. "The closest thing to an enemy, from what I read of the diary, is *us*. All of our problems stem to when an Augmetic warship attacked Albion— potentially to try to *rescue* our ancestors.

"They destroyed the fort guarding the prisoners with a weapon of incomprehensible power, creating Daleheart Bay. Then the people at Caledon destroyed that warship—in a way that resulted in her crashing *into* Caledon and wrecking the magical artifacts that were transforming Albion to a place humans can live."

No one in the room was stupid. The situation being laid in front of them was entirely outside their context, but they were competent, intelligent people, and all of them were following so far.

Coral could tell by the sick horrified expressions.

"So...there's *nothing* we can do?" Nevin asked.

"That depends on how much we trust the words of a dead man whose job was to make sure our ancestors never escaped," Coral pointed out drily. "Commander El-Ghazzawy? Is there any further background you think we need?"

"Only that I cannot tell from Findlay's journal *why* the Stelforma ever would have left Hibernia. They had a city with the magic and engineering of a people powerful enough to reshape our entire world. And yet they live on islands with buildings much like our own.

"After the first war, they captured enough ships to duplicate our engines and hull forms, but since then, they've kept up with us in terms of ship engineering well enough. The first war was a *disaster* for them, though. Only a few pieces of their High Magic allowed their wooden steamers to attack our defenses at all."

"Something different must have happened at the southern pole," Coral agreed. "We don't know what it was. We're going to find out, though."

That cheerful statement drew everyone's attention and Coral smiled thinly. She rose and joined El-Ghazzawy on the stage, gesturing to the old CUNE map.

"From what I understand of Findlay's final journal entry, there is a set of magical artifacts somewhere on Albion that are driving the hellfrost storms," Coral told her people. "They're *supposed* to be helping keep Albion habitable but instead are slowly freezing the northern half of our world.

"Sometime after the Great Fleet had sailed, Findlay found the key that takes control of those artifacts," she continued. "But when their last disaster destroyed any chance of him leaving the City of Spires, he had no hope—except that someone would find his journal and that key.

"We did. And if we trust that this long-dead man wrote the truth in his final hours, I now hold the key to preventing the slow death of our world and every living thing on it."

She tapped the old map.

"This was their map of our world," she noted. "I don't know what magic or engineering they created it with, but it is entirely accurate for the areas we can compare it to. Except, of course, for a few notable exceptions like Daleheart Bay and the ice that chokes this northern hell."

"If we have this key...does that mean we've already saved everyone?" O'Connor asked.

He knew better. Coral *knew* her chief of staff knew better—but he was asking to make sure the plan was very, very clear.

"No. Because a key needs a lock," she told them all. "And that lock, in this case, is what Findlay called a 'Mind.' A creature of great power—that is both the master of and, in some way I do not understand, the city of Hibernia itself."

"Here," El-Ghazzawy said, pointing to the bottom of the map. Well past the area the Republic's cartographers had access to. Past the area where they even had *guesses* based on conversations and trade with the Stelforma.

Well past the line of the Southern Doctrine, where the presence of a Republic warship would be met with overwhelming force—even without the war that everyone knew was about to begin anyway.

"So, what do we do?"

O'Connor's question was directed solely at Coral. Her people knew her well enough to know that she'd already made her decision and that all of this had been to lay the groundwork for her orders.

250

"There may be more information here in the City of Spires," she told her people. "We can't just abandon our investigation and excavation on the second day. That said, our orders were to find an answer to the hellfrost storms, and I believe we have found that."

"My people were watching the ice depth the whole way up," Captain Oliversen noted slowly. "I wouldn't have wanted to sail into the unknown without *Icebreaker* leading the way, but now we know, with some confidence, how deep the ice is between here and open water.

"*Cloudwatcher* can break through that."

Every ship the Republic had ever built was equipped with an icebreaker bow—it was the only hull form they really knew worked with their engines and paddlewheels. Knowing what she now knew about the Great Fleet, Coral understood *why* most of the evacuation transports had been equipped with icebreaker bows, too.

Findlay had been forced to make massive choices around what he could and couldn't put in the ships for his civilians. The internal combustion engines had given the ships the power to break through the ice that had been starting to blockade their harbor, so they'd built the ships to use that power.

And now, two hundred years later, that decision had come full circle and would allow a Republic battleship—which, while it shared the *form* of the evacuation ships, was notably larger and vastly more heavily armored and reinforced—to retrace the Great Fleet's route.

"Then that becomes the course we must take," Coral decided, the last piece of her plan falling into place. "Captain Jernigan and the cruisers will maintain the Bloodspeech relay between *Cloudwatcher* and North Dale Base. *Cloudwatcher* will remain here to continue investigating the City of Spires and see what more can be learned of our past and origins.

"*Icebreaker* will sail south. We will use the Bloodspeech relay to coordinate refuel and resupply as we head south." She turned to look at the map they'd taken from the ruins.

"We are over sixteen thousand kilometers from Hibernia," she noted. "Once we are clear of the ice, we will maintain full cruising speed twenty-six hours a day. Including the time to clear the ice, it should take us thirty days to reach the south pole and the old Stellar Terraforming base there.

"Once we have reached Hibernia, it may take us some time to find the Mind itself. We don't know enough about what we're going to encounter there—but Findlay *did* know, and he believed that strangers who knew nothing about the truth of our world could find the Mind and deliver it the key.

"Since we are *exactly* the type of clueless people he was expecting to find his journal, I have to hope he believed correctly." She spread her hands. "I *do* believe that, given enough time, we can find the lock for this key once we're in Hibernia.

"And I believe that us spending weeks finding the Mind and delivering this key will be time better spent than almost anything else we might do."

Her officers waited in silence for her to finish. Coffee was sipped thoughtfully, though much of the breakfast food was starting to go cold.

"What about the Stelforma?" Captain Nevin finally asked. "We are planning to violate *every* part of the letter, spirit and intent of the Southern Doctrine."

"Oh, worse than that, Captain," Coral warned. "We are, unless I am severely mistaken, about to sail a ship of people their faith says are damned right to the place their faith says is a paradise they were stolen from.

"I *intend* to attempt diplomacy. We will make at least a few copies of Commodore Findlay's journal as we sail south. We will provide the Stelforma with a copy. Hell, with the original, if need be.

"They are as doomed as we are if we do not complete our mission," she reminded her people. "I want to believe that they will understand that and work with us. They have to know something about Hibernia and what's down there.

"They may even know more about what we've discovered of our

past. This is no longer a matter of our nations, people. This is a matter of our *world*."

"And if the Stelforma don't see it that way?" Nevin asked.

"Then this is the most powerful battleship in all Albion and we will smash our way through their fleets to save them from their own stupidity," Coral said flatly. "We are going to save our world, people. We are going to save *everyone*.

"We cannot allow ourselves to be slowed or stopped. We will talk as long as we can. We will argue, we will convince, we will negotiate, we will *bully*. But we will not fail. This ship will reach Hibernia. We will deliver the key to the Mind and save our people's future.

"And we will not let *anyone* stop us."

CHAPTER 38

CORAL DIDN'T EVEN LET them wait for the hellfrost storm to lift. Based off their prior experiences, it could take days, maybe even a week or more, for the mind-numbing cold and ice bombardment to cease.

And now that she had an answer, she was grimly aware of the calendar inching toward winter for the north of the Dales. She didn't know if unlocking the "orbital terraformers" for Mind Hibernia would ease that season for people like the folk of Keller's Landing. She *did* know that if nothing changed, people were going to die this winter.

Either she was wrong and all of this was a waste of time and resources—or every day she delayed cost the people of the northern settlements the lives of those they loved.

And Coral Amherst did not think she was wrong.

So, she stood at the front of the flag bridge, staring out at the storm through a window that really shouldn't have been open, and watched her flagship crash into the ice once more.

Icebreaker Squadron was down to a single ship now, but thankfully no one had been so foolish as to suggest that Coral give up command or something silly like that. In her quiet moments, she was hoping that the Republic would be able to send her more ships as she traveled south.

But *Cloudwatcher* had to stay at the City of Spires, and her cruisers were the only thing providing the City with a communication link, however tenuous, back to the Republic.

"Sir!"

Coral turned to look at the young rating who'd approached and dropped into parade rest.

"At east, sailor. What is it?" she asked.

"Communique through the Bloodspeaker relay, sir," the woman replied, holding out a folded sheet of typewriter paper.

"Thank you."

The sailor stayed at attention as Coral took the dispatch, then saluted and retreated back to the Bloodspeaker's station between the flag bridge and the main bridge.

Coral unfolded the sheet of paper and studied the typewritten note. Bloodspeech was audio only, between trained Daleblood magi, which meant that a communique like this would have been typed, recited back to its originator, and then retyped and the two versions compared to make certain it was correct.

And that would have been repeated every thousand kilometers or so of a very long trip to Daleheart city and the Citadel.

FROM: ADMIRALTY COMMISSION

TO: REAR ADMIRAL CORAL AMHERST

COMMISSION HAS REVIEWED INITIAL REPORT. INFORMATION LIMITED AS WE DO NOT POSSESS SOURCE DOCUMENT. CANNOT, REPEAT CANNOT, MAKE JUDGMENT ON RECOMMENDED PLAN.

POTENTIAL COMPLICATION TO CROSSING STELFORMA WATERS: WAR IMMINENT.

PARLIAMENTARY VOTE AND ACTIVATION OF WAR PLAN BLUE FIRE EXPECTED WITHIN FIFTY-TWO HOURS.

TANKERS FROM ORIGINAL ICEBREAKER SQUADRON WILL RENDEZVOUS AS REQUESTED.

NO FURTHER ASSETS AVAILABLE.

THE REPUBLIC PLACES OUR FAITH IN YOUR JUDGMENT AND YOUR PLAN.

COMPLETE YOUR MISSION.

NO HIGHER PRIORITY.

Coral read the message three times, then chuckled softly, remembering a long-past conversation with her father when he'd asked her how she was doing one evening.

She'd been studying for the Navy Academy entrance exams, a single day of intensive testing where success or failure would decide her entire future. Her father, who had probably understood even better than her what she was getting into, had gripped her shoulder comfortingly and said a handful words that had stuck in her head ever since: *So, no pressure, then?*

"No pressure, then," she echoed. She folded the communique up and put it inside her jacket, with Findlay's command sigil and datakey.

O'Connor looked up as she stepped back into the central U of tables and double-checked *Icebreaker*'s position. Right now, of course, that was an estimate—but they guessed they were still a day away from breaking into open water.

"Any change to the plan, sir?" he asked.

"No. Not for us."

He gave her a quizzical look.

"Parliament is voting on war, today or tomorrow," she told him. "Given everything we *have* been told, that means they've probably found the Stelforma invasion fleet."

"War Plan Blue Fire," O'Connor said after a moment's thought. "Fuck. And us out here, running south on a straight bloody line."

"That's what the Commission said, yeah." Coral was surprised her chief of staff had leapt to the specific war plan from just what *she* had told him.

"I'm a planning officer, Admiral," he reminded her. "I worked on an update to the Fire War Plans last year. Blue Fire is...aggressive."

"That's one way to put it." She looked around her flag bridge and shrugged. If anyone in there was going to betray them to the Stelforma, they had no way to communicate *to* the enemy. "As I understand it, all of the Fire Plans called for either attempting to force a major fleet engagement or allowing the Stelforma to court one, allowing us to neutralize their capital ships with superior numbers and firepower."

Except that from her earlier conversations with El-Ghazzawy, it was quite possible that the Republic Navy had neither of those things. And thought they did.

"Basically. The Blue Fire, Green Fire and Teal Fire variants are all war plans predicated on attacking the Stelforma's ability to land an invasion," O'Connor agreed. "Blue Fire and Teal Fire assume we know, roughly, where the invasion fleet and its associated battle fleet are."

He paused, waiting to see if Coral knew the assumption that underlay Blue Fire specifically.

"While I have copies of the war plans in my safe, I am not briefed on the full details of Blue Fire, Colonel," Coral said quietly. Her first duty upon receiving a notification of the formal activation of War Plan Blue Fire would, in fact, be *to* read the copy of said plan in the safe.

Though her orders also absolved her of following up on Icebreaker Squadron's theoretical role in that plan. No higher priority, and all that.

"Blue Fire assumes we've lost our numerical superiority due to an intelligence failure," her chief of staff said bluntly. "Once it's activated, *every* battleship is ordered to a rendezvous in the southern Westerling Sea.

"It calls for us to concentrate our entire capital-ship strength into a single heavy battle force, leaving cruisers behind to handle security in zones we normally protect with battleships. The commander of this fleet, most likely Admiral Moreno, as Home Fleet will be the first formation to arrive, will wait on the most up-to-date possible intelligence on the location and potential course of the invasion fleet.

"Once he has that intelligence, he will intercept that fleet. The brutal calculation of War Plan Blue Fire is that the Stelforma have to assume we still have battleships in those other posts and will hopefully send their own battleships in pinning operations or raids. That will allow us to put the entirety of our capital-ship strength against perhaps seventy-five percent of theirs, sacrificing cruisers to gain a numerical advantage at the key point."

Coral considered the scenario and shivered. For most of the peacetime roles of the Republic Navy, cruisers could take over for battleships easily enough. Battleships had slightly longer range and somewhat better endurance against storms, but cruisers would serve well enough.

But if the Stelforma sent battleships against those anchorages expecting to fight battleships, the Republic would lose a lot of cruisers—and would likely lose several of their less-well-defended shore bases, with all of the human cost entailed in that.

"The brutal calculation" summed it up quite neatly and horrifically.

"We are ordered to complete our mission," she told O'Connor softly. "Whatever War Plan is activated will not directly impact us, though hopefully the Navy will keep us informed of what is going on. If nothing else, drawing the Stelforma into a major battle for control of the sea should keep them from getting in *our* way."

She was all too aware, though, that her mission was for everyone on Albion, Stelforma included. She was surprised to realize that she didn't *want* a war at all, now she knew more of their shared and separate history.

"This whole damn conflict between us and the Stelforma is over ancient history between people who have been dead for two hundred years," she told O'Connor.

"If the Commission is activating Blue Fire, the Stelforma are ready to invade," her chief of staff pointed out. "We have never started the wars with them."

Coral chuckled softly.

"*That*, Colonel, while *technically* true, is definitely twisting things a bit," she admitted. "A lot of people are going to die. Worse, in some ways, if the war has kicked off, we're not going to have a chance to talk to the Stelforma about what's at Hibernia.

"And given that their ancestors abandoned their 'paradise,' I suspect we *really* need to know what we're getting into!"

CHAPTER 39

IT WAS three days later and a thousand kilometers farther south when the news of the declaration of war finally arrived.

"That's that, then," O'Connor concluded, standing in the center of the flag bridge. He held the sheet of paper Coral had just read from and read through it himself. "Current estimate of Stelforma naval strength is *forty-five* battleships?"

"El-Ghazzawy had warned me, quietly, that Intelligence was revamping their estimates, but they didn't have anything *solid*. Just steel-purchase numbers that didn't line up with their known new hulls." Coral shook her head. "Apparently, we have a solid handle on where they're making armor plate but not so much on where they're actually building the damn ships."

O'Connor grunted with dissatisfaction and turned to study the chart table.

"I'll get Blanc and the ops team started on reviewing status updates, and we'll get the chart updated on where all of our ships are," he told her. "I'm presuming we'll want to avoid the war as much as possible?"

"Unless you think we can convince everyone to sit down and

shut up while we save everybody," Coral said grimly. The Republic's numerical disadvantage wasn't fatal—the Stelforma still had casemate battleships in commission, and the Republic Navy didn't—but it required the immediate offensive called for by Blue Fire.

A defensive posture against an enemy who had fewer ships than you was one thing. A defensive posture against an enemy that *outnumbered* you was another. The Stelforma could make a landing anywhere along the coast of the Dales, and once they had an army on the continent, dislodging them would be hell.

The Republic, on the other hand, didn't *want* to conquer any of the Stelforma nations. An invasion force they landed on a Stelforma island would, at *most*, have land access to perhaps a tenth of the Stelforma industry and population before needing to launch another amphibious assault.

It was a strategic imbalance that had left the Republic determined to maintain enough of a naval force to keep the Stelforma from their shores. An objective that they appeared to have finally, dramatically failed at.

Hence War Plan Blue Fire, a do-or-die throw of the dice for a major fleet action to decide control of the sea—but also an attempt to destroy the transport and landing ships necessary for the Stelforma to land their soldiers on the Dales at all.

"Well, I guess I'm authorized to remove this from my safe now," Coral finally said, tapping the black *TOP SECRET OPEN ON AUTHORIZATION ONLY* folio sitting on the table next to her. Since the Commission had given her advanced warning, she'd removed the war plan from her secured safe and had glanced at key sections.

"Do we have the rendezvous code ID?" she asked O'Connor. She hadn't looked at all of the details at the end of the message. She'd only read out the war notice to her staff herself. Not least, the final section was just a list of numbers and letters that required decryption—decryption that one of the signals noncoms had been doing while they spoke and now slid over to O'Connor.

"Zulu-Oscar-Seven," her chief of staff replied. "That's about twelve kilometers directly northwest of the York Republic. It's *in* Stelforma waters."

Coral opened the folio to the page with the potential rendezvous coordinates. There were twenty-six possibilities, each referred to by a random three-character code that had then been encrypted to conceal them further.

"Mark it on the map," she ordered, passing the page to O'Connor as she turned her focus to the big chart.

She was tracing the coordinates in her mind as her chief of staff put a blue flag on the spot, confirming her fears.

"Does our intel include any estimate of the location of the Stelforma invasion fleet?" she asked.

"No," O'Connor said. "But if they're using ZO-Seven..."

He studied the map, then pulled a trio of orange flags from the drawer.

"It's in one of these three harbors," he concluded, putting the flags down. One was the York Republic's main harbor. The other was a bit farther away, the secondary harbor of the Hertz Princedom. The third wasn't labeled on the map.

"What's that?" she asked.

"A large natural lagoon," he replied. "It's not close to any cities or bases we know of, but if they dredged out the entrance, it's large enough for the invasion fleet they launched last time."

"And since it's not a city or normal harbor, they would have expected us to miss it," Coral murmured.

"Exactly. Planning flagged it when we were revising the war plans, and Intelligence was supposed to get agent eyes on it."

His hand lingered over that flag, then he tapped it firmly.

"I'm guessing they're here," he said. "They learned about closing harbors to civilians and mustering fleets in them last time around; we learned what they were up to well in advance. I suspect that one of the final points in favor of war was Intelligence finally getting reports from the agents investigating the lagoon.

"If it's been updated to a base and is anchoring an invasion fleet, well…"

"That's pretty damned obvious," Coral agreed. "And pretty damned in the way."

The course they'd plotted to Hibernia was as direct as they could manage while still skirting most Stelforma territory. And that course took them basically directly between the assembly point for the Republic fleets and the lagoon O'Connor was flagging.

"We could adjust our course," he suggested.

"We're already looking at twenty-nine days," Coral replied. "Still fifteen thousand kilometers."

They'd pass the fleet rendezvous point well before that. At five hundred-ish kilometers a day, sailing all night at cruising speed, they'd hit the fleet rendezvous in sixteen days.

"The timing is tight enough, we could join the fleet for the attack," O'Connor murmured. "Which…we can't risk. Not with the key aboard."

"No. We can't risk it." She shook her head and measured the distance between the flags in her mind.

"We didn't need a damn war," Coral finally said. "I need thirty damn days. *One fucking month.* If our friends and enemies could keep from killing each other for one damn month, we can save everyone from the death of our world."

"What do we do, sir?"

"We make the run to Hibernia," Coral replied. "We avoid the war if we can. But we listen and we learn what's going on. We have a mission."

And in the back of her mind, she wondered if the answer to the war itself lay in the document being feverishly retyped in the intelligence office belowdecks.

CHAPTER 40

ICEBREAKER RENDEZVOUSED with the fuel tankers after ten days. The battleship's fuel tanks had been drained by the demands of smashing through a thousand kilometers of ice, leaving her at less than a third of her immense capacity when *Chorus of Dawn* and *Song of Children* met with her.

"El-Ghazzawy, have we completed one of the copies of Findlay's journal?" Coral asked her subordinate as she watched teams haul the hoses between the three ships.

"Just one so far, though a few are close," the intelligence officer replied. El-Ghazzawy looked *exhausted*, which suggested she hadn't been leaving nearly enough of the work to the yeomen she'd been assigned.

"One will have to do," Coral decided. "We'll transfer it to *Chorus of Dawn* and they'll transport it to Daleheart."

"I'll talk to my people immediately and make the arrangements."

"Good."

The younger woman saluted crisply, leaving Coral on the flying bridge with a handful of *Icebreaker*'s crew.

For the first time in weeks, the massive battleship was at rest.

Massive sea anchors limited her movement, allowing the tankers to focus on pumping as much corn oil into her tanks as possible as quickly as possible.

Coral had agreed with Nevin to let the crew rest for the day. They were far enough south that it was safe for the crew to sun themselves on the deck, and some brave souls were even using one of the ship's launches as an impromptu dock for swimming.

Even Coral wouldn't have put that much strain on her magic by choice! But there were at least fifty of the crew in the chilly water, with a couple of the stronger swimmers keeping a *probably* unnecessary eye on the cluster of Daleblood crew.

Watching her people swim for fun in water that would have sent any Seablood into hypothermia in moments, she was reminded of Findlay's description of her people: *Augmetic super-soldiers.*

She still wasn't sure what an "Augmetic" was—other than a name for a Daleblood—but she could guess at "super-soldier." Her people were a creation of a mighty magic from the worlds beyond. An *artificial* upgrade to create a modified human that made a better soldier.

It explained one of the oddities of relationships between Dalebloods and Seabloods. While there were some who argued for purity standards, the truth was that any child of a Daleblood mother or father had the same magic as any other. Only a single Daleblood parent was required for the child to be a Daleblood.

The strength of the magic varied between individuals, but that variability didn't seem to be affected by any standard of *purity*. Even Coral, who was as pureblooded a Daleblood as was physically possible and had long leaned on the superiority of that blood, thought purity standards were stupid.

The more she thought about what her people apparently were, though, the more she understood why her ancestors had collectively decided to bury their history when the Seabloods had arrived. For whatever reason, the Great Fleet had arrived without their command ships, which had limited the knowledge base and history they'd brought with them.

The Dalebloods, though. They had to have known and remembered everything. They knew they'd been prisoners, the Seabloods of the Great Fleet their jailors. But they'd *also* seen Fort Hearth destroyed by fire on high, and when the Great Fleet arrived as refugees, they'd decided that reconciliation was more important than revenge.

Was more important, even, than remembrance.

Her ancestors had chosen to bury the grudge against their jailors' children—and had done so by burying any knowledge of the history that shaped it.

To Coral Amherst's ancestors, the lives of the desperate refugees who'd washed up on their shores had been more important than all of the reasons the Dalebloods had to hate the strangers.

It was a thought-provoking realization, one that was rattling around her brain toward an unknown conclusion as she stared out at seas empty of anything except her three ships.

"THE ADVANTAGE of actually making physical contact is that we got a bunch of updated intelligence," El-Ghazzawy told Coral later, after the Admiral returned to the flag bridge.

The space was mostly empty, with most of the crew *frolicking* elsewhere. A pair of dutiful ratings who'd presumably aggravated their chiefs were providing what support was available, but with O'Connor, Coral and El-Ghazzawy clustered around the chart table, there were more officers in the room than crew.

"We now have the expected arrival times of the various squadrons at the ZO-Seven rendezvous point," O'Connor added. "As well as what the Admiralty knew about Stelforma positions as of the declaration of war."

"Lay it out," Coral ordered.

"The Northern and Eastern Squadrons are going to be last units to arrive at the rendezvous point," O'Connor told her. "Those will be the last ten battleships, bringing what's been designated *Third Fleet* up to a strength of thirty-six two-turret battleships and *Swordbreaker*."

Coral considered that number and sighed.

"There's going to be a lot of worried engineers and exhausted engineering techs in that fleet," she noted.

Of the forty-two battleships the Republic had in commission, Coral had one and had left one at the City of Spires. That left forty, of which, under normal circumstances, a *minimum* of eight—and more likely ten—were undergoing some level of refit or repair.

If Admiral Moreno had thirty-seven of those forty ships, that meant the Navy had suspended any refits or repairs that *could* be suspended—and had probably issued those orders weeks past.

"Not just engineers. Admiral Moreno is too damned smart not to know that at least five of his ships should be in a yard, not a battle line," O'Connor agreed.

There was a *reason* a Seablood who shouldn't be at sea was commanding the Dales' primary striking force—and it was because Admiral Aster Moreno was universally acknowledged as the best fleet commander *Albion* had produced in the last century.

Coral hoped that whatever measures his staff were taking to keep the old man comfortable and healthy aboard his flagship were working. They needed the man's brain to be as sharp as ever, not distracted by his own frailties.

"The last Eastern Squadron ships will arrive at the rendezvous point in six days," her chief of staff noted. "About two days before the earliest we're likely to get there. Admiral Siena and the Northern Squadron should get there around the same time."

"By then, Moreno, at least, should know what the Stelforma are doing in response to the declaration of war," El-Ghazzawy said. "Intelligence has confirmed Colonel O'Connor's guess."

She replaced the three orange flags on the map with a single red flag at the lagoon.

"It looks like the Stelforma Chosen started using their own resources, separate from the member nations, to convert the Adelaide Lagoon into a fleet anchorage at least five years ago," she told them. "The entrance channel was dredged—and then dynamited when it still wasn't big enough.

"In its current state, Adelaide Lagoon can provide anchorage for several hundred vessels and has an entrance that can pass three battleships abreast," she said grimly. "Intelligence estimates put the invasion fleet at two hundred transports, with eighty cruisers and somewhere between thirty and forty battleships for escorts."

"They concentrated their fleet, too," O'Connor said grimly. "Everyone is trying to make sure they have the edge at the main point of contact."

If Moreno pulled off the intercept, it would be the largest fleet battle in Albion's history. Coral had to wonder, though, if it would be the largest such battle in *human* history.

"The best option for Moreno is to bottle them up in the lagoon," Coral noted. "On the other hand, *they* know that too. How good do we think their intel is?"

El-Ghazzawy shrugged.

"That's not an estimate the Admiralty decided to share with staff intelligence officers," she admitted. "My own guess would be that they definitely know Home Fleet has sortied from Daleheart, and they likely know the Western Squadron has sortied from Bluecollar.

"Unless they have a *lot* more capital ships than even our worst-case estimates, the only force they have capable of challenging the combination of Home Fleet and the Western Squadron is in Adelaide Lagoon. They'll have to launch their invasion, however ready or unready they are, to avoid getting trapped.

"They know Moreno by reputation and have to consider the likelihood that we've discovered the Adelaide Lagoon anchorage and that the Admiral is taking at least Home Fleet to try and blockade it."

Coral shook her head.

"I have to assume the enemy is smart," she noted. "Which means they've got twenty- and thirty-centimeter shore-defense batteries along the outer reef. They'll lose accuracy with indirect fire from the ships trapped in the lagoon, but they'll have enough guns to bury Home Fleet on its own."

"I agree. But I doubt the Stelforma Admiral wants to fight a battle with his fleet trapped in a lagoon," El-Ghazzawy replied. "They'll sortie."

Coral nodded, tracing a course on the map. "It will have taken time for them to learn about the declaration of war," she observed. "At least a week to inform their fleet commander. They don't have Bloodspeech, but we know they have telegraphs and some of those cables run across the shorter ocean crossings."

And for all she knew, some of the closely held Stelforma High Magic would allow them to warn the fleet too.

"Assuming they weren't already on the edge of launching the invasion right then, it could easily be another five or six days before they're ready to move. So, they'll sortie..." She chuckled grimly. "Around when the fleet finishes concentrating. Assuming Moreno has agents at the Lagoon with Bloodspeech, he'll move as soon as they sortie, and they'll meet...here."

Her finger stabbed down on the map, and she studied the entirely empty and ordinary patch of ocean.

"How close will we be in seven days?" she asked O'Connor.

"Assuming we stick to the same course, about five hundred kilometers north by northwest," her chief of staff said after a moment.

"And if we were to change course and go directly there?"

"We'd still be three hundred klicks away by the time the fleets start shooting."

"At cruising speed. And our tanks are full," Coral murmured.

"I thought you wanted to avoid the battle, sir?" El-Ghazzawy asked.

"I do. But I also need to know what the Stelforma know about where we're going," the Admiral said slowly. "And the more I know about where we all came from, the more I think the whole damn *war* should be avoided.

"Go find Nevin, Colonel," she ordered, a decision finally snapped into place. "Our course is for the battlefield. And we're going to prep every fucking blue flare we have—because thanks to a dead man, I know how to save us all, and I will *not* stand by and watch a quarter-million people kill each other while I have that answer."

CHAPTER 41

TO: ALL COMMANDS

FROM: ADMIRALTY COMMISSION

BLUECOLLAR BASE ATTACKED AT TWENTY-FIVE HUNDRED HOURS NOVEMBER TEN.

ONE BATTLESHIP, TEN CRUISERS, ATTACHED DESTROYER FLOTILLA.

BLUECOLLAR REMAINS IN REPUBLIC HANDS. BASE DEFENSES BADLY DAMAGED. STELFORMA NOW AWARE THAT WESTERN SQUADRON HAS SORTIED.

ENEMY MAIN FLEET HAS SORTIED.

FLEET ACTION EXPECTED IN NEXT FIFTY-TWO HOURS.

ALL COMMANDS TO HOLD DEFENSIVE POSITIONS AND STAND BY FOR NEW ORDERS.

THE REPUBLIC EXPECTS EVERY OFFICER TO DO THEIR DUTY

Icebreaker's engines complained underneath Coral's feet as she tossed the dispatch down on the chart table. They were close enough to be receiving Bloodspeech updates from the southern communicator posts now, though the dispatches were meant for the cruiser

273

Captains stuck patrolling zones where they expected battleship-led attacks.

New orders could be a lot of things, but Coral could guess what the decisions hung on. If Third Fleet smashed the Stelforma invasion fleet, the cruisers that had been left to secure the Dales would be called forward to escort Republic landing ships for a counter-invasion to force peace talks.

If Third Fleet *lost*, the Admiralty would recall the cruisers for a desperate strike to sink as many invasion transports as possible, hoping to stave off the actual landings.

If it was an inconclusive battle, the other commands would have to brace for attacks like the one on Bluecollar as the war expanded and both sides tried to find a different advantage. Both fleets would be hoping for a decisive victory in the Westerling Sea.

And Coral was hoping for something different. *Icebreaker* was now up to her full thirty-kilometer-per-hour maximum speed, burning corn oil like mad as they tried desperately to reach the Stelforma before the battle was closed.

"We're within Bloodspeech range of Third Fleet, sir," O'Connor pointed out as he skimmed the dispatch himself. "You could talk to Admiral Moreno."

"The problem, Colonel, is that if I can't convince the Stelforma to listen, Admiral Moreno has to fight," she said quietly. "And if I *can* convince the Stelforma to listen, I am quite certain that Admiral Moreno will listen.

"I somehow doubt that the man who had three flagships sunk underneath him in the last war will turn down a chance to avoid further bloodshed!"

"And what if we get the timing wrong?" El-Ghazzawy asked. "If we're trying to talk to the Stelforma and then Moreno starts shooting?"

"We have to put some things up to chance and others up to communication," Coral murmured. "If the Stelforma agree to talk, we'll inform the Admiral. Until then, though, I don't want to interfere with his operations.

"We're the long shot, an attempt to find common ground and common cause after the war has already started. The only reason I'm prepared to consider this is because *Icebreaker*'s armor gives us a solid chance of taking their first shot and surviving to clear the field for Admiral Moreno."

"There are a lot of ways they could turn this into a trap, sir," O'Connor warned. "I feel like we should inform the Admiral in advance."

"It would be a distraction, Colonel, one Admiral Moreno doesn't need."

And if Coral told *anyone* off *Icebreaker* what she was planning, she was quite certain she'd be ordered not to try. But so long as she didn't explain her plan to her superiors, nobody could stop her!

Dawn stretched pale and warm across the Westerling Sea. After weeks at temperatures low enough to freeze the mercury in the thermometers, Coral was glorifying in the thirty-plus-degree heat. It had its own dangers—not least that if it was thirty degrees at dawn, it was going to be a *lot* hotter by noon—but the magic in her blood could handle those as easily as it handled the chill.

"Sir, we have a signal from the north," Nevin's signal officer told the Captain and the Admiral. "One of Third Fleet's cruiser screen has spotted us. We're being interrogated."

"Get the Bloodspeakers to order them off," Coral replied. "*Icebreaker* is on special duties for the Commission."

"Yes, sir."

The signal officer gave orders to a rating, who vanished back into the hull. For her own part, Captain Nevin made a vaguely strangled noise in the back of her throat, earning her a sharp glance from her Admiral.

"Yes, Captain Nevin?" Coral asked calmly.

"Does anyone actually know what we're about to do?" Nevin asked.

"You probably should have asked that a few days ago," Coral pointed out. "My staff certainly got into me on it yesterday. You're the one person with enough authority to have gone over my head to find out."

The blonde Daleblood Captain chuckled, the sound still vaguely choked.

"You're going to get us all killed, Admiral," she told Coral. "I'm guessing we're asking for forgiveness, not permission?"

"Oh, I'm not planning on asking for forgiveness," Coral replied. "More presenting the Admiralty with an established fact. We *are* going to make contact with the Stelforma. We *are* going to negotiate at least a temporary cease-fire, and the Republic Navy *is* going to honor it.

"And then we're going to get Stelforma permission to sail right through their territory, find Hibernia and fix our damned world."

Nevin's answering chuckle was even more strained than the last one.

"I didn't realize it was all that straightforward," she finally said.

"'Complete your mission. No higher priority,'" Coral quoted back at her subordinate. "My *mission* is to save the Dales from freezing to death over the next decade. According to my orders, even the war is a lower priority.

"So, since the war is getting in my way, we're going to end it."

"You realize that you are..." Nevin trailed off.

"'Eager and overly confident'?" Coral asked brightly, echoing Admiral Tse's not-quite-criticism from her meeting with the Commission.

"That is one way of phrasing it," her flag captain conceded. "I was thinking closer to reckless. Foolhardy, maybe? Foolish?"

"Mad," Coral said softly. "I am following the last instructions of a man who's been dead for two hundred years, Captain Nevin. Reckless, foolhardy, foolish, irrational...even mad. But I believe that if we do not act with the key Findlay left us, we will all die. Seabloods and Dalebloods and Stelforma alike.

"If I complete my mission, we will save the Stelforma, too. They will help us."

"Or destroy us—and any hope of using that key with us."

Coral glanced around the flying bridge, then back at Nevin and smiled.

"You are *Icebreaker*'s Captain, Ekaterina Nevin," she reminded the other woman. "You and you alone can stop me, if you think I'm wrong. If you think I'm going too far.

"*I* think I'm right. I think I'm doing the right thing to save us all. So, what do you think?"

Nevin held her gaze in silence for several seconds, then glanced to the north at the cruiser neither of them could see.

"I have seen a city killed by the hellfrost ice," she murmured. "I will risk much to spare my home that. Lead on, Admiral. And if you are mad, *Icebreaker* will be lost alongside you!"

CHAPTER 42

"Smoke on the southeast horizon! *Lot* of smoke!"

"It appears the Stelforma are nothing if not punctual," Coral observed. "Captain Nevin, set a course. Signals officer—hang the blue flag and ready the blue flares."

The flare code was meant for time of peace more than times of war. They were supposed to be used to enable communication and *avoid* conflict well before it started. Today, though, Coral needed to talk to the Stelforma commander before the fighting started.

So. Blue flares—code for *We need to talk.*

Surprise alone might buy them the chance they needed. If nothing else, *Icebreaker* was now sailing toward the Stelforma formation at thirty klicks and closing the distance *fast.*

"Range estimate, forty klicks," the lookout called down.

"If they haven't updated their average gun elevation, their range is twenty," Nevin observed. "Ours is twenty-four."

"So, we have four kilometers and about ten minutes to *not* fire as proof of our good intentions," Coral said. "Fire the first flares as soon as we have visual from the crow's nest."

That would be around twenty-five kilometers. They could see the

279

smoke from a lot farther away—Stelforma diesel burned notably blacker than Republic corn oil—and the *flares* would be visible around thirty klicks...but Coral wanted the Stelforma to know she only had one ship.

Icebreaker was the most powerful battleship on the planet, with armor she wasn't convinced the Stelforma could penetrate at all, but she was still only one ship. Coral suspected they could take the ship straight through the Stelforma formation and come out the other side...well, afloat, if not intact...but she couldn't defeat an entire fleet on her own.

"Estimate closing speed, forty-five klicks. They're making twenty across our bow."

"Do we know where Third Fleet is?" Coral asked.

"Best guess is that Moreno is about sixty klicks directly ahead of them," O'Connor told her. "A day's wages says at least one of his cruisers has spotted the smoke and given him a bearing."

"Not taking that bet, Colonel," she replied. "I'm only making one bet against the odds today."

"Visible hulls! *Lot of fucking hulls.*"

"Flare up!" the signals officer snapped in response to the lookout's not-overly-detailed report. A moment later, the first rocket blazed into the air from the back of the battleship citadel.

"Get a count of the battlewagons, at least," Coral called up to the lookout. "We'll pass that and their exact position and course to Admiral Moreno, no matter what happens."

There was no response to the flare. Coral let a minute pass per her chronometer, then glanced up.

"Range?"

"Twenty-three thousand five hundred and eighty meters," the lookout read off their range finder. "In range!"

"Another flare, please, Signals," Coral ordered flatly, and glanced at Nevin.

"Permission to load and elevate the guns?" the Captain asked.

"Granted. Do we have that capital-ship number?"

"I make it thirty-eight battlewagons," the lookout shouted down. "At least four or five times that in cruisers and transports!"

A blue flare sent a harsh color change flashing over the flying bridge as it blazed into the sky and Coral watched it go up grimly.

"Pass the numbers, position and bearing along to Admiral Moreno," she ordered. "And ready more flares. One a minute until they acknowledge us."

"Or start shooting," Nevin added grimly.

"Or start shooting," Coral conceded.

EVERY MINUTE, a blue flare fired into the sky from *Icebreaker*'s central armored citadel. Every minute, the battleship closed another three-quarters of a kilometer toward the Stelforma invasion fleet.

Every minute, Coral's people were taking more and more detailed notes on the strength of the invasion fleet. The Blood-speakers were rotating their trances, keeping at least one of them broadcasting to Third Fleet at all times.

"Twenty kilometers," Nevin said aloud. "We are now in range of their main guns."

Coral nodded silently. There were a *lot* of guns over there. They weren't yet certain of the breakdown between the older ships with casemated eighteen-centimeter guns and the new ships that carried the same two twin twenty-centimeter turrets as modern Republic ships.

If it had been her putting the enemy fleet together, there wouldn't have been a single casemate battleship on the other side. If nothing else, the casemates lacked the elevation of turreted guns, which meant the older battleships were heavily restricted in terms of range.

"Seventy-six turrets versus three," she murmured. "If they don't know what *Icebreaker* is, it looks pretty clear, doesn't it?"

"Flare spotted!" the lookout shouted from above them. There was a long pause. "Red flare, sirs."

Coral chuckled.

Surrender or be destroyed.

"I was expecting that," she admitted. "Fire another blue flare in immediate response, then return to the pattern."

The rocket whistled into the air behind her, barely audible over the sidewheels groaning away around her.

"They could fire at any time," Nevin pointed out.

"They could. They also know we could have fired fifteen minutes ago," Coral replied. "They're confused and concerned and want to see what the hell we're after, but they want to do so under *their* terms."

"I presume we're not going to do that," the Flag Captain said.

"Not a chance in that frozen hell we just left," Coral confirmed. "No. I need to talk to them, but if they won't talk, we need to get to Hibernia regardless."

She studied the smudge of smoke on the horizon, the last spark of the red flare barely visible even to her.

"Get the lookout to identify which ship launched the red flare," she ordered. "Then adjust our course. We're going to go right for the prick in charge and see if he's willing to talk."

"The likelihood that even *this* ship will survive to ram and board is quite low, sir."

"Even *I* think that level of aggression is too much, Captain Nevin." Coral smiled as another blue flare lifted into the air behind her. "We'll break south at three kilometers if we don't have an acceptable response."

That was the first time she'd said aloud that there was an exit strategy, and she could *feel* both Nevin and O'Connor release some of their tension at her words.

"Second red flare," the lookout reported.

"Launching a blue flare in response," the signals officer added before Coral could say anything.

Her people knew what they were doing, and she clasped her hands behind her back and faced into the wind. The next twenty minutes would decide a lot of things—including whether one Coral Amherst lived or died.

And everything hung on how curious the Admiral in command of the Stelforma was.

"Sir! Message from Third Fleet for you!"

Coral didn't even look at the Signals rating, simply holding out a hand for the typed communique.

It was very, *very* short. Admiral Aster Moreno didn't mince words or avoid profanity when asking what she thought she was doing.

"There will be no response yet," she told the rating, her gaze still focused on the enemy. "But there *will* be a response. Shortly."

The first flare was instinct. A hostile ship in weapons range that wasn't shooting. Give it a chance; see what happens when you demand surrender.

The second flare was doctrine. There was no rule in the Book for a ship making full speed toward your position in a time of war without firing and with blue flares up. Doctrine regarded that ship as a potential threat, not to be allowed to close range.

The third flare, though...

By now, it would definitely be the fleet commander making the call. It didn't matter *what* they'd been doing when *Icebreaker* hauled into range, they were either on their flag bridge or the flying bridge of the flagship now.

The Stelforma officer was almost certainly staring at her ship, wondering what she was doing. If Coral was only a *little* bit lucky, they weren't the kind of officer that would shoot first and interrogate prisoners later. They were, after all, the officer the Chosen Mother had selected to command her greatest fleet.

So, the question was what the supremely intelligent, supremely capable and supremely *loyal* Admiral the Mother would have picked would decide. Coral had presented them with an enigma wrapped in a threat, sailing under a flare of truce.

"Flare!" the lookout snapped. "Wait, no! Double flare!" There was a long pause, as if the woman was making sure she'd seen what she thought she'd seen.

"Green and blue! Repeat, *green and blue flares.*"

Coral watched the horizon, focusing in to see the rising rockets that told her that at least the *first* part of her plan had actually worked.

Acknowledged and *We need to talk.* She had to take that as an invitation to approach.

"Captain Nevin," Coral snapped. "Keep the guns loaded and crewed—but turn the turrets away from the Stelforma fleet. We will proceed on the assumption that we have safe passage—but we *are* going to be coming under the guns of their entire fleet. We will be careful."

The irony was that *Icebreaker* was actually *safer* at close range than at long. Once they were close enough that shells were coming in horizontally, they were going to hit the adamantine belt. Even at the current range, the shells would have come in from above and hit the deck armor. *Icebreaker*'s deck armor was impressive, but it was still limited to the armor the Republic could make.

"Understood. We'll, uh, keep moving?"

Coral chuckled and turned around to find the Signals rating who'd brought the communique from Admiral Moreno.

"I need a message sent to Admiral Moreno," she told the youth. She waited a moment as he produced a notebook and a pen to take her dictation.

"We are engaged in critical discussions with the Stelforma with regards to *Icebreaker*'s priority mission," she said slowly, watching to make sure the rating got every word. "*Icebreaker*'s Bloodspeakers will continue to provide updated information on the course, numbers and position of the Stelforma fleet while the discussions proceed.

"In exchange, I need—emphasize *need*—Third Fleet to refrain from engaging the Stelforma until our discussions are complete." She paused, trying to consider how to phrase the final piece.

"I have absolute faith in your judgment of the overall threat to the Republic," she finally said. "Per the Commission, there is no higher priority than my mission. Balance this as you must."

The rating finished scribbling and passed her the notepad to review.

It had to be the right tone. Coral needed time—but she *also* needed to know that the Stelforma weren't going to take advantage of her impromptu truce to do a run around Third Fleet.

She trusted Moreno to know when he could no longer wait to attack. She had to trust him to wait *until* then, to give her a chance to save them all.

CHAPTER 43

The first surprise Coral found herself swallowing was the nature of the Stelforma flagship. She'd expected a turret ship, of course. That the Stelforma had been building turreted capital ships had been common knowledge for a while now.

She had *not*, however, been expecting a three-turret ship. The other battleship was still smaller than *Icebreaker*, but she carried the same number of heavy twenty-centimeter guns.

Coral got a better look at the ship than she had at any Stelforma capital ship before, too, as the baroquely decorated battleship advanced from the main fleet line to rendezvous with *Icebreaker* in open water, roughly a kilometer from the invasion force.

The only Stelforma ship she'd ever seen this close up before was *Dancer*, but *Dancer* was, at least officially, a warship of the Williams Princedom.

Apostle of War was not. She was a battleship of the Stelforma Chosen and she resembled nothing so much as a cathedral on the waves, with statue grotesques mounted on the central citadel and her lookout post mounted on a church-style *bell tower*.

Every square centimeter of the warship had been painted or

sculpted into gorgeous art. Coral found herself half-hoping that the statuary and sculpture were wood or plaster, for the sake of the battleship's crew—and half-hoping that it was actually stone, which would badly impede the ship's function.

The two ships came to a slow halt with their turrets conspicuously pointed away from each other, roughly a hundred meters apart. Blue flags hung from the signal posts on both ships, marking a truce that Coral doubted they'd expected when the day began.

"Forty degrees Celsius, sir," O'Connor warned. "The Stelforma are going to need you to go inside their ship if you're talking to them."

"There are risks we have to take," she agreed, watching as her launch was slowly lowered into position beside *Icebreaker*'s deck. "And there are risks we do not."

She held out a package wrapped in black silk to her chief of staff. It was shockingly small and light for the weight it contained. The small wooden box inside had been her mother's favorite jewelry box, storing the most precious—though not the most *expensive*—pieces she'd owned.

The jewelry had been left to Coral's sisters. The *box* had been left to her, and while some might have taken that as an insult, Coral knew it had actually been a sign of how well Mariela Amherst had known her daughters.

Until that morning, the hand-carved and enameled box had held the insignia of every rank Coral had held prior to Rear Admiral. Now it held the fate of the world, wrapped in further black silk.

O'Connor took the silk-wrapped box with an awed expression that told her he knew *exactly* what was in it.

"I *think* we're in the right place to talk to the right people," she told him. "But if I'm wrong, that key still has to make it to Hibernia, Colonel. I'm trusting that to you."

"I will not fail you, Admiral," he promised. "Upon the Blood."

"I know. Upon the Blood."

A<small>POSTLE OF</small> W<small>AR</small> turned out to have a specialty elevator mounted on the port side of the ship, allowing Coral and her trio of Marines to step easily from *Icebreaker*'s launch onto the platform, which then clanked its way up the attached chains to deliver them to the main deck.

A surprisingly familiar woman in the cassock of a Priest-Captain was waiting for her at the top of the elevator, saluting crisply as Coral stepped onto the deck.

Coral returned Priest-Captain Angelica Carrasco's salute and bowed her head slightly.

"Priest-Captain Carrasco, this is an unexpected surprise," she told the other woman. "You appear to have risen in the esteem of your masters."

"I have the honor to serve as the Apostle-Admiral's operations officer," Carrasco replied. "I see congratulations are in order on your promotion, Rear Admiral Amherst."

The Apostle-Admiral? That was...quite the title.

"Thank you. I believe that the Apostle-Admiral, then, will be the one I must speak to."

"So the Apostle-Admiral Luke believed," Carrasco agreed. She glanced back at the line of armed guards that both she and Coral had ignored so far.

"I am commanded to bring the Admiral to the Apostle-Admiral Luke," she told the guards. "You will escort us, but you will not interfere."

"You cannot allow the Cursed to bear arms into the presence of an Apostle!" a Stelforma Marine officer snapped, her hand on her sword.

"This was his command," Carrasco replied. "Will you defy His Holiness?"

There was a long silence, and Coral winced in sympathy for the Stelforma Marines.

"Please, Priest-Captain," she finally intervened in the staring contest. Removing her weapons belt, which already only held her Dalesteel sword, she passed it to Brivio. "Sergeant Betje Brivio and her team will accompany me for now but not enter the Apostle-Admiral's presence. And the Sergeant will carry my arms, so that I meet with him unarmed.

"Is this sufficient for your security?"

The more she saw of *Apostle of War*, the more she was certain that *Icebreaker* could have crushed the smaller battleship *without* her adamantine armor, matched main guns or not. Even if the decoration was wood and plaster, it still had weight—and given the ship's shorter length, she had to have paid for the decoration and her three turrets either with engine power, armor or *both*.

Captain Nevin could sail circles around the Stelforma ship while being basically immune to *Apostle*'s fire, even at this range. If this "Apostle-Admiral Luke" tried something stupid, the worst he could do was kill Coral. Her people would still be able to complete the mission and get the key to Hibernia.

She was surprised by how much that reassured her. Coral attached a great deal of value to her own life, but having read Findlay's final entries...she recognized that there were callings beyond that.

She was going to save the damn planet. If that required giving up her life, she'd do it. She'd fight a bit harder for her pride, she'd admit that to herself at least, but that was why *she* was offering to give up her weapon.

That way, no one had forced her to.

~

As aboard *Dancer*, the Stelforma blue-and-green-orb-on-golden-sun symbol was everywhere aboard *Apostle of War*. The battleship's armored citadel was carpeted with a thick fabric that was already showing why that was a terrible idea, as grease and boots stained and wore it to pieces.

Coral was escorted to what would have been her flag mess aboard *Icebreaker*. Like *Dancer*, the mess was far more thoroughly decorated than any Republic warship. It put even *Dancer* to shame, with more of the thick carpet, rich wood paneling and heavy curtains with the Stelforma world-on-sun.

The curtains were pulled back to reveal portholes with open armor shutters. Through them Coral could glimpse her own ship—and the main occupant of the room was studying *Icebreaker* through the window.

Her Marines had, grudgingly, waited outside the door to honor Coral's promise, but she and the shaven-headed officer at the window weren't alone. Half a dozen senior priests in full black-and-jeweled-green vestments were arrayed along one wall, and a matching array of senior officers—some of them *also* priests—lined the wall opposite them.

The tables, which Coral suspected shared the same inlaid Stelforma symbol as the single table in *Dancer*'s receiving mess, were covered in charts and papers. She realized, after a moment, that vertical glass panels like those in her flag bridge had been tucked behind the curtains to conceal them from her view.

Apparently, the Apostle-Admiral used this space as his flag bridge—but, being an Apostle of the Chosen, anywhere he went was also automatically a clerical space.

"Apostle-Admiral, may I present Rear Admiral Coral Amherst of the Republic of Dales Navy," Carrasco introduced her, standing a good four meters back from the man at the porthole.

The Admiral turned and Coral met his gaze across the room. The Apostle-Admiral wasn't a big man in any sense, but something in his presence filled the room. He wore the same cassock uniform as Carrasco, but his was pure, shining white.

In stark contrast to the uniform, its wearer was darker-skinned than most people Coral had known, with a sheer slope to his face that was unusual in the Republic. It might have been more common in the Stelforma, but Coral had met very few Stelforma.

"Admiral Amherst," he greeted her, his voice a soft baritone. "Welcome aboard *Apostle of War*."

He smiled.

"I am Luke Chang and I have the privilege of *being* our Apostle of War," he noted. "I am the Apostle-Admiral of the Stelforma Chosen, the blade our Mother commanded to finally bring the Dales to their knees."

There was a depth to his eyes and his gaze that Coral almost fell into before she steeled her will. This was a dangerous, *dangerous* man.

"I request an audience, Apostle-Admiral Luke Chang, for the fate of all Albion," Coral told him, letting formality carry her words.

He cocked his head at her.

"So I presumed," he told her. "You have risked much to stand here, Admiral. There are those who would strike down any Cursed who dared approach an Apostle. Even now, it is only my command and my will that keep my Guardians from killing you where you stand."

There were no armed guards visible in the room. Coral was not so foolish as to assume that meant the Apostle-Admiral was unprotected.

"Beyond that, you have brought the most powerful warship in the Dales Navy within my reach," he noted. "My people could storm your vessel at any moment, claiming her for the Chosen and tipping the balance in the battle to come."

"That would be awkward," Coral told him brightly. "I'm not sure I have enough people to crew both of our ships."

There was a moment of utterly shocked silence as the Stelforma officers in the room realized just what she'd said, and she held Chang's gaze through its entirety.

She wasn't exaggerating or bluffing. Not only were *Icebreaker*'s crew Dalebloods one and all, there were also almost two hundred

Daleblood Marines aboard the battleship. Any attempt by the Stelforma to storm *Icebreaker* would almost certainly result in *Apostle of War* changing ownership.

"The strength of your conviction and your faith in your people are impressive," Chang finally told her. He seemed somewhere between amused and pleased, despite the shock clearly showing on the faces of his subordinates.

"So, tell me, Admiral, what calls for all of these risks?"

"I suspect you know some of it," she noted. "Your ships, after all, intercepted mine south of the Northern Doctrine Line."

"We did," he confirmed. "Because we knew your mission was to violate one of the Great Necropolises, and the dead, Admiral Amherst, should be able to rest without being poked and prodded. But Admiral Martins and Keeper Hayden are dead. Our attempt to preserve the sanctity of the Great Necropolises ended in tragedy."

"Did it ever occur to you that there was a reason we were seeking the City of Spires?" Coral demanded. "Or did you just assume you knew better?"

"The Republic wallows in its ignorance of the truths of our world," Chang told her. "You do not know enough to know what is wise, to know what is reason."

"'The truths of our world,'" Coral echoed. "I suppose those are why I am here, Apostle-Admiral. Tell me, does the name Alistair Findlay mean anything to you? How about Maria Keely?"

The change in tone in the room was instant, and a divide among the Apostle's followers became clear. Two of the senior priests clearly recognized the names and were staring at her in undisguisable horror. The rest of the room, though, was simply picking up Apostle-Admiral Chang's surprise and shock.

"I see," he finally said. For the first time since they'd started speaking, he stepped away from the window, surveying his officers and priests like he hadn't noticed any of them except Carrasco before.

"Leave us," he ordered. There was no give in his tone. No flexibility or uncertainty.

"My lord—" one of the senior priests began to object.

"*Leave us.*"

It took a minute, but then Coral was alone with the man tasked to conquer her nation.

"Sit, Admiral," he instructed, gesturing to a table as he swept the charts up in his arms and dumped them haphazardly on a different table.

He took a seat opposite her and leaned on his hands.

"Those are names to conjure with, I suppose," he admitted softly. "Maria Keely's name is known only to students of the Seventh Mystery. The Chosen Mothers do not use the names of their birth, so the name of the *first* Chosen Mother is kept among the Mysteries. Alistair Findlay, though... That is a name very few living beings will have heard."

"He was the commanding officer of the Caledon military base and the northern terraformer," Coral murmured. "Not necessarily concepts I understand, no, but I know who he was."

"That is fascinating, Admiral. I suspect, then, that you did in fact reach the Great Necropolis at the City of Spires? And you found some names within it?"

"I found Commodore Findlay's journal, Apostle-Admiral, of the fate of Caledon and the damnation of our entire world," Coral told him. "I know why our world is dying and I know how to fix it."

She watched his face and smiled thinly at his lack of surprise at the descriptor of their world as *dying*.

"And you are not surprised to learn that we are all doomed," she murmured. "Which, combined with what I know of the *north* of Albion..."

The pieces fell into place, and she realized that *this* war, at least, had never been about religion.

"Your southern islands are becoming uninhabitably hot, aren't they?" she asked. "Our southern polar regions have been super-heated to provide a counter to the chill in the north?"

"You are an extraordinary woman, Admiral Amherst," the Apostle-Admiral told her, his gaze unfathomable as he regarded her steadily. "You guess, from *fragments*, secrets that the Chosen have concealed for centuries. To answer your question, I would have to break my most sacred oaths as an initiate of the Final Mysteries. And yet, I am tempted."

"Is the Final Mystery that Stellar Terraforming was a business venture, never a religion?" Coral asked flatly.

There was a very long silence, then Luke Chang rose from his seat and pulled a bottle and two cups from a sideboard. Without asking, he poured them both a solid shot of a black liquor, then swallowed his own before answering.

"No," he said. "'Stellar Terraforming,' in fact, isn't a name I know. Yet what you say fits in the gaps in the Mysteries. I have no doubts about the mission that the First Mother left us, Admiral. In the Teachings and the Mysteries, we find the structures of our societies and our future.

"They were created to preserve knowledge and allow us to rebuild from very little. They warn us about your people, the Cursed, and that this whole world had been built as your prison until you broke it."

That was...an accurate, if slanted, description of what Coral understood the history of Albion to be.

"Admiral Chang," she said softly. "I need to know what happened to Hibernia. I know what happened to Caledon. I know what happened to the City of Spires. I may not understand all of the details, but I know how our world broke.

"Alistair Findlay left behind a key that could save us all. But to use it, I must reach Hibernia and commune with the Mind there. I need to know why your people fled."

He slid a cup over to her and poured himself a third measure. Coral hesitated for a moment, then took a sip. The black liquid had to be at least fifty percent alcohol, and it burned sickly sweet down her throat.

"You ask me to betray the Mysteries," he told her, staring down into his cup as she coughed. "The Final Mysteries, in fact, the ones not even shared with all of the Apostles. And yet..."

"I have no desire to lead you into apostasy or broken oaths, Admiral," Coral told him. "I want to do two things. First, I want to fix our world. Secondly, I'd love to stop our people killing each other—and if I fix our world, I think that's a damn good step in that direction.

"I need your help," she admitted. "I need to know what's waiting for me in Hibernia. I could *use* permission to go there, from the highest levels of the Stelforma. I'd *love* a commitment to a cease-fire while I sort out the mess our ancestors left us."

"The purpose of the Teachings and the Mysteries is to guide us in restoring humanity to paradise," Chang finally said. "I think you, Coral Amherst, more than any other I have ever met, understand that purpose."

"I will do whatever it takes to fulfill Alistair Findlay's last command," she told him. "A dead man left the tools to save the world and a book telling us how to use them. I will neither dishonor that sacrifice nor condemn any of our people."

"I think, Coral Amherst, that you may better serve the true cause of the Apostles than many who have worn the white."

"Will you answer my questions, then?" she asked.

"I am sworn to preserve the Mysteries," Chang told her. "But before I was sworn to preserve them, I was sworn to serve my people."

He looked up from the cup and met her gaze, deep brown eyes seeming to stare into her very soul.

"Ask, and I will answer as best as I can."

CHAPTER 44

"I ALREADY ASKED," Coral said, but there was no bite to the complaint as she took another sip of the fiery black liquor. "Why did the Stelforma leave Hibernia?"

"We did not choose to," he told her. "I don't know all of the details. I know there were no ships of a size sufficient to endure the storms already sweeping the southern seas. But the First Mother and her people had greats birds of burden they had used for a thousand tasks, large enough to carry tens of thousands of people north.

"But only people. All of the magics and engineering of Hibernia were left behind. A single chest of arcana was brought, to allow us to wield a small number of the High Magics, but our ancestors worked those birds of burden to death.

"And as each bird died, the survivors had to do more work. Our ancestors could risk bringing less and less with them, the last groups arriving with the clothing on their backs and not a single possession."

That sounded more voluntary that Coral had generally seen it depicted in paintings of the Abduction of the Chosen, but it also aligned with Findlay's description of the evacuation of Caledon. She didn't know what the "aircraft" Findlay referred to in his journal were, but she suspected that they were the "birds of burden" of the Stelforma story.

"But why did they leave?" she repeated.

"We were driven from Hibernia by the spirit of the place," Chang told her. "Sent into the north as the power of our paradise was turned to a greater task—and warned that we could never return, on pain of death by fire."

He shook his head.

"We know, roughly, where Hibernia is, Coral Amherst," he said. "And we are merely human. The commandment not to return has been breached at least once a generation for the two hundred and eighty years of the Stelforma's existence."

It made sense, she supposed, that the Stelforma had fled Hibernia closer to the Seabloods abandoning Caledon than the Seabloods fleeing the City of Spires.

And the kind of desperate evacuation he described explained much of why the Stelforma seemed to know little more of Albion's true history than the Republic did.

"And what happened to those who tried to find Hibernia?" Coral asked.

"They died, Admiral. A few turned back, their ships driven before storms of heat and hellfire. Others saw empty ships wash up on shores far from their origins. Others were never seen again.

"You may wish to reach Hibernia, Coral Amherst, but our sacred oaths say no one may pass—and our own fools have well proven that the spirit of that place will turn her power against any who try to reach it.

"It is within *my* power, perhaps, to grant you safe passage through the Isles to the south pole," he conceded, "but no mortal hands can bear a ship to our ancient home. Your quest is brave, your drive admirable, your desire for peace and salvation beyond laudable.

"But your mission cannot succeed."

Like her own flag mess, there was a map of Albion painted on the wall of Chang's working space. It was probably more accurate in the south than hers—and hers had likely been more accurate in the north, even before they'd pinned the CUNE's original map up next to it.

"Do you know, Apostle-Admiral, what bars the way to the City of Spires?" Coral asked softly.

He shook his head.

"Captain Carrasco does. She was trapped in what my people call the hellfrost storms," she told him. "Storms that are so cold, they flash-freeze the ocean around ships. Where unprotected crew are killed in moments and the thermometers themselves freeze rather than give you a temperature.

"We sailed into that to reach the City of Spires. We breached a thousand kilometers of ice, climbed mountains carved by the fire of ancient failures and entered a tower barred by ancient magics. I have walked into the hell of ice and frost and death, Apostle-Admiral Luke Chang.

"My crew are Dalebloods. Armed with the best of the magics and knowledge of our Seablood cousins, we can live where they would die. We can sail where they cannot. And we can go where *your* people cannot.

"No Stelforma can complete the task before me, I see that," she told him. "No Seabloods could either. Only a crew of the Daleblood —only the very Cursed you have sought to subjugate—can save you.

"Only the power of the prisoners this world was transformed to hold can free us all."

The room was silent for a very long time, Chang studying her in silence as she returned his regard. Coral *knew* she was right. Only her crew could make the journey to the southern pole—and it was fitting, too.

Their ship had gone to the northern extremes of their world to find the answer. It was only right that the same ship and the same crew go the southern extremes to finish the task.

"You ask the impossible," he finally told her. "To allow a ship of the Cursed through all of our waters, to seek our holiest of holies."

"Which is more unacceptable, Chang?" Coral demanded. "To risk our passage...or to risk the death of our entire world to fire and ice? My mission is to save your people as much as my own. We *must* work together, as one humanity if not one nation or one faith, or our world will die and all of our people with it."

The silence hung around the room like a wet blanket as she met the gaze of the Stelforma's most powerful military commander. She could make the journey without his permission or his help, but it would be easier to escape her current position with his aid.

And if she made the journey south against the will of the Stelforma, *Icebreaker* would see a lot of fighting before they ever reached Hibernia—and Coral did not expect reaching the Mind itself to be easy once she made it there.

"I am the Apostle of War," Chang told her, his voice very quiet. "All Apostles are equal, but some are more equal than others. I am the right hand and the raised blade of the Chosen Mother, the servant she trusts above all others.

"If anyone must break with all we have believed to honor the oaths we swore, it can only be me."

She waited. She'd won, she could tell that, but a man like Chang would have terms. She doubted they'd be anything she couldn't accept, but they would exist.

"You will bear my personal pennant as you sail through our waters, marking you as traveling under the authority and protection of the Apostle of War," he told her. "No one *should* dare to bar your way, but I suggest you avoid our islands if you can.

"Also"—he held up a hand—"you will carry a contingent of Keepers with you. I will have to discuss, but I believe that among the High Magics we carry aboard *Apostle* herself is one that should shield them from the heat of the south.

"It could not shield a ship, but it should be able to shield a few rooms. They will bring other Magics, as they judge fit, to aid in the mission. As you say, it is by acting *together* that we will save ourselves."

"And the war, Apostle-Admiral Luke?" Coral asked.

"I assume that Admiral Moreno is somewhere along my course between here and the Dales, with the majority of your capital-ship strength," Change said drily. "I will send a cruiser ahead under blue flares and offer a one-month cease-fire to permit the completion of your mission.

"Both of us, I think, are rushing to conflict from fear of the other —and fear of the creeping death of our world to the north and south. Let us breathe and see if you can undo the fate that binds us all."

He smirked.

"Assuming, of course, that Admiral Moreno is amenable to laying aside our blades for a time. Peace, after all, requires two parties."

"I believe the Admiral will be agreeable," Coral said. "I thank you, Apostle-Admiral. I will not fail in the task I have taken up."

"No, I don't believe you will, Admiral Amherst," he said softly. "I know you don't share our faith, but I look at you and I understand, truly, what it is meant to be Chosen. *You*, Coral Amherst, were Chosen to save us all.

"The weight of all our ancestors rests on your shoulders. I will clear the way for you as best as I can, but I must remind you: no ship has entered the polar zone and lived in over two hundred and fifty years. If you fail, if *Icebreaker* shares the fates of those who went before you, I will have no choice but to complete the task laid before me by my Chosen Mother and do all within my power to subjugate the Dales."

"And the Republic will stop you," she told him. "A bunch of people will get killed for nothing—because if I fail, I don't think we have more than another century left before our Albion kills us all."

CHAPTER 45

"Sir!"

Nevin, O'Connor and El-Ghazzawy were all waiting as Coral climbed over the edge of *Icebreaker*'s hull onto the main deck. They were clearly trying *not* to hover and ambush Coral with questions the moment she arrived.

They were failing on both counts.

"With me, the three of you," Coral ordered, walking past them briskly toward the citadel and her office. The three officers obeyed, falling in behind her as the Marines scattered back to their barracks belowdecks.

Once she was in her office, Coral poured herself a cup of chilled coffee from the urn her steward kept refreshed in these temperatures. A long swallow hopefully put enough coffee in her system to counteract whatever the *hell* the liquor the Apostle-Admiral had served her was.

"It's done," she finally told her subordinates. "We will be receiving a party of guests from *Apostle of War* shortly. They will be bringing...*things*. I'm not entirely clear on the nature of their tools, but it is a group of Keepers of the High Magic.

"I *presume* the Keepers will be coming with guards, though that wasn't mentioned. We will put them and any escorts they have up in the port staterooms. They will be restricted to those staterooms except as necessary to perform their tasks."

"They...are putting *Keepers* aboard a Republic ship?" O'Connor asked, stunned. "That's...new."

"It was the Apostle of War's requirement for his cooperation," Coral told him. "When they arrive, they will be bringing a number of flags and pennants with them that we will need to fly as visibly as possible. We will sail under the personal protection of the Apostle-Admiral."

"That...should be enough, yeah," Nevin said. "But what are we going to do with the Keepers?"

"They are apparently going to bring some magic with them to protect them against the heat as we go south," Coral said. "And other magics to help with our mission when we reach Hibernia."

"The heat," El-Ghazzawy murmured, then audibly swallowed a curse. "An opposite created to maintain balance. Hibernia is as hot as the north is cold, to maintain some area in between that is habitable for humans."

"Exactly," Coral agreed. "And their southern islands are becoming uninhabitable as quickly as our northern shores. That's what this war is about, not their demands for our capitulation and conversion. They need somewhere to evacuate their people who can no longer live where they are."

"The habitable zone is shrinking fast," O'Connor said. "We're running out of time."

"We may, in all honesty, *have* run out of time," Coral admitted. "That doesn't leave this room, people. But I don't know enough about the magic of these 'orbital terraformers' to know whether they can undo the damage already done. It is possible we have found Findlay's key too late.

"We cannot act on that fear, however. We must complete the mission we have set ourselves."

"So, what did you learn about Hibernia?" O'Connor asked. "The heat, I'm guessing, will be a problem?"

"It's more than that," Coral told them. "According to the stories they passed down, the Mind of Hibernia sent them away, warning that it would burn their paradise to preserve the world and that any attempt to return would result in their deaths.

"And people have tried," she warned grimly. "None have returned. Walls of heat and even fire upon the seas have been reported from those who have turned back. Ships, empty of all crew, have drifted ashore years later.

"I believe that Dalebloods can pass where Stelforma could not. But more than that, I believe that we must deliver the key to Hibernia."

O'Connor took the silk-wrapped box from inside his jacket and put it on her desk.

"Speaking of."

"Thank you," she acknowledged. "Thanks to the Keepers coming aboard, El-Ghazzawy should be able to *gently* interrogate them about what they know of the southern waters. From what the Apostle-Admiral told me, they won't know the story of why their people left Hibernia, but they likely know what lies before us."

"I can't believe they're letting Keepers onto a Republic ship," El-Ghazzawy said.

"I can't believe *we're* letting Keepers onto a Republic ship," Nevin replied. "But I understand. If their magic can make a difference..."

"We have to accept their help as the price of our passage through Stelforma waters without violence," Coral said. "But I'm hoping that Stelforma High Magic may clear what paths Daleblood power cannot. It is Seablood engineering and adamantine from their ancient home that will bear us through the waters to Hibernia.

"It is Daleblood endurance that will allow us to crew *Icebreaker* and make it to the end. It is fitting, I think, that Stelforma magic makes its contribution."

"Three peoples, one humanity," O'Connor said, unknowingly echoing her words to Apostle-Admiral Luke.

"And, unless I am being even more pessimistic than I think, one chance."

CHAPTER 46

"Permission to come aboard, Captain!"

"Granted."

Coral stood on the flying bridge, watching the onboarding of the Stelforma contingent but leaving the greetings to Captain Nevin.

One by one, twelve Stelforma in colored cassocks climbed over the edge. The first, Coral recognized, was Priest-Captain Carrasco. The Apostle of War seemed to think the woman had some special in with Coral—or, perhaps, just wanted to use someone he *knew* could deal rationally with the Dalebloods.

Carrasco was the only one of the priests in the black cassock of a naval officer. Five wore the dark jeweled green of the Keepers, the priests tasked with the security and use of the Stelforma High Magic. The other six wore dark blue cassocks Coral had never actually seen in person.

They were the protectors she'd expected. Guardians of the Chosen—with a reputation to match the Dalesguard of the Republic and armed with weapons forged of the High Magic itself.

Carrasco gave Captain Nevin a crisp salute as she stepped ahead of the Stelforma party.

"I am Priest-Captain Angelica Carrasco," she introduced herself. "I have been charged to lead this delegation and join your mission, for the good of all humanity."

"Your assistance is welcome, Priest-Captain. I am Captain Ekaterina Nevin, commanding officer of the Republic of Dales Navy battleship *Icebreaker*. Your companions?"

Coral mostly tuned out the names, turning her attention to the cases the last two Guardians were now bringing up from the boat beneath. She'd known that Stelforma High Magic required equipment in ways that Daleblood magic, being entirely internal, didn't.

It was still fascinating to watch the uniform dark gray cases, each about a meter long and half that wide and tall, come up onto the ship and be neatly stacked on the deck. The four Guardians not doing the lifting had formed a seeming casual barrier between the cases and the rest of the deck.

The last two cases lifted up onto *Icebreaker* were larger than the rest. Where the first ten cases had all been identically sized, these two were each the size of a coffin. Two meters tall and a meter squared, something about them sent a shiver of concern through her blood.

Coral might not have recognized the coffin-scale boxes, but something in her Daleblood did. Something very old.

Hopefully, that meant the coffins contained something that would be useful against whatever magics guarded Hibernia. For now, though, she was looking for a more mundane tool—and so was Captain Carrasco, she realized.

"Where is the pennant box?" she asked the Guardians.

One of the two hauling boxes up shrugged.

"Not ours," he told Carrasco. "So, deal with it."

Coral found herself suddenly in need of something snackish as she focused her attention on the confrontation. While the Guardians of the Chosen didn't answer to a Priest-Captain like Carrasco normally, Carrasco had been placed in charge of the Stelforma party.

Which meant the Guardians *should* answer to her now—and if

they didn't, that would be interesting. Also potentially problematic for Coral, but she wasn't going to interfere in the dynamics of the Stelforma party.

The Priest-Captain clearly recognized the challenge to her authority for what it was, but her body language was relaxed and amused.

"As you wish," she told the Guardian. "Keeper Fischer? Please fetch the pennant box from the launch."

It was phrased as a request, but it was definitely an order.

"You can't have a Keeper do manual labor!" the Guardian objected as a blonde woman in a green cassock—the closest Keeper —started toward the side of the ship.

"If Keeper Fischer understands the importance of our mission and obeys instructions, then I will do exactly that," Carrasco said calmly. "And your refusal to do so will be remembered as requiring just that."

The standoff continued for a few more seconds as the blonde mage stepped up to her respective protectors and bestowed them with a smile that Coral suspected would make *anyone* weak at the knees.

"Is the box ready to be transported?" Fischer asked.

"We are on it, Keeper Fischer," the Guardian said, his tone dark as he turned to call down to the boat beneath.

Coral, for her part, was taking mental notes. She was impressed—both with Priest-Captain Carrasco and with Keeper Fischer for playing along. She wasn't entirely sure that the Keeper *would* have done the physical labor herself, but Fischer had certainly been willing to give the Guardian the *impression* that she was!

YELLOW-GOLD FLAGS with crossed swords hung from both *Icebreaker*'s bow and stern masts, as well as the fighting tops and crows' nests. It was probably excessive, but Coral had let Nevin and Carrasco do what they judged was necessary.

She felt *slightly* better as she watched a Stelforma turret-cruiser sail past them, equally done up with the Apostle-Admiral's banners. Blue signal flags hung above the gold ones on the cruiser, marking her as the Apostle of War's envoy to the Republic fleet.

Coral had watched *Apostle of War* use a heliograph and semaphore flags to send instructions to the rest of the fleet, until the cruiser had pulled close enough alongside the battleship for them to set up a gangplank and transfer physical documents.

Studying the cruiser, she had a moment of realization that forced her to take a second look.

"So, *that's* what you did," she said aloud.

"Sir?" O'Connor asked. The chief of staff was also on the flying bridge, watching the deck as the Keepers and Guardians finished moving their cargo to their designated staterooms.

"I've been wondering how they packed four turrets onto ships that didn't look any bigger than our three-turret cruisers," she told him. "Take a closer look at that one."

The cruiser was two kilometers away, but that was nothing to a Daleblood's sight. At this range, Coral could see that while the Stelforma ship had one more *turret* than her Republic counterpart, she actually had two less *guns*.

"They're single-gun turrets," O'Connor finally realized. "Because they were having problems getting their turret-support mechanisms down to a size that would fit on their cruisers; we knew that."

"So, they went down to one gun rather than trying to fully minia-turize the two-gun system from the battleships," Coral concluded. "Four turrets on the centerline with one gun each, the central two elevated above like the mid-gun for our three-turret ships. Not a bad design, but it falls short against dual turrets."

"The problem, of course, is that their next design will be four dual turrets," her chief of staff pointed out.

"And on a battleship, at that," she agreed grimly. "I know we're working on quad-turret cruisers for an eight-gun salvo, but..." She shook her head. "The citadel for the wheels takes up a lot of real estate on the deck. There's been talk about putting a turret on *top* of the citadel, but that's too much topweight."

She watched the cruiser continue to sail away for a few moments, then turned to O'Connor.

"Anything stopping us from getting on our way?" she asked.

"Nevin is waiting until we've got the Keepers and their friends tucked away with all of their gear," her chief of staff told her. "I'm curious what magic they're planning on using to survive the heat. It's already forty degrees at noon, and you're saying it gets hotter as we go south."

"It will," she agreed grimly. "But they've been living on these islands for a while. They're probably more used to this heat than we are, which will help for a time."

The battleship's circulation pumps were now set to pull air from the outside into the lowest parts of the ship to chill, then send that air throughout the rest of the vessel. Given the inevitable nature of the bilges, that added a definite edge to the air inside the ship, but it brought the temperature in most of the ship's interior down to a bearable high twenties.

Except the engine rooms, of course. Coral was worried about those. Even for Daleblood crew, those spaces around *Icebreaker*'s immense combustion engines were going to be brutally hot. There were limits to the magic in their blood.

Though, to be fair, the *sea* would start boiling at around the same time her Daleblood crew started dying.

"Admiral Amherst, sir!"

Coral glanced at the entrance to the citadel to find one of the signals ratings standing waiting.

"Sailor," she greeted the boy. "What is it?"

"Message from the Bloodspeakers, sir. Admiral Moreno has requested a direct discussion."

That, she supposed, had been unavoidable.

"Have the signalers inform him I will blood up and be in contact shortly," she ordered.

~

CORAL'S OFFICE was enough cooler than the outside that she suspected that the circulation system had been set up to send extra air, warm or cold, to the flag spaces. She hadn't noticed the heat when everything had been cold, but she noticed the cooler air now.

It was at least one piece of relief as she pricked her finger and drew the runes of communication on her forehead. Focusing on the location of Moreno's fleet, she sent her voice and will winging across the waves.

"Admiral Moreno, this is Rear Admiral Amherst, as requested," she said to the air.

It took a moment before she felt the mental click of the connection forming, then the older Seablood Admiral's personal Bloodspeaker spoke before she could say a word, echoing Moreno's words.

"What, in the name of seas, skies, fires and ash, are you *doing*, Amherst?" he demanded.

"I was ordered by the Commission to complete the mission before me," Coral said mildly. Tradition required, after all, that she treat the junior officer relaying Moreno's words *as* the Admiral. The Bloodspeaker couldn't speak to her like that. Admiral Moreno *could*. "A giant war was going to get in my way, so I fixed it."

The stunned shock of the middleman carried perfectly across the tenuous voice connection, until it faded into a bitter chuckle, followed by them repeating Moreno's response.

"I see why we sent you north," the Bloodspeaker told. "What do you mean by 'fixed it,' Amherst?"

"There is a courier ship on her way to find your fleet right now," Coral advised him. "And no, I didn't tell Apostle-Admiral Chang where to find you. He'd worked out that you were going to be in his way and roughly what your strength was going to be before he and I exchanged a word."

"I'm not surprised. Chang and I have met, in several senses," Moreno said through the relay. "What message is this courier carrying?"

"He is requesting a thirty-day cease-fire to see if my mission has the impacts we hope," she explained. "He has authorized me to take *Icebreaker* all the way through Stelforma waters to the south pole, to seek Hibernia per my prior reports."

The silence was less stunned this time.

"They weren't ready for this," Moreno noted. "They're not going to mind an extra month. They'll scatter the transports to a dozen ports and make it impossible to predict their next axis of attack."

"We weren't ready for this either," Coral countered.

"Yes, but *our* shortfall is that we need another dozen *Sword-breaker*s. Those will take years to build. *They* need more time to exercise their amphibious-assault units. Thirty days may make the difference in their preparation, Admiral. There's a reason he picked that time frame."

"Maybe, sir, but I need to complete this mission. As the Commission instructed me: no higher priority."

"I find this whole affair difficult to believe, Amherst," Moreno admitted. "Myths and legends and dead men and great magics."

"Our northern shores are freezing. The Stelforma's southern islands are burning. Albion is dying, Admiral. I have seen it with my own eyes, and I have felt the chill of the hellfrost storms in my own bones. I will not quietly stand by while our world and our people die.

"And since the Stelforma are driven to sharper conflicts by the growing dangers of their southern islands, I think that solving the greater problem will solve the more immediate one."

"*No higher priority*," Moreno echoed. There was a pause, potentially a conversation between the Admiral and the Bloodspeaker the latter was instructed not to relay. "This is madness, Amherst. To risk our most powerful ship in a blind quest to fulfill a legend. And yet..."

"And yet we know our world is dying," Coral told him. "Is it not worth a great risk to defy a greater danger? Even if all we can push back is the war itself? Thirty days of peace is not nothing, Admiral. It might be enough to lay the groundwork for more, even if I fail."

"I know Luke Chang," Moreno's relay repeated, sounding a bit thrown by their Admiral's words. "I have fought him at sea, I have dueled him on land, I have danced with him, and I have *bedded* him. If you convinced him to buy into this enough to offer a cease-fire, I have to see that as a weight on the scales.

"And you are right. A month is not nothing. I will stay my hand and wait. Short of sending a line of cruisers trailing after you, there is no way we can maintain communications."

"I think that a Bloodspeech relay would be imposing far more on the Apostle-Admiral's goodwill than we can afford," Coral admitted. "I suspect he has effectively pledged his honor, his career, and potentially even his *life* on me being right."

"The Stelforma are not usually ones to execute lightly," Moreno noted. "But I fear you may be right. For the Apostle of War to take this risk, it must not fail. You convinced him enough to take on that risk.

"I was born in one of the northern Landings, Admiral Amherst. I have read the letters from my home. For their sake—for *all* of our sakes—if the path you have found is true...do not fail."

"I will not."

CHAPTER 47

"Well. How is our new friend doing?"

Coral's question was as much amused as anything else. The Stelforma ship, trailing them by about ten kilometers, was outside their gun range of her and *inside* her range of them. They'd clearly come close enough to see the Apostle-Admiral's flags flying and were now...confused.

But since the destroyer *might* mass a thousand tons and have half a dozen ten-centimeter guns, Coral wasn't exactly worried about her. The real concern was that the destroyer might go and get friends —and since Coral was reasonably certain Chang's fleet had all of the battleships that could actually hurt *Icebreaker*, she wasn't really concerned about that.

"She's been sitting at ten klicks for the last few hours, since she came in close enough to see the Apostle-Admiral's flags and skedaddled back," O'Connor told her. "I doubt she can stick with us much longer."

The chief of staff leaned over the chart table and studied their current position.

"We haven't left Stelforma waters yet," Coral noted. They'd spent the last week skirting around the main Stelforma islands while cutting through their territory as quickly as possible. They'd lost enough distance avoiding trouble that they still had a week left to reach Hibernia. Thirty-five hundred kilometers.

They'd come a long, *long* way in just over three weeks. But they still had a long way to go, and the destroyer tagging along behind them was worrying her.

"We're still in their waters, yes, but we're four hundred klicks from the nearest harbor that can actually fuel and supply even a destroyer," her chief of staff said. "Even giving her, say, a third again the range of our destroyers, she's only got two thousand klicks' worth of fuel aboard."

The ratio was probably the other way around. The Republic hadn't advanced their engine designs in the last two hundred years —attempts to improve the efficiency of the system had generally done the opposite—but the Stelforma had never fully managed to replicate them, either.

The southerners had stolen versions and had managed to get *close* to the efficiency of the Dales' system for their battleships, but their destroyers didn't get either of those.

"So, even if she's from the closest harbor and heading back there, she has to turn back soon," Coral murmured, nodding. "And it's not like she can tell anyone we're here *without* turning back."

"We're basically ignoring her, anyway," O'Connor said. "We're probably spending more time thinking about her than we need to."

"I dislike being followed, Colonel," Coral replied. "We're sailing under a flag of truce, so I can't do anything about it, but I don't *like* it."

"Sir! Flares from the destroyer!" the lookout shouted. "Multi-color sequence. Looks like...blue, green, yellow, orange?"

That wasn't part of the codes agreed between Stelforma and the Dales. It had to be an internal Stelforma code—and the Republic's intelligence on Stelforma ship-to-ship communication was mixed at best.

"Fascinating," Coral said, studying the destroyer for a moment and watching the same sequence repeat. It repeated again about thirty seconds later, and then she saw the ship turn to the east.

"I think I need to speak to our guests," she told O'Connor. "Because that destroyer was very determined to send us a message before she turned away."

APPROACHING THE PORT STATEROOMS, Coral felt the temperature begin to drop. Whatever magic the Keepers were using to protect themselves from now-*fifty*-degree noon temperatures was powerful enough to spill out into the areas of the battleship around them.

Two Marines stood just outside the door to the section of the ship reserved for civilian passengers—normally civil or diplomatic officials, but it worked for this purpose as well.

"How are our guests, Sergeant Brivio?" Coral asked the senior Marine.

"Calm, cooperative. Not friendly—though we mostly only see the Guardians. Keeper Fischer seems nice enough, and Captain Carrasco is...sane," Brivio reeled off swiftly. "With their air cooling, people are starting to argue *for* this posting."

"I assume Captain Nevin is being kept in the loop to make sure that doesn't become a problem?" Coral asked. "And Major Carlevaro, for that matter?"

Major Lainey Carlevaro commanded the half-battalion of Marines aboard *Icebreaker*. Coral hadn't interacted much with the woman, but the Marines were Carlevaro's responsibility.

"We're watching it, sir," the noncom confirmed. "Between the cooling from their magic and what I think are half a dozen incipient crushes on Keeper Fischer, the guard posting is probably more popular than it should be. The Guardians do their best to control that themselves, though."

Coral remembered the attractive blonde Keeper who'd played

along with Captain Carrasco to bring the Guardians in line when they'd boarded. Fischer was far too young for her—*Carrasco* was a more appropriate age for her own interests—but she could certainly see the Marines' interest in the Stelforma mage.

"Remember that she is a priestess of a religion that says we are all irredeemably damned," she reminded the Marine noncom.

"Oh, I know that. So do the other Sergeants. But young Marines, regardless of what's in their pants, tend to think with it more than they should."

Coral chuckled. "So I've heard. Been a long time since I counted as *young*, though."

Brivio, who was closer in age to the "young Marines" she was judging than to the Admiral, let that one hang unchallenged.

"I need to speak to our guests. Keep your ears peeled, just in case they do something stupid."

"Seems unlikely, but we're just on the other side of this door." The Sergeant paused. "I'd be more comfortable if one of us went with you, sir," she admitted.

"I am Daleblood, Sergeant," Coral pointed out. "I'm reasonably sure I can survive twelve Stelforma long enough to reach the damn door."

"Yes, sir." Brivio paused again, clearly considering a different argument, then shrugged and knocked on the hatch. "Admiral Amherst is coming in," she called through the metal before opening it.

One of the dark-blue-cassocked Guardians was standing on the other side of the door, doing his best imitation of a statue carved from well-oiled wood and blue steel. Like the Marines outside the door, he was visibly armed. Where the Marines had the Navy's standard bolt-action carbines, however, the Guardian was equipped with a single pistol.

It was a *big* pistol—and its lines were familiar to Coral. She didn't know the nature of the weapon the Stelforma Guardian carried, but it looked more like the sidearm Alistair Findlay had been holding when he died than any gun Coral had ever carried.

"I need to speak to Priest-Captain Carrasco," she told the silent warrior after a few seconds when the man didn't move to let her past.

The silence continued for a few seconds, and then the man grunted and stepped against the bulkhead.

"It's your ship, I guess," he told her.

Coral gave him a respectful nod and walked forward into the small mess that was attached to the staterooms. It wasn't quite up to the standard of the flag or Captain's messes, but it was definitely a step above even the regular officers' mess.

The Stelforma had added their own touches as well, mostly tablecloths with their green, blue and gold world-on-sun symbol. The room had a handful of couches and was the only gathering space in the civilian staterooms that they'd put aside for the Stelforma.

Coral was surprised to find that it was mostly empty. She'd expected the Keepers and their Guardians to be in the mess rather than their staterooms—though she understood that the six state-rooms in this section were almost as large as the mess themselves.

Fortunately, the two occupants of the room were Priest-Captain Carrasco and Keeper Fischer, both sitting at the same table and sharing a pot of tea.

Both looked up as Coral entered the mess, and Carrasco gestured for her to join them.

"Please, Admiral, sit," she said.

"I need to ask you some questions," Coral told the Priest-Captain, exchanging a nod with the blonde Keeper at the table as well. Fischer seemed inclined to let Carrasco carry this conversation, which was fine by Coral.

"I'd invite you into my office, Admiral, but I'm afraid it's in the same room as my bed and that would get me some *lectures*," Carrasco said with amusement. "The Guardians are...unenthused with this situation."

"They will learn," Fischer added. "If you need confidentiality, Admiral, I can return to the stateroom Angelica and I are sharing."

"That won't be necessary," Coral said. She chose not to interrogate the concept of Carrasco being lectured over having Coral in her bedroom. Or, for that matter, the concept of being invited into Carrasco's bedroom.

"We made contact with one of your destroyers as we were approaching the southern limits of your claimed waters," she explained. "They shadowed us for half a day, then fired off a four-flare code three times before they had to fall back to their base.

"I'm not familiar with your multi-flare codes, and I was hoping you could tell me what they were trying to communicate."

The Keeper and the Priest-Captain were probably at least *aware* of Bloodspeech as a concept, but Coral wasn't going to draw attention to the fact that the Republic Navy didn't actually use flare codes or signal flags for their own intership communications.

"Four colors?" Carrasco asked.

"Yeah. Blue, green, yellow and orange."

Up to that moment, the conversation had been calm and friendly —even cheerful. Carrasco had definitely been glad to see her—and Fischer, so far as Coral could tell, was either glad to see *everyone* or very good at projecting that.

But as soon as Coral listed off the four flare colors, every scrap of cheer vanished from Carrasco's face.

"That's a warning signal, Admiral. For dangerous weather. And we are very far south. I've never *officially* heard about anything unique down here—but remembering the hellfrost storm at Keller's Landing..."

Coral caught the woman's meaning and grimaced.

"I don't suppose the chiller of yours can be souped up?" she asked.

"No," Fischer said sadly. "It is already requiring a twice-daily ritual of refresh. We are cooling as much as we can. I have concerns about our ability to keep these rooms habitable as we get farther south, but we do have some more workings available.

"But I have nothing I could use to protect the entire ship."

"Damn," Coral conceded. "Thank you, Captain Carrasco. I think I need to go pass that warning on to Captain Nevin and see what we can do."

"Good luck, Admiral. For all of our sakes."

CHAPTER 48

CORAL DIDN'T KNOW how the destroyer had known what was coming their way, but the Stelforma ship's warning gave them just enough time to come up with a plan for if the storm was what they feared.

Barely three hours after the destroyer had fled, their lookouts saw it coming.

"Funnel cloud on the horizon! Another...multiple...*many* funnel clouds on the horizon!"

Beneath Coral's feet, she could hear the thrum of the corn-oil feed pumps. Designed as an emergency system to pump water out of the ship, no one had ever thought to use them the way the chiefs were working on at that moment.

"Watch out, sir!"

Coral half-stepped, half-jumped out of the way as a working party brought one of the big hoses they used for refueling the ship past her, unrolling it as they went.

"Tornado storm," she said to Nevin. "I wish I was more concerned about the tornados than the heat."

"Me too," the Captain agreed, watching the hoses get strung all across the main deck. "I suggest we relocate inside, sir. We're just getting in the way, and the deck is going to be very hazardous shortly, in multiple ways."

"Hopefully the right ones," Coral replied, but she nodded her agreement. She *hated* not being able to see what was going on with her own eyes, but she had no interest in slipping over the side of the ship when they *intentionally* poured water all over her decks.

The temperature was rising. It had been fifty-two degrees at noon, shortly before the destroyer had broken off, but had dropped to forty-eight before they spotted the storm.

Now it was back to fifty-two and Coral didn't like the speed of the increase.

"How's our water supply for everyone?" she asked.

"We've had the desalination plant running basically nonstop," Nevin told her. "Everyone is under orders to refill their canteens every hour and to drink the damn things dry. Rather have a quarter of the crew in the head pissing than lose a tenth to dehydration and heat stroke!"

Daleblood endurance could do a lot, but at these temperatures, regular water consumption was going to do just as much. Reminded by the Captain's words, Coral took a long swing from the canteen she was carrying.

The distillation process left the water tasting vaguely flat and flavorless—though it was at least cooler than the air around her as they reentered the battleship's citadel.

"Those tornados do worry me," Nevin said. "Our upper works should be able to take them, but avoiding them is better."

"Steer as you see fit, Captain," Coral told her subordinate. "We can dodge tornados, mostly. But if the temperature keeps rising..."

"We'll make it work, sir."

Coral nodded her agreement—but as she entered the flag bridge, she saw the thermometer on the external bulkhead.

Fifty-six degrees. The temperature had gone up by four degrees in the five minutes she'd taken to walk through the ship.

ICEBREAKER RAN WEST AHEAD of the tornado swarm, and the temperature continued to creep up. At sixty degrees, the chiefs were finally ready for the "emergency cooling system" to be activated.

The pumps had been primed and tested, triple-checked to make sure they could handle the volumes in the reverse of their usual direction. Hoses had been dug out of storage, repurposed from other tasks, and in some cases permanently damaged to serve their new purposes.

But even Dalebloods couldn't endure temperatures over sixty degrees Celsius for long. The air circulation inside the battleship's hull would keep the temperature lower than the outside for a time, but not forever.

"Pumps...on," O'Connor reported softly. "If anyone wants to see something damn stupid and spectacular, check out the window."

"If it's stupid and it works, it isn't stupid," Coral pointed out. She didn't even need to walk over to look out the window. After the first few seconds, the windows were partially blocked by an intermittent waterfall—draining from the top of the citadel, where one of the main fueling hoses was dumping a *lot* of water.

"We've sealed all the watertight hatches," her chief of staff said. "This *should* all go overboard. But it's risky."

Coral checked the interior temperature.

"And it's now forty degrees in here...and sixty-six outside," she told him. "I don't care how much our people are drinking; if it gets much hotter, we're going to start losing crew. Permanently."

"And if we overload the ship with water, we all drown."

"Nah, we just put the pumps back to their usual emergency purpose," Coral replied with a chuckle. "We'll be fine, Colonel. I wouldn't have agreed to the plan if I thought it was going to be more dangerous than the heat."

"External temperature at seventy," one of the ratings reported a moment later.

"Someone check on the lookouts," Coral ordered. "We *need* them up there, but no one should be out in this for more than five minutes."

"Captain Nevin and the chiefs are probably on that," O'Connor pointed out.

"And we are going to triple-check that, because I am not *losing* anyone because we forgot to make them come in out of the heat."

A staff noncom was promptly commissioned to back up the bridge crew on that point, and Coral turned her attention to the chart table.

They weren't losing ground versus their destination, but they weren't gaining any, either. Running due west, and the storm seemed to be *following* them.

"Again with the malevolent energy," she muttered. "I swear, these storms *hunt* us."

"Thankfully, they're slow?" O'Connor said. "Lookouts put this one at about twenty-five klicks. Though the winds that are hitting us are up to about a hundred and twenty."

"And the temperature is up to seventy-five," Coral said. "Forty-six inside. We can't take it much hotter, Colonel. Even with everything we're doing. And those winds..."

"The lookouts are being careful," he reminded her. "Everyone else is inside the hull or the citadel. No heat casualties reported yet; everyone is drinking their water and hunkering down."

"Even in the engine rooms?" she asked.

"From what Nevin said, the chiefs have basically hooked straws into canteens on the engineers' belts and told them to not *stop* drinking," her chief of staff said with a grim chuckle. "We can take this heat for a bit. I'm hoping that it doesn't get this hot *permanently* at Hibernia."

Coral grimaced.

"I'm expecting around this," she admitted. "I don't know how the Stelforma are planning on coming in with us. It's going to be hard enough for—"

The sensation of the entire ship being struck by the hand of a god cut her off, and she barely grabbed onto the chart table for balance. *Icebreaker* was twenty-five thousand tons of steel, fuel and adamantine. She shouldn't *buck*.

"Report!" she barked.

"Funnel cloud came down right on top of us," someone relayed from the bridge. "Stern fighting top is...*gone*. Three lookouts with it."

There was no saving those people. Even if they'd survived the tornado tearing the crow's nest away from the fighting top, *Icebreaker* would never find them. Coral had to hope they'd died instantly.

She could do nothing else for them.

"Captain Nevin is turning us south again," O'Connor reported. "Max power run to try and get around the flank of the storm."

Coral would have given a *lot* for the storm to include such minor things as *rain*. Instead, wind and tornados battered her flagship while the murderous heat hammered into them.

She stood at the chart table, listening to the reports as they ran along the tornado front. There was nothing she could do. Captain Nevin was in command of the ship, but even she was dependent on the lookouts and her navigators to make the right calls.

"Temperature is seventy-four degrees," O'Connor murmured after an hour of near-silence. "That's the first time I've seen it go *down*."

"Night's almost here," she replied. "That has to help."

"Wait, sir—*rain!*"

Coral managed not to run to the window to confirm the rating's report, but it was a near thing. Even through the sheet of water pouring down from their hoses, she could see it. The sky had finally broken, the funnel clouds drifting away to the east as clouds faded to black and unleashed a torrent of rain.

"I never thought I'd be *glad* to be looking at a hurricane," she said drily. "But today...today I'm glad to see any rain at all."

The rainfall and winds hammered *Icebreaker*, the water beneath the capital ship already angrier to Coral's fine-tuned senses. But even as the battleship crashed through the waves challenging her, the temperature began to plummet.

Seventy degrees.

Sixty.

Fifty.

The hoses cut out around fifty-five degrees, letting the water from the storm do the job they'd been pumping seawater to achieve.

"The decks are going to *stink*," O'Connor observed as the temperature stabilized around forty-five degrees. "Though I suppose the rain might wash the salt and whatever else got pumped up with the water away!"

"It should," Coral agreed. "And the fact that a torrential downpour and hundred-and-twenty-kilometer-an-hour winds are the *nice* weather for this trip should say everything, shouldn't it?"

This was weather *Icebreaker* and her crew could endure. It felt less actively malevolent than the heat storm they'd just endured, too. This was...ordinary weather. The heat storm, though... That had been part of what they were fighting.

That, Coral knew, had been a symptom of their world's accelerating death.

CHAPTER 49

"We have traveled farther south than any ship ever has and returned."

Priest-Captain Carrasco stood at the window of the mess the Stelforma shared. There was a chart spread out on the table behind her, and Coral was leaning on the chart—where she'd just marked their current position for their guests.

The invitation to join Carrasco and Fischer for tea had filtered up through the Marines over the course of several days. It hadn't occurred to Coral to meet with them herself, though as soon as she'd finally received the invite, she'd found herself surprisingly pleased.

Now she sipped a cold tea and tried not to pay too much attention to how the tightly tailored cassock framed the Stelforma Priest-Captain's figure.

"I wasn't sure how much information on this place is known versus concealed behind Mysteries," Coral admitted, glancing over at Keeper Fischer.

"A lot is hidden about the Southern Sea," Fischer admitted. "We do not wish to encourage people to attempt a journey that has killed everyone who tried. But for this mission, the Apostle of War made an exception to the Mysteries and gave us as much information as he possessed."

Coral nodded, realizing she *probably* should have spent more time with her guests and picked their brains.

"We are within a thousand kilometers of the landmass," she told them. "I am not entirely certain where we need to make landfall, though. That wasn't in Findlay's diaries."

"We don't know much more than you do," Carrasco warned. "I know more about the Abduction of the Chosen than I did before the Apostle-Admiral briefed us, but much of what we *do* know are the reasons why we *don't* know more.

"Very little could be transported on the birds of burden that carried our ancestors away from Hibernia before it began to burn. Few personal possessions. Barely any more documents. Like the Seabloods, we have journals and drawings of what people remember from afterward, but many of those are apparently hidden behind the Mysteries."

"The First Mother put a great deal of information and knowledge into our oral and written traditions," Fischer said. "Much of it was focused on the sacred duty of preserving our people. Very little spoke to the past before.

"There are Mysteries, I believe, that died with the first Chosen," the Keeper concluded. "But we have seen ourselves the barriers that guard the approaches to Hibernia. The hellstorm that battered us. The unrelenting heat."

It was midafternoon at that moment...and just over sixty degrees outside. Inside the Stelforma staterooms, their magic brought that down to a mid-thirties that now felt almost chilly to Coral.

"The chart you have, from the Great Necropolis in the north, shows all that any of us know," Carrasco concluded. "But I think, Keeper, that you may know more of what to read on it than myself or the Admiral."

"You may believe I know more than I do," Fischer said. She bent over the chart, tucking her hair behind her ear to keep it out of her view. "You say we are here, Admiral?"

She tapped the map.

"Within twenty or thirty klicks, at least," Coral confirmed. "The storm mucked with our reckoning a bit, and we haven't seen land since to recalibrate. The stars and compasses get us close, but our exact location is..." She spread her hands in a shrug.

The chart was a copy of the one from the City of Spires, copied line for line by El-Ghazzawy herself. Coral had full faith in the replica, though she wondered if they should instead be using the charts El-Ghazzawy had created that were a fusion of the most recent information they had for known places and the highly detailed ancient maps.

"This map doesn't really give a lot of detail on what is on the island," Fischer said. "It looks like the entire landmass is the Necropolis. Which doesn't help us find the seat of the Mind at all."

"No, but we are limited in where we can anchor a battleship," Carrasco suggested. The Stelforma officer stepped back to the table and looked over Coral's shoulder at the map.

Coral took a moment to get over the distraction of the other woman's closeness and focus on the map. Studying the edges of the landmass, she could see why Caledon in the north had possessed ships and Hibernia hadn't.

There were no good harbors there. There weren't even many *bad* harbors.

"Topography suggests that these are beaches, not cliffs," she pointed out. "We can anchor off just about anywhere, which doesn't help us find anything. And we're vulnerable to the heat storms."

"Any of us who go with you will have about twelve hours before they have to turn back," Fischer told her. "The armor can only go that long without a ritual of refresh."

Coral hadn't heard anything about *armor*, though she supposed some High Magic armor suit would help the Stelforma survive the heat. And there had been those two coffin-like boxes when the Keepers had come aboard.

"While I hope not to need you, given the Apostle-Admiral *sent* you, I'm going to try and have some of you around," Coral replied. "So, we'll want, at least at first, to be looking for somewhere within ten hours' decent hike of the shore."

"Here," Carrasco said, reaching over Coral's shoulder, her arm brushing Coral in a moment that sent a surprising spark down the Admiral's torso.

It appeared she had no grounds for complaining about the Marines crushing on Fischer after all.

Putting that thought aside, *firmly*, she followed Carrasco's finger to the point she was indicating.

"It's not much of an inlet, though the scale might be deceptive," Coral murmured. "But it's the only sheltered anchorage anywhere around the island."

"*If* the iconography on this map lines up with anything I've learned of our Mysteries, it's close to this point as well." Fischer tapped a strange symbol of interlocked and overlapping circles. "That might not be the Mind's seat, but I suspect it will have some connection there."

"And what is that?" Coral asked.

The two Stelforma exchanged a look and Carrasco chuckled. "I am bound to service the flock and guard the islands," she pointed out to the Keeper. "*I'm* not even privy to whatever Mystery that is."

Fischer sighed.

"It is the symbol of the atomic fire, the Divine energy we use to power our High Magics," she said. "And never tell the Guardians or the other Keepers I said that.

"But if this is a power source for Hibernia and is still operational, at this point it can only be feeding the Mind. It gives a starting point, if nothing else, and it looks like it might only be a few kilometers from that bay."

"We'll set our course for the bay, then," Coral agreed. "I see it as part of the deal I made with the Apostle-Admiral, Keeper, that I must know as many of your secrets and Mysteries as are needed to complete this mission—and that I will take every one of them to my grave.

"Do you understand?"

Carrasco chuckled, still *far* closer to Coral than was necessary.

"You're not going to get a better oath, Keeper Fischer," she told the other Stelforma woman. "I once risked the lives of my entire crew on this woman's word."

"And so you ask me to risk the greatest secrets of our people."

"You already have, Keeper. And you will do so again, because the Apostle Luke chose you, of all the priests he could have sent, because you understand the consequences if we fail."

There was something to that statement, and Coral gave Keeper Fischer a questioning look.

"My father was a Keeper before me," Fischer said softly. "When I was a child, we realized that the heat was creeping north. He and several other Keepers secretly acquired a ship, reinforced it with the most powerful of the High Magics that they could muster, and they took it south.

"The ship returned two years later. Washed ashore on the Isles of Morgenstern, a wreck with no living crew. A hole was carved clean through it, from front to back, like no weapon or act of nature I have ever seen."

The Keeper shook her head.

"My family understands the task before us, Admiral Amherst. We have already striven for the goal and sacrificed for it. That is why I speak for the Keepers who accompany us. Carrasco is here because you know her and she speaks the language of wave and steel.

"I am here because my family has defied the Mysteries to challenge the fate of our world, and yet shrouded by that shame, I have still risen as high as any scion of my lineage. The Apostle-Admiral knew who he was sending with you.

"I will hold you to your promise, Coral Amherst, to take these secrets to your grave. And in turn, you have my promise that I will withhold nothing that could serve the mission."

"Thank you."

Coral knew she didn't fully understand just what the Mysteries meant to the priests of the Stelforma Chosen. But she grasped, if only loosely, how much Keeper Fischer was risking.

She was about to say something else when a bolt of lightning hammered into her skull. Coral threw her hands onto the table, barely managing to absorb her convulsive lunge without injuring herself as the Blood boiled within her and a voice Spoke inside her skull.

"You are entering the Hibernia Exclusion Zone. Turn back immediately. The Exclusion Zone has been established for the safety of all humans on Albion. Turn back immediately. Autonomous defenses are active.

"There will be no further warnings. Turn back immediately."

Never in her life had Coral received Bloodspeech without performing the rituals to awaken the link. Never in her life had she heard a voice that bored through her skull with that much force.

Never in her life had anyone who was *not* of the Daleblood ever spoken to her through her blood.

CHAPTER 50

"Admiral? Amherst? *Coral?!*"

That was the first time Angelica Carrasco had ever used Coral's first name, and she retained enough consciousness to mentally note that she would have preferred *far* more pleasant circumstances.

Coral raised her hand as Carrasco gently shook her shoulder.

"I'm okay," she half-gasped. "That was...unpleasant."

"What in the names of the Chosen *happened?*" Fischer asked.

"The Mind can use Bloodspeech," Coral said grimly. "Except that it does so with a foundry's drop hammer."

Fischer very clearly understood what Bloodspeech was. Carrasco looked less certain, but both of them seemed to get the idea. Neither, clearly, had received the warning from the Mind.

"Are you all right?" Carrasco asked.

Coral chuckled as she levered herself back upright. She didn't like showing weakness in front of *family*, let alone people who were, at best, uncomfortable allies.

"I am fine," she told them. "But I need to go check on my people. That was an unpleasant experience—and one every Daleblood on the ship will have shared."

The Priest-Captain looked slightly hesitant to take Coral's word for it—but that might have been wishful thinking from the part of Coral that didn't necessary use her *brain* for its evaluations.

"Go," Fischer urged. "We'll be ready when we reach the island. Make sure your people can get us all there!"

Coral nodded to the two Stelforma women, concealing a deep breath as best as she could, and rose firmly to her feet.

She had work to do.

Sergeant Brivio was still standing watch outside the hatch to the Stelforma quarters. She was alone, though, where she'd had another Marine with her when Coral had gone inside.

"Report, Sergeant. You okay?" she asked.

"I...was at least trained in receiving Bloodspeech," the Marine said slowly. "Most of the junior Marines haven't. Corporal Satine blacked out for at least twenty seconds before I got her back on her feet and sent her on to the infirmary."

"Which is probably swamped," Coral guessed grimly.

"I'm guessing the same, but when a Marine collapses and cracks her head against the wall, I'm sending her to the damn infirmary."

"Agreed, Sergeant," Coral told the Marine. "Do you have backup coming?"

"Yes, sir. But I can handle the Guardians if they get uppity."

Coral held her peace on that. She had her suspicions about the weaponry available to the Guardians—but she'd also accepted that Fischer was *definitely* in charge of the Keepers and definitely on her side. Unless she was mistaken, for the Guardians to access anything except their sidearms would require Fischer's permission. They might not always honor *Carrasco*'s authority, but the Guardians served the Keepers.

"Hopefully, that won't be necessary," she finally said. "But keep an eye on things. I'm heading back up to the flying bridge."

"Sir...what in the frigid hell *was* that?" Brivio asked as Coral turned away.

"I believe that was the entity we are trying to find," Coral replied.

She could hear the Marine swallow hard as she headed down the corridor. They had come all this way to find the Mind Hibernia, and now they'd at least heard it speak—and in doing so, the Mind had basically flattened half of Coral's crew.

Passing through the ship, she saw repeated evidence of that. No one appeared to be down and out, but there were definitely a lot of Daleblood crew staring blankly off into space like they'd been hit on the head.

CORAL FOUND Captain Nevin on the flying bridge. The Captain was grimly holding on to the rail and staring south.

"Captain."

"Admiral," Nevin replied. "How's your head?"

"Like a god just yelled at me. You?"

"Same. And those of us with just a headache are probably the best-off third of the crew. I've ordered the ship to halt for an hour while we deal with this mess."

"How bad?" Coral asked, joining Nevin at the rail.

"Fifteen percent of the crew, give or take, are fully trained in Bloodspeech," the Captain pointed out. "That includes every command-ranked officer and a good chunk of the Chiefs and Sergeants. So far as I can tell, everyone who is Bloodspeech-trained is fine. A headache, a momentary blackout, no worse.

"Of the rest, about a fifth are in a similar state to the trained...and then the rest are various gradations of worse."

"How bad are the worst?" Coral asked flatly.

"There's a couple dozen of the crew in the infirmary who are still unconscious," Nevin said grimly. "I *think* everyone will wake up over the next couple of hours, but we have *no* records of this kind of mass high-power Bloodspeech transmission."

Coral had to wonder if they *should* have been able to handle it. If the Mind *also* had access to what they called Bloodspeech, it had to be a leftover from the time before Caledon fell. She doubted the Mind had intentionally attempted to flatten the ship, only to communicate a warning.

So, either her people now lacked the control of their magic that their ancestors would have had—or the Mind had gone so long without interacting with humans of any kind, it hadn't realized that its message would hurt the Dalebloods this badly.

"Good call on stopping the ship," she told Nevin. "We'll check on the injured, make sure everyone is fine, and we'll resume our course once we're ready."

Captain Nevin was silent for a few seconds. "No turning back, no," she finally said. "We've come too far and there's too much at stake. But...that *was* Mind Hibernia, wasn't it?"

"Most likely," Coral agreed. "I can't think of anything else that would be this far south and warning us off. Plus, it did say the *Hibernia* Exclusion Zone."

"This could get ugly, couldn't it, sir?"

"We have no idea what kind of weapons systems the Mind may command. We have to hope that the armor we took from that Seablood transport suffices to withstand its power."

The two women stared at the sea in silence, both of them pausing to drink water against the brutal heat.

"If it can talk to us by Bloodspeech, we should be able to talk to *it*, shouldn't we?" Nevin finally asked.

"Maybe," Coral said. She hadn't thought about it—she'd been a *bit* distracted—but it made sense. "Ask for volunteers in the Signals team, Captain. I have the grim suspicion that attempting to Speak to the Mind is going to be more dangerous than we can possibly anticipate."

CORAL WAS WRONG, as it turned out. She and Nevin watched the Bloodspeakers paint the runes on their foreheads and reach out to the south with every scrap of training and power.

There was a medic on hand to provide first aid, and the junior Signals crew were standing by on their typewriters while the two senior officers listened.

And...nothing. It was at least safe for her people, she supposed, but they weren't finding anything.

"We're not even getting a link. It's like there's nothing there," the Lieutenant with the runes on his forehead admitted. "Except we *know* there's something there, because it just dropped a hammer on our heads twenty minutes ago."

"It doesn't want to talk to us, then," Captain Nevin said grimly. "That's a damn shame. I was hoping we could *tell* the damn Mind we were delivering the key it needed."

"I don't even know what the Mind *is*," Coral admitted. "Only that it controls Hibernia. *Is* Hibernia, in some way. And that delivering the datakey Findlay left behind should let it fix the planet.

"I have to assume that something that can fix *Albion* is both powerful and well capable of defending itself. Being able to tell it that we're coming would be very, very useful."

"I'm sorry, sirs," the Bloodspeaker told them. "There's nothing. Whoever is sending that message either shut down their ritual completely or..."

The officer trailed off.

"Or?" Coral prodded.

"Or it can Speak...but cannot Hear," the younger man suggested. "If it only works one way for the Mind..."

"Then we'll need to get a lot closer," Coral concluded grimly. If it wouldn't listen to Bloodspeech, they'd have to find *other* ways to make it listen. "But I was expecting that."

No one in the Signals office looked overly enthused at the idea, but no one argued with her, either. They had all seen the hellfrost storms of the north and the hellstorms of the south. They had nearly died in ice, and they had nearly died in fire.

Nothing was going to stop them now.

CHAPTER 51

"LAND HO!"

The noon sun was *broiling* Coral and her crew at this point. It hadn't dropped below fifty degrees, even at night, for two days. The maximum seemed to have, thankfully, plateaued around sixty-five, but that was enough that Coral was concerned for even her Dale-blood crew.

The desalination plant tucked away near the main diesel engines was running flat-out twenty-six hours a day. The Stelforma, she'd noted, were drawing more water than they should have, but there was still enough for every member of the crew to be drinking nonstop.

And the last she'd heard, Nevin had limited the engine crew to fifteen-minute stints. Even that worried her—at least once, the temperature in the engine rooms had reached a hundred degrees Celsius and forced the crews to abandon them completely.

Land was a promising sign of the end of their journey.

"How far and what bearing?" Nevin shouted up.

"I make it twenty-five klicks dead south. Might even be the bay we're looking for, sir!"

"That would be some well-deserved good luck," Coral murmured to the Captain. "Sail your ship, Captain Nevin."

At this point, Nevin didn't even bother to acknowledge Coral's unnecessary commentary. They'd sailed into two varieties of hell together. Ekaterina Nevin knew exactly how much crap her Admiral would take—*and* that the level was far higher for any member of *Icebreaker*'s crew than anyone else now.

Icebreaker turned, a delicate dance of the two steering paddle-wheels rotating in opposing directions while the main drive wheel lifted out of the water.

"We *should* be close to the bay," Nevin told her. "The storm threw us off but not that badly. We know where we are, so if the CUNE map is correct..."

"I know, I know," Coral conceded. "But remember that map is two hundred and eighty years old *and* we got chased for half a day by a wall of tornados. Forgive my hope for good luck, Captain."

Nevin chuckled, her gaze clearly focused toward the south, hoping to see the landmass. After a moment, she shook her head. "I'm going up top," she told the flying bridge crew. "I need to see with my own eyes."

Coral could have stopped Nevin, she supposed, but given that *she* wanted to do the same thing, she couldn't bring herself to be that much of a hypocrite. She remained on the flying bridge, looking for the smudge of land along the horizon.

"Don't slip," she ordered instead, watching the battleship's Captain head for the crow's nest and the fighting tops.

Per the map, it should still take over an hour for them to reach land unless they sped up—and salving the Admiral's impatience wasn't worth the fuel and risk to the engine-room crew that maximum power would require.

"Definitely the harbor," Nevin shouted down once she'd made it to the top. The Captain was leaning out farther than she should have, with one hand on the multibarrel anti-boarding cannon to keep her balance.

"Have the helm adjust course three degrees west; that will bring us right into the bay mouth," she continued.

After everything they had seen and endured, the thought that their journey might be almost over was hard to grasp. Of course, reaching Hibernia wouldn't be the end of it, but Coral held on to the rail and watched the horizon begin to discolor as they approached.

First, it was just a shadow, a reflection of the land on the water and sky as much as anything else. Then, as they drew closer, she could finally make it out clearly from the flying bridge. For her eyes, picking out details at ten kilometers was easy enough, though not everything was *instantly* clear.

Nothing about the shoreline looked unusual at first glance. There were structures set back from the water, half-concealed behind long-dead trees, but Coral judged them to be homes of some kind.

As they drew closer, she could see taller buildings farther inland. None were quite as tall as the City of Spires, but the construction looked *very* similar—the same mix of steel, concrete and glass.

Initially, she thought the shadow that loomed up behind the buildings was a mountain. She'd been focusing on the smaller structures until El-Ghazzawy made a choking sound.

"Commander?" she asked, turning to check on the intelligence officer.

"That isn't a mountain, sir," the younger woman said softly. "Look up."

Coral did, following the lines of the shadows up to the top of the...structure. The lower portion of it had been covered in dirt at one point, lending to the illusion of its being a natural formation, but as she looked farther up its side, dirt gave way to concrete and steel.

Massive vents, of a scale that was impossible to judge, given the alienness of the structure, belched steam and smoke that billowed high into the sky. Coral had seen volcanoes in her career, but this was something else.

Volcanoes were things of the planet, a vent to Albion's inner core.

This was a thing of magic and steel and engineering and power, an artificial mountain that towered above any structure she could conceive of being built by human hands.

"What the *hell* is that?" Coral whispered.

"I think...I think that's the terraformer, sir," El-Ghazzawy told her. "From the diary, there was one at the north pole, too, at Caledon. That's what the crashing ship destroyed."

And Coral could see why it had required a massive ship at immense speed to destroy Caledon now. This wasn't a structure built by humanity. It was a mountain shaped by *gods*.

Those gods had been human. That was the legacy of their ancestors, a birthright that the falling ship had taken from them three centuries ago.

"Well, we know where we're going," Coral said. "To the mountain."

They could check out the power plant, as the Stelforma had suggested, but now that she could see the terraformer itself, she knew that was where they had to go. Even if the Mind had retreated from the outer parts of the city, it would be in the terraformer.

"I knew that we did not fully understand what our ancestors were capable of," El-Ghazzawy said quietly. "But this...this is unbelievable."

"Our ancestors apparently turned an uninhabitable ball of ice into the Albion we know," Coral pointed out. Or, at least, the Seabloods' ancestors had.

"We *knew* that. This is simply the tool they used for it." She shook her head. "You're not wrong, though. Transforming a world isn't a thing we can really wrap our minds around. But a mountain made by human artifice...*that* we can comprehend."

"Sort of," El-Ghazzawy muttered.

Coral snorted and turned her gaze to a somewhat more immediate concern. They were heading toward a bay that would have enough space for *Icebreaker*. Depending on what infrastructure and docks were present, the old harbor could make their lives a lot easier.

The bay was the first spot where she noticed structures right down to the water. There was a raised promontory around one side, providing much of the shelter the bay offered against the elements. It had been flattened for some unknown purpose, but she could see the natural lines beneath where humanity had sliced it off.

Following the headland down, she could see that there were more structures on the beach. They were odd things, squat structures uglier than most buildings she'd seen in the Necropolises.

And they were...*moving?*

A brilliant flash and a sound like stars dying tore apart Coral Amherst's world—and *Icebreaker*'s armor rang like a struck gong.

CHAPTER 52

"Turn, turn, turn! Full power to the engines! Crew the guns!"

Nevin's orders were barked with the confidence and competence of long practice. Whether they were the *right* orders for the circumstances, Coral didn't know—but they were the orders Nevin knew to give.

"Forward turret is crewed. We need a target!"

"There!" Coral snapped, pointing at the squat structure she'd spotted just before it had opened fire. They were still ten kilometers distant, but whatever it had hit *Icebreaker* with had followed a perfectly flat trajectory.

She hadn't *seen* the attack. She had an afterimage in her eyes that she took a moment before blinking away, but the flash of light had been over too quickly for her to consciously register its presence.

The second attack was the same. She barely registered it *happening*—but *Icebreaker* rang underneath them as a line of fire momentarily connected the battleship to the shore battery.

But Coral's shouted direction *had* apparently been heard, and someone had passed the bearing to the forward turret crew. They'd been outside the turret, hiding from the sunbaked oven of their duty station, but the hydraulics had been freshly tested.

A handful of seconds after the second blast struck the battleship, her own guns responded. Two hundred-kilo-plus shells hammered into the source of the enemy fire and detonated.

"*Damn* good shooting," Nevin shouted from above—and for about five whole seconds, Coral thought that was that.

Then the shore battery fired *again*, and this time, *Icebreaker*'s entire twenty-five-thousand-ton mass *lurched* under her.

"Damage report!" Nevin shouted.

"First two hit the adamantine. We've got cracking on the support frame, but the armor's intact," someone shouted back up. "Third hit the steel belt. Ammo lifts for port secondary three and four are just fucking *gone*, sir, but there was no ammo in them when it hit."

"Hit them again!"

The stern turret fired almost as Nevin was speaking, another pair of shells hammering into the shore position. Sand and concrete were blasted into the sky, and Coral left the destruction of their current attacker to Nevin and her crew.

Her fear was what else was positioned along the outer edge of the bay. She'd spotted one battery before it had fired—honestly, one *gun*, since it didn't seem like there were multiple weapons in the structure—but a second or third could easily overwhelm *Icebreaker*'s ancient, enchanted armor.

The fourth shot was aimed with some level of malevolence. Coral didn't know what was shooting at them—there certainly weren't any *people* on Hibernia, with the temperatures they were enduring— but it knew enough to identify a threat.

A line of fire connected the shore structure to the forward turret, and Coral swallowed a shocked exclamation of fear. Metal exploded away from the hit, shrapnel slicing across the main deck with lethal effect, but the turret somehow endured—and fired in chorus with the central turret a few moments later.

This time, one of the shells found *something* in the sand and concrete, and a secondary explosion lifted a building-sized storm of dust and debris. Coral held her breath for a second, waiting for a second hit that the forward turret would *not* survive, but the debris cloud settled without further fire.

Except for the stern turret putting another pair of twenty-centimeter shells into it, anyway.

"I'm turning us away," Nevin said flatly. "We can't risk taking more hits like that!"

"Get us back over the horizon and prep for long-range fire," Coral agreed. "I *think* I've picked out two more batteries, but they apparently can't shoot what they can't see.

"And *we* can."

It was a strange flaw for a magical defensive system built by ancients with access to the full near-divine magic of the original Stelforma and CUNE. Whatever had hit *Icebreaker*—and as Coral examined the crater in the side of the forward turret, she had to concede she had *no* idea what the weapon was—was very clearly line-of-sight.

"Four dead," Nevin said behind her, the Captain's voice as cold as the City of Spires. "Eleven wounded, but they'll be fine."

"And the targets we identified?" Coral asked.

"We're dropping sea anchors now, and we'll shell them from here. Lookouts in the fighting tops think they put eyes on two more that you didn't see. They might not be gun batteries; might be some poor idiot's house on the beach."

"I don't care," Coral told her flag captain. "If it's positioned to fire into the harbor, shell it to pieces."

The turrets carried the thickest armor on the ship at twenty-five centimeters of face-hardened steel. The main belt—though it had the adamantine layered on top—was only twenty. And as they'd seen when a shot had hit just beneath the port casemate guns, *that* hadn't been enough.

The twenty-five centimeters on the turrets had been. Barely. The turret was still structurally intact, but Coral wouldn't have counted on the remaining armor withstanding a normal shell from a ten- or twelve-centimeter light gun, let alone whatever hellweapons Hibernia was guarded by. It looked almost like it had been turned liquid and *flowed* downward around the impact point.

"While I know that you and I are not as worried about our hearing as a Seablood would need to be," Nevin murmured, "we should probably not be standing *right* under the guns when we start shelling the beach."

Coral chuckled and gestured for Nevin to lead the way back to the citadel.

"That's fair. Any ideas for deciding when it's safe to go in?"

"In all honesty, sir? I think we want to send people in on the launches first. Sweep the shores with Marines after the guns have pounded them for a bit. I'm *hoping* that the boats won't draw as much attention as a battleship did."

Coral's sense and tactical brain argued with her impatience...but her impatience lost. Nevin was correct.

"I won't even insist on accompanying them," she said with a sigh. "But I need to be on shore with Findlay's legacies sooner rather than later."

"I understand," the Captain agreed. "And that is part of why we're about to fire a quarter of our magazines at what I'm hoping are just beach houses."

Coral shook her head as the hatched closed behind them.

"Some of them might be beach houses," she conceded. "But some of them have more of...whatever the *fuck* that gun was."

The battleship shivered around them as all six main guns fired as one.

"Agreed. And that is why we're going to blow everything we can pick out from the crow's nests to debris and dust," Nevin told her. "Get used to the sound of the guns, Admiral. We'll be at this for a bit.

"The guns will last longer if we fire once every few minutes instead of a few rounds every minute—and I don't want to assume we've found Hibernia's last secrets!"

"I guarantee you, Captain Nevin, that you and I will never see the entirety of Hibernia's secrets," Coral said. "But I hope we can at least find enough of a breach in her defenses to talk to the Mind."

"And that the Mind can actually fix things."

Coral met her flag captain's gaze and shrugged.

"I can't allow myself to consider any other possibility, Ekaterina," she murmured. "I have to focus on pulling it off."

CHAPTER 53

SEVENTY SALVOS HAMMERED the beach before they were ready to take any chances. For four hours, the battleship shuddered every four minutes like a steady metronome as Captain Nevin's gunners carefully lined up their shots, made sure all three turrets were firing together, and worked their rain of fire and steel along the beach.

It was eighteen hundred hours and the beginning of the evening when the Marines finally lowered two of *Icebreaker*'s launches into the water and forty of the Dales' finest troopers headed toward shore.

Coral stood on the flying bridge and watched them go. She couldn't see the shore from there, and she could not, no matter how she looked at it, justify going ashore with the first landing parties.

"If there are any of those batteries left, those boats are doomed," El-Ghazzawy said grimly next to her. "We lost people *inside* the turrets, the Jimmy said."

"Hit armor hard enough, stuff comes off the other side even if you don't breach it," Coral agreed. "The launches might survive because the shot goes right through them. It will suck for the poor Marine in the path of the shot."

El-Ghazzawy stared after the boats.

"When do you plan on letting the Stelforma ashore?" she asked.

"When I go ashore," Coral replied. "I'm not sure who Fischer is going to let go on land or even how they plan on surviving this heat, but they'll go ashore with me and the party of Marines I'm not going to be able to avoid."

The lead boat passed out of sight over the horizon, and Coral caught herself holding her breath for a few seconds. Only the sound of engines broke the night. The boats' distant motors were barely audible over the sound of *Icebreaker*'s own systems.

The ship's main engines might be slowed to a minimum, but feeding the desalination plant and the pumps and the air circulators and the other systems desperately trying to keep the crew alive in sixty-degree heat required them to be running.

It didn't take long for even the sound of the boats' engines to vanish into the evening wind and the steady rumble of *Icebreaker*'s pulse.

"They're to return by nightfall," Major Carlevaro told her. Coral hadn't even realized the white-haired Marine officer had joined them on the flying bridge, and she glanced back at the woman.

Carlevaro was far younger than the impression her stark-white hair gave. Even after weeks in the brutal southern sun, she was still shockingly pale, and her eyes were equally pale in a way Coral had rarely seen.

The woman answered to Nevin, not Coral, but since she was *there...*

"Your assessment, Major?" Coral asked.

"I don't think we know a damn thing about what we're walking into, sir," Carlevaro said bluntly. "Half of my stock of Dalesteel blades are with the landing party, along with a quarter of my grenades and half my armor-piercing rockets.

"I'm *hoping* they don't fire a shot, but I've given them every advantage we can. I'd like to think nothing survived four hundred shells, but I looked at the forward turret, sir."

"We have no idea what did that," Coral conceded. "Which means we have no idea what your people are facing."

"They're to secure the bay and check for anything with line of sight on it." Carlevaro looked toward the island, like her strange eyes could pierce its secrets more than any other Daleblood's. "We might be okay."

"We just dropped a hundred tons of ammunition containing over three thousand kilos of our best explosives onto those beaches," Captain Nevin pointed out. "What could survive that?"

"*Icebreaker* just took four hits from some kind of fire lance of the gods," Coral said. "Putting that together with what Captain Fischer said, the last ship that made it this far was holed from prow to stern, Captain. We survived."

"Let's not underestimate the survivability of the original Stellar Terraforming defenses."

The flying bridge was silent as they all stared to the south, waiting for the return of their first landing parties.

THEY WERE FUNCTIONALLY *at* the south pole, which put nightfall very late. It was still twilight and shadowed when the boats returned. Gas-fed illuminators on the front of the boats and on *Icebreaker*'s port side guided them home.

Coral did a headcount instinctually as the landing craft approached the battleship, and breathed an unconcealed sigh of relief when she realized they were all there.

"Once they're aboard, I'll meet with the Sergeants of those squads in the flag mess," she decided aloud. "Captain, Major—make sure the rest of the Marines from the landing party get whatever special rations or treatment we can give them here. They took a hell of a risk."

"The Sergeants may not regard dinner with the Admiral as a reward, sir," Carlevaro warned.

"I know and I don't care," Coral replied. "I need their honest opinions on what they saw immediately, and I'm not enough of a stone-cold bitch to make them talk to me *before* they've eaten."

"I'll let them know what's coming," the Major said drily before vanishing into the citadel.

"El-Ghazzawy." Coral was looking at the island again, thoughtfully.

"Sir?"

"Check in with Keeper Fischer, please," she told the intelligence officer. "If she or Carrasco has a way to join us for this briefing, I think that would save us all some time."

"Yes, sir."

"You are also to be there."

"Yes, sir."

Coral's subordinates scattered and she gave Albion's south pole a calm smile.

"You will be saved, Hibernia," she whispered to the dark artificial mountain in the distance. "Even if you don't realize that we're your saviors, we are going to get through. We will save *everyone*."

They'd made it this far, after all.

Lieutenant Bolkvadze, the young officer responsible for Coral's flag mess, outdid himself. The line between "give the NCOs a damn good meal for taking a literally incalculable risk" and "flaunt that the Admiral eats better than the crew" was a very thin one, and he had walked it impeccably.

It probably helped that the difference in quality of food available to officers versus enlisted aboard Republic ships *wasn't* immense. The difference between line officers, bound by regulations that specified *exactly* how much more per person the officers' mess was allowed to spend versus the enlisted and Chiefs' messes, and flag messes, which had no such restrictions, was usually larger.

Coral understood the value of impressions in *every* direction. That meant that she had a freezer full of the most expensive and intricate delicacies tucked away in the back of the mess kitchen that was kept for entertaining nobility, dignitaries and other Admirals. She'd kept a similar freezer aboard *Songwriter*, for special occasions.

It also meant that she ate the same food as a Rear Admiral that she'd eaten as a Captain, which was the same food as the rest of the officers. Her food was generally eaten in greater privacy and came directly from a kitchen to wherever she was, but it was the same food as the line officers and her staff.

Bolkvadze and his stewards had mostly stuck to that concept. If the steaks were noticeably higher-quality, well, even the Chiefs' mess got steak every so often. If the greens were probably the last fresh greens on the ship, well, *Coral* hadn't had anything but blanched frozen greens herself for a week.

She wasn't actually sure where her people had found anything resembling fresh greens on a ship that hadn't dropped below forty degrees Celsius in weeks, if she was being honest, and she wasn't going to ask.

But the relative simplicity of the meal seemed to calm some of the potential nerves of the four Marine noncoms Carlevaro led into the room for dinner. Coral had also kept the numbers down, so while the noncoms were outnumbered, the *Marines* outnumbered the Navy personnel.

She had the Captain, El-Ghazzawy and O'Connor with her. The four Marine Sergeants, led by Sergeant Adrichem, she noted, had Carlevaro to provide a shield from too much officer headweight. None of the Stelforma had joined them, the heat limiting what the Keepers could safely do.

"Eat, Sergeants," Coral told them as they gingerly took their seats. "We had no idea what you were going into earlier today. Your courage and that of your Marines did not go unnoticed and will not go unrewarded."

She smiled. "Dinner is the least I can do, and it will not be the last."

The names of every Marine who'd gone ashore had already been noted down in reports and records. So long as *Icebreaker* made it home herself, every one of those forty Marines was going to find the next steps in either military or civilian life significantly smoother.

Part of that was the authority any Admiral—indeed, any Captain —had to smooth the paths of the sailors and Marines under her command. Much of it, though, was the wealth and power of the Amherst family.

Valentina would soon know their names, and the family took care of those who served their causes.

Coral managed to sustain her patience through the main course. As the plates were cleared away, one of the stewards brought out beer bottles that had clearly spent a portion of the meal in the freezer. Chilling *anything* in this heat was impressive, and several of the ship's freezers and chillers had already died on the journey.

All four Sergeants took the chilled beer bottles with almost-awed expressions, and she chuckled.

"All right, Sergeants," she told them. "Lieutenant Bolkvadze managed to find you cold beer. You've *half*-earned it already, so tell me what you saw."

Adrichem, who had at least spent time around Coral in person before, was the first to speak.

"The beach was...about what we'd expected after the shelling," he noted. "We didn't want to trust the docks we saw—they seemed most likely to be defended—so we went ashore through the rubble anyway.

"It's hard to say what was and wasn't a gun platform in the wreckage. We *think* there were at least three more, two at the mouth of the bay and two on the inner shore. Seems like an odd layout for defending against ships, but..." He shrugged.

"We surveyed the bay shore and the immediate surroundings. Nothing on the bay that was intact looked like weapons. We found a few places back from the shore a bit that appear to be gun platforms, but they can't aim low enough to engage the harbor."

"What do you mean?" El-Ghazzawy asked.

"They're built with dome housings, with clearly visible retractable gunshields," one of the other Sergeants answered. "And while we saw six, one of them was open and had the gun up. It couldn't depress below about five degrees, and the position was at least ten meters above sea level.

"If we hadn't seen that the weapons have no arc for over-the-horizon fire, I'd say that was what these were for. As it is…they can go to vertical but they can't aim at the bay."

"Like they're designed to shoot down the 'birds of burden,'" El-Ghazzawy muttered. "They didn't build the defenses to stop a seaborne attack. They built the defenses to stop someone coming from the *air*?"

The Sergeant who'd just spoken nodded slowly. Sergeant Martyna Abbasi, Coral recalled the woman's name—one of *Icebreaker*'s handful of combat engineers.

"That would fit," Abbasi agreed. "Not a scenario I would consider or plan for, but…"

"We know the Stelforma left this place carried by massive birds of some kind," Coral said grimly. "It would make sense, if those were that common, for their defenses to be predicated on that kind of threat. *And* we know that part of what doomed us was an attack from beyond the sky—which, again, would require defense against the air."

"This may be our only saving grace," Captain Nevin said softly. "Even the adamantine armor belt can't take more hits like that. If they had a proper anti-sea battery based on the gun they hit us with…" The Captain shivered.

"A little bit of bad luck, and the shot that breached the main belt would have hit twelve-centimeter ammunition going up to the secondaries in the casemate. The secondary explosion from that…"

Coral joined Nevin in the shiver. The *best*-case scenario there was that they lost one of the steering wheels. More likely, they'd have lost most of the port side of the ship and *Icebreaker* would have sunk.

"Fortunately, it sounds like we should be safe to advance into the bay now," Coral noted. "Sergeants?"

"We triple-checked the docks and everything around them," Adrichem confirmed. "There was one of the...anti-air gun batteries. But the only security position for watching the dock itself was clearly intended to have people in it. And, uh..." he coughed. "We blew up the only gun we thought might surprise us."

"And the route forward?"

"Everything on the island is dead, sir," Abbasi said bluntly. "And I don't think there's been ice here for two centuries. So, roads that might have been destroyed by plants or freezing anywhere else on Albion are perfectly intact.

"I didn't see much in terms of signage, so we have no idea what the road network looks like outside of the area around the bay, but it exists and should lead to places."

"Our main destination is hard to miss," Coral replied. They'd been planning to head to the "atomic fire" location the Stelforma had identified, but none of them had realized the terraformer itself would be quite so obvious.

"The problem is going to be finding an *entrance* into the terraformer, but, presumably, the roads will lead right to one."

"Assuming the ancients built this city on the same rules we would, that follows, sir."

That was a dangerous assumption, but Coral at least accepted that all of the ancient mystical places of the world—the "Great Necropolises," as the Stelforma called them—had at least been built by humans.

Somehow.

"Then our next steps are clear," she said, looking over to Nevin. "We *carefully* go into the bay after sunrise, keeping all guns crewed and loaded, and then I'll take a party ashore to see what we can find."

"Would now be the time to recommend *against* sending the Admiral in the shore party?" Carlevaro asked.

"You may recommend it, yes, Major," Coral told the Marine. "It won't make any difference. I am the one charged with Findlay's legacy. I, and whoever the Keepers send, will make the journey to the heart of Mind Hibernia and deliver the key.

"I won't go alone, I won't unarmed and I won't go blindly—but I *will* go."

"It is your decision, sir," the Major said, her tone heavy and resigned.

"It is," Coral confirmed. "And I will be entirely reasonable and practical inside that restriction, Major, but we're going ashore in the morning, and I'm going directly to that mountain pretending to be a building, and I am going to *find* the being we came here to find."

"And if you get shot to pieces by an antipersonnel version of the gun that nearly wrecked *Icebreaker*, sir?" Carlevaro said bluntly.

"Then I hope that the key and sigil survive—and I *know* that you will take up my burden," Coral replied. "Because we cannot afford to fail, people. Albion is dying. Our people will die with her if we don't turn back the clock."

Nothing in Findlay's diary made her or El-Ghazzawy think there was any help coming from humans beyond the sky. The Commodore had expected that help within decades. By the time the City of Spires had been abandoned, *something* had clearly happened to the Commonwealth of the United Nations of Earth.

Coral had no idea what...but she also knew that she only comprehended what the CUNE was in the vaguest of details!

CHAPTER 54

THE NEXT MORNING, as *Icebreaker* slowly made her way up to the ancient concrete dock, Coral found out how the Stelforma were planning on joining her on shore.

She was standing on the battleship's deck, watching the crew—mostly stripped to the absolute minimum of clothing in the heat—guide the warship close to a dock that had never been meant for a ship of her draft and length, when she heard a sound that could *maybe* be described as footsteps.

Maybe.

Turning to see what the noise was, she saw a pair of what she honestly thought were statues for a moment walk out of the citadel onto the main deck. The two Stelforma—it had to be them, though she wasn't sure which ones—were covered from head to toe in a smooth armored shell that looked to be made of some kind of melted stone.

From the sound of their steps, it had to weigh at least two hundred kilos on top of the Stelforma inside, but they moved with surprising grace as they crossed to where the crew were preparing to lower a gangplank. If the occupants of the suits noticed the consternation they caused amongst the Dalebloods, they genteelly ignored it.

For her part, Coral walked over to join them.

"We're waiting on the gangplank before the first party goes ashore," she told the two Stelforma. "Two squads of Marines are going to sweep the dock, then we'll be heading toward the mountain with a platoon in escort."

She eyed the mobile statues.

"I honestly thought the Sacred Arms of Power were a myth," she said. "I'd seen drawings, but…"

"They may as well be," Keeper Fischer's voice emanated from one of the statues.

"That is not for the outsider to know," the other Stelforma barked, to which Fischer chuckled.

"Either this is going to work, Guardian Koff, and we'll be heading into an age where the secrets of Keepers and Guardians will need to be shared far and wide, or we'll all be dead anyway," she told her subordinate. "And it hardly hurts for the Admiral to know that these are among the last Sacred Arms of Power left."

Coral inspected the suits and nodded. There were no tooling lines. Few visible lines at all, in fact, though the suits moved easily with their wearers. Parts of the smooth stonelike exterior flexed almost like skin to allow rotation and bending.

"They're impressive," she said. "I'm guessing they're the cause of the twelve-hour limit you mentioned?"

"Indeed. After twelve hours of use, they must rest in their sarcophagi, where they are refreshed by the atomic fire," Fischer told her. "We can push a bit, if needed, but given that we are running their climate canticles at maximum, I would prefer not to risk it."

"While I imagine the terraformer is farther than it looks, I can hope that it's less than six hours' hike away," Coral replied with a chuckle, glancing out toward the looming artificial mountain. As if to drive home its size and power, a plume of steam that had to be wider than the bay at its base blasted up into the sky from one of the side vents.

"It should be," Koff growled. "Certainly for the Sacred Arms, if not for merely human feet."

"I suspect Daleblood feet might surprise you," Coral told the Guardian. "We shall see if you can keep up."

The ramp finally connected to the pier, and the last anchors slid into place with a soft cheer from the crew.

"Marines first," Coral reminded the Stelforma, gesturing for Carlevaro's people to lead the way.

For their part, Adrichem clearly was making sure his people had full canteens as a final check before they went ashore. Twenty Marines would need to carry a lot of water in this heat.

Hopefully, they still had *some* ammunition for their carbines!

As Coral's own landing party assembled around her, she realized she didn't need to worry about bullets. The Marines had clearly stripped their gear down to the minimum, added a *layer* of linked canteens between the base harness and their packs, and *then* slung on ammunition and portable armor-piercing rockets.

"How many of the rockets do we have?" she asked Brivio, whose squad had clearly been attached directly to her.

"One per Marine," she replied. "And yes, for a platoon-strength deployment, that's half of the damn things aboard *Icebreaker*. But the Major has the sneaking suspicion that, well..."

Brivio covertly gestured at the two Stelforma in their Sacred Arms.

"She figures that anything we run into on the island is either going to be a fort like the gun batteries or look like that. Apparently, she has some family stories of metal warriors that she's worried about."

"Prepare for the worst we can imagine," Coral said quietly.

"Because we probably can't imagine what this place what built to defend against."

"Yeah. You don't go first, sir," the Sergeant told her bluntly. "The Stelforma are welcome to. Those suits will take a lot more shooting them my people."

"I'll let them know that they can be our walking shields," Coral said with a chuckle. "Are we ready?"

"You've got your Dalesteel blade?" Brivio asked.

"I don't leave the ship without it in *normal* times," Coral replied. "El-Ghazzawy?"

The intelligence officer was wearing much the same harness as the Marines, though where the Marines had packed rockets, *she'd* packed a camera and a stack of notebooks.

Coral supposed the terraformer, at least, would hold still long enough for photographs.

"Sir!"

"Are you armed in that, uh, *array*?" Coral asked, gesturing at the harness the Commander wore. "And how much water do you have?"

El-Ghazzawy shrugged.

"I have my sidearm and one of the Marines' Dalesteel blades," she confirmed. "And Sergeant Brivio may know more about how much water I have than I do. She made sure I was kitted out."

"The Commander is very good at her job," Sergeant Brivio said carefully. "*I* am very good at mine. Everyone is as ready for a day-long hike in an oven as it's possible for us to be."

The Marine paused thoughtfully and looked over at the two mobile statues of their Stelforma companions.

"Well, I have no idea how ready the Stelforma are," Brivio admitted. "But given that my understanding is that those suits can take *more than one* of our armor-piercing rockets to take down, I'm assuming they're ready."

CHAPTER 55

WHILE THE OVERALL layout of Hibernia's road network was still a mystery, it was relatively straightforward to pick out the route to the terraformer. Coral had been counting on there being a straight path there. She hadn't quite thought through the fact that the terraformer was the logical recipient of just about any cargo arriving at Hibernia.

The ancients might not have planned for most of their cargo to come in by water—the preponderance of weapons systems aimed at the sky was proof of that!—but they'd made allowances for it. A massive thoroughfare, easily thirty meters wide, led directly toward the mountain.

As they trekked along it, Coral saw several other thoroughfares of a similar scale. Each led to an elevated area that had been artificially flattened, much like the promontory that shielded the bay. Those spaces, she guessed, were where the birds of burden had landed and taken off from.

A guess swiftly confirmed when Fischer suddenly stopped, staring at one of those connecting roads, and made an incoherent choking noise.

"Keeper?" Coral demanded.

"Look at the side of the road, Admiral," Fischer half-whispered. "Time has done its work, but..."

Coral followed the pointing arm of the Sacred Arms and swallowed as she saw what the Stelforma was indicating. As she said, time had eroded away the scattered possessions, but it was still clear where the fleeing people had abandoned possessions, vehicles, even suitcases of clothing along the side of the route to the aircraft sites.

It was one thing to hear the Apostle-Admiral explain that the evacuation had worn the birds of burden down, requiring each wave to bring less and less with them. It was something else entirely to stand at one end of the road toward the evacuation site and see the trail of things precious enough to attempt to bring...but not more precious than lives.

"Your people survived," Coral told the Stelforma woman. "And when this is over, we'll reclaim what was lost. For *all* of our people. None of us were meant to lose as much as we did."

"Agreed," Fischer said firmly. "Apologies, Admiral. That was...a surprise I should have perhaps expected. I knew, after all, that the Chosen were driven from this place upon ever-weakening birds."

"But it's still a shock to see the debris of that process and know what your ancestors left behind," Coral agreed. "Come on. Let's find the Mind. Let's end this."

Despite Coral's breezy threat to try to leave the Stelforma behind, the Sacred Arms proved more than capable of keeping up with the pace that the Daleblood Marines set. Despite her own fitness and general skill with the powers of her blood, *Coral* was having some difficulty keeping up after the first hour.

But it was over twenty kilometers from the end of the bay to the base of the mountain, according to both the battleship's range finders and her own instinctual assessment of distances—a minor power of the Dalebloods.

For most of that distance, only silence and the wind greeted them. There were more signs of the evacuation as they drew closer to the mountain, including spots where large vehicles unlike anything Coral had ever seen had been moved to the side of the road and just...abandoned.

The first sign that the evacuation had been anything but voluntary came when they hit the ancient blockade fifteen kilometers in.

"Take cover," Brivio barked, suddenly pulling Coral behind one of the big transport vehicles. The thing had eight sets of four wheels and towered at least six meters tall. Whatever it was, it was hopefully proof against most weapons.

"What is it?" Coral demanded.

"There's something across the road. Well, a bunch of somethings. Take a look—but be careful! Based off the shore batteries, we can't be sure ancient defenses are dead."

Coral grimaced and nodded, carefully poking her head out and focusing her vision to see what blocked their way.

Like everything in the necropolis, wind had eroded large chunks of the barriers that had been set up across the road, but the armored vehicles remained. Eight of them formed a perfectly even line across the road, the space between them still half-filled with broken barricades—*wooden* barricades, of all things.

"Do those...do those vehicles have *turrets?*" Coral asked.

She was not unfamiliar with the concept of using diesel engines for land vehicles. The trackless train-haulers that powered the Dales' inter-city economy were about halfway between the vehicles she was eyeing and the transport she was hiding behind in size, and there were *some* smaller vehicles in the Republic.

They were generally the transport of choice for people at least as wealthy as the Amhersts and far more concerned with showing off said wealth. *These* vehicles, while smaller than the twenty-four-wheeled behemoth she was hiding behind, were very clearly war machines of some kind.

And each of them carried what resembled nothing so much as a battleship turret on a minuscule scale.

"It looks like, yeah," Brivio agreed. "I'm hoping they're dead, because I don't want to find out what the ancients thought was worth mounting twelve wheels on and sending to war!"

"Fischer, do you have eyes on the vehicles?" Coral called across to the Stelforma Keeper.

Everyone had stopped around the same time, seeking various forms of cover to protect themselves from the potential fire of the long-stopped vehicles.

"I do," the Keeper replied. "But I don't know any more about them than you do. Wait..."

Coral waited.

"Canticles of Warning just activated on the Sacred Arms," Fischer told them grimly. "At least one of those vehicles is alive."

"I'm so glad we found a way to know that from here," Sergeant Brivio said in a sick tone. "Because I was about to send a team forward to check that."

"Which leaves us, unfortunately, with the question of just what do we *do* with an operational, probably armed war machine of the ancients? Given the warning we got from the Mind...I think we have to assume it's hostile."

"WHAT's the range on those rockets you're all carrying, Sergeant?" Coral asked Brivio, running down her list of options.

Focusing on the vehicles carefully, she realized that two of the eight were...*glowing* slightly to her eyes. Could her blood let her pick out which ones were active? That would be useful and would make sense, given that her ancestors had designed their powers to fight their enemies.

"About five hundred meters," Brivio replied. "And accuracy is trash beyond two hundred, even in Daleblood hands. Hundred is better."

They were just over a kilometer from the blockade. If the vehicles were hostile, there was no way even Dalebloods were crossing eight hundred meters at a run. Even if all they had was the equivalent to the multibarrel anti-boarding cannon on *Icebreaker*, her people wouldn't survive that zone.

"Fischer, Koff," Coral called over to the two Stelforma. "Our rockets and grenades might hurt them, but we'd have to get close. Any options in those Sacred Arms worth mentioning?"

"Likely I can get close enough to engage them," Koff replied, which was probably the first time Coral had heard one of the Guardians be helpful. "But it's possible these vehicles have some weapon intended to fight the Sacred Arms."

"Koff might make it, he might not," Fischer agreed. "And I judge our weapons to have about the same effective range against those vehicles as your rockets."

"We can also go around," Coral noted. "They don't seem to have responded to us yet, and even if they're *alive*, I'm not convinced they can *move*."

Time was a concern. They'd already burned two of the hours the Sacred Arms could operate. Going around, without knowing how far they'd have to detour to avoid the vehicles' fire or if there would be other barricades...

"I'm going to *guess* that the Sacred Arms will stick out like a sore thumb to any kind of ancient war machine," Brivio said quietly. "We might be better off with a more...quiet approach."

"I'm listening, Sergeant," Coral told the other woman.

"There are enough ruins and vehicles and other trash around here that I can get close. There's a few of the vets in the platoon I think can pull it off as well. We can sneak around the side, worm our way in on our stomachs where we have to. Get to range of the rockets and wreck the things."

"That'll take longer than if I charge," Koff pointed out.

"There are two of them alive, Guardian," Coral told him. "You might get one of them. The other will rip you to pieces."

"Well, if the Guardian wants to be ready to charge in as backup if they do decide to start shooting, I'd appreciate that," Brivio replied. "But I think a couple of us need to borrow some other Marines' rockets and get to crawling, sir."

"I'd rather not lose anyone, Sergeant," Coral murmured.

"As I understand it, sir, it's take some risks or lose *everyone*. I've had to sneak through worse. I won't turn down fire support from everyone else if the things start moving, but I think I can take four Marines in with, say, three rockets each—and if those things can take half a dozen rockets apiece, we have bigger problems."

"All right, Sergeant," Coral conceded. "Everyone else, get ready to pepper the damn things with whatever we've got—to distract them, if nothing else."

CHAPTER 56

CORAL WAITED NERVOUSLY, watching as the team of five brave Marines crawled forward, laden down with rockets. She held Brivio's carbine, the flanking team having left behind their standard weapons in favor of carrying more of the anti-armor weapons.

The irony was not lost on anyone, she suspected, that the weapons had almost certainly been intended as a counter to the Sacred Arms worn by the two Stelforma about to provide a distraction.

"Halfway there," El-Ghazzawy muttered.

It had taken the Marines fifteen minutes to cross five hundred meters, but they were now inside the theoretical maximum range of the rockets. The two active vehicles continued to pulse a faint orange color to Coral's eyes, more clearly now that she was focusing on it, but neither the aura nor the vehicles themselves appeared to have moved.

There was no warning when the situation finally changed. The sky tore with the same star-breaking sound as when the batteries on the shore had fired on *Icebreaker*, and a streak of light connected the right-hand active vehicle with the lead Marine.

The woman was *obliterated*, an effect only added to by the detonation of the rockets she'd been carrying. One moment, she'd been moving up ahead of the rest of the fire team. The next moment, only a smoking crater marked where she'd been.

"Fire, fire, everyone *fire!*" one of the Sergeants who'd remained behind bellowed—suiting their actions to their words and opening up with their own carbine.

Coral joined in. Every Daleblood learned to shoot as a child, and the Blood lent its gifts readily to the process. Even at a kilometer's range with a short-barreled rifled carbine, few Dalebloods were going to miss a target several meters across.

Whatever ancient spirit was driving the war machines failed to judge the difference in threat between thirty people peppering them with solid bullets from a kilometer away and four Marines sprinting toward them with rockets.

A pair of sky-tearing booms assaulted Coral's ears, and the massive vehicle she was hiding behind *lurched* in her direction, spitting debris everywhere.

Then Guardian Koff stepped out from behind his cover. He'd unslung the long rifle he'd carried on his back for the entire journey so far, and for the first time, Coral realized the weapon was far too square and thick-barreled to be any weapon she was familiar with.

It didn't have the smooth elegance of the ancient firearm she'd seen in the CUNE base or the sidearms she'd seen the Guardians carry. This was a block of metal a hundred and twenty centimeters long with a simple horizontal grip halfway down its length and a pistol-style grip ten centimeters from its end.

Several artists had spent untold hours beautifying the weapon, but at its core, it was a just a straight block of metal, and Coral wondered just what the hell it was.

Koff ignored the explosion as one of the vehicles hit the ground near him, propping the big gun on his shoulder and aiming carefully before pulling the trigger.

Coral saw nothing initially...but she felt the power of the weapon ripple down her spine and glanced downrange to see armor *boil* off the left-hand vehicle. Whatever the Guardian's weapon was doing, it wasn't visible to the human eye, but it was visibly melting the target vehicle.

And at *that* point, whatever spirits drove the machines recognized the threat.

The sky tore again, and whatever hellshot the ancients used slammed into the Guardian. Koff was *flung* backward, even the massive weight of the Sacred Arms failing to keep him in place. A second bolt of light blazed through where he had been standing— and Coral could *see* the two turrets, now haloed in red in her vision, adjusting to target the fallen Guardian.

Except that while they'd been focusing on Guardian Koff, Sergeant Brivio and her three remaining Marines had given up on crawling and *run* forward. All four of them crossed the hundred-meter line, dropped to one knee and launched the first salvo of rockets.

Two rockets hit each vehicle, rocking them back on half-rotted wheels. One vehicle lost several centimeters of height as the wheels disintegrated under the impact—but both now were training their guns toward the Marines.

And then Koff fired again. The Guardian wasn't even fully back on his feet, barely up on one knee as he aimed the arcane cannon at the ancient vehicles. His invisible blast hit on the blast marks where the rockets had connected on the right vehicle—and punched clean through.

The halo around that vehicle flickered and faded as ancient magics and engineering alike failed—and a blast from the other vehicle blazed just above the Guardian's armored helm.

Brivio and her team had grabbed their second rockets while Koff was disabling the first war machine, and now four rockets hammered into the remaining vehicle as one. For a few long seconds, Coral thought it was *still* going to fire again...and then, mid-rotation, the turret stopped moving.

The light slowly faded around it in her vision as she exhaled a sigh of relief.

"Report," she snapped. "Keeper Fischer, check on your man. Sergeants, check on your Marines!"

THEY REGATHERED ten minutes later next to the old barricade, where Brivio was poking at one of the intact vehicles.

"They were just left here," she told Coral. "Not even locked. I'm consider—"

"No," Coral cut the woman off before she finished. "Whatever you were about to suggest, *no*. As we saw with the two partially alive ones, whatever spirits ran these things are determined to destroy anyone who comes near."

"It may be even more complicated than that," Fischer pointed out. The Keeper still looked like a statue had stepped out of a Stelforma church—but her Guardian companion very much did not.

The stonelike surface of Koff's Sacred Arms was cracked and blackened. Coral suspected, though she couldn't be sure, that it was actually *thinner* than it had been, some kind of magical movement smoothing the damage to restore as much function and protection as possible.

"What do you mean, Keeper?" Coral asked. "And how are you holding up, Guardian?"

"It is entirely possible that we're looking at two separate sets of... instructions, for the spirits, let's say," Fischer said grimly. "The autonomous exclusion protocol, the warning you all received from the Mind as we approached, is likely more limited in terms of its area. The external defenses, definitely, and likely defenses on the terraformer as well, are bound by the exclusion protocol and will fire on anyone.

"But the lesser spirits that drove vehicles like these? They are not part of the Mind or bound by its instructions," the Keeper guessed. "*They* are engaging on old threat-detection canticles and…"

She sighed.

"Our founder *hated* your people," Fischer concluded. "So, if this place was run by people who answered to Maria Keely, those spirits recognize your people, specifically, as enemies. Hence why they didn't fire on Koff until he shot at them."

"And I am fine, Admiral," the Guardian added. "Broke a rib, I think, but I've carried on through worse." He chuckled. "We'll send someone else in with you tomorrow if needed, I think, but I can make it through the rest of today."

"We're not turning back," Fischer said fiercely. "Unless your people need to, that is?"

Coral considered the situation, glancing at her own people. Two of the Marines were dead, and half a dozen were wounded. Most of the wounded could walk, enough so that she could send all of them back, but none of them could really protect themselves.

"It would…help if Guardian Koff escorted our wounded back to *Icebreaker*," she suggested. "That way, we don't need to put them at further risk but the rest of the party can continue."

And Guardian Koff, who Coral was willing to bet had broken more than *one* rib, had a good excuse to bow out for the day as well.

CHAPTER 57

No other ancient war machines or hostile spirits barred their way along the ancient road. A second blockade, farther up the road, barred their way, but it had been assembled without the armored vehicles. The debris of the blockade was easily shifted, and the party finally came face-to-face with the reality of the Hibernia terraformer four and a half hours into their mission.

It was potentially, Coral reflected, not quite as mountainous as it seemed. The tapered tower was perhaps *only* half a kilometer high and the same across the base. Versus the mountains across the Dales, it was a pale imitation of the creations of nature—but as a building crafted by human hands, it dwarfed anything else she'd ever seen.

And its doors were sealed. The road led up to an open courtyard area with three separate sets of doors. Two sets were large enough to admit a trackless train-hauler—or the transports they'd seen abandoned along the roads of the Necropolis.

Both of those were smooth-faced panels of the same material as the Sacred Arms Fischer wore. There were no mechanisms Coral could see. No handles, no controls. They were clearly doors, meant to admit the cargo haulers that had fed Hibernia's magics, but whatever engineering or magic lay behind them was beyond Coral's party.

There was thankfully one more door, a more human-scale entrance to the side of the cargo doors. As Coral moved up to examine it, though, she realized it was of much the same design as the big ones.

"How in hell do we get in?" she finally asked aloud. "Ask nicely? Hibernia, can you please let us in? We're here to help!"

If the Mind heard her, it didn't reply. Fischer and El-Ghazzawy joined Coral next to the door, the Keeper's Sacred Arms looming over the two Daleblood women.

Coral looked over at her intelligence officer and concealed a grimace. El-Ghazzawy was too dark-skinned to look *that* pale.

"Commander, drink your damn water," she snapped. "And eat an energy bar. You're making your blood work too hard to protect you in this heat. Drink!"

El-Ghazzawy started, then nodded and pulled a canteen from the collection the Marines had hung on her. She kept drinking for a good ten seconds, which was more confirmation than Coral needed that the woman hadn't been drinking enough.

Suiting her actions to her words, Coral drew one of her own canteens and drained it as she glared at the smooth door.

"Thoughts?" she finally asked her companions. "I'd prefer not to have to go back to the ship for explosives, but it might be our best option. I'm not sure even Dalesteel will get through this."

"Findlay implied that he'd left us everything we needed to get to Hibernia," El-Ghazzawy replied. "The sigil was supposed to let us in, but I don't see a way to use it."

Coral considered the door for a few more seconds, then reached into her jacket and took out the box holding the two pieces of ancient magic they'd come all this way to use. The gold medallion of Findlay's rank was cool to the touch, the metal protected from the heat around them by the box.

All things were relative, though, and she suspected it was far warmer than she currently perceived it. Holding up the sigil with the branch-flanked circles of the CUNE, she stepped closer to the door and waited to see if anything happened.

"Touch it to the door," Fischer told her.

"What?" Coral asked.

"I've never seen anything like this *door* before," the Keeper said quietly. "But I *have* seen command-access sigils before. They are used for the most sacred of the archives and vaults in the Hall of the Keepers.

"Touch the key to the door. It should awaken the spirit."

Coral had been expecting... She wasn't sure what she'd been expecting. Some kind of clear *insert sigil here* receptacle, she supposed. Following Fischer's direction, she placed Findlay's command sigil, ship side down, against the door.

For a moment, nothing happened, and she was about to at least *attempt* the Dalesteel option, then there was an awful tearing sound. Coral stepped backward, her free hand falling to the sword hilt, and then the door smoothly and silently slid sideways, revealing an opening into the heart of the mountain.

"What the *hell* was that noise?" she asked.

"Even the magic of the ancients gets...stuck," Fischer said with a chuckle. "That was probably rust or something similar breaking."

"Huh."

Darkness beckoned through the door. Whatever Mind Hibernia was, it held their answers, and it lurked somewhere within its ancient artificial mountain.

"Marines, to me," she ordered. "Lanterns and guns. Let's see what the past has waiting for us!"

STEPPING through the door brought two swift realizations: one, that even Dalebloods needed *some* light to see by—which Coral had anticipated, hence the lanterns—and two, the Hibernia terraformer might be blasting steam into the sky to help raise the global temperature, but it was also cooling its own interior.

Coming in from an outside temperature hovering in the mid-sixties, survivable only by various forms of magic, to a temperature that was probably in the high twenties felt positively *frigid*.

"Well, that's...refreshing," Sergeant Brivio said brightly, her lantern flickering around what seemed to be a small antechamber. "We also appear to be in a box, sir."

"Security checkpoint," Coral guessed aloud. "Same as we have in the Citadel back home. Let me see what the sigil can do."

Only two of the Sergeant's Marines had managed to squeeze into the unexpectedly tiny antechamber with the two officers, the noncom, and the Stelforma in her Sacred Arms.

There was, at least, enough room for Coral to find the inner door and press Findlay's sigil against it. There was no tearing sound this time. The interior door had clearly been protected from whatever had almost locked the outer door in place, and it slid open in perfect silence.

Coral knew she *should* have waited for the Marines to go in first. Or perhaps at least Fischer, whose suit could, demonstrably, withstand the arms used by the ancients. But her impatience took the lead, and she was through the door the moment it finished opening.

At which point, Hibernia demonstrated that they didn't need the lanterns. Ancient light sources came smoothly to brightness, without any of the flickering Coral was used to with oil lamps.

She stood at the entrance to a grand lobby. Sixteen meters high, with three galleries around the exterior of the higher floors.

A profusion of doors led off deeper into the mountain in every direction, and Coral felt a moment of complete overwhelm, forcing her gaze to focus on *something* specific in the immense room.

The sculpture at the heart of the room drew her gaze, and she chuckled softly as she saw the full three-dimensional version of the Stellar Terraforming logo. A two-meter-wide sun, presumably plated in gold rather than made from it, hung in an armature at the center of the lobby. Also attached to the armature was a perfect globe, exactly half green and half blue, that began to slowly orbit the sun as the ancient magics awoke again.

"The floor, sir," El-Ghazzawy said quietly. She'd apparently chosen a different point to focus on, and Coral followed her directions and swallowed.

The floor was some kind of smooth and polished stone, surprisingly clean, given the centuries of neglect. There were no breaks in it, no sign that it had ever been carved or inlaid or shaped—but at the cardinal points around the central sculpture of Stellar Terraforming's logo, the stone bore the crossed-branches-and-circles of the Commonwealth of the United Nations of Earth.

"Looks like we're where we should be," Coral murmured.

"I hope so," Fischer replied. "We've come a long way to be in the *wrong* place."

"Stellar Terraforming in the middle, Commonwealth on the floor," Coral listed off. "Even if it wasn't the only damn half-kilometer-tall tower spitting steam into the air, I'd still guess we were in the right place. Now we just need to find the Mind itself."

And at that moment, of course, it all went to hell. El-Ghazzawy and Brivio stepped into the lobby to join them, and suddenly, *new* lights—crimson ones—flashed to light on the wall and a siren tore through the air.

"Alert, alert. Facility has been compromised. Augmetic intruders on site. All defenses activated. All personnel report to secure locations. Repeat, facility has been compromised. Augmetic intruders on site."

"Well, shit," the Sergeant swore.

CHAPTER 58

FOR THE FIRST FEW MOMENTS, at least, the siren and lights were the only reaction. Coral's Marines piled into the room, forming a defensive perimeter around the officers. The problem was that if anything came through that required the armor-piercing rockets, Coral had a pretty good idea of what the explosions and rocket exhaust would do in a confined space.

Nothing attacked them after a minute or so, and Coral growled, shaking her head to consciously suppress the sound of the sirens.

"Well, this just got a lot less comfortable," she said loudly. "But we need to finish the job. Marines, watch the doors. El-Ghazzawy, Fischer...there are too many possibilities in play here. We need to find some kind of map or directions."

"The building is five hundred meters high," Fischer noted precisely. "*Most* of that has to be the machinery of its magic, so it shouldn't be *that* bad."

"Except we can't split up," Coral pointed out, already heading toward the back wall. Hopefully, there was some kind of reception desk or directory there. "We have to assume this place has defensive spirits and mechanisms as well. We'll need every hand, every gun we have to get through this place alive."

Despite the vast openness of the space, there was only a single small desk at the back of the lobby. Coral presumed that there had been more people in there than just one receptionist, but they'd been expected to stand. Or maybe the furniture for most of them had been removed during the evacuation? She wasn't sure.

What she was swiftly sure of was that the desk was empty. Completely. There were no papers, no directories, no sign that any information had ever been kept there. There was just...a chair and a plain surface.

A surface with the CUNE logo emblazoned on it and a small recession just below and to the right of the logo from the perspective of someone sitting in the chair. A recession the exact size and shape of the sigil still in Coral's hand.

"Well, here at least there's a clear *insert sigil here* sign," she muttered. "Any sign of trouble?"

"Not yet," El-Ghazzawy told her. "That may not last. Your call, sir."

"Always," Coral agreed—and slid Commander Findlay's command sigil into the receptacle on the desk.

It fit perfectly. She wasn't entirely sure what she was expecting the reaction to be, though part of her wasn't really expecting *anything*.

She was not expecting a thirty-centimeter-tall woman to appear out of nowhere, standing on top of the desk and turning to face her.

"Welcome to the Hibernia Terraformer Facility," the woman said in a bright voice. "We are currently under a lockdown and have imposed a security exclusion zone. Please report to the nearest evacuation site for immediate transport off-island."

"I need to find the Mind Hibernia," Coral told the tiny person who'd just appeared on her desk.

"Welcome to the Hibernia Terraformer Facility," the woman

repeated, in the same bright voice. "We are currently under a lockdown and have imposed a security exclusion zone. Please report to the nearest evacuation site for immediate transport off-island."

"Commodore Findlay sent me," Coral snapped at the tiny person. "I need access."

The woman flashed, and for a moment, Coral could see through her. This wasn't actually a person, she finally realized, but some sort of magical illusion.

"C. U. N. E. N. Command override recognized," she told Coral. "Standing by for instructions."

"Are you the Mind Hibernia?" Coral asked carefully.

"This unit is a non-sapient administrative secondary intelligence," the desk told her. "The lockdown prevents any network connection to Mind Hibernia."

"Can you stop the spirits from attacking my people?" Coral demanded.

"Query not understood. Autonomous defense protocols have been activated by the presence of Augmetic infiltrators."

Coral grimaced. She and whatever spirit occupied the desk clearly shared a language sufficiently to communicate—but they didn't share enough *understanding* to make it straightforward.

"Can you shut down the 'autonomous defense protocols'?" she asked, carefully echoing the alien syllables.

"This unit is a non-sapient administrative secondary intelligence," it repeated. "Such a security override would require access to the central security control systems."

"Could Mind Hibernia shut down the protocols?" Coral asked.

"Mind Hibernia is under lockdown," the desk replied. "If lockdown is lifted, Mind Hibernia would have full control of the secondary autonomous systems via the central network."

"And how do I lift the lockdown?" It appeared that she was going to have to prod the strange spirit for every piece of information needed.

"Unknown. That information is not available to this unit's databases."

Coral looked helplessly past the illusion at Keeper Fischer.

"It won't listen to me," Fischer warned. "It's locked to the sigil and you right now. But...ask it where the Mind is."

As Fischer had suggested, the spirit standing on the desk didn't respond to her speaking at all.

"Where can I connect with the Mind Hibernia?" Coral asked, carefully picking and choosing words from what the illusion had said to her.

"That data is secure."

Coral eyed the spirit for a long-suffering moment, then considered its earlier words.

"Override that security," she ordered.

"C. U. N. E. N. Command override recognized. Mind Hibernia is in full security lockdown, and all secondary access terminals have been disabled. Connection is only possible for external actors via the central quantum core on level minus twelve."

Coral didn't understand half of the *words* the spirit was using, but she could get the gist. Hibernia was protecting itself by making sure only the terraformer could talk to the Mind. To access the Mind, she had to go to its brain—which was twelve levels underground.

"How do I get to the core?"

The figure pointed.

"That door provides access to the secured elevators to the sublevels. Override will be required to reach level minus twelve. Proceed left from the elevators, and you will pass through security to the quantum core."

"Thank you," Coral told the spirit. It stared blankly back at her, then vanished when she retrieved the sigil and looked at her companions.

"That's what we needed, isn't it?" El-Ghazzawy asked.

"It was," Coral agreed. "I'm just worried about what other security measures the spirits of this place have ahead of us. It's been noisy so far, but that's it."

"We can't delay," Fischer told her. "We're too close."

"I agree. Come on. Brivio!"

THEY MOVED AS A GROUP, the Marines forming a living shield around the core trio as they crossed to the indicated door. At least *inside* the terraformer, the doors had clear handles, allowing them to be manually slid open.

Past the door, they followed an austere corridor for about ten meters—past several closed doors that Coral suppressed her curiosity about—into another, much smaller lobby.

This one had a lot fewer doors leading out and was clearly centered on two doubled doors that Coral recognized from the City of Spires. Remembering the elevators in that ruined tower, she smiled grimly.

"Who's ready to jump down an empty shaft again?" she asked.

"'Again'?" Fischer replied.

Before Coral could explain, the elevator she was approaching made a soft chiming noise and the doors slid open.

"The City of Spires didn't have power," Coral noted. "We had to climb down empty elevator shafts. Here, though..."

"Hibernia has power. That's why it's our hope," Fischer agreed. "We're only going to fit a few of us in there, especially with the Arms."

The Keeper paused. "It's cool enough," she noted after a moment. "I could—"

"No," Coral barked. "You're staying in that damn armor, Keeper Fischer, because I do not trust this place for one damned second. Brivio, you're with El-Ghazzawy, Fischer and myself. Have the rest of the Marines ready to follow."

She walked steadily into the elevator, hoping that it would be *relatively* clear how to get it to go down to level minus twelve.

The elevators *she* was used to, though, had a *wheel*. And usually an operator who knew by sound what floor they were on. This had a glass panel to the left of the door, blinking between a set of numbers and words and an image of the exterior of the mountain as Coral tried to read it.

"Um. Fischer?" she asked after a moment.

"Put the sigil to the panel," the Keeper suggested. "Then find the level number and touch it."

That sounded unlikely to work to Coral, but the Keeper did know more of these magics than she did. Coral touched Findlay's sigil to the panel and almost dropped the thing as the numbers and light resolved into a steady, calm light showing level names.

This looked more like the directory that Coral had expected to find at the front desk...but she guessed that the triangle at the top, above level twenty-five, marked some way to access levels even higher in the terraformer.

But the lowest level that the screen contained was minus twelve —labeled as *HIGH SECURITY – QUANTUM CORE*.

Hesitantly, Coral touched that label on the glass. It flashed and the doors swiftly shut—fast enough that she nearly jumped back into Sergeant Brivio's arms.

"I'm not sure we'll be able to bring others down without the sigil," Fischer warned as the elevator shivered into smooth motion. "It may be just the four of us."

"Much as I hate suggesting it, perhaps the lady in the giant suit of armor should lead the way?" Sergeant Brivio said. "That is my job, but..."

"No, Sergeant, you are entirely correct," Keeper Fischer replied. "The Sacred Arms should withstand anything this floor throws at us. If you are all comfortable hiding behind a priestess and a scholar, I shall endeavor to keep you safe."

"When the priestess and scholar is wearing the same armor that

I saw stop an ancient weapon once already today, I'm fine hiding behind her," Coral said drily. The elevator came to a halt—far too swiftly to have traversed twelve floors, but the panel *said* they were now on level minus twelve.

The moment of truth awaited.

CHAPTER 59

FISCHER LED THE WAY, the Sacred Arms allowing the Keeper to act as a mobile wall. Nothing immediately lashed out, but the moment Coral walked out into the entrance lobby of level minus twelve, she knew they were going to be in trouble.

The weapons might change, but a kill box was a kill box. The way the lobby narrowed down toward a single exit point to the south told Coral everything.

"Careful," she ordered her companions. "If there is anywhere in this place that is guarded by the spirits of that autonomous defense protocol, it's here."

She drew her sword. She wasn't sure if guns would do anything against the defenders of Mind Hibernia, but she had faith in the speed of her blood and the sharpness of the Dalesteel blade.

Both El-Ghazzawy and Brivio followed suit, spreading out slightly behind Fischer as the Arms-clad Keeper strode toward the kill box.

"Fischer!" Coral barked. "That is a trap."

"And there is no other way forward," Fischer replied. "Better triggered with the Sacred Arms than unleashed upon fragile flesh."

The Keeper didn't give Coral time to raise any counterarguments. She kept walking forward and entered the narrow zone of the security point. Coral held her breath, but nothing responded to Fischer.

"There's a door here," Fischer called back. "I think we'll need the sigil to get any deeper."

"Okay." Coral looked around. There *had* to be something there, but it hadn't responded to Fischer. "I'm coming."

"The building didn't declare an alert until someone *other* than you and Fischer entered," El-Ghazzawy reminded her. "It is watching for Augmetics—Dalebloods. Findlay's sigil marks you as authorized, but Brivio and I will *definitely* set it off.

"I suggest we stay back here and wait until you've opened the way with the sigil, if nothing else."

"We do not even *begin* to understand how the defenses of this place think," Coral said. "But...you're right in how the lobby responded."

She sighed, then nodded.

"Wait here, both of you."

Coral followed the path that Fischer had taken, her sword in her hand as she listened and watched for any sign of the spirits responding to her. But she didn't know what signs she needed to be aware of—and she reacted too late.

Either the sigil wasn't enough to clear her way—or the presence of Augmetics in the lobby *without* the sigil triggered an entirely new alert. The moment Coral stepped into the choke point leading away from the elevators, everything changed.

Two panels none of them had spotted in the walls slid open, so quietly that even the Dalebloods didn't register the sound. There was enough sound, *barely*, for Coral to hear the concealed guardians move—but it took her a second to realize what the soft whirring even *was*.

She turned back in time to see the squat machines emerge from their alcoves and fire, the sky-tearing boom of their ancient guns deafening even to Dalebloods in the confined space.

Brivio had the instincts of years as a Marine, diving to one side before the guardians fired.

Aldith El-Ghazzawy didn't. As much a historian as a naval officer and *never* a front-line fighter, the Commander never stood a chance. She might never have even been aware that the machines were there before she died—and there was no way she ever perceived her death.

The hell-cannon destroyed her entire head and neck, leaving her decapitated body to slump to the floor like a mangled puppet.

That image would stay with Coral for a long, long time—and even as she moved backward, she couldn't look away from her subordinate. Her *friend*, the woman who'd made their entire mission possible. Who'd finished Coral's father's work and found the armor that had made *Icebreaker* nigh invulnerable. Who'd read Findlay's diary and provided Coral with the second brain to be sure they were doing the right thing.

Then the ancient weapons spoke again, stone exploding behind where Coral had been a half-second earlier. She drew on the full power of the Dalebloods, leaping the full length of the elevator lobby in a single blurring bound, landing next to her dead friend as another ear-tearing boom sounded next to her ear.

She dodged back to the left, letting another round shatter stone on the other side of the room, and then she was within reach of the guardian. Dalesteel, infused with the blood and power of her people, flashed in the artificial lights, and the guardian's long-barreled weapon parted at the blow.

The machine tried to turn, likely activating some secondary weapon, but Coral didn't give it a chance. Her sword flipped up from the one-handed strike that had disabled the guardian's gun, and her other hand grabbed the base of the hilt—and she brought the century-old weapon down in a perfect two-handed strike that cleaved the ancient machine in two.

"Coral, *down!*" Fischer's voice bellowed across the underground room, her words sounding oddly slurred and slow.

Coral obeyed, sweeping her own feet from underneath her as the second guardian fired at her. It would have missed, she realized, since Brivio was wrestling with the thing—but the Sergeant's Dalesteel sword was on the floor, thrown aside by the machine as it brought out a blade of its own.

Except that it hadn't thrown aside the blade, she realized. It had disarmed Brivio—*literally*. The Sergeant's hand and most of her forearm was still attached to the sword now several meters away from her!

But the ear-shattering *crack* that filled the room after Coral hit the ground didn't come from the guardian. The machine seemed to freeze, slowly rotating toward Fischer...and then whatever munition the Keeper had fired into it detonated.

Sparks of arcing lightning covered the guardian, flinging Brivio back from it with a crackling blast, and the machine stopped.

Coral took one glance back at Fischer and realized the Keeper had one arm of the Sacred Arms fully extended and pointed at the guardian. Some iteration of the same hell-weapon the ancient machine used was clearly built into the armor the Stelforma wore—and the machine, it appeared, was as vulnerable to the damn thing as any mortal.

"Sergeant," Coral snapped, half-running to Brivio's sound. "Sergeant, talk to me."

The Marine coughed wetly, and Coral realized that while the guardian hadn't managed to shoot the Marine, the blade it had produced had done a lot more than remove her forearm. Brivio's chest was covered in blood from at least four separate stab wounds, several of which had to have pierced the woman's lungs.

"You got it?" Brivio whispered.

"The Keeper did. I got the other one," Coral said grimly as she tore into Brivio's first aid pouch. "*You*, Sergeant, need to remember that the Daleblood can only fix you if it's on the inside!"

Brivio chuckled weakly but presented her stump for Coral to roughly tourniquet.

"Admiral...she's not going to make it," Fischer said softly.

"Never assume a Daleblood is dead," Coral barked, working her way swiftly and brutally through Brivio's wounds. The Marine was silent, focusing her energy internally, but Coral had a pretty good idea how much the antiseptic bandages she was wrapping the woman's chest in would hurt.

But as she'd told Brivio, the Daleblood could only save her if it was still *inside* her. Coral had been trained in two *very* different types of first aid, and she agreed with Fischer. If Betje Brivio had been Seablood or Stelforma, she'd have been dead already.

But the Sergeant was *Daleblood*, and that meant she could survive. So long as there was enough of the magic in her blood and enough of her blood still inside her to sustain her.

"Eat this," Coral ordered, handing the wounded woman the tablets contained in the first aid pouch. Brivio grimaced and obeyed.

"What *are* those?" Fischer asked, the Keeper watching this process from several meters away.

"Amphetamines to keep her heart beating and circulating her blood, wrapped in pure sugar to keep the Daleblood itself fed," Coral replied absently as she finished tying the bandages and checked the Sergeant for more wounds.

Brivio leaned back against the wall and exhaled very, *very* carefully.

"I think I might make it, sir, but I need to sit here for a while," she told Coral. "And you and the Keeper...you need to go save the world. The Blood's staying inside, and that's all you can do.

"Go!"

Coral hesitated for a moment. One of the companions who'd gone into the City of Spires with her was gone. They'd lost half a dozen Marines traveling through the city—a dozen crew to the shore batteries.

Her roster of dead was growing faster than she'd feared, and she didn't want to add the Marine to it.

"Go," Brivio repeated. "I will be fine."

Or, at least, if she wasn't fine...there was nothing more anyone else could do for her there.

"Okay."

CHAPTER 60

COMMODORE ALISTAIR FINDLAY'S command sigil opened the door on the other side of the choke point.

Coral walked forward with her sword in hand, Keeper Fischer at her side. She was half-expecting more mechanical guardians, but all that was on the other side of the door was another door.

Each of the doors would have rivaled bank-vault seals in the Dales, but they slid softly aside as Coral pressed the command sigil to them. Five doors in total, each a good forty centimeters thick and made of the same adamantine they'd armored *Icebreaker* in, barred the way to the "quantum core."

Coral wasn't sure what she'd expected the Mind to be, but the room on the other side of those doors wasn't it. It looked like nothing so much as the file archives in the basement of the Daleheart Citadel. Rows of black boxes, each a perfect one-meter cube and separated by exactly fifty centimeters, stretched seventy-five meters into the distance.

Five parallel rows. Above them, racks made of adamantine held a second set of rows. Two hundred and fifty perfect black cubes. They were linked to each other by the adamantine racks and also by lines of crystal braiding so perfect as to be transparent.

There was no sign that this place had ever been intended for humans. There were no chairs. No desks. No sign of any mechanisms to interact with the Mind.

Then a light flickered in the middle of the room and an illusion of a tall woman dressed in an elegant but alien-seeming long dark-green dress appeared in front of them.

"Augmetics have entered the core. Initiating shutdown protocol."

"My *name* is Admiral Coral Amherst of the Republic of the Dales," Coral shouted at the being she'd come so far to find. "I bear the sigil and authority of Commodore Alistair Findlay, and I *forbid* you to do *anything* drastic, for the sake of all of the people on our poor, forsaken Albion."

There was a long, long silence. Coral knew nothing about the Mind, but she suspected that silence was longer for Hibernia than it was for her.

"I am not subject to the same unthinking overrides and command protocols as a sub-sapient processing intelligence, Admiral Amherst," the Mind told her. "But you do bear the Commodore's sigil and are accompanied by a non-Augmetic."

"What it does it hurt to hear me out, anyway?" Coral asked. "I don't know enough of what you are to hurt you, let alone stop you from committing suicide if you choose. Please."

Silence echoed through the strange chamber and Coral somehow knew she was being regarded with a thousand senses she could never name.

"You are an Augmetic. You are the enemy."

"I am half a dozen or more generations removed from anyone who even knew what the word *Augmetic* meant," Coral pointed out. "Let alone the people who fought the CUNE. I am here because our world is dying, and Commodore Findlay's last words tell me that *you* can save it."

"Even if Commodore Findlay survived the destruction of Caledon

—probably twenty-six percent, plus/minus seven—it is a zero-order probability that the Commodore survived long enough for you to have met him," the Mind told him. "Unfortunately, stabilization of Albion's climate is of a similar order of possibility.

"The limits of what can be achieved by counter-heating and the use of the limited solar reflectors under my control were crossed one-hundred-and-two-point-three standard years ago, at which point irreversible temperature decay began. Albion cannot be saved. My duty and principles require me to salvage as much time for her inhabitants as possible, but I will not risk compromise of my core intelligence.

"Leave this island. I will do what I can. I can do no more."

"Listen to me, Mind Hibernia," Coral demanded. "Commodore Findlay has been dead for two hundred years, yes. He *did* survive the destruction of Caledon and led an evacuation that settled his people farther south.

"But not far enough south, so they were forced to evacuate *again*. He stayed behind, waiting for an expedition that went into Caledon, looking for what he called 'the key.' They succeeded, but the Commodore was unable to get the results of their success south.

"Now the north of Albion is freezing. The south of Albion is burning. Left unchecked, how long do we even have?"

She hadn't meant to ask that question. She wasn't even sure she *wanted* to know.

"Destabilization of the climate is accelerating. This facility is incapable of further counter-heating," the Mind told her. "The last of the secondary power sources failed two-point-seven standard years ago. I am relying solely on geothermal power."

"So, the Stelforma islands aren't going to get hotter, but the north is going to keep getting colder?" Coral guessed. So long as she kept the Mind talking, it wasn't killing itself. If it was anything like humans, she suspected that the more she could *engage* the being, the less likely it was to suicide at all.

"Assuming the Stelforma islands are the southern hemisphere

archipelago the Stellar Terraforming personnel were evacuated to, fundamentally correct," Hibernia replied. "Ice-sheet expansion will continue at a growing rate. Catastrophic weather events will begin to sweep the entire main continent in fourteen-point-two years, plus/minus one-point-seven years.

"It is possible—approximately forty-two percent, plus/minus five percent—that Albion's eventual new equilibrium will include a small habitable zone, as existed prior to terraforming measures. More likely, however, the ultimate failure of this facility and the inherent ecological instability of a failed terraforming will result in a full ecological collapse.

"Most likely scenario—fifty-three percent, plus/minus six percent—is loss of all animal and macroflora inside forty standard years, plus/minus three-point-five years."

Fourteen years until hellfrost storms swept all of the Dales. Forty until *everything on the planet* was dead.

"My god," Fischer whispered. "Surely, it can be stopped?"

"This facility has expended every resource available for three standard centuries—approximately two hundred and eighty local years—in the attempt," Mind Hibernia told them. "I am a Class Three Artificial Mind, the support intelligence for the Class Two Artificial Mind present at Caledon.

"I am vastly more intelligent than any human. I have run out of resources. I have bought humanity three centuries on this world."

"But you don't have the orbital terraforming network," Coral said.

Vastly more intelligent than any human or not, *that* was clearly a surprise to the Mind.

"I do not," it confirmed. "The entire orbital network, with the exception of a small set of orbital reflectors above the southern pole, was under Caledon's direct control. It was locked down under security protocols when an *Augmetic* ship attacked the planet."

"I don't even know if my ancestors had anything to do with

that," Coral pointed out at the Mind's shift in tone. "*I* certainly didn't!"

"The orbital network is out of my control in any case," the Mind told her. "The security created by a Class Two Mind cannot be breached by a Class Three Mind. Not while also dedicating sufficient function to maintain the limited terraforming processes that have permitted your people to live."

"There was a fail-safe, Hibernia," Coral said. "Findlay's people found it. They brought it to him. He died with it—but we found him. And his last journal instructed us to bring it to you."

"*GIVE IT TO ME!*"

The demand came without preamble or warning, issuing from a dozen hidden speakers in the room with enough force to buffet even Daleblood ears.

"That's why I'm here," Coral told the Mind. "But I don't even know—"

The floor in front of her split open, a metal podium rising up to about waist height with several receptacles, including one sized for the sigil—and one that resembled nothing so much as a lock. A lock suited for the datakey she carried.

"I have spent three hundred years knowing I could not succeed," the Mind said, instantly calm again in a way no human could have managed. "I am a backup, and my primary made a mistake that damned every human soul on this world.

"For all of my power and all of my resources, I could not save this world. I stretched to the point where I will break before it dies—I will not live to see your people die in the cold and ice, but they will die, nonetheless.

"But with that key—"

Coral had already opened the box and drawn the datakey. Now, even as the Mind came as close to begging as a being of its power *could*, she plunged it into the lock meant for it.

Hibernia was silent. The whole room was silent.

"Hibernia?" Coral asked quietly. "Did it...did it work?"

"Assessing."

That was it. One word. For five whole minutes, Coral and Fischer waited. Then, finally:

"I have released the security lockdown on the island of Hibernia," the Mind told them. "None of your people were actively in danger from the security systems, but while they were operating in autonomous mode, I would not have been able to prevent them from terminating any Augmetics they encountered."

"Thank you," Coral said. "But...did it work?"

"It worked, Rear Admiral Amherst," the Mind told her. "I have full control of the orbital surveillance and terraforming networks." There was a pause. "I am still refining whether I will be able to fully restabilize the planetary climate."

"Is there anything we can do?" Coral asked. "The Stelforma can't survive on your island in its current state, but Dalebloods can. If human hands can help you..."

"That was not a possibility that I could have considered previously," Hibernia admitted. "My last human contact was Maria Keely. You do not, Rear Admiral Amherst, understand how thoroughly Administrator Keely despised, hated and feared the survivors of the Augmetic Liberation Forces.

"Your ancestors killed her parents, husband and daughters in the Collier Bombardment," the Mind told her.

"I have no idea what that even means," Coral admitted.

"And that, Admiral, is why I am prepared to let your Dalebloods come to my island," Hibernia said. "It is...easy for a Mind to fail to realize that things can be *forgotten*. While a conflict endures between the Stelforma and the Dalebloods, the alliance and integration I am processing between the Dalebloods and the *Seabloods* augurs for a better future if you work together."

"You...can see that?" Fischer asked.

"I can now," the Mind replied. "The orbital surveillance system only possesses six months of storage on board, but I am processing all of their data while we speak."

It paused.

"I would find it extremely helpful if your nations were not to go to war while I need your help," Hibernia noted. "It appears that you two, specifically, may have contributed to postponing that conflict. That is, again, promising."

"If you can save Albion, we can talk our governments out of fighting," Coral promised.

"I will hold you to that," the Mind replied. "In the short term, I will need the assistance of *Icebreaker*'s crew to reboot at least one of the secondary fusion plants. That will require reactivation of a desalination plant and electrolysis plant to provide deuterium to the facility."

Fischer coughed.

"The terms...are not what you use," she said slowly. "But we have a small-scale atomic arc battery aboard *Icebreaker* with us, including a fuel-purifier system. And *Icebreaker* herself has a quite-effective desalination plant."

"I will need the specifications," Hibernia replied. "It is possible that we can use your existing facilities to accelerate the reboot. I require the fusion plants to have sufficient spare power to operate the fabricators.

"Without the fabricators, I cannot even produce spare parts for my own systems. With the fabricators and control over the orbital network, I should be able to produce additional terraformer satellites and even surveillance platforms.

"Given the correct raw materials."

"What kind of raw materials?" Coral asked.

"Iron and unrefined petroleum would be the most useful for filling my reserves," the Mind told them. "Once we have the power plant online, I will need to negotiate with your governments for those supplies."

"For the salvation of our world, I don't think it will be difficult for us to provide as much petroleum from the tar sites as you need," Fischer promised, removing the helmet of her Sacred Arms to allow her to look over at Coral. "But our iron mines are...limited. We may not be able to spare sufficient metal from our own needs to meet yours."

"The Republic can," Coral promised. "I think that Mind Hibernia has it correct: our people must work together with the Mind to save us all. Republic iron and Daleblood engineers matched with Stelforma petroleum and...potentially some of what is concealed in your Mysteries."

"I will need to train anyone you send me from scratch, even from your Keepers," Hibernia said, a touch of grouchiness to the Mind's tone. "But yes. Combined, your nations can provide what I need to save you. Now, at least, that Findlay's key has unlocked Caledon's security barriers."

"A new beginning, then." Coral nodded. "We can make it happen. I should head back to my ship. Bury my dead. Will I be able to send others here to speak to you?"

"That will not be necessary," Hibernia told her. "Now that the security lockdown is lifted, I will access the network across the island. We will need to double-check the compatibility of my transmitters with your neuro-organic nanotech radio transceivers, but I should now be able to communicate with you anywhere on the planet.

"You will be my voice and my ambassador, Admiral Amherst. We will save our planet together."

"For the Blood," Coral swore. "For our world. I will serve."

Coral and Fischer carried Brivio into the elevator, leaning the barely conscious but alive Marine against the wall of the capsule as it began its ascent.

"We've got a lot of work to do, Admiral," Fischer said firmly.

"First, we reboot this fusion core of Hibernia's. Then we both go home and convince our governments to save the planet together. No pressure. No higher priority."

Fischer chuckled.

"Weirdly, I'm not worried about that," she admitted. "It'll be hard, but...we managed this." She waved around at the building.

"I have to agree," Coral said. "Now the Mind isn't going to *shoot* at anyone who comes near, we can help it help us. We'll make it work."

She sighed and shook her head, checking Brivio's pulse again to make sure the Sergeant was still alive.

"I'm worried about what comes after that now," she admitted. "I know that I don't fully understand what the 'transceiver net' Commodore Findlay wrote of was, nor do I understand what the CUNE were or what the whole damn war was about.

"But I know that Findlay expected help long before the City of Spires was abandoned. We know what wrecked our world. But we don't know what happened to the rest of the CUNE."

"Let's save Albion first, then worry about the universe, hey?" Fischer said lightly. She tapped her fingers against the helmet.

"But speaking of things that come after," she continued, "I need you to promise me something, Coral Amherst."

Coral gave her a questioning look.

"I have spent *weeks* now sharing a room with Angelica Carrasco," the Keeper told her bluntly. "When this is all over, the Chosen are going to throw a stupid huge party to celebrate the peace treaty. At that party, when the barriers to such things are no more, you will ask Angelica to dance. *Please.*"

JOIN THE MAILING LIST

Love Glynn Stewart's books? Join the mailing list at:
GlynnStewart.com/mailing-list

Be the first to find out when new books are released!

ABOUT THE AUTHOR

Glynn Stewart is the author of *Starship's Mage*, a bestselling science fiction and fantasy series where faster-than-light travel is possible—but only because of magic. His other works include science fiction series *Duchy of Terra*, *Castle Federation* and *Exile*, as well as the urban fantasy series *ONSET* and *Changeling Blood*.

Writing managed to liberate Glynn from a bleak future as an accountant. With his personality and hope for a high-tech future intact, he lives in Southern Ontario with his partner, their cats, and an unstoppable writing habit.

VISIT GLYNNSTEWART.COM FOR NEW RELEASE UPDATES

CREDITS

The following people were involved in making this book:

Copyeditor: Richard Shealy

Proofreader: M Parker Editing

Cover art: Elias Stern

Typo Hunter Team

Faolan's Pen Publishing team: Jack, Kate, and Robin.

 facebook.com/glynnstewartauthor

OTHER BOOKS
BY GLYNN STEWART

For release announcements join the
mailing list or visit **GlynnStewart.com**

STARSHIP'S MAGE
Starship's Mage
Hand of Mars
Voice of Mars
Alien Arcana
Judgment of Mars
UnArcana Stars
Sword of Mars
Mountain of Mars
The Service of Mars
A Darker Magic
Mage-Commander
Beyond the Eyes of Mars
Nemesis of Mars *(upcoming)*

Starship's Mage: Red Falcon
Interstellar Mage
Mage-Provocateur
Agents of Mars

Pulsar Race: A Starship's Mage Universe Novella

DUCHY OF TERRA
The Terran Privateer
Duchess of Terra
Terra and Imperium
Darkness Beyond
Shield of Terra
Imperium Defiant
Relics of Eternity
Shadows of the Fall
Eyes of Tomorrow

SCATTERED STARS

Scattered Stars: Conviction
Conviction
Deception
Equilibrium
Fortitude
Huntress
Prodigal *(upcoming)*

Scattered Stars: Evasion
Evasion
Discretion
Absolution *(upcoming)*

PEACEKEEPERS OF SOL

Raven's Peace
The Peacekeeper Initiative
Raven's Course
Drifter's Folly
Remnant Faction
Raven's Flag *(upcoming)*

EXILE

Exile
Refuge
Crusade
Ashen Stars: An Exile Novella

CASTLE FEDERATION

Space Carrier Avalon
Stellar Fox
Battle Group Avalon
Q-Ship Chameleon
Rimward Stars
Operation Medusa
A Question of Faith: A Castle Federation Novella

Dakotan Confederacy
Admiral's Oath
To Stand Defiant
Unbroken Faith *(upcoming)*

VIGILANTE
(WITH TERRY MIXON)
Heart of Vengeance
Oath of Vengeance

Bound By Stars: A Vigilante Series
(With Terry Mixon)
Bound By Law
Bound by Honor
Bound by Blood

TEER AND KARD
Wardtown
Blood Ward

CHANGELING BLOOD
Changeling's Fealty
Hunter's Oath
Noble's Honor
Fae, Flames & Fedoras: A Changeling Blood Novella

ONSET
ONSET: To Serve and Protect
ONSET: My Enemy's Enemy
ONSET: Blood of the Innocent
ONSET: Stay of Execution
Murder by Magic: An ONSET Novella

STAND ALONE NOVELS & NOVELLAS
Children of Prophecy
City in the Sky
Excalibur Lost: A Space Opera Novella
Balefire: A Dark Fantasy Novella
Icebreaker

Ingram Content Group UK Ltd.
Milton Keynes UK
UKHW011312130623
423377UK00001B/141